# THE SERVANT OF STONE

MÓRDHA STONE CHRONICLES
BOOK 8

KIM ALLRED

STORM COAST PUBLISHING, LLC

The Servant of Stone
Mórdha Stone Chronicles, Book 8
KIM ALLRED

Published by Storm Coast Publishing, LLC

Copyright © 2023 by Kim Allred
Cover Design by Amanda Kelsey of Razzle Dazzle Design

Print Edition July 2023 ISBN 978-1-953832-22-1
Large Print Edition July 2023 ISBN 978-1-953832-23-8

*To Mom*
*I'll never be lost with you watching over me.*

"An adventure may be worn as a muddy spot or it may be worn as a proud insignia. It is the woman wearing it who makes it the one thing or the other." Norma Shearer

# 1

---

*Saint-Malo, France - 1805*

AJ Moore-Murphy stood inside the doorway and gave the room a quick scan. It had more appeal than the typical inns she was familiar with, but of course, this wasn't any ordinary inn. This was L'éventail Bleu, an upscale brothel on the northwest coast of France. It was a tactic Beckworth, the Viscount of Waverly, had used when he'd rented a room for her missing friend Stella in Bournemouth while evading Gemini's men in England.

After watching Beckworth stumble around the room for the last five minutes, Stella nowhere in sight, AJ touched the tips of her ears, positive there would be smoke if not downright flames coming from them. All the miles and all the worry, she'd been so close. Now, within mere hours, they'd missed her.

"Where's Stella?" She kept her tone light but firm. What she wanted to do was stand in front of his face and scream at him. Stella had been on the ship when they'd arrived in Saint-Malo. Finn had confirmed it before tracing Beckworth to this brothel.

Beckworth stared out the window, his gaze on the street below. Maybe Stella was running an errand. But if that was true, why did Beckworth look like someone had just gutted him? When he turned toward her, she could barely hold his stare. The hollowness, bleakness, failure—a mirror into his tumultuous soul.

She had to maintain focus, or she'd be swallowed up by such despair.

"They took her."

She sucked in a deep breath and almost choked on the scent of stale perfume. She counted to ten, but her mantra for inner peace wasn't going to work. Not for this.

"Who took her?" Her words were measured. She'd tried for a softer tone as before but caught Finn's side glance and knew she'd failed. Instead of steady reassurance, she'd only managed the edge of calm, her emotions clearly leaking into outright fear with a side of anger.

Beckworth's gaze fell away, and his expression became dazed. He kept reaching for his head. Had someone attacked him? She glanced at Finn, who shrugged.

This was a Beckworth she'd never seen before, even at his darkest hour when he'd been stuck in Baywood, Oregon. There had been fear then—and anguish at the thought of never going home. But he still had a spark. That instinct for survival. Now, it seemed as if his inner flame hadn't been reduced but utterly extinguished.

Before she could ask for Finn's advice, he was already on the move. He strode to the table, picked up a clay pitcher, sniffed it, then grabbed one of the goblets. Red liquid streamed into the cup, and she almost smiled, knowing how much Stella must have appreciated the wine. It was doubtful she'd seen much of it while on the run.

He approached Beckworth, wine in one hand, his other outstretched toward the bed. "Come sit down."

When Beckworth didn't move, she thought Finn might force the issue, but after a few minutes, he moved on his own, ignoring the bed and stumbling to the table where he collapsed on a chair. When Finn placed the wineglass in front of him, Beckworth picked it up and drained it.

Finn pointed to the other chair and waited for her to take a seat. That was when she noticed the origami swans, several of them, arranged around the candlesticks like a centerpiece. Tears stung her eyes when she picked one up—proof her friend had been there.

Finn sat and rested a hand on her arm before glancing at Beckworth, whose focus had turned to the swan in her hand. He tapped the table until Beckworth turned a startled gaze to him as if he'd just now realized Finn was in the room.

"Tell us what happened."

Minutes passed before Beckworth poured the last of the wine and ran a hand through his hair several times, wincing when he touched what appeared to be a sensitive spot. After a long sigh, he turned to AJ.

"I thought we were safe. At least for a night. We'd been running nonstop, and after the ship and storm, she needed to rest." His voice was rough, probably the first words he'd spoken since waking. He held her gaze. "She's been so strong. You'd be proud of her. But we had a hard time staying ahead of them. I originally thought of going to Hensley, but Gemini was certain to send men there if she hadn't already. The earl's manor seemed too far to run, though maybe that would have been the best." His voice trailed off, and he pushed the empty goblet away. "The only place that seemed safe and out of reach was the monastery." A slight smile touched his lips. "Everyone always ends up there."

AJ flicked a glance to Finn. Those were the exact words he and Ethan constantly drummed into her. If this were any other day, Finn would have teased her about it, but his expression remained stoic. This wasn't any other day.

"Gemini? Is that who you've been running from?" Finn asked.

Beckworth shot a look at him and grabbed his head again. "Yes, although I haven't seen her since we escaped from an abandoned farmhouse south of Basingstoke."

"Basingstoke. You were there?"

He nodded. "Her men were everywhere. I thought heading for a ship would be the last place she'd think to look, but with the stones involved, I should have known better. We were halfway to Southampton when I discovered she'd sent most of her men south." He glanced around the table, looked in his empty cup, and pushed it away.

"Was it her men who took Stella from this room?" Finn managed to keep his tone supportive.

Beckworth snorted. "I don't know. Gemini might have discovered what port we sailed from. There could have been one or two of her men hiding in Bournemouth, but I never sensed them. It would have taken time to get word to her, wherever she was hiding. It just doesn't make sense." He gave Finn a quick glance before settling his gaze back on AJ. "If it had been her, or even Gaines, that took her, they wouldn't have sneaked in. Gemini is too prideful. She would have made her presence known, and I seriously doubt you would have found me alive."

Finn pointed to Beckworth's head. "Maybe she thought she'd killed you."

"She wouldn't have taken a chance with something as unreliable as a hit on the head." He touched his head and winced. "No matter how effective at knocking me out."

"How did you meet Gemini in the first place?" Finn's question surprised her. Hensley had already told them, but as much as she didn't think it to be true, perhaps Beckworth had an ulterior motive. The question had to be asked.

"She'd been watching me since she wormed her way into my holiday hunting party, playing the role of Lady Penelope Prescott. No doubt one of many parts she's played. Her trusty bloodhound, Gaines, followed me to London and noticed the shady characters I'd been meeting with. They assumed I was running my own information ring outside Hensley's purview, not realizing it was an assignment orchestrated by the spymaster."

He leaned back in the chair and gazed about the room. His eyes were unfocused, either from the realization Stella was truly gone or from the hit on his head. "Gemini knew about the duke and Reginald and more than she should have about the stones and the books. She thought I could fill in the gaps from what she'd already learned." His wicked laugh sent chills down her spine. "One of Gemini's weaknesses is making assumptions before validating her facts."

"Whatever possessed you to run instead of playing out the role? You could have gained valuable information from her." Finn, having worked for Hensley for many years, understood the advantages and the risks of working undercover and blending in. He'd spent eighteen months traveling to find the Heart Stone.

"And you were in the same town where Gemini had set up the meeting with Finn." AJ couldn't keep her mouth shut any longer.

Beckworth's brows shot up at that, and he gave a derisive snort. "Why doesn't that surprise me? No wonder she wouldn't reveal the location of the meeting."

AJ glanced down at the paper swan she'd been holding to find the poor thing had been mangled in her clenched fist. Regardless of her attempts to straighten it, the swan's wings drooped. She stuck the wilted figure in her pocket, her original fear stoking the flames of anger. "So, why did you run? Another couple of days, and we could have gotten you out of there."

Beckworth pushed out of his chair and paced the room, his arms waving. Whether anger or fear drove him, she couldn't tell and wasn't sure it mattered. He was no longer the confused viscount. "Well, excuse me. I thought you would be more interested in removing Stella from the middle of danger, not have me guess at whatever plan you might have cooked up. Gemini never revealed the location of the meeting. I had no idea we were in the vicinity, and none of her men had been aware, other than perhaps Gaines. And god knows I tried. I spent an entire evening getting them good and drunk."

He gave her a scathing look. "Oh, and Gemini discovered who killed Dugan."

She paled. "So?"

"Gemini and Dugan were lovers. And while she's now intimately involved with Gaines, she still pines for Dugan. I worried she wouldn't wait for Murphy's arrival before killing the person who took her lover from her. She is a bit mad."

She glanced at Finn, and though his gaze was tender, the heavy hands of guilt settled on her. "I'm sorry." But the words did nothing to console her. She ran her hands through her hair before picking up a goblet and throwing it at the wall, where it bounced before rolling toward the window.

Beckworth ignored her outburst and tugged at his sleeves. "We still have an advantage. Whoever took Stella didn't just select a random person in a boardinghouse. We have to assume the people that took her are either working with Gemini or a rival faction."

Finn pounded a fist on the table. "That's all we need, two different groups searching for the Heart Stone." He stood, and it spurred AJ to follow. The room seemed to press in from all sides.

"Either way—" Beckworth moved to the bed and pulled on a boot, "—there's only one reason they took Stella. Someone still believes she's you. They'll want to barter to have any hope of getting the Heart Stone. And we know where they're going."

AJ shook her head and grumbled. "The monastery."

# 2

When they exited the boardinghouse, Lando was waiting with four horses, three of them complete with saddlebags and weapons. AJ's bow and quiver hung from one saddle.

"Hello, little man. It's been a trial catching up with you." Lando nodded to one of the horses. "Hope you don't mind me picking up your ride."

Beckworth scowled. "How many times have I asked you not to call me that?"

"Not enough to sink in, I'd imagine." He tossed Beckworth a small, wrapped package before handing one to AJ and Murphy. "Your breakfast. You're welcome."

Beckworth stuffed the meal in his jacket pocket, not particularly concerned about squashing it. Then he threw his saddlebag over the horse before taking its reins. The lump he'd received was still sensitive, and he pushed on it until his eyes watered. He deserved the pain—needed it. After everything they'd been through, he'd allowed Stella to slip from his grasp. He shouldn't have been so brash strutting around town, thinking they were safe simply by stepping foot in a different country— war or not.

Once everyone was mounted, he followed them as they maneuvered through the edges of town, keeping their heads down and avoiding any place soldiers might congregate. They walked their horses until they were a couple of miles out of town, giving them time to eat while moving, noting that AJ only picked at her food.

He wanted to say something. To apologize for losing Stella. For not taking better care of her, although he wasn't sure what else he could have done other than perhaps take her elsewhere. Maybe they should have gone to London after all. They could have waited for Hensley if he wasn't already there for the season. He had contacts Gemini wouldn't have known about. If only Stella could have seen the flower vendors in Whitechapel. It was too early in the season for lilacs, but the daphnes would be in bloom. He could have dressed her in the finest gowns and introduced her to Dame Elizabeth Ellingsworth. There were so many other things he could have done had he been thinking straight.

AJ gave him side glances, but Murphy kept her close to him. He couldn't blame the man and didn't think it had anything to do with him. Murphy and Lando were both watchful, keeping eyes out for French soldiers if he had to guess.

She had to be curious and would want to know everything there was to know about Stella. How was she holding up? Was she scared? Was she getting enough coffee? He snorted. They were the same questions running through his head. Even if she was frightened, she'd always adapted, and she would this time as well. His worst fear was that she'd blame him for failing her. No. He wouldn't think that way. She'd confided not more than a day ago that AJ trusted him. That she trusted him. She'd be spitting mad and defiant, but she had to know they'd come for her. That *he* would come for her.

Then another thought raised the hairs on the back of his neck. Had they found her pistol, or had she been able to keep it hidden? It hadn't been in the room, and he'd scoured the place, making sure he had what little of her belongings had been left behind. And it hadn't missed his attention that the nightwear he'd given her had been tossed on the chair, and her pants and shirt were gone. She must have changed at some point during the night because the kidnappers wouldn't have given her the time, though he had found her purse with the coins she'd stolen from Gemini. He reached for the swans he'd stuffed in his pocket. The simple touch of the paper birds somehow kept her close.

They rode for several hours, maintaining a steady pace, until they turned down a small trail, following a creek for a quarter of a mile. They rested the horses while Lando pulled out another wrapped package for everyone.

"What do you think is waiting for us at the monastery?" AJ moved her food around, nibbled at a bit of cheese, then sat back with her skin of water.

Murphy shrugged. "The monastery doesn't have any protection, and it would depend on the size of Gemini's force—assuming it's Gemini that took Stella. The *Daphne* should be in the bay by now."

"And would Gemini know of the iron door?" Lando asked. He kept his gaze on the trail, forever the watchful sentry.

AJ and Murphy turned to Beckworth as if he were one of Gemini's inner circle.

"How would I know?" He stared off at the trees, sensing their gazes on him. He released a sigh. "I don't remember her mentioning the monastery, only the stones. She knew the book had been split into pieces but didn't indicate if the information was recent or something she'd learned from the duke. The biggest surprise for me, besides Stella being mistaken for AJ, was this new incantation that allows a traveler to select a specific day and location, though it seemed it wasn't completely accurate. Gaines showed up two days late from his jump to the future, and I got the sense the jump they tried before had been more accurate."

"She didn't give any other names? Who might have given her the incantation?" Murphy's questions were reasonable, so he played along.

"No. She gave me what she knew, or suspected, was common knowledge. I don't think she had the stones, though she seemed to know where they were. She also suspects two are missing."

"How the hell does she know that?" Murphy seemed skeptical, and Beckworth couldn't blame him. He'd been mystified himself.

He shrugged. "For some reason, she suspects you have one. She'd probably piss herself if she knew I had it." He'd picked up a stick and had been drawing odd shapes in the dirt. He scratched through them, realizing they had been designs for a new garden bed. Something he'd wanted to share with Stella. He stabbed at the dirt until he'd created a small hole. Could he make it large enough to bury his head in it?

"There was one thing I found odd," he continued. The others had gone back to their meals and inner musings, thinking he'd finished with what little he knew. He held their rapt attention again, and AJ's expressive gaze, full of hope, almost broke his heart. "Gemini was obsessed with locating Maire."

Murphy straightened. "We'd heard she was looking for the translator. We assumed it was Maire."

He nodded. "It was one of the questions Gemini wanted me to ask Stella. Of course, she thought I was speaking to AJ, so it was a logical assumption I might garner an answer. She assumed if anyone knew where Maire was hiding, it would be her." He gave AJ a quick glance before dropping his gaze.

"Was that her exact word—that Maire was hiding?" Murphy asked.

He thought back to their conversation. "She assumed Maire was in hiding, continuing her translation of *The Book of Stones*, or at least a section of it. She also assumed Hughes was with her and never gave any consideration that they might have jumped to the future with you."

"Well, that's helpful." Lando sliced a piece of apple with his knife. "Not good that they're looking for Maire, but they have no idea the two of them are with us."

"So she's on the *Daphne*?" Beckworth asked.

Rather than giving him a direct answer, AJ's voice rose an octave. "What if Gemini's men went to the monastery? What if they have her?"

Murphy laid a hand on her shoulder. "You're getting ahead of yourself again. Neither Jamie nor Ethan would let her off the ship without knowing the conditions at the monastery. Jamie would have sent Fitz and a small team in first."

She jumped up to pace back and forth. "You're right. I hate going back to the monastery when we don't know who's running the place." She stopped and gave Murphy one of her pleading looks. "Maybe we should try the iron door first, and if that doesn't work, we head down to the beach and signal the ship."

"An excellent idea." Beckworth stood and gathered the remains of his lunch. "The three of you should head for the ship while I enter through the front door."

The three of them were repacking saddlebags when they turned and stared.

"What is this, little man? What game are you about?" Lando's words should have cut him, but he understood their confusion.

"I have no desire to get myself shot, but we need someone

inside, and I have a better chance of talking my way in than any of you."

"You should at least wait until we've checked with Jamie." AJ's concern for him was touching, if unwarranted.

"Beckworth's right." Murphy took AJ's packaged leftovers and water skin. "We can monitor from the road. If guards are outside, we'll know the monastery has been compromised. But it's also possible they won't have enough men to post sentries. After five minutes, if Beckworth doesn't wave us in, we go for the stairs and the ship."

With somewhat of a plan, they returned to the road in time to meet a small group of travelers headed in the same direction. After a few short words, Beckworth ascertained they were getting as far from Paris as possible, heading for family along the coast, and the team fell in behind them.

When they grew closer to town, Murphy suggested they stop at Guerin's Inn in case they had news of the monastery. But two miles shy of town, Lando called a warning.

"Four riders. They've grown closer the last few miles, but now they seem to be pacing us." Lando turned his horse and pulled out a spyglass. "They appear to be French soldiers."

"Let me have your field glasses." Murphy held out his hand to AJ.

When she gave him the binoculars, Beckworth scowled. "Are those mine?"

AJ gave him a wicked grin. "If you mean, are they the ones you stole from the sisters, then yes, they are."

He snorted. "Edith had several lying about the house. I doubt she's even noticed them gone."

"They're wearing uniforms, but something is off about them." Murphy continued his surveillance. "Ah, that's the problem." He handed the field glasses to Lando. "Their uniforms don't seem to fit well."

"They're staying back with the size of our group. They'll wait until after town, then try to overtake us before we reach the monastery." Lando handed the glasses back.

Murphy smiled. It was that friendly smile that didn't reach his eyes. The one Beckworth had come to know well. Murphy had a plan, and most likely a devious one.

"Aye. But let's see if we can change the setting a bit. Our visit to Guerin's will have to wait for another day."

After another mile, a narrow road branched off to the south-west. Rather than follow their fellow travelers, they bid farewell and took the road that skirted the town. When Beckworth lifted a brow, Murphy flashed his grin.

"This road leads to a cave Sebastian uses to store his smuggler's inventory. Ethan and I helped unload a cart or two while we waited for a ship to England."

Beckworth nodded, knowing the story of how Murphy and Hughes had followed him and AJ after they'd left for England on the *Daphne*.

The terrain was rocky and would be difficult for carts to travel, which was why the smugglers' cave had remained safe from French troops. And he noted there were several opportunities for the perfect ambush. They traveled a half-mile past a trail Murphy said led to the cave before they stopped to set their trap.

Murphy and AJ would stay with the horses and cover Lando and Beckworth, who would hide behind a grouping of large boulders until the riders passed. Their decision to leave no one alive, assuming they weren't indeed soldiers, made AJ irritable. Still, she seemed to understand Murphy's reasoning—take them out here or face them again when the numbers might be against them. For now, they were evenly matched.

Everything went without a hitch. The four men were focused on the narrow road and not their surroundings. When he and Lando quietly closed ranks behind the men, an arrow took one to the ground. Lando dispatched a second one while Murphy's shot rang true, taking out the third. Beckworth shot the fourth man, who had been taking aim at Lando. He'd been wrestling with the first man, who'd been struck by the arrow.

The four of them gathered around the remaining man. Blood seeped through the shirt where an arrow stuck out of his abdomen. He grimaced in pain, one hand grasping the shaft of the arrow. Beckworth was surprised the man had fought as hard against Lando with what appeared to be a severe injury. The struggle for survival wasn't anything to take lightly.

AJ stared at the carnage. "Maybe we should have confirmed they weren't really French soldiers."

"They would have been an equally difficult problem," Beckworth said.

"Sebastian would have talked to them." She turned away as the injured man continued to stare with unrepentant defiance.

"We don't know who has control of the monastery, and we don't need to fight two fronts." Lando took weapons and coin bags from the dead.

Beckworth glanced at the others. "Why don't you ride ahead? I'll see what our friend can tell us." He sighed when he caught Lando looking at Murphy. "Fine, Lando can help. We need to hide the bodies anyway. Give us thirty minutes."

When he and Lando caught up with AJ, he put her mind at ease. "They killed the soldiers just outside Saint-Malo. Lando took the horses back to where the road split and sent them back the way they'd come."

"And the last man?" Murphy asked.

"He was stubborn and native French. Of that, I have no doubt. But other than what happened to the soldiers, the only thing I was able to get was a single name—Belato."

AJ's head swung up at that, her brows knit together.

"Do you know who that is?" Murphy asked.

She squinted, drawing her brows closer together, but then she shook her head. "I've heard the name before but can't remember where or when."

"Let's keep moving." Murphy took the lead, and they followed single file.

Beckworth let everyone go on, insisting on watching their back. He stopped every quarter mile or when they crossed a ridge, waiting to see if anyone else followed. It gave him time to resolve what he'd done to the mercenary. God knows he'd done worse in his time but thought he'd grown beyond that. But with every question he asked of the man, he never really saw him or the blood as he worked for answers. All he saw was Stella. The way she'd looked with fear when he'd first spoken with her. Or her greater alarm when he returned to her room later that evening, when all she saw was someone sneaking into her room after everyone else had passed out. The look in her eyes when she stared at the dead mercenary he'd shot. Then he remembered how quickly she'd adapted. She didn't want to kill anyone but hadn't seemed to mind when he had to do it. She understood survival.

After his vision had finally cleared and he stared down at the man, the defiance now erased by fear, his senses returned. The man had been bleeding out from the arrow in his stomach, and there wasn't any way to save him, even if he had a mind to. He'd been surprised when the man grabbed his wrist, his strength waning but firm enough to hold on.

When the man pulled him down and whispered the name into his ear, he questioned if the man had given him a false lead. Until the man uttered his last words, a thin trail of blood leaking from his lips and staining his teeth.

"They're all mad."

He waited five minutes, and when no one else appeared on the trail, he turned and spurred his mount to catch up with the others. The last few miles were uneventful, and they didn't stop until they reached the final curve in the road that took them to the monastery. They left the horses and moved cautiously over the rocky terrain to see what Beckworth would be riding into.

"Oh god, they've already posted guards." AJ had a hand to her throat, no doubt worried about Maire.

"They're guards, all right, but not mercenaries." Lando moved the spyglass in a slow line before dropping it. A huge smile added sparkle to his gaze. "They're sailors."

Murphy laughed. "Jamie has added a defense perimeter."

They scrambled back to their horses and raced to the inner courtyard. The sailors guarding the front of the building raised their arms in greeting and opened the doors for them. They'd barely dismounted before Maire raced out the foyer doors to greet them, Hughes a single step behind.

Tears streamed down her face, and his chest clenched. Not Stella. Please don't let this be about Stella. AJ had gone pale as she caught Maire in her arms.

"Sebastian is gone. They took Sebastian."

# 3

---

Stella groaned, and before opening her eyes, listened for sounds. She'd lost count of how many days she'd been in this hellhole called England, though it was unfair to blame an entire country because of one crazy woman with a battalion of mercenaries. For however long she'd been in this time period, it was long enough to not take waking up for granted. Her behavioral conditioning now included listening for anything that might tell her where she was and whether she was safe before ever cracking a lid.

She started with a physical review because the pounding in her head told her she better prepare herself for bad news. Without moving, she couldn't tell whether she had any further injuries other than what might be a concussion. This headache was not the same as her no-caffeine-induced ones. She slowly rolled over, pretending to still be asleep. Sore muscles forced a low moan, but that might have been from the cold room and the hard floor beneath her.

The previous evening was a blur. She'd been in a warm brothel and had eaten a decent meal with equally decent wine. She'd gone to bed with Beckworth—rephrase—shared a bed with Beckworth and had expected to immediately fall asleep, but it seemed too intimate to lay next to him in layers of lingerie. Once she'd confirmed Beckworth had been asleep, she'd crept out of bed and changed into her pants and shirt. What happened after that?

Another groan escaped. Someone had dragged her from the bed. More than one someone. She'd struggled, and Beckworth had tried to help, but he had his own intruder to battle. Then a blow to the head. That explained the headache.

She pushed her concern for Beckworth aside until she could figure out where she was. Her senses lit up, and a sinking feeling swept through her, leaving her chilled to the bone. The ground moved with a soft rolling motion and a rhythm that matched the low creaks she knew too well, and she wrinkled her nose at the damp smell of seawater. She was on another god-forsaken ship.

There wasn't any reason to postpone the inevitable, so she opened her eyes to darkness. She blinked, then noted there must be a lantern because her surroundings appeared with a soft golden glow. She sat up, then stopped as the pounding in her head increased. It settled to a gentle thrum after she took several long, deep breaths.

She was still in her pants and shirt, grateful she'd changed, then felt weird. Had she somehow known they'd come for her? She shivered. The downside was she had no shoes. At least she'd been wearing socks.

Next came a quick scan of her surroundings, checking to see if she had company. But other than noting she was in one of four cells in what appeared to be a cargo hold, there wasn't a guard. She did spot the lantern that hung a few paces from the only visible door.

She surveyed everything a second time but at a much slower pace. Her cell was ten-by-ten with iron bars. A bucket sat in the corner closest to the door, and a tin cup sat on the other side.

There was a thin sleeping pad, though she wasn't on it. They must have just dumped her without a second thought. These accommodations made Gemini's seem like a five-star hotel. Well, maybe a four-star one.

She closed her eyes and quieted her breathing, determining what else she might be missing. It was impossible to tell what time of day it was or how long it had been since she'd been kidnapped for a second time. Now, she understood what Maire had gone through—how dangerous this time was for her and how brave it would be for her to return to this century. That alone stopped the pity party she'd been planning.

There were no voices that she could discern, but every once in a while, the ship seemed to hit something. There was a soft scraping and gentle clanging sound. When she put it all together, she smiled. The ship was docked. She might not know where, but land was land as far as she was concerned.

She looked up. She wasn't sure how many decks this ship had, but some cargo holds could be reached from the top deck. Her muscles proved to be as stiff as she feared when she pushed herself up from the floor. She grabbed one of the iron bars to steady herself as she waited for the headache to calm to a manageable level. Once the ache receded, she returned to her task of scanning the ceiling. She moved to the front of the cage, her eyes searching until she found it.

The square hole was right above the alleyway between the two sets of cells. There was a rope ladder, but it had been tied up, so it hung about eight feet above the floor. She stored the information for later and redirected her focus to the cell door since she was standing in front of it. It wasn't a padlock she was familiar with, but after looking at the lock in the cell across from her, she didn't think it would be any more difficult to pick.

She instinctively checked her pockets. They were empty. Her heart sank. She remembered leaving the beaded purse on the table rather than her pants pocket. Not only did she not have anything to pick the lock, if she was able to get out, she didn't have a single coin to her name.

She collapsed onto the pallet, bemoaning her current situation while avoiding any thoughts of Beckworth and whether he was still alive, when a soft shuffling came from her left.

It sounded larger than a rat.

She squinted into the next cell, having assumed they were all empty, though she hadn't taken a close look into the shadows. A lump slowly rose, and Stella froze like a bronze statue.

The lamplight wasn't strong enough to provide any additional help. She'd have to move closer if she wanted to know more, but decided it best to wait to see what the other prisoner did. Assuming it wasn't her guard just using the spot for a nap.

She couldn't make out the figure. It still looked like a lump, just taller. Since she couldn't discern a head, she couldn't be positive, but she'd swear whatever it was was staring right at her.

Then it rose like an apparition and drew near. She almost peed herself, then snorted instead when the dim light revealed someone in a robe approaching her—not a ghost. They stopped when they reached the iron bars.

"Come closer, child, so I can look at you." A slim, pale hand reached through the bar then waved for her to follow his directions. "I won't hurt you. I want to make sure you're all right. The guards were rather rough when they brought you in. You hit your head on the floor when they dropped you."

She reflexively rubbed her head and squinted when she found two sensitive spots. One must have been when they hit her in the brothel, the second when they'd quite literally tossed her in the cell. She considered the cloaked figure. Her situation couldn't possibly get any worse by stepping closer and seeing what was under the hood.

He grabbed the bars with both hands as if they held him up.

They were old and wrinkled, his nails stained. At first, it looked like dirt, but the curiosity that would probably get her killed before she saw Baywood again urged her forward. She couldn't be certain with the limited light, but rather than dirt, the stain could be from ink. AJ had written a story for the Baywood Herald on the history of printing presses. There'd been a couple of pictures from the early days of men with stained hands. It wasn't the same thing, but for some reason, she was positive this guy wrote with quill and ink—a lot.

He didn't speak, and she sensed his eyes following her every move. Then he shook his head. "I'm sorry. I thought you might be someone else." He turned toward the front of the cell and mumbled, "I could have sworn I heard them say AJ Murphy." When he took a step away, Stella had to take a chance.

"Do you know AJ?"

The man stopped, then turned to give her a longer look. It appeared he was going to grab the bars again, but this time he reached for his hood and lowered it. He was as old as she suspected, yet his gaze was clear, and his eyes sparkled with intelligence.

"I know her well enough to know you're not her. Yet they—" he nodded toward the door, "—certainly think you are." He grasped the bars again, then tapped a finger along it, and she guessed he might be contemplating the possibilities.

"Who are these guys? Did they kidnap you, too?"

"In a manner of speaking, I suppose."

"Do you know what they want?"

"Something I cannot give them."

The kidnappers could talk to this guy for hours and end up going around in circles. Though he appeared fragile, she had no doubt he'd never crack under pressure. Tough old bird.

Now that she was up and talking, her throat felt raw. She studied the cup by the door, then picked it up. It appeared to be water, but with her sensitive stomach, she didn't want to gamble. "Is this safe to drink?"

"It's water, though it tastes stale. It won't harm you."

Though she wanted to down it all, she only drank half. Who knew how often the refills came.

"How many are there?"

He gave her a quizzical look, then his eyes shifted up, hopefully doing some mental calculations. After several seconds, he shrugged. "I've seen five different men since I've arrived. There have also been two young boys who clean the buckets. But there will be many others if they plan to sail."

"How often does the food come? Does the water come with it?"

"Twice a day, and yes, more water is brought with each meal."

She gave him another perusal. His whiskers were light and more than a five-o-clock shadow, but not quite a beard. "How long have you been here?"

"Two days, maybe a bit less, maybe a bit more. I don't think they bring the food at the same time, but that has been the only way for me to track the time."

She nodded. Without any windows or portholes, passage of time would be difficult to track. If they kidnapped her during the night, and depending on how far they traveled, and how long she'd been out, it might still be morning. "Have they brought food today?"

"Not yet.

"So they should be bringing more in, what, the next few hours?"

"Most likely sooner."

Something wasn't adding up, and she was all over the place with her questioning, feeling out of sync with the linear timeline. She hadn't expected this old guy to know AJ. And why wasn't Beckworth here? Surely, he'd be an important captive.

She closed her eyes, her heart beating double-time. He had to be alive. Frantic and out of his mind that he lost her, but alive. AJ would be so mad at him. But that was better than being dead.

She turned on him so fast, the old man took a step back. "Have you seen a woman?"

"What?"

"A woman. Was there ever a blonde woman with the men?"

He shook his head.

Damn. But in a way it made sense. Gemini couldn't have gotten to France so quickly. Her headache was making it impossible to think. It didn't matter. There couldn't be another explanation for the kidnapping. Certainly not for plucking someone from a brothel with a man lying next to her.

"If you're not AJ, then who are you?"

"I'm Stella." She tilted her head, crossed her arms over her chest, and took in his hooded robe that scraped along the floor. "You're not from the monastery, by any chance?"

He smiled and then chuckled. It was a hearty one that brought tears to his eyes. "And you're not from this time period. Or am I wrong?"

# 4

Stella stepped back and appraised the diminutive man. Her synapses began firing, and she ignored the hunger pains and coffee cravings as she studied him. Why would he suspect her of being from another time? He knew AJ, so he might know about time travel, but if he was just guessing, she should keep it to herself.

"Who are you?" She wasn't going to say anything more until he did, and she glanced away to avoid his steady gaze. Her eyesight must be adapting to the low lighting because she noticed her raincoat and boots lying next to the cell across from her. Why wouldn't they have dropped the items in her cell? Maybe they'd make her answer questions, then feed her clothing to her one boot at a time, assuming she didn't freeze to death first.

"I'm a friend."

The old man's words brought her back to the conversation. "Look, enough with the cryptic answers. I'm not the one that put us in a cell. I gave you my name, the least you can do is give me yours." She hesitated as she took in his robes. "It's the polite thing to do."

His eyes sparkled with mirth, and she wondered if he was getting something more potent in his mug of water that made this situation so amusing. She wanted a glassful of whatever it was.

"You have such fire. Even more than AJ, I think."

A heavy thud that shook the cell bars came from above, like someone dropped a compact car on the deck. She ducked involuntarily.

"They're fixing a broken mast. At least that's what I heard the guards say earlier. Nothing to worry about. We're still in port."

She eyed him but refused to say anything more until they were on the same playing field. Before turning away from him, she gave him her till-hell-freezes-over look.

He must have seen the look before because he just nodded. "Not one for patience, I see, but these conditions don't always bring out the best in people."

She scowled. "You're not making friends here, old man."

His laugh was warm and addictive, and she had to work hard to stop her own grin.

"Fine. I don't know why you're being so difficult. You must be making our captors mad as hatters." She stepped to the bars again and gave him a more thorough look. He seemed to understand her motive because he lowered his hood to reveal a cloud of white hair. It could use a brush if it didn't remove what little hair he had left. His face was kind and gentle, but his eyes shone with intelligence, and only because she knew herself so well, an edge of craftiness.

She barked out a short laugh. "Good god, don't tell me you're Sebastian?"

His eyes brightened. "You've heard of me?"

She shook her head in dismay. Did Beckworth know Sebastian had been kidnapped? He'd given no indication that he wasn't expecting him to be at the monastery. She'd doubted him before, hadn't been convinced she could trust him, remembered the hurt in his eyes when she'd told him AJ didn't trust him. No. She wasn't going to second-guess his actions in bringing her to France. They'd been in a sticky situation with little time to plan out a strategy, and he couldn't have known how much she already knew. It was all water under the bridge at this point. She'd listened to everything AJ, Finn, Maire, and Ethan had discussed about this time period. Who the players were, the towns, and who she could trust.

It was time to pull on her big-girl panties and start using her head. The intelligence that had impressed Beckworth. She'd hold on to that, and the knowledge that whoever had kidnapped her hadn't killed him. She closed her eyes for a moment and pushed back the emptiness that filled her thinking he might be dead. Then she shook herself like a cat coming in from the rain. She might not be AJ, but she could be more difficult to handle than her friend. They were messing with the wrong woman.

She looked at Sebastian, who was watching her with the same gleeful look, and tried to understand why she had to go through a guessing game just to get his name. The only thing that came to mind was that he'd been testing her. She gave him her most radiant smile, the one that was on almost every bus stop bench in Baywood. The smile Beckworth had noticed.

"I have heard of you. I've heard many wonderful things. Like how you stood up to the duke and took the monastery back from Reginald."

His eyes lit up, and he glanced at the door before stretching out a hand through the bars. She grasped it without hesitation. "Then we are not alone, child."

A huge sigh escaped her. "Thank god."

"Yes, thank God, and our mutual friends as well."

"So, what's the plan?"

He released her hand and shrugged. "They seem to be

waiting for someone. I would have expected to be interrogated by now, but they've only attempted a couple of questions, and when I remained silent, they simply went away."

"Yeah, that sounds like they aren't supposed to hurt you. Just keep you in storage..." Stella glanced around. "Or cargo, until the important kidnappers show up. And I have a feeling I might know who that is."

"Really? I have to say, I'm at a loss at who that could be. I didn't think there was anyone left who knew of the stones."

"Does the name Gemini ring a bell?"

His eyes became unfocused. "Possibly. But it was a long time ago, I think." He shook his head. "My memories become harder to retrieve as the years go on. It's best if I let the name sit with me awhile."

"Fair enough." Now that she had a friend, it was no longer about just her getting out of this. Whatever plan they devised would require them both getting out. Otherwise, Maire would have her head on family night's dinner platter for leaving him behind. "So, this is the third day you've been here, and our captors come twice a day to feed us and empty the buckets." She eyed the lantern. "They leave the lamp burning during the day. What about nighttime?"

"They leave it lit."

Another reason why Sebastian could only guess how long he'd been down here. He'd have to count the number of meals since there was no separation of day versus night in the hold. She paced the edge of the bars circling her enclosure, and her stomach gave a low growl. "Do you think it will be much longer before they bring food?"

"I imagine soon."

"Maybe they'll give me my clothes," she muttered and glared at the lock on the cell door. "Not that I have anything in the pockets to open this."

"Here, child."

She turned to find Sebastian holding out his robe to her. His monk's garb wasn't too dissimilar to his robe other than it slid over his head rather than being tied in the front with a rope belt. His shoes looked sturdy, though she'd been expecting sandals.

When she didn't make a move toward it, he shook it at her. "I am warm enough until they give you your clothes." He nodded toward the pile outside their cell. "They must mean to give them to you."

She glanced down at her woolly socks and wiggled her toes. If she only had her raincoat, but it wouldn't be nearly as warm as his robe. She took it since it seemed to make him happy. "Thank you." She slipped it on and reveled in the warmth of his retained body heat.

"You don't have some type of narrow pin or wire, do you? Something I could use on the door lock." If she ever got out of here, she'd need to build a survival kit. Coffee beans and a lock pick were the first items that came to mind.

He shook his head, then paused. "Check the pockets."

She did. A skeleton key was in the right pocket. "This isn't the key for the iron door, is it?"

That same cheery gaze. Did anything ever get this man riled up?

"No, child. I never remove it from the monastery. Only a small group of people know where I keep it." He smiled. "Though I do have a tendency to move it around."

She smiled then felt the left pocket. A few coins wrapped in paper, which explained why they didn't jingle. Then something poked her finger. "Ouch."

Sebastian smiled.

She pulled it out. It was a cross that hung from a thin strip of leather. She gave him her wicked smile and a wink. The cross was thin, almost pointy on the end. It might be long enough, but it depended on the lock. She could also try the skeleton key, but she didn't have experience working with those. Her gaze flashed to the door when it creaked open.

She took off the robe and shoved it back through the bars, but slid the cross into her pants pocket. "It's better this way." He took the robe and hustled back to his pallet. She moved to the back of the cell, staying in the shadows, wanting to get a good look at her captors before deciding the best way to play the situation.

"Grab the lantern then close the door behind us. How difficult can it be?" The French-accented voice was a bit high-pitched and irritated, but it was definitely a man.

"Why can't you do it?" It was a deeper, English voice. Interesting.

"Because I'm holding a tray with both hands. For all that's holy, where in the hell did they find you?"

"I'm a good soldier."

"Yeah, well keep your lips shut while I check on our guests." He giggled like a little girl as he limped down the aisle, then stopped where the two cells met. His eyes were cold and calculating and seemed at odds with his tall, skinny frame as he shifted from one foot to the other. When he did, it was obvious one leg was shorter than the other. He hadn't shaved in a couple of days, and based on the grime on his face, hadn't bothered with a bath, either. She couldn't smell him from where she stood and decided to keep as much distance as possible. He circled, as if looking for a place to set the tray. "Get over here and pull this stool over."

The second man, much larger and beefier than the first, lumbered to follow, then kicked the stool until it hit the bars of Sebastian's cell. He didn't seem to have much in the brains department, so she assumed he was the muscle. And what he had was impressive enough. The question was how fast he was.

The first guy, who she named Slim, peered in at Sebastian. "Here's your breakfast. Now stay on your pallet while Henry gets your bucket." He turned to huge man. "Well, get the bucket. And don't ask me why you have to do it each time. Just put it outside in the hall and bring over the clean one."

Henry pulled out a ring of keys and fumbled as he found the one he needed. While he struggled with that simple assignment, Slim took a few awkward steps to peer into Stella's cell. "Come out where I can see you."

When Stella didn't move, he swore something under his breath. Then he glanced over at her pile of clothes. "If you want your coat or boots, you need to let me see you. Don't worry, I've already felt the merchandise on the ride back to the ship." His grin produced an ugly smile of stained teeth, and the one behind his left eye tooth was missing.

Her skin crawled at the thought of his hands on her. At least she knew one of the men that had been at the brothel. She assumed Henry had also been there. She didn't think she had any bruises so he must not have done too much harm. She needed her coat, so she stepped into the dim light.

The door to Sebastian's cell clanked shut. A bowl of food had been placed next to a glass of water, and the big guy carried a bucket to the door.

"You're a fine woman. I wonder why the captain gets all the pretty women." Slim licked his bottom lip, and Stella tried not to throw up in her mouth.

"Because ship's captains have money," Henry said as he trudged back to the cell with a clean bucket. Not as dumb as she thought. She'd have to keep an eye on him.

"You can step back now. You don't want to mess with Henry. He could snap you in two by accident."

Henry frowned. "That's not a nice thing to say to a lady." He opened the door to her cell and peered at her through the bars. "I don't want to hurt you, so stay on your pallet."

She backed up until she stood on the thin bedding. It would be best if she appeared docile and beaten. Once the food and water had been placed inside, Henry peered into the bucket. "She hasn't used it yet."

"Then leave it," Slim growled. "Must I always think for you?" He used his boot to push her clothes to the bars of her cell. "It will be another day or two before they start asking questions."

He picked up the tray and Sebastian's bowl from the previous night. "You'll get another meal later tonight. I suggest getting some sleep. You won't be going anywhere."

She decided not to ask any questions. They'd already given her enough information to consider, and she needed to know what else Sebastian could tell her. She waited for them to trudge out, which they did with a sharp crack of a closing door. She raced to the cell door and listened. She didn't hear a lock and sincerely thanked whoever was watching over them.

# 5

AJ paced the room, noting that Finn kept an eye on her like she might do something rash, and stopped at one of the tall-backed wooden chairs and leaned against it. Still too antsy to sit, she used it as a touchstone.

She gave a quick glance toward Ethan, who held Maire against him as she battled with her fear for Sebastian. She understood Maire's concern. They were all upset, but Maire was remembering their vacation to the monastery. Sebastian remained a prominent historical figure among the brothers. However, there had been no record of his death. It was as if he was there one moment and gone the next. Maire had to be thinking this might have been the moment that Sebastian disappeared, never to be heard from again.

There was one way to know for sure. They simply had to go into the tunnels, back to the smuggler's meeting room and see if Sebastian's journal, the one Maire retrieved during that vacation, was already there waiting for them.

Maire had been on her way to do that when Ethan forced everyone into this room because the men wanted to talk about it, mull it over, strategize, whatever. AJ pushed her hair back and stared at the ceiling, then gave the room another long study. She remembered this room. It was where they'd met the duke to discuss the stones. When Maire feigned illness so the two of them could be taken elsewhere to search for *The Book of Stones*. How naïve they'd been, and what luck that Sebastian had found them.

The room looked different. All the duke's extra ornamentation had been removed, and while not completely stark, was certainly more austere than their first visit. Their second visit had turned into another battle, and more time had been spent cleaning and repairing than touring.

"Can you tell us again, Brother Leclair, the last time you saw Sebastian?" Finn had taken over the questioning since Ethan was busy restraining Maire from running off.

Jamie and Lando, who were originally standing at the entrance to the room like a pair of avenging angels, were now sitting at some distance from two young monks, who sat rigidly on the sofa. Thankfully, Fitz had been sent to check the perimeters at all the entrances, including the iron door.

Brother Leclair was the oldest of the two, but if AJ had to guess, he wasn't much older than her, somewhere in his late twenties, maybe early thirties. He'd been at the monastery for less than a year and had missed the previous excitement with Reginald and Dugan. The second monk, Brother Ignatius, was even younger but had been at the monastery longer. He hadn't been away when the duke ruled as if some monarch, but he clearly remembered them and their battle with Reginald.

"As I stated before—" Brother Leclair stopped to mop his brow. He was a short man with a heavy girth and a pleasant smile before the interview had begun. Now he was as nervous as a mouse surrounded by starving cats. "It was shortly after morning service, three days ago. Sebastian was to lead a work party, moving crates to the smuggler's cave. But he received a message while the crates were being loaded. He told me he had to run an errand, and he would meet us at the cave. He packed a small bag and took one of the donkeys. That was the last we saw of him."

"And who delivered the message?"

"I didn't see them." He mopped his forehead again, then pulled on his ear. His unfocused gaze turned toward the hearth where a fire chased the chill from the room. "I originally assumed it came with the morning kitchen delivery, but now I think that might be wrong."

Finn waited. He leaned back in the chair, one leg resting on a knee, as if they were simply having a casual conversation. The monk must have subconsciously noticed because he relaxed back on the sofa, and the monk next to him followed his actions.

Still tugging on his ear, he began to nod. "There may have been a rider from town."

The second monk, Brother Ignatius, fidgeted and plucked at the sleeve of his robe. He was taller than Brother Leclair, with a thin frame and round glasses. If he were transplanted to her time, she'd think him a geek. "The message couldn't have come with the morning deliveries. The cook would have had it sent immediately, but I remember Sebastian coming in asking for water to be brought down for the men. He also wanted a lunch packed for them since the trip to the cave and back would take several hours."

"Yes, I remember Sebastian leaving us." Brother Leclair became more animated, his arms starting to wave in expressive gestures as he explained, "We were just outside the iron door. I was checking off the boxes as they were carried out of the tunnel and before they were taken up to the carts. He had planned on only taking one cart load but decided to take three carts because he'd heard from Louis earlier that two ships had arrived at the docks. If anyone was riding out this way and noticed the carts, they would assume we were headed to the docks to pick up supplies."

"He was always a crafty old man." Ethan chuckled, and Maire nodded, though she didn't do anything more than lay her head on his chest. But she was paying more attention to the monks than she had earlier.

"He left, saying he had to go to the kitchen and make sure there would be food and water for the workers." The monk tucked his handkerchief in a pocket. "He never returned, which is why I assumed the message came with the kitchen delivery."

"But I was in the kitchen, and I never saw anyone hand him a note." Brother Ignatius pushed his glasses up and shrugged. "I wasn't there the entire time. I was still helping with moving food to the pantry, but if he had a message, someone would have given it to him right away, and that didn't happen."

"How else would he get a message?" Finn tapped his fingers on the armrest and lifted his gaze to the ceiling as if he was working out the puzzle himself.

After a few seconds of listening to wood snap and sizzle in the hearth, Brother Leclair snapped his fingers. "Maybe the messenger never made it to the monastery."

Brother Ignatius nodded, a smile appearing. "The stables. It's possible a rider went directly to the stables and left the message."

Finn shot a glance to Lando, who for a large man, made a quick and discreet exit out of the room. He'd be on his way to the stables. "That's very good. Is there anything else you can think of?"

The two monks glanced at each other, shared a few words, spoken too lightly for AJ to hear, then they both shook their heads.

"It was a busy morning. It's all we can think of." Brother Leclair looked apologetic and not as afraid as he'd been earlier.

"Thank you, Brother Leclair." Finn stood and walked to the sofa. "We've kept you from your tasks for too long." The monks stood and shook the hand Finn held out to them. "Do you expect the prior back soon?"

"Not for another few days," Brother Leclair said. "But I know he'd want us to shelter you and provide whatever assistance we can offer to help find Sebastian. He would never leave without a note, not if he wasn't planning on returning."

"Don't worry. We'll find him." Finn's words almost reassured AJ, if she hadn't known the forces that seemed to be coming at them from multiple directions.

Once the monks left, Jamie stood and walked to the hearth. "Let's hope Lando discovers something more. I still don't understand how Gemini could have gotten here before us."

"If she knew about the stones and the monastery," AJ chimed in, finally having something to say, "It's possible she'd sent men ahead of her."

"So, why didn't they simply storm the monastery and take what they wanted?" Ethan asked.

"Maybe they weren't sure who was here," Jamie suggested. "They seem to be patient. Perhaps in luring Sebastian away from the monastery, they hoped to garner more information before bringing in more men."

"What about this Belato fellow?" Beckworth, who AJ had forgotten was in the room, stood from the corner where he'd dropped into a chair and had mentally shut down since first entering the room. He didn't move any closer and appeared to be hurting more than the rest of them. She'd never seen him like this before, but she assumed he was gripped with guilt. And she hadn't helped. Stella's kidnapping hadn't been his fault. From everything she'd seen in that room at the brothel, he'd taken care of her and had tried to keep her focused and strong. He'd even claimed she'd be proud of how strong Stella had been. But instead of thanking him for all he'd done, she'd been too angry and scared to tell him. It had been easier to just take it out on him. She'd have to rectify that.

"Who?" Maire sat up and wiped her eyes.

"Belato." AJ left her spot at the chair and moved closer to the group, closer to Beckworth, who had also taken a few steps toward Maire. She directed her next statement to him. "That was the name you got from one of the men who followed us from Saint-Malo before he...died." No reason to mention any torture that helped with the interrogation or the fact he'd been struck with her arrow.

"You're positive he said Belato?" Maire was alert, her gaze sharp.

"I remembered the name but couldn't remember much more than that." AJ began pacing. "I'd forgotten all about it once we discovered Sebastian gone." She thought she'd heard the name before, and the fact that Maire recognized it gave her hope it meant something important.

"There wasn't anything more to remember." Beckworth tugged at his sleeves but didn't look at the team. "The man had nothing else to say until the end, and it was the single name." He must have also picked up on Maire's enthusiastic response because whatever fugue state he'd been in seemed to evaporate.

"I think he was the monk that Sebastian had trained before he turned on Sebastian." Maire pushed away from Ethan and stood. "That's why the stones and book were hidden in the first place. Why the Heart Stone was sent to Radcliffe."

"Are you positive?" Finn asked.

Maire shrugged. "I think so. Sebastian told us about him while we were hiding from the duke. He must have recorded it in one of his journals."

"When was this?" Beckworth asked.

Maire rushed to the door. "During the Terrors. Belato had

left the monastery for some reason, and when he returned, he'd brought others with him. A brother, perhaps his father, I don't remember the details."

Everyone followed Maire out the door. Beckworth remained, staring at the fire.

AJ wanted to race after everyone, but she knew where they were headed, and if Maire had to find a journal, it would take her a while to find the right one.

She stepped toward Beckworth, but he didn't seem to notice. "I'm sorry."

He stood straighter, but he didn't take his gaze from the fire, and his response was gruff. "What do you have to be sorry about?"

She flinched at the harshness. "For yelling at you. We were so close to catching up with Stella. I'd thought for sure we'd find her at the brothel. That we could take her home. I didn't think about what you'd been through. What it must have taken to keep her safe."

His shoulders slumped, and he turned his back to her, now fully engrossed with the flickering flames. "I'm the one who should be sorry. I'm the one who lost her."

AJ snorted, and though he didn't say anything nor turn around, she thought he might have smirked. "You stole her away right from under Gemini's nose. You ran in the direction you thought would be the safest. I don't know that I would have headed south, but any direction would have been a crapshoot. It's easy to second-guess a person's actions after the fact. It's quite different when there aren't many options and the bad guys are breathing down your neck."

She stepped closer. "When Maire and I ran from Dugan while on the road to South Hampton, there had been other options. But they weren't so clear at the time."

He turned toward her but didn't look at her, still keeping his gaze firmly on the crackling wood, probably replaying his days on the road with Stella.

"I've known Stella a long time." She took a step toward him. "She never wanted to travel to the past. It terrified her. It's rare to see her frightened by anything. She tends to get mad and temperamental."

"Did you know she was terrified of horses?"

The question startled her. She hadn't expected it. She moved until she stood shoulder to shoulder with him and extended her arms as if she was warming her hands by a campfire. "No. But horses in our time are mostly for pleasure riding, racing, or working a ranch. Finn and I never thought to ask her on one of our trips to visit our horses. She's a city girl, and I just figured it wasn't her thing."

"She's also frightened of enclosed spaces and gets terribly seasick."

"I knew about those. We made her go on a boat tour while vacationing in France. It was a calm trip, but she was nauseous for hours afterward."

"We found an apothecary, and I was able to procure several herbs. They worked well until the storm. Even then she never gave in." He turned to her for a half-second and smiled. "In the middle of the storm, as wet as a sewer rat, she crawled across the deck and saved the captain's niece, who'd been injured."

"She's always had a gentle heart, willing to help whoever needed it." AJ snorted again. "After living through a storm or two at sea myself, it's hard to imagine her crawling across the deck to do that, but at the same time, it's not that strange."

His head fell back as he barked out a laugh. "She is definitely a complex woman. And an excellent shot with a flintlock."

"You gave her a firearm?" AJ was taken aback. "What were you thinking?"

This time he finally turned to her, and she recognized the

Beckworth she'd come to know. His expression was perplexed, but he had a twinkle in his eye, and a grin hovered. "She hounded me day and night until I finally agreed to show her how to use one. Said she'd been trained to handle firearms since she was a kid. And based on how quickly she adapted to the flintlock, I had no reason to question her. And honestly, I couldn't stand the constant blathering on about it."

AJ stared at him for a moment, then burst out laughing. "I didn't know she could handle a gun, but it's not something one typically needs in my century." She shook her head. "I never had a clue."

They turned back to stare into the fire, AJ now satisfied the tension between them had disappeared.

"I'm worried about her," Beckworth finally said.

"It sounds like your prepared her for this time period the best you could."

"I'm not worried about whether she's prepared. She adapted rather quickly in my opinion. But now that she has the ability to survive on her own, she'll likely take risks. And that could end up getting her killed."

He was right. Stella wasn't one to just sit back and wait for rescue. If AJ's first option of choice when under Dugan's thumb had been escape, Stella would be thinking the same thing.

"She still has one thing going for her."

Beckworth turned, almost eager to hear any kernel of hope.

"They still think she's me. And they still need the Heart Stone."

# 6

Finn waited for AJ and Beckworth at the door that led to the subbasement and tunnels under the monastery. He'd never understood the relationship those two had developed. Not really. They'd all had a rocky beginning, and Beckworth absconding with her from Baywood and stealing her away to the past should have left some type of rift between them. Instead, whatever they'd endured before he and Ethan had caught up to them was something lost to him.

If he considered his friendship with Ethan, it had its own unsettling start. If he hadn't found Ethan in that glade, a time that seemed so long ago considering all they'd withstood since, events could have played out quite differently with the duke.

He didn't begrudge AJ her friendship with Beckworth. The man had proved himself trustworthy, helping them out of scrapes many times. And if he viewed his own friendship with Stella, while not quite the same, it gave him a bit more understanding.

AJ had been keeping a watchful eye on Beckworth, and he had to admit there was something wrong with the man, had seen it the moment they found him in the room at the brothel.

Beckworth's sense of guilt was like looking in a mirror. He'd fallen under its grasp many times over the course of his own questionable decisions, especially where AJ was concerned. And several other times when in service to Hensley. The weight of regret and second-guessing was something Beckworth would have to work out himself, but if AJ could give him some peace, then so be it. They needed Beckworth at the top of his game.

He turned when he heard footsteps approaching and smiled at AJ, who had Beckworth in tow. Something had improved, but nothing he'd be able to put his finger on, other than it seemed a bit of the burden Beckworth was dragging around seemed lighter.

"Something smells delicious." AJ was perkier. Her eyes shined with whatever success she believed she'd achieved with the man behind her, who wasn't smiling, but at least the sour scowl was gone.

Finn breathed in the heavenly aroma of roasted lamb from the nearby kitchen, and he grinned when AJ's stomach grumbled.

"Maire arranged for a late meal that's being kept warm by the fire." Finn smiled down at her, then gave Beckworth a nod. "They've also arranged for rooms on the second floor. I guess friends of Sebastian earn some concessions."

"If it's all the same to you, mate, I'll see if my room below is available." Beckworth brushed past them and jogged down the stairs.

AJ sighed. "I thought I talked him past the guilt."

"It will take a while." Finn continued to stare down the stairs where Beckworth had disappeared. He suspected there was something else going on with Beckworth, but he decided to keep it to himself. AJ had enough worries about Stella. Besides, by now, his sister undoubtedly had pulled down volumes of Sebastian's journals, probably covering an entire table, searching for the one she needed.

He wrapped an arm around her and pulled her in for a kiss. It lasted longer than he planned but it was always that way with them. He could never get enough of her. His salvation. His love. He pressed his forehead to hers. "Let's see if Maire found anything."

When she grabbed his hand, kissed the tip of his nose, and tugged him down the stairs, he couldn't seem to wipe the silly grin from his face.

---

**B**eckworth raced down the stairs and stormed past a few rooms he was familiar with. Then, for no particular reason, turned left, slowing when he realized he'd never been to Sebastian's sanctuary. He stopped and braced a hand against a wall, not feeling the sharp edges of stone that hadn't worn away with time as they dug into his flesh.

He appreciated AJ's attempt to salve whatever injury to him she thought she'd committed. But as he'd told Stella, he had a thick skin. He understood why she'd been angry at the brothel, and though it had been directed at him, she'd been striking out at the closest person at hand. They were all scared for Stella.

What bothered him most was that it wasn't just Stella's safety that worried him. When he'd woke and found her gone, it felt as if someone had reached into his chest and ripped everything out. He had to find her, and as much as he wanted to race back to Saint-Malo to pick up the trail, he had to know what he was riding into. And this team, who seamlessly fell into place whenever there was a problem with the stones, they were the people who found answers. Once he had some, then he'd make his own plans.

He let out a shuddering breath and looked around. It was apparent that he needed the team just to find Sebastian's sanctuary. He'd been close when he'd retrieved Sebastian from the cell Reginald had locked him in. There was a statue, but he had no idea how to find it or what it meant, other than it was a clue to where Sebastian's workroom was located.

He backtracked to where he left the main hall and ran into Murphy and AJ. "These blasted halls are impossible to navigate." He glanced at them and realized they were most likely waiting for him. He scanned the walls and nodded to himself. This part seemed familiar. "Well, go ahead. That sister of yours has probably already found the correct journal, deciphered where Sebastian has wandered off to, and is already on her way to the iron door to head out on her own."

Murphy grinned as he turned the wall lamp, then pushed in the fourth stone below it until a click sounded and the door popped open. "Unless she drugged Ethan, then she hasn't gotten far. And if she went out the iron door, she'd have a long walk to wherever she thought she was going."

Once they'd reached the next floor, Murphy held out his lantern to AJ. "You know the tunnels better than either of us, as Beckworth has already proven."

Beckworth ignored him and tugged on his sleeves.

"Right." She took the lantern. "After seeing what this all looks like two hundred years from now, it will take me a moment to get reacquainted with this century's version." She scanned both directions the tunnel took from the stairs, but barely gave the passage to the right a second glance. It appeared to be more of a reflex to look both ways before moving on.

She led them down two passages before stopping at the statue of the old warrior Beckworth remembered passing several times. When AJ pushed on one of the stones behind the statue, he realized the statue did more than mark the general vicinity to Sebastian's sanctuary. It was the way in.

The door popped open with a rush of air, and the murmur of voices leaked out. The distinct deep rumble of Lando, who must have caught up with Hughes and Maire, filtered out. Beckworth followed AJ in, and Murphy closed the door that locked with an audible click.

It wasn't a large room, but the long table fit comfortably with eight high-backed chairs. Stuffed bookcases filled two walls, and a workstation ran along a third immediately to the left. The workstation held shelves of labeled bottles and jars. Two jugs, most likely filled with water, sat at the end. A teapot hovered over an unlit candle warmer. An opened journal sat next to an inkpot, quill, and various vials. The old monk had been concocting some potion, and if he remembered correctly, it would be some type of curative.

Maire sat at the table, opening and closing journals as fast as Hughes could take them from a shelf. Lando stood behind Hughes and replaced them once Maire was finished with them.

AJ fussed with the teapot, emptying it and refilling it with fresh water. She opened jars, giving each a sniff before finding something she liked, then sprinkled it into the teapot. Murphy sat at the opposite end of the table with another journal. He ripped out a blank sheet of paper and pulled another inkpot to him, though he didn't open it.

"Have you found anything?" Murphy asked.

Beckworth doubted he'd expected a positive response or else they wouldn't still be searching through the books.

"We're close. I can feel it." Maire pushed a journal to Lando while pulling another one to her. After skimming a couple of pages, she tapped the table. "I think this is it." She glanced at the next two books Hughes placed on the table. "Pull the next two, just in case."

"What are you looking for?" Beckworth asked. No one else seemed inclined to ask, though Lando turned from shelving the last book to look at Maire.

"When AJ and I first met Sebastian, he brought us to this room and showed us one of the sections of *The Book of Stones.*" She pushed back wayward strands of hair that had fallen out of her braid, then tapped her foot. "He told us how the book had been split into four pieces, what he referred to as chronicles, and why he decided to hide the torc and smaller stones while sending the Heart Stone away."

"I remember now." AJ slid into a chair, leaning over to look at the journal Maire was reading. "That's when he mentioned this Belato. Wasn't he another monk?"

Maire nodded. "Yes, he was Sebastian's student, being trained to handle and protect the artifacts, which was part of the monastery's role. But Belato got greedy, or maybe it was his family. Either way, he was involved."

"When was this?" Lando asked.

"It was during the Terrors." Maire tapped her finger on a passage. "Here it is. He wrote this a couple of months after Belato was removed from the monastery in 1795."

"Ten years ago." Beckworth took a seat next to Maire. "The duke arrived in France a year or so after that. He spent his first year at a villa just outside Paris."

"In time to meet this Belato?" Murphy asked.

Beckworth shrugged. "Perhaps. From what I'd been told, the duke heard about the stones about that same time period. I'd just moved into Waverly and received a letter from him every three or four months." He scratched his head. It had been years since he thought of this, had hoped to forget it all. "So much has happened since then, but the name means nothing to me. Not when the mercenary uttered it several hours ago, nor now."

"Maybe he didn't hear it from Belato," Hughes suggested.

"Perhaps he heard it from someone else, but this Belato has somehow been keeping watch."

"I want to hear what Sebastian wrote. Maybe there's a clue." AJ brought the teapot over and poured a cup for Maire. "Anyone else? I'm afraid it's only tea and not very hot but it's steeped well enough." When they all shook their heads, AJ poured a cup for herself.

"Can someone bring me an extra lantern?" Maire asked. "This is written in French, and I need to translate." When Murphy placed it on the table, she sipped her tea, ran a hand over the page, and began to read.

*"I only feel safe recording this now that it's been six months since Brother Belato has left the monastery. There are rumors from Paris that he is dead, but very little truth comes from the city these days. Brother Belato came from a poor family in a small town several miles outside Paris. He was to be my intern, to someday fulfill my role once I am too old to carry on. He was a kind young man, though more curious than a monk should be."*

"He continues in some detail to list the tasks and behaviors of Belato. I'll need to read it and see if it tells us anything, but let me jump ahead to something more pertinent."

The group waited, no one wanting to break the spell Sebastian's words had already cast. After several minutes, Maire nodded. "Here we are. This is after the start of the Revolution and the early days of the Terrors."

*"I didn't know until weeks later that Brother Belato had written messages to his oldest brother. His parents were long deceased, and he was the youngest of the three boys. He told his brother about the stones and the magic they were purported to hold. I don't know that either of them believed the stories, but it wouldn't matter. Many would pay handsomely for the chance it was real. By this time, I had begun to worry that Brother Belato was not the right person for the role he'd been given. In Paris, his brother had turned his luck and became*

*powerful in the new regime. Powerful enough to be given oversight of the monastery and all its holdings. I discovered the deceit—the betrayal—only hours before they stormed the building. With the prior and several trusted brothers, we hid as many treasures as we could. There were many passageways and secret rooms I never divulged to Brother Belato. I had suspected his main interest was always in the stones, and regretfully, the prior and I both felt it was necessary to break* The Book of Stones *apart. It seemed the best option rather than destroy it.*

*"I hid the four parts, which the prior referred to as chronicles, within the various subfloors and rooms. We also decided to separate the stones and torc. From what little I knew of the stones at that time, I determined the largest stone, the Heart Stone, most likely held most of the power, although we considered the stories to be nothing more than fanciful tales. I convinced the prior that it should be sent away from the monastery. The details of where everything was hidden is in a separate journal, marked for those most trusted."*

Maire sat back and closed the journal. "I think we know the rest of the story. The Heart Stone was sent to Radcliffe, everything else was buried here but has since been moved again after everything that has happened with the duke and Reginald."

"So, whatever was in this separate journal that only his most trusted brothers could read is no longer accurate information." Murphy leaned his elbows on the table and looked at each person around the room. "If Belato had somehow discovered a way to get that journal, he'd be working with outdated information."

"If somehow this Belato learned everything had been moved..." Hughes kept his gaze on Maire. "The easiest way to find the new locations would be from Sebastian himself."

"That might be part of the kidnapping." Beckworth didn't sound convinced. "I think they need something more." He nodded toward Maire. "He needs a translator."

Murphy nodded. "I agree with Beckworth."

Lando snickered.

Beckworth grinned. "It's bound to happen occasionally." There was a time he'd take offense to Lando's response. It said something about how far he'd come to see it for what it was— simple jesting.

"The first question we have to consider," Murphy continued as if he hadn't been interrupted, "is whether Gemini and Belato are working together, or are they competitors?"

Hughes paced in what little space was available. "We don't have enough evidence to tell us one way or another."

"The most we know is that Gemini is probably the one that enticed the duke about the stones." Beckworth paused to recall the evening Gemini shared part of the story. He had no reason to believe she lied. She was too arrogant, always assuming she had the winning hand. "Whether she had good timing or had spies at court, I believe that this happened just prior to the duke being expelled from England. It wouldn't be a stretch to believe that while the duke was in Paris, he sent Dugan out to search for information on the stones. As much as he abhorred living at the monastery, he was far from the eyes of Napoleon's court, and had all the time he needed to pursue the story of the stones. When his guards discovered a stone, it made the story all that more real."

"But how did Gemini know of the stones?" Lando asked.

Beckworth laughed. "And that's the real question we need to answer. If I had to guess, I'd say it's all connected, and everything we've been through these years has come full circle."

Murphy growled. "And we've been the unwitting flies in the soup. Somehow staying one step ahead of messing up Belato's plans." He ran a finger over a groove in the table, worrying it over and over. "But we still don't have the evidence that the two are connected. We have to consider Gemini and Belato are working alone."

"How does that help us find Stella and Sebastian?" AJ hit the mark as far as Beckworth was concerned. It was critical to know who was giving the orders so they could determine their plans for the stones, but getting Stella and Sebastian out of harm's way was the priority. If they knew all the players in the abductions, that alone might provide all the answers they needed.

Maire collected the journals on the table. "I'll take these upstairs and read through them. Perhaps they'll provide more clues."

"We need to go back to Saint-Malo." Beckworth stood, wanting to leave right then but it would be foolish to ride through the evening with soldiers about.

"Why?" Maire asked.

"To see if we can narrow down who took Stella. I don't care that it was the middle of the night, someone's always awake in Saint-Malo. And this wasn't a single person. There were at least three of them, I would guess at least another holding a coach. It hasn't quite been a full day, so if I can get there quickly, I can question people before their memories fade."

"That seems like a long shot." Hughes took the journals from Maire. "Let me carry these for you."

Beckworth tamped down his temper, but it wasn't easy. "I know it may not yield anything, but you don't need my help to plan the next steps. This is how I can be the most useful. If I find nothing, then we don't have to wonder."

"Let's discuss it in the morning." Murphy stood and rubbed his face before striding to the door. Instead of opening it, he slid the blind open to confirm there wasn't anyone in the passageway.

"We have another task this evening." Maire closed the journal she'd been writing in and stuffed it in a pocket.

"What would that be?" Hughes asked.

"We need to visit the smuggler's meeting room," AJ answered.

Everyone looked to Maire, even though AJ had answered the question.

"When we visited France in the future timeline, we found a trail to one of Sebastian's journals that he'd left for me. It has the locations of what he referred to as the *Mórdha Stone Chronicles*. Since I've already read the journal, I know the locations of the individual chronicles, including the one still here in the monastery. Now I need to know if Sebastian has already left the journal."

AJ led the way since she was the most familiar with the maze of tunnels. Beckworth remembered most of the path, but he might have made one or two wrong turns. When he saw the stone bench that sat outside the smuggler's room, it reminded him of Stella. Two hundred years from now, she would stand in this very spot. Was she still alive as he'd told everyone he believed? Had she been hurt? The thought of it made him want to hit something, and he held his hands behind his back to prevent him from doing just that.

They followed Maire into the room. AJ was a step behind her, holding one of the lanterns high overhead as she followed Maire around the table to the far wall. Maire grabbed the lamp farthest to the left and twisted it to the right. A grating sound came from the lower part of the wall, and everyone gathered around, two more lanterns raised high to give her more light.

Maire was quiet when she removed a journal. She gave AJ a long stare, who nodded in return. He didn't know what to make of that but made a note to ask AJ if his curiosity wasn't appeased. Maire moved to the table and opened the journal. She only read a few lines before she closed her eyes and then the book.

"This is the same journal he left for me." She glanced at AJ, and he thought he caught tears in her eyes. He definitely needed some answers. "I'd like to take some time to copy the pertinent information, just to validate my other notes. I don't feel comfortable taking the journal from here. If we don't find them in the future..."

"It's not a problem." Murphy strode back to the door. "We'll be in the kitchen preparing the dinner that was left for us." He motioned for Lando, Beckworth, and AJ to leave before turning to Hughes. "She has one hour. No more. She can always come back in the morning."

When Maire started to protest, Hughes pulled a chair out for her. "No problem. We'll be up soon."

# 7

Beckworth woke early, but not as early as Maire, who was already in the smuggler's room reviewing Sebastian's last journal. Ever the perfectionist, she wanted to be positive she hadn't missed any clues as to the whereabouts of *The Mórdha Stone Grimoire*, otherwise known as the druid's book, and the torc. After getting a quick breakfast of porridge in the kitchen, he decided to stop by Sebastian's workroom. Murphy and Hughes appeared to be going through the entire room, inch-by-inch, in case they missed a secret hiding place. Unable to provide any help, he returned to his room to pack his saddlebags.

His patience was wearing thin. He understood the importance of what they were doing, but for him, it was wasting valuable time. The trail in Saint-Malo was growing cold. He was of no use to anyone here, and if he didn't do something proactive, he'd end up at Guerin's, spending the day getting drunk, and that helped no one at all.

He reached into his pocket and plucked out the delicate paper swan. One of his favorite memories was of Stella sitting on the bed in the brothel, her hair catching the firelight as it dried. His fingers brushed over the swan involuntarily, as if they were stroking the soft auburn tresses. She'd been making her birds, her teeth nipping her lower lip when she made certain folds. He could watch her all night.

He shook himself and went back to his task of gathering his things, including a few items of Stella's that had been left behind. He picked up her beaded purse, her remaining coins still in it. Not wanting to take her money, he'd discreetly negotiated a loan with Jamie, who could retrieve what was due him from Barrington, should he not make it back to Waverly. With enough coin in his pocket, he took nothing from the monastery. He would stop in town and gather more supplies. Items Stella would need, like two coffee pots and decent beans. He grinned at her obsession.

Once he had everything packed, he left the saddlebags by the door to the outer courtyard and returned to Sebastian's workroom to find Murphy. He found Lando pushing on stones behind the worn statue of the warrior. The team decided to keep all secret doors closed when not in use, just in case there was a spy or two at the monastery. It wasn't up to them to reveal Sebastian's secrets.

"You're too far down, try the one right behind the bloke's head." Beckworth leaned against the rock-hewn wall and watched Lando try two more stones before taking his suggestion.

When the door clicked open, Lando grinned. "You do come in handy, little man."

Beckworth shook his head, deciding that if he stopped grousing about the nickname, the big man might get bored and stop saying it. He pushed his way past him and entered the room, letting Lando close it behind them.

AJ was at a bookcase, pulling down a book, searching through it before replacing it. Murphy was at the table, scanning a journal by lantern light. It was Jamie that surprised him. He sat at the far edge of the table, several maps had been spread out, and he jumped from one to another and back again.

"Isn't this a fine scholarly group? Can any of you read these books?" Beckworth pulled out a chair and dropped into it, resting his boots on the table.

"Most of them are in French, which I can read. If I think it might hold something useful, it goes into a stack for Maire for further review." Murphy set the book he'd been scanning onto a tall stack. Beckworth doubted it was the one for Maire.

"And I'm taking a look to see if there are any secret compartments Finn or Ethan might have missed." AJ took the stack Murphy had reviewed and began setting them back on the shelves. "I've picked up a few French words, though I do spend more time asking what something says than being of much use."

"You're doing fine. Searching for hidden treasures is a painstaking effort which is why most pirates turn to plundering." Murphy winked at Jamie.

"Aye. It's much easier risking one's life running down a ship, boarding her, and daring a fight with her crew in the hopes of a better bounty."

AJ snorted and rubbed the back of her neck. "We've been at this for a while. I think I'll check on Maire's progress and take any books you'd like her to review." She picked up the short stack Murphy pointed at then went through the door Lando had opened for her.

Once she was gone, Beckworth tugged on his sleeves and gave Lando a long look before settling his gaze on Murphy.

"What is it? Not that I don't already know." Murphy pushed the journal away. "There's been something eating at you since last night. Is this about Stella?"

"Of course, it's about Stella. And Sebastian as well. I understand the need to know where all the valuables are buried. It gives us an advantage. But that doesn't mean we can't be doing more than one thing at a time. We shouldn't wait for the kidnappers to contact us."

"What do you propose?"

"I'm familiar with Saint-Malo. I spent time there when I worked for the duke. Some of my old friends must still be around. One or two that might be able to steer me in the right direction."

"This would be to gather information. No interference. No one can know you were there."

He understood the game. Uncover as much information as possible—how large was the crew, did they have their own ship, or did they have a safe house close by? If he was lucky enough to discover where Stella and Sebastian were being held, they could plan a double strike. While one team negotiated for an exchange, a second team could run the rescue operation. But he was getting ahead of himself.

"I'll be nothing more than a shadow." Beckworth buckled a knee, making it look like one leg was shorter than the other. He hunched his shoulders and gave Murphy a sketchy grin. He changed his speech pattern. "Even if they have someone on the crew that's met me or seen me, they won't recognize me." He cackled before straightening to his normal stature. "I wouldn't do anything to put Stella in harm's way. I guarantee that."

Murphy studied him for several seconds, and Beckworth refused to break the contact. He'd already said too much, and he didn't want anyone second-guessing things he refused to examine.

"You shouldn't go alone."

"I'm better on my own without someone getting in the way." He moved to the blind to check the outer corridor. Satisfied no one was there, he opened the door. "Give my regards to the rest of the team, but I think I should leave now. It would be better if I get there before dark."

He shut the door and heaved a sigh. The task of locating Stella was daunting, but she had to be near if the kidnappers had any interest in finding the Heart Stone. The question was where.

———

Beckworth grabbed his saddlebags and walked across the courtyard. A good night's rest, a supply of food the monks refused to let him leave without, and a loan from Jamie. He felt like a new man, or at least a better-prepared one. He dropped the bags by a post and retrieved his horse from a stall.

He'd just tied the horse to the post when soft footsteps approached. He released a sigh, hoping to avoid this conversation. But there had been little doubt he'd make it out of the courtyard without her tracking him down. He picked up a brush and hurried through the ritual.

"You were really going to leave without saying goodbye." AJ sounded hurt, and she had every right to be.

"I'm not in the mood for a lecture." He dropped the brush in a bucket then leaned over to check the horse's hooves.

She snorted. "I don't lecture."

He barked out a laugh as he walked around the horse. It couldn't be helped. After all their time apart, she still knew how to push his buttons, as they called it in her time period. "Perhaps I'm not prepared for your advice."

She leaned against the post and folded her arms across her chest. "I suppose that's better, but I wasn't going to give you any. I wish there was some to give."

"We've been in sticky situations before. We'll get through this as well." He walked across the aisle to gather the saddle and bridle.

"I wanted to thank you for searching for Stella. Finn believes the work we're doing here is important, and I agree, but I'd rather she not spend any more time than necessary with whoever took her." She bit her lip and glanced away.

"There's nothing for me to do here so I might as well be doing something I'm good at."

"Selecting fabric for a new waistcoat and how to plant a proper English garden." She grinned.

"You have to admit, most of the country could learn something from my tutoring." He couldn't help but return the smile, the first that made him feel better since Stella was taken.

"It wasn't your fault. No one would have expected someone to be waiting for you in France." AJ pet the horse's cheek, watching Beckworth tighten the girth and fuss with the saddlebags.

"It doesn't make it any easier to bear." He turned to her and was a bit surprised when she stepped back. Her brows furrowed as she studied him, and he wasn't sure what she saw—guilt, torment, a desire to flee. He wasn't certain of his own emotions.

"No. It doesn't." She handed him the bridle. "We haven't heard from the kidnappers. They must know we're at the monastery. Wouldn't they have sent a message by now, or someone to negotiate a trade?"

"It's too soon. They're probably waiting to hear back from those blokes who were following us. They'll give them another day before they conclude they won't be coming back. They know we're here. Maybe they're waiting for us to make the next move."

"Why would they kidnap Sebastian if they have Stella?"

"They kidnapped Sebastian before we landed. And as I said last night, if they can't locate Maire, they need another translator. Or maybe it's as simple as needing another hostage if Stella was lost to them."

AJ fed the horse a handful of hay. "What about the person

who came up with the new translation for the time travel? They got closer than Maire did."

"Yes, I was thinking about that. My best guess is that their translator, if they even have one, might have gotten lucky and just happened to stumble across it. Or perhaps this Belato monk learned more about the stones than Sebastian was aware."

When AJ glanced away, he leaned against a stall wall. "You're worried about something. And I don't mean Stella and Sebastian being kidnapped or someone trying to steal the stones and all their secrets. It's something deeper than all that. There's something you and Maire aren't sharing."

He remembered the look they'd given each other when Maire found Sebastian's journal in the smuggler's room. It was almost as if she hadn't wanted to find it. When the minutes ticked by and the urgency to leave swept over him, he decided she wasn't going to tell him. But when he took a step toward the horse, she wiped her eyes and her lips trembled.

"It's Sebastian."

He waited, giving her the time to put her words in order.

"When we took that holiday trip to France and visited the monastery, we were delighted that the monks and staff knew about Sebastian. There was even a statue of him in the courtyard." Her laugh was melancholy. "But no one could tell us how he died. There isn't a single record of it, nor any hint as to whether he left the monastery or died of some illness." She stared up at him and couldn't hold back the tears. "What if this is when he dies?"

Her words took the breath from him. Of all the things she could have said, this hadn't even occurred to him. He wasn't sure he had any words of encouragement for her, so he said the first thing that came to mind. "No one can control another's fate. I liked the turn of phrase I learned in your time period. We play the hand we're dealt. Some hold onto their chips, waiting for that perfect hand. Others go all in, risking chance on the next card. There's no right or wrong way, and we'll never know if the path we chose was the best one. If this is Sebastian's time, you can't blame yourself. We're not the ones who put this game in motion. And have you considered there might be other reasons why Sebastian didn't leave a trail as to his death?"

She nodded. "We thought it might be because he thought we'd come back already knowing when and how he would die."

"And that sounds like the most likely reason. But remember, they need a translator, and if they can't find Maire, Sebastian is the next best thing. Either way, they still need the Heart Stone. Stella is safe for now." If he only believed his own words.

"You have to find her." She laid a hand on his shoulder. "I don't mean to pressure you, but you're the best we have at this type of thing."

"Only sending in your best?" he chided, but her banter increased the lightness of his mood. He didn't mind the pressure. It barely touched the remorse he'd already placed on himself. "I won't let you down." He patted her hand. "She truly does make excellent coffee."

AJ swatted him. "Well, at least we have our priorities. Be safe."

"That goes without saying." He mounted the horse, and with a quick bow, he kicked the animal into a trot. He didn't look back, but he felt her gaze on him. He had to keep his promise. Almost as necessary as finding Stella, he didn't want AJ to lose her faith in him.

# 8

Beckworth kept his head down as he rode through town. His intent was to ride straight to Saint-Malo, but he decided it might not hurt to see if anyone might be staying close to keep an eye on the monastery. The town's two inns were the best places to hear gossip. He stayed for an ale at the inn across from Guerin's, then stumbled on his way across the street. It was doubtful that anyone watched him, but one could never be sure, and he might as well start his ruse now.

After an hour at Guerin's, he'd gained nothing but a decent bowl of stew and two pints of ale. Unsure what condition Stella's clothes might be in, he stopped at the mercantile and picked up a pair of pants, shirt, and jacket. He wished he could buy a stylish dress, but for now, pants were the best option.

In addition to blankets, hard tack, and a few other small items, he bought two coffee pots and a pound of beans. He was a fool, but he rationalized it had more to do with keeping his sanity rather than hearing her complaints, which could go on for hours if she was intent on torturing him. The thought made him smile. He'd put up with it, just to know she was safe.

He was on his way out the door when he noticed a display

case of jewelry, hairbrushes, and hand mirrors. His gaze locked on a hairpin. It was emerald green and cut in the shape of a leaf. He stared at it long enough that the store clerk hurried over.

"Is there something that caught your eye? A hand mirror or perhaps a broach?"

"The hairpin. The green one." Beckworth was being ridiculous, but he remembered how she kept pushing her hair out of her face when making her swans. And could the pin be any more perfect? Not only would the green look stunning against her dark auburn hair, but the leaf reminded him of all the times she'd brushed them from her hair after climbing out of a bush.

He couldn't stop the grin as he handed over the coins and took the wrapped hairpin, which he tucked inside his jacket. With one more stop at the apothecary, he stuffed the purchases in the saddlebags and mounted the horse.

With the time he spent at the inn and shopping, he kept the horse at a moderate pace. He would arrive in Saint-Malo well after dark, but since he'd already made all the necessary purchases, he could wander through town to scout at his convenience. More importantly, it opened up options of where he could stay that would keep him off the streets and away from the boardinghouses.

When he was about five miles from town, he slowed and turned into some trees. Several minutes passed before the quick pace of a single horse drew close. He waited until the rider passed before spurring his mount on to chase the man. It took less than a minute for the rider to slow and quickly turn his mount around, his sword out.

"Easy." Beckworth held up his hands, no weapons in sight. "I just thought if you were going to follow me all the way to Saint-Malo, we might as well ride the rest of the way together."

"One day, your surprises will get you killed, little man."

Lando turned back toward Saint-Malo and moved his horse at a slower pace.

Beckworth caught up and rode by his side. "Will Murphy ever trust me?"

"It has nothing to do with trust. If these men are part of Gemini's crew, she's proven to be unpredictable. If the abduction was Belato, we have no idea how many men he has. You need someone to watch your back, whether you think you do or not. There's too much on the line to lose you, too."

"It's comforting to know there comes a point in our numbers where I become valuable." His words belied the sense of camaraderie he felt hearing Lando's words. He wasn't one to gush over praise. He'd sought it from the duke for too many years to count. Hearing it from men who put loyalty above all else made him sit his horse a bit straighter.

"I have to admit there was a time I didn't think I'd ever come to trust you." Lando glanced over his shoulder, ever the watchful one.

"What made you change your mind?"

Lando rubbed his cropped hair then his jaw. "I've questioned your motives several times. Most would probably think it was when you continued to search for Finn after he was captured by Dugan."

That made him pause. "I thought most people assumed I was the traitor."

"They did—in the beginning. But each time it appeared your motives were all about Waverly, your assistance came at great jeopardy to yourself. You could have gone into Waverly and eventually wrestled it back. You were smarter than your half-brother, but don't let that comment go to your head. Reginald wasn't that bright."

Beckworth laughed. No one in this group would ever give too much praise—it wasn't their way. They proved their loyalty through action, something he'd taken for granted but wouldn't any longer. The silence stretched as they rode, and he assumed Lando had nothing more to say on the topic. Whether he'd been mulling over the right words or had needed the time to provide the right answer, Beckworth didn't know. But as it turned out, Lando wasn't finished.

"I didn't understand at the time why you stopped me from chasing after Dugan's men when they captured AJ outside Corsham. I thought you mad or possibly working for Reginald. But I surely would have been killed had you not stopped me. It wasn't difficult to see, once I gained my head, how worried you were for AJ, though you wouldn't admit it at the time."

"I don't know what made me see the light as to what I'd been doing in my attempts to gain approval from the duke. Maybe it was my time in the future, never knowing if I'd find my way home. But after all those miles spent with AJ and watching how much Murphy's men trusted her on the ship..." He glanced off to the distance. This was a difficult conversation he wished he hadn't started. "Let's just say she was the first one to see something different in me, and I suppose it rubbed off."

"As I said, little man, don't let it go to your head."

"So, tell me, did you volunteer to follow me, or did Jamie select you for this task?"

"Someone had to make sure you didn't get yourself killed, or worse, lose AJ's friend again." With that, Lando nudged the horse to a faster pace.

Beckworth could have taken offense about losing Stella, but like earlier in the monastery, he understood Lando's words for the jest they were. Lando had his back and that was all he needed to know. He kicked his horse to catch up, and they rode in silence until the lights of the city came into view.

"What was your plan?" Lando pulled out his eyepiece and scanned the area in the moon's stingy light. "It's hard to see much. It's possible the kidnappers are no longer here and moved them closer to the monastery. But I imagine you did a bit of investigating while making your purchases."

"The innkeeper at Guerin's remembered me. The town's on edge after hearing Sebastian was taken. They're more watchful. It's possible that one or two men might be overlooked, but no more than that without drawing attention."

Lando nodded. "So where do we start?"

"The pubs, but we need to find a base to work from. I have an idea or two on that."

"Not the boardinghouse."

He grimaced. "No, not there. I no longer trust them. Though I might go back and have a word or two with them. Someone should have seen something of that night, but I'd prefer to leave that as a last resort."

They spent the night a few miles from town, close enough to watch the slowly diminishing lights but far enough away that a fire wouldn't be noticed unless someone went out of their way. They ate hard tack and Beckworth made coffee, remembering to crush the beans as Stella had done. It didn't taste like hers, but it was close.

The following morning, Beckworth explained his plans for a more permanent location, then gave Lando directions. It would be better to travel apart. Not knowing who was involved, someone might recognize him, but no one should know Lando. They would enter town from different directions and uncover as much as they could.

An hour later, Beckworth turned down a deserted alley after circling the streets closest to the old dock. This part of town was in disrepair and most ships tied up at the newer docks. But no one stopped anyone from docking at the old pier. At this time, only one ship was using the dock. While the name of a ship said little about its origins, the name *The English Rose* suggested an

English ship. He turned away from the dock and rode to an alley three blocks away. Only a handful of the buildings were in use, nothing more than warehouses on the cheap.

The wood building was deteriorating from time and weather, but it was still standing and would require a few more years before it toppled. He opened the delivery door, which was wide enough to accommodate carts, and walked his horse in, dismounting to shut the door. After tying the horse to one of the posts, he left the saddlebags on the horse and climbed the narrow staircase to the second-floor offices. He found three oil lamps and a windowless room.

When he heard the door of the warehouse being pulled open, he jogged down the stairs to meet Lando. "Tie your horse to a post. There's an office upstairs with decent ventilation and no windows. We can have a fire in the evenings."

"How did you know about this place?"

"An old friend used to run his ill-gotten gain through it. This was several years ago when more ships docked here."

"The duke's people didn't know about it, did they?"

Beckworth gave Lando a long look, wondering if the man still thought him a spy. "If they did, it would make this a horrible decision on my part. I assure you, I'm smarter than that."

Lando smiled. "That you are, little man. So, what's the plan for the rest of the day?"

He almost cringed at Lando's pet name. How long did he have to ignore it before Lando got bored with it? "It will be safer for you to check the town."

Lando nodded. "I can check the pubs and inns as I walk the streets, but I doubt anyone will be congregating in groups."

"They won't be parading Stella or Sebastian around. But my guess is they've been docked here a while. Someone will make note of it. Keep your ears open."

"And what will you be doing?"

"I can't say why, but I think the docks might hold our answers."

"You think they're on a ship?"

He shrugged. "It's just a feeling. They could have them in a building like this one. They might not even be in Saint-Malo anymore. We should know for certain in the next couple of days. Let's meet back here in four hours and see what we can put together."

F our hours later, Beckworth had spoken with someone from every ship in port. He'd started with the ships docked closest to town. If someone had prisoners, they wouldn't want to be close enough for anyone to hear screaming, but he wanted to be methodical and not rule anything out. So he moved from the less likely ships until he narrowed down his options. The more sailors he spoke with, two ships stood out as possibilities, and he shifted his tactics until he had a prime target.

Of the two ships he was left with, he again focused on the most unlikely. It was an English schooner—a smuggler. England wasn't fond of smugglers, but Napoleon embraced them.

After fifteen minutes of watching the ship and the crew, he approached the sailor that seemed to be in charge. It was a dangerous approach; they all had been. It was unfortunate Eleanor wasn't here. Her ability to change someone's appearance through skills learned as a dressmaker in London's theater would have come in handy. He scratched his couple days' worth of beard and smiled. It would have to be enough.

He limped toward the man, his gaze focused on the ground, only rising every couple of steps until the man stopped shouting orders and glared at him.

The sailor slapped another man on his shoulder and pushed him away. "Not like that. Go find Billy and have him show you the proper way."

Before the man walked off, Beckworth bent and untied the ropes used to haul cargo off the dock and into the hold. He retied the ropes then slapped the crate. "That should do it," he said, using his best Cockney accent.

"You looking for a spot on board?" The man, who might be the second mate, gave him a more thorough look.

"Something to get me back to England. I'm not fussy about the port. I work hard."

"Well, at least you know your knots. I have a spot, but we'll be working our way down the coast. We won't be seeing England again for at least a month or two."

Beckworth scratched his head, then slowly shook it. "I've already been gone too long."

"That's the best I can do. We leave at dawn. If you change your mind, ask for Smithy."

He nodded. "I'll give it some thought." Then he turned and limped away. Before he made it five paces, the man called after him.

"You can try the ship at the end of the pier. I hear they're headed for England with the next tide."

He turned and gave the man a wave, continuing on with his limp and a grin. Now, if fate was with them.

# 9

"Two guards." Lando shifted his position as he and Beckworth squatted behind stacks of barrels and crates. "One is on the deck, but he spends most of his time aft. He makes it to the bow every fifteen or twenty minutes. The one on the dock spends most of his time starboard. The rest of the men look to be preparing the ship for sail."

Beckworth had returned from making a perimeter sweep after tying the horses a hundred yards away in case they made a sound. It was a couple of hours before dawn, and Lando had been monitoring the ship since he had more experience in knowing how quickly it would be ready to sail.

They would have arrived earlier, but Lando had discovered a possible location perfect for holding prisoners. The only problem was that they had to wait for the cover of darkness, and they'd barely gotten past the men guarding the facility. Instead of finding the kidnappers, they'd found themselves surrounded by unsavory mercenaries. They hadn't been spotted, but it was impossible to leave until the men had settled down for the evening, which had been an hour earlier.

The mercenaries had something to hide, but it wasn't Stella.

At that point, Beckworth just wanted out of there. Now, they had little time to ascertain if this was the right ship, but with the crew preparing to set sail, he wasn't sure what they could do.

"The crew is lazy, maybe half asleep." Lando tapped Beckworth on the shoulder, then moved to a closer spot near the bow and behind a cart. He pulled out his spyglass. "There's not enough light to make out much else."

Beckworth scratched his beard. "We could grab one for questioning, but it wouldn't be long before he was missed."

"Maybe. Sometimes men just disappear."

"Not sure I want to take that chance." He peered around the other side of the horseless wagon, but the different angle didn't provide any new information.

"The only other option would be to board her, but it will be tricky." Lando tucked his spyglass away.

"It doesn't appear I have much of a choice. If I get caught, just head back to the monastery. Someone needs to report back to Finn and Jamie."

Beckworth took two steps when he heard a sound to his left.

"Psst. Beckworth."

He spun around. Was he hearing things?

"Over here."

"Stella," he whispered, turning to a canvas-shrouded stack of crates.

Lando was beside him, partially turned to watch the men on the ship.

The canvas parted like the curtains at a theater, and Stella, dirty but apparently unhurt, tiptoed to them.

Before he knew it, he was hugging her. He wasn't sure if he pulled her in or if she jumped into his arms, but it didn't matter. Not wanting to let go, and sensing Lando watching them, he pushed her back.

"Are you hurt? Where have you been?" Beckworth held her

at arm's length and gave her a thorough perusal. Her clothes were wrinkled, her hair was a rat's nest, but her smile warmed his heart.

"I'm fine. And I've been over there." She nodded toward the ship. "I woke up in a cage in a cargo hold."

"Then why aren't you there now?" Lando asked.

She turned toward him, twisting out of Beckworth's hold. "And who are you?"

Beckworth grinned. She hadn't lost her spunk.

Before Lando could answer, she waved a hand. "No. No. Don't tell me." She stood with one hand on her hip, a finger resting on her chin. One of her thinking poses. She looked him up and down, tapped a foot then snapped her fingers. "Lando."

Lando shook his head but couldn't hold back a grin. "At your service. Now, please, time is of the essence. How did you manage to get off the ship?"

"Yes. Exactly. Well, the cage has a rather simple lock, but I didn't have anything to pick it until Sebastian lent me his robe..."

"Sebastian is with you?" Beckworth interrupted.

"Yeah. Sorry. Probably should have mentioned that first. Anyway, he had this little silver cross in the pocket of his robe that with a little bit of bending was able to fit in the lock. I came out last night after the evening meal. Sebastian said once they left a meal, they didn't return for hours, so I thought I'd check out our situation and see if there was anyone out here to rescue us." She winked at them. "Guess second time is a charm." She focused on Beckworth, giving him the same quick study he'd given her. "But what happened to you? I was so busy trying to get away from the kidnappers, but they were too strong. I thought I saw you fighting with someone, but then it was lights out for me."

"I woke the next morning. Or I should say AJ woke me, mad as a hatter."

"AJ and Finn found you?" Her eyes misted over. "I can't believe I didn't ask. I should have known when Lando was with you." She grabbed his wrist. "Is she okay? Are they all okay?" Her head dropped. "I can't believe how close they were."

"This can be discussed later. Why didn't you get Sebastian out and then escape?" Lando asked.

"What a grand idea. Gee, why didn't I think of that?"

Beckworth grimaced. Based on her touchy mood, he guessed she hadn't been given any coffee. Probably nothing more than water and leftovers from the crew.

She continued on after giving Lando an apologetic shrug. "That was our plan if no one came before sunrise. But we have no money and no transportation. Sebastian has friends near here, but it would be a long walk. We didn't think we'd have gotten far if we tried before now. Any other questions before we get Sebastian?"

Lando gave Beckworth a sympathetic grin. "It must have been an interesting journey running from Gemini."

"You don't know the half of it." Beckworth glanced back at the ship. "You said they're sailing in the morning? We heard they were sailing with the tide."

"I'm sure they said morning."

She didn't sound that convinced, but at this point it didn't matter. They had to go back aboard to get Sebastian. They'd have to be quick about it.

"Okay. Tell me where they've been keeping you, and I'll go get him." Beckworth glanced around the crates to see what the crew was doing. He couldn't be sure, but it seemed like there was more activity.

"I have to show you."

"No," both men declared at the same time, shaking their heads in unison.

"It's like a maze down there. It took me half the first night to figure out the turns and remember them. It's pitch black down there without light."

Beckworth rooted around in his saddlebag and pulled out a small candle. He turned to Lando. "You know what to do if we get caught?"

Lando nodded then ducked back down behind the cart.

He took Stella's arm. "Show me where you board her."

She led him back to the ship then paused. "How did you find us?"

"Let's discuss that after we get Sebastian."

He glanced up, curious how she'd gotten off the ship in the first place.

She stepped closer, keeping her voice low, her expression serious. "I worried they'd killed you."

He tapped his knuckles on his head. "It's quite hard."

Her lips twitched for a moment. "I didn't freak out when I woke in the cage. It helped that Sebastian was with me. But I'm not sure what I would have done if you hadn't shown up." She wrapped her arms around her middle and stared into the darkness of the dock.

He grabbed her shoulders and turned her face to him. "You're standing on the dock after picking the lock of your cage and sneaking out under the noses of more than a dozen men. You could have run at any time, but you stayed because of Sebastian. Being courageous isn't always the same as being fearless. Now, let's get our monk and get away before they notice."

She studied him for an instant then nodded. After glancing around, she stepped on a crate and then a stack of two before reaching the gun port. When she grabbed the edge and slithered through the opening, he could only stare, slack-jawed.

After a second, she popped her head back out and asked with a loud whisper, "Are you coming?"

---

S tella waited next to the cannon, shifting from foot to foot. She wasn't sure if she was shaking because she was cold or because she'd actually found Beckworth. Or rather, he'd found her.

He'd come for her.

Funny how she never questioned it. She assumed it was because of all the stories AJ and Finn had shared with her. Beckworth always seemed to come through. Even Maire, who had every reason to dislike him, had changed her opinion of him. Although, being Maire's way, she did get frustrated with him. If she was honest with herself, there were times he drove her mad. She smiled. Those were the times she enjoyed being around him the most.

A soft thud and an arm brushing against her woke her from her daydreaming. Beckworth fumbled in his pocket, and then a flame cast a yellow glow for several feet around them. He lifted it to let the light creep into the darkness.

"What made you think of the gunports?" He sounded amazed.

She tucked her hair behind her ears and shrugged. "I considered the hatch, but I couldn't reach the rope ladder. I didn't think I'd be able to sneak past anyone if I took the stairs. I smelled the gunpowder when I was trying to find a way out, then I remembered the gunports on the *Daphne Marie*. I thought I might be able to squeeze through."

"It was a tight fit. Where from here?"

She turned to the bow. "This way." They moved swiftly but had to douse the flame when the sound of footsteps approached, the light of a lantern heading their way. Beckworth pulled her to a far corner where the shadows would be the darkest and held her against him. It rekindled memories of the long days on horseback. When the footsteps went upstairs and Beckworth relit the candle, she regretted the moment hadn't lasted longer.

They moved into the hold where Stella and Sebastian were being kept, and Beckworth doused the candle. The monk was lying on his pallet and looked asleep, but when they reached the door to the cell, he sat up.

He took a moment to stand then smiled when he saw his visitors. "Ah, Lord Beckworth. It's good of you to rescue us. Stella was certain you would."

She didn't dare look at Beckworth and focused on the lock. "You know I'd say anything to keep our spirits up." She sneaked a glance at him. Heat warmed her cheeks, and she turned her back to him as she fussed with her task. Honestly, how could any woman not blush like a schoolgirl with that look in his eyes? Thank the stars she hadn't been wearing the lingerie when she'd been kidnapped.

She'd barely opened the door when the ship shifted, and she lost her balance. "What the hell?" Beckworth caught her elbow before she went down.

Sebastian, not expecting it any more than her, wasn't as fortunate, and he fell on his backside. He didn't stay down for long and rolled to his knees. Pretty spry for an old man. But the ship pitched again, and he struggled for his balance.

"Damn it to hell. I think we've lost our chance. Stay here." Beckworth pulled the candle from his pocket and slipped out the door.

She hung onto the bars of the cell. Sebastian did the same as the ship rocked. She closed her eyes and cursed at not getting Sebastian off the ship sooner.

It seemed like hours before Beckworth returned, though it was more like ten minutes. He was carrying a saddlebag.

"What's going on?" Stella backed up, her stomach already starting to churn from the rolling deck.

"I thought you said they weren't sailing until morning?" He didn't look happy, and rather than look at her, he searched through the saddlebag, nodding as he did.

"They said morning. I'm sure that's what they said." She sounded defensive, and it irritated her, but she might have missed the part about the tide. She couldn't believe she'd made such a colossal mistake.

"What they actually said was that we'd sail with the tide in the morning." Sebastian returned to his pallet and sat down.

"I thought that meant sunrise." Her voice was barely audible to her own ears. It had been a really bad assumption. And now she'd put Beckworth in danger.

"There's nothing for it now." He didn't sound angry, but he had to be questioning the wisdom of coming back for her. "We can't change our circumstances, so we need to plan how we can use this to our advantage." He closed the saddlebag and stood. "Did they mention where they were headed?"

"Southampton," Sebastian answered.

He nodded. "Give me a minute." He strode to the door and took the lamp off the hook, then began walking the perimeter of the hold.

She watched him, curious what he was thinking when he hesitated at the back of the cells. The lamplight wasn't strong enough to brighten the entire hold, and she'd never wandered over there. He returned the lamp to the nail.

"Do they always keep the lamp lit?" Beckworth asked.

Sebastian leaned his head against the bars. "They have while we were in port, but they also bring one of their own."

"How are we going to hide you?" Stella stared at the saddle-bag, refusing to look at him.

He picked up the saddlebag, walked to the farthest corner of the room, then returned without it. "Tell me their full routine."

"They come twice a day with food and stay long enough to taunt us while they change out buckets." Sebastian gave Stella an encouraging smile that only scratched the surface of her remorse. "The only other time I've had visitors was the first day when a man came in alone, but he only stared at me before leaving. And of course, when they brought Stella."

Beckworth nodded. "The oil lamp won't reach the corners of the room, and unless they have a reason to come farther than your cells, and I stay perfectly still, we might get lucky."

"How did you get the saddlebag?" Stella's cranky side was coming to life. She was filled with dread about the Channel crossing and worry for Beckworth if they discovered him. Would they kill him in front of them or just toss him overboard?

He gave her a long look, though she dropped her gaze after the first few seconds. "Lando. If I got caught, he was to stay hidden so he could report back to Finn. If their plan was to sail with the tide, we should have had enough time to get off the ship. I don't think either of us expected them to set sail so quickly. Either something made them sail sooner than expected, or they have a green crew, which would explain the rough start. The sails weren't set properly against the tide."

"That doesn't explain the saddlebag." Stella knew she was harping on all the wrong things, but she couldn't help herself. The fact the ship set sail before the tide didn't lessen her guilt.

Beckworth shrugged as he walked into her cell and looked around, his eyes locking on the thin pallet and raincoat. "Lando would have known we'd run out of time, and he knew where we boarded. He took a chance to climb up and toss the bag in. With everyone busy setting sail, no one would have paid attention.

And while I had two saddlebags, he rightly assumed one would be difficult enough to hide."

"They'll be coming soon, son. We should be prepared." Sebastian lay down and closed his eyes.

"Right." Beckworth stepped to Stella and squeezed her shoulders. "Don't worry. I know you were hoping to be back home by now. I'm sorry you have to go through all of this again."

"I can't believe how stupid I was. Now, I've gotten you in trouble. What if they catch you?"

"Let's deal with one issue at a time." He took her hand and placed her beaded purse in it.

She blinked back the tears and opened the bag, dumping the coins into her palm. "If I remember your lesson, this is a lot of money."

He nodded. "And it's best you keep it. If they do catch me, they'll take it. I doubt they'll think to search you again. If you have a chance to escape, with or without Sebastian, you have the money to find your way to London. Hensley should be there for another month or two."

She stared at the coins for another few seconds before nodding and stuffing them in the bag.

"If you make it to London, buy a decent day dress and go to the gentlemen's club at 28 St. James Street. Can you remember that?" When she nodded, he continued. "They won't let you in, but tell the doorman that the Viscount of Waverly sent you. Ask for Phillip. He'll arrange a coach to Hensley's manor."

"I don't like this."

"It's just a precaution. I don't plan on getting caught."

She nodded, unable to say anything else.

"Now, back to your cell, and don't even glance toward the back of the hold."

"I'm not that much of an amateur."

He chuckled. "No. You're not. And I almost forgot." He

reached into his pocket and retrieved a pouch. "There are smaller individual bags inside. They're close to the same colors as before."

Her heart beat faster, and her insides felt like mush. He remembered to bring herbs for her seasickness. Her eyes watered, and she kept her head lowered, blinking rapidly to dry them. She snorted, but her voice was thicker. "Well, someone planned for a voyage."

He grinned. "Another precaution."

"Thank you." He'd planned everything except for an earlier-than-expected departure. She didn't know what else to say, so she stepped to Sebastian's cell door and relocked it. Then she stepped into her own, repeating the action with the door before shoving the tool into her pants pocket.

Beckworth grabbed the bars and peered in. "Get some sleep if you can. It's best if we stay quiet. It might be a while yet with the ship getting underway, but we can't be too careful." He reached in and squeezed her arm before moving to the back of the hold.

She watched him disappear into the shadows. Other than strange noises she couldn't place, it was as if he'd evaporated, like walking into the fog.

She pulled on her raincoat and curled up on her pallet. The tears fell without warning, and she knew they weren't for herself or for Sebastian. She'd led Beckworth into a tenuous position while he was trying to save her. If anything happened to him, it would be her fault.

## 10

Finn watched his wife pace along the windows that overlooked the bay where the *Daphne Marie* was anchored. She didn't notice the warm spring day, the light breeze blowing in from the south, or the white puffy clouds emblazoned on a rich blue sky. He understood her misery. Once again, Beckworth and Stella were gone. Though from Lando's explanation, not on purpose. For some reason, the ship had left before the tide. Maybe what the kidnappers had told their hostages hadn't been true or plans had changed. Either way, they'd lost another member of their crew.

AJ hadn't seemed to hear most of what Lando had shared, or perhaps she was simply ignoring it. And now, she began mumbling, her hands balling in and out of fists. He didn't think it possible, but she was working up her anger again.

He didn't dare try approaching her. His own anger was hidden beneath the surface, and though he shared her concerns, he couldn't see how anything could have been done differently. At least they knew where Sebastian was. If only Stella had gotten Sebastian off the ship as soon as she could have. But then what? Where would they have gone and not have dozens of men after them?

Part of AJ's problem was that she'd convinced herself that Stella had gone a bit mad from her kidnapping and her first days alone with Gemini. Even after listening to Beckworth paint a very different picture—a woman far from crazy and quickly adapting to her surroundings—AJ fell back into the old paradigm whenever she became stressed.

Then there were the kidnappers. Nothing they were doing made sense. Gemini might have been unpredictable in her actions, but her goal had been clear—use the power of the Heart Stone, and the torc if possible, to travel to the future, gain important information, then sell it to the highest bidder. He didn't think many people knew there was a second Heart Stone —the original. If this group was working for Belato, he would know they needed the Heart Stone, even with the torc. So, why leave without bartering for the one item they needed? Unless they thought Sebastian could find something more in *The Book of Stones*, or worse, force him to lead them to the torc. Again, why leave?

"What's taking her so long?" AJ bit out the question, which made him lift a brow. She dropped into a chair and bent over, holding her head in her hands. "Sorry. Sorry. I know Maire works at her own pace. I'm not understanding what point fate is trying to impart with Stella always slipping away from us."

He gave in and approached her, running a hand along her back. "I find myself with the same dilemma, but perhaps we're too focused on wanting to see Stella. We want to know for sure that she's safe and unharmed. To see it with our own eyes. The only word we had was from Beckworth, but now Lando has met her. And his observation didn't portray her as someone who had lost their wits, but a woman focused and determined."

"But she hasn't been involved in these schemes before. She doesn't understand how ruthless they can be."

"Doesn't she?"

AJ sat up, and Finn massaged her shoulders and neck. She leaned into his ministrations and sighed as the knots released. "Her entry into this time period was worse than mine. No matter how mad I'd been with you, you taught me how to survive."

"And hasn't Beckworth done the same thing? They might have only known each other by sight, but they knew us. After hearing Beckworth's tale about their journey to France, I'd say Stella is fitting right in."

She laughed, took his hand, and kissed it. "Thank you for being my touchstone."

"Perhaps we should go to our room and wait." He pulled back her hair and kissed her neck, knowing it tickled her. He pulled her to him when she giggled and tried to get away. "Oh no, you don't."

They both broke away when running footsteps, heading their way, sounded in the hall. Maire ran through the door, almost toppling a desk as she bounced off it, moving too fast to make the turn and sliding on the polished stone floor.

"I've got it. The last name and location." She was out of breath and holding her side. "Maybe I should have spent some time running with you." She plopped a book and several sheets of paper onto the desk, then collapsed into the chair. "I don't know why Sebastian bothered to encrypt the names after all he did to hide his journal, which was already written in Celt, but he might have suspected a spy."

Bootsteps echoed down the hall, hurried but not running. A few seconds later, Ethan broke through the door. "I had no idea you could move that fast. One minute I was gazing out the window talking about the new herbs in the garden, then I turned around to find you gone."

Maire blushed. "Sorry. I would have thought the rustling of pages as I gathered everything up would have been a clue."

He kissed the top of her head. "You obviously aren't aware of how often you rattle paper without moving from your seat." He gave her shoulder a squeeze before joining Finn and AJ near the windows.

"I suppose that's true enough." Maire laid out the pages and opened a journal. "I assumed since Sebastian had sent two chronicles to England that the last one would have been sent there as well. As it turns out, the last one is right here in France. Bréval to be exact, just west of Paris."

"Who did he send it to?" Finn's jaw tightened with the news, and AJ squeezed his hand, understanding the dilemma. Paris during a time of war wasn't a safe place to travel.

"That's the other strange thing." Maire wrote a note on one of the pages. "He sent it to a woman, the Countess Blanchet. At the time of his notes, this would only have been a year ago, so they should still be in the same location."

"What do we know of this countess?" Finn didn't want to travel deeper into France, but it didn't appear they had a choice. He rubbed his ribs which were long healed since his beating by the French soldiers, but the memory would last a lifetime.

"I've asked Brother Ignatius to join us," Ethan said. "He seems to keep track of the political powers in Paris."

"Yes. Sorry for being late, I had to finish a response for a messenger." Brother Ignatius entered, his hair standing up on one side, his glasses skewed. He acknowledged everyone in the room before taking a chair near Maire.

"I didn't think the monastery was political." AJ took the opportunity to slip from Finn's grasp, and he let her go, expecting her to pace, but she went back to her spot near the window.

"It isn't," the monk said. "But after the raid during the Terror,

Brother Sebastian felt it important to keep an eye on what was happening outside the monastery. He thought we'd be better prepared for changes in policy."

"Smart." Ethan rolled out a map that Finn hadn't noticed him carry in. "When I went into town with Louis for supplies, there was talk at Guerin's about a shift in local command. There will be an increase in troop movements between here and Paris. This could be a problem for us."

"Maybe." Finn's answer was returned with skeptical looks. "Let's hear Brother Ignatius's information before we settle on a solution. Can you tell us anything about this Countess Blanchet?"

The monk smiled. "Oh, oui. She is well known around here because of her humble beginnings. She was raised at the convent not far from here. She came with several other young women to help at the monastery as a maid and was one of the few Sebastian allowed in his workrooms. She was quite devout, though I remember Sebastian mentioned once that he hadn't thought her meant for a solitary life of the convent. He asked an old friend if they would take her in for one year to see if a life with a well-placed merchant would suit her better."

"This was before the Revolution?" Finn asked.

The monk nodded. "Many years before. She never returned. Instead of working as a maid, the merchant's wife had connections at court. She educated the young woman, who attended royal functions with the couple. She caught the eye of Count Blanchet and eventually married him. She never lost contact with Sebastian except during the Terror. Sebastian worried that the count and countess would meet Madame Guillotine, but the count was a wise man and changed his political stance before the Revolution. While he didn't approve of Robespierre, he knew enough to keep his head and his land. He and the countess became popular in Napoleon's court, though as I understand it, the countess continued her work outside the court helping the poor."

"And it appears, at least a year ago, Sebastian trusted her enough to send her one of the chronicles." Maire had a light in her eyes that Finn had seen hundreds of times. She was cooking up a scheme. "I've looked for recent communiques that Sebastian might have kept, but I haven't been able to find any."

Brother Ignatius shook his head. "There was at least one, about seven or eight months ago. She had taken ill, but the doctors felt she'd make a full recovery."

No one said anything. They didn't have to. It was quite likely the woman hadn't recovered. "Is the count still alive?" Finn didn't like the direction this was taking, but when he'd heard the locations of the other two chronicles, he understood what they would have to do. No one was going to like it.

"As far as I know," Brother Ignatius answered. "I continue to monitor Sebastian's correspondence and respond where I can."

"Now that we have our three locations, we have enough to make plans. We need Jamie, Fitz, and Lando. And Brother Ignatius, I'd appreciate your opinion as well."

"Of course. It's almost time for tea. I'll have something set up in here if that's acceptable."

Once the monk left, Ethan broke the news so Finn wouldn't have to. "It seems we have no choice but to break up the team."

---

AJ didn't like it. Not one bit. They worked better as a team, not broken up into little segments with no backup. But she held her tongue to see if Finn agreed, though he hadn't batted an eye when Ethan suggested it. She felt a knot forming, and she rubbed her stomach. She'd brought antacids for Stella but maybe she'd need them long before she caught up with her best friend. It appeared Stella was fine on her own with Beckworth watching over her.

She dropped into a chair, and suddenly Finn was next to her. Thankfully, Ethan had taken Maire out to get some air and ask one of the sailors to get the men.

"Are you going to be all right?"

"No."

He chuckled, but it was half-choked out. Her poor husband probably didn't know whether she was joking. He massaged her neck. "Relax. Are you more concerned about the team splitting up, or that Stella is once again in trouble?"

"I told Beckworth to find her, not take off with her. And our missions are barely successful with dozens of men, how can we succeed in smaller groups? Gemini and now this Belato. We have no idea how outnumbered we are."

This time his laugh could probably be heard all the way to Sebastian's secret workroom. He pulled her from the chair and dragged her to the sofa. She wasn't feeling cooperative, knowing a lecture was at hand, and wondered if this might be comparable to being taken to the woodshed. She couldn't even muster a smile at the thought of Finn bending her over for a spanking. Well, perhaps a slight twitch of the lips escaped, but then she forced the frown to return, though it was difficult. She wasn't going to let Finn weave his Irish blarney to make everything seem logical—even if it was. She wasn't in the mood.

Finn sat and tugged her off her feet. She fell against him, and he grasped her in a fierce hug. "Now, you're going to sit here and listen to me before everyone returns. You keep getting way ahead of yourself, and now you've worked yourself up to the point of feeling ill."

When she remained silent, he continued, "First, let's talk about Stella. There's been good reason to worry about her before we caught up with Beckworth. Now, I'm not saying we shouldn't still be worried, but as crazy as this might sound, it's worry for a different reason. In just over a week, she's learned to survive with or without Beckworth. You know how smart she is. And I realize she sometimes acts before thinking things through, but there's enough of that behavior to go around with our team. Based on what Lando shared, Stella had waited until the last moment before chancing an escape with Sebastian. It was luck that Beckworth and Lando found her at all. But no one was to blame for the ship departing before they had the tide." He gave her a kiss on the cheek. "If you were in Stella's shoes with the options she'd been handed, what would you have done?"

Her head rolled into his chest. "The same thing."

"She has Beckworth watching out for her. And now, we know where Sebastian is. I'm not sure what to think of those three together."

She laughed, and it was an honest one. "And why do we have to split up?"

"Several reasons, but the main one has to do with how far apart the chronicles have been spread. We need to hit fast. And while having dozens of men at your back can make one feel more secure, sometimes the easiest solution is a small strike force, who can move and adapt quickly."

"If you have the right team." They both turned to see Jamie stroll in with Fitz and Lando behind him.

"Aye," Fitz said. "Remember that time just south of Belfast? You decided to send me and Jamie in to steal..." he coughed, "I mean, borrow those barrels of whiskey."

Finn laughed. "I didn't know I had to tell you not to open one before you got them all onboard."

Lando almost choked, and tears ran down his face. "They couldn't see what they were doing in the dark. I think they stopped at a pub before completing their task."

"It must have been weak wood for the barrel to have split like that," Jamie insisted, though his smile was wide enough to split his face.

"What happened?" AJ asked, unable to stop her own grin that came more from seeing the men so jovial rather than the story itself.

"The two of them came back, one barrel short, soaking wet, and smelling of a distillery," Finn managed to get out.

"The barrel had split open, and the pressure inside blew the whiskey all over them. They were bathed in it." Lando held his belly as if it would burst open like the barrel.

Finn waved a hand. "Sorry, Ethan, this was a tale for the record books."

"I'm afraid we caught most of it," Maire said with Ethan in tow. She attempted to appear shocked and disappointed, but she couldn't stop the laughter in her gaze.

Brother Ignatius entered in time for everyone to settle, and three of the kitchen staff followed with trays. Maire and AJ rushed over to clear a table for the platters. As was their way, they discussed trivial matters while they ate, then updated Jamie, Lando, and Fitz on the third location and the unknown health of the countess.

After the trays were removed, Ethan and Jamie spread out their maps—Ethan's of France and Jamie's of England.

Ethan pointed to a spot southeast of their current location and just northwest of Paris. "From here, it will take a little over four days by horseback, another day or two by coach, to reach Bréval. We don't know if the count is aware of the chronicle should the countess's health be an issue. But assuming a team is able to collect it, the best path from there would be to catch a ship in Le Havre."

"The team can find a ship heading to England at one of the two smuggler ports just west and east of there." Fitz brought over a small tray with a bottle of Jameson and several glasses. "They'll most likely be heading toward Southampton or one of the smaller ports like Bournemouth." He poured a glass for everyone, even AJ and Maire, who usually preferred wine, but they both took the proffered glass.

Jamie tapped on the map of England, somewhere along the western side of the country. "Worcester. Northeast of Hereford. We have the name but other than the general location, we have little else to go on. We're hoping Maire can find more details in Sebastian's journals to help with that. The only question is whether Gemini already has a team on their way or if they've already been there."

"So that leaves London." Maire leaned over the table to get a better look. "Or, more accurately, Ipswich, northeast of London. This one shouldn't be a problem, assuming this person is healthy."

"Each team will need at least a day or two for reconnaissance." Finn refilled a few glasses. "Once the teams have completed their mission, we should meet in London."

"Why there?" AJ asked. Not that it mattered, she was just curious.

"Hensley will still be there, and we might need his help." Finn took a long swig and appeared to relish the burn. "Sooner or later, Gemini and Belato will come looking for us. If Beckworth and Stella manage to get Sebastian away from whoever kidnapped them, my money is on them getting to London and trying for Ipswich."

"Will he leave Sebastian with Hensley?" Maire perked up at the thought.

Finn nodded. "Aye, most likely."

"Then we divide our resources between Worcester and Bréval. Afterward, both teams head to Hensley's." Ethan said.

"So, who goes where?" AJ asked.

"We need a small team for Bréval," Jamie said. "In foreign land during wartime, the team needs to be invisible."

"AJ and I will go." Finn looked to Lando. When the big man nodded, he finished with, "And Lando."

"Leaving us for Worcester. I suppose that makes sense." Ethan smiled.

"In what way?" Maire asked.

Jamie tapped the map, pointing at Worcester, then moved his finger a short distance southwest. "Hereford is close. They can offer protection if needed."

"That's perfect." Ethan nodded and turned to Maire, who smiled in turn. They would get to see the earl again. AJ almost wished she was going with them. "We could use Thomas's surveillance team."

"Then we have it." Finn sat back, appearing satisfied, but he wouldn't let anyone see anything else, regardless of his true feelings.

AJ doubted Finn was comfortable with the situation. "How are we going to get that close to Paris? As soon as either of us speaks, they'll know we're not from around there."

"That's where my Irish will pay off. They know we don't get along with the English." He gave Ethan an apologetic grin. "We can stick with our original cover story that AJ is from America. The English aren't happy with the loss of their upstart colonies. We're simply looking for sanctuary in exchange for hard work. It's not ideal, and we'll do our best to stay off the main roads as much as we can."

"I'm guessing that the *Daphne* won't be able to pick us up?" AJ had grown comfortable onboard the *Daphne*, and the thought of a different ship where Finn didn't know the captain made her queasy. She braced for the answer she knew was coming.

"We'll need smugglers," Finn answered. "They shouldn't be too hard to find. Brother Ignatius, could you get a message sent to Hensley in London? I think it's time to give him an update. It might not get there before us, but I'd like to try."

"It will not be a problem. If you could have your post to me by morning, I can get it to town and on the next available ship."

"We appreciate your help. We'll do everything we can to bring Sebastian back to you."

AJ studied her husband. He meant every word of his promise, but once again, the road was filled with danger, and this time, like no other, their enemy was a ghost, and no one knew their end game.

Finn squeezed her hand, his expression as solemn as she'd ever seen it. They were in a game of winner take all.

# 11

---

Beckworth pulled one of two blankets from the saddlebag then, raising the candle as high as he could, scanned the back of the hold again. The cells were ten feet high with bars running across the top. They were built close to the hull but left an aisle of about two feet on both sides. The back of the hold, beyond the last of the cells, was another ten feet of space with two stacks of crates about head high that gave him something to hide behind. There wasn't much space, and it wouldn't be comfortable, but he wouldn't be spending the entire trip there.

He glanced up to the top of the last cell. People rarely looked up, and his saddlebag would probably be safe, but he'd need one of the crates to place it up there. And it would be risky each time he needed to get to it. Best if he found a way to hide it within reach.

The candle sputtered as he poured the melted wax to form a base, and he smiled when he remembered teaching AJ the trick. He set the candle in the soft wax then opened the saddlebag for a closer inspection of its inventory. His first relief came when the first thing he saw was a coffee pot and a bag of beans. Besides the blankets he'd already removed, there was half of the hardtack as well as leftover cheese and meat from yesterday's meal. It was enough to get him to England, but they'd have to find food straightaway if they managed to escape. The rest of the bag held two knives, a pistol with a belt of cartridges, more candles, and a couple of mugs. He pulled out a small portion of hardtack and pushed the saddlebag behind the crates, following behind it. He cursed, then backed out to dowse the candle he'd already forgotten about. He peeled the warm, drying wax from the floor, shaped it into a ball, and dropped it into the bag. Then he crawled behind the crates until he was out of sight.

He pulled the blanket over him. In the dark, if the men checked this far back and considered looking behind the crates, the dark blanket might give the appearance of more darkness. At this point, everything was a gamble. He settled in and nibbled at the food until the door to the hold burst open.

"Watch where you're walking. You almost made me drop the tray." A gruff English voice pierced the silence of the room.

"That would be a shame if they only got to eat what we picked up off the floor." A higher-pitched French voice responded.

These were the kind of men who could stir trouble if not controlled with an iron fist. Since Stella hadn't been bothered to this point, he didn't believe the sail across the Channel would change the situation. Men were most bored when at port with idle hands. Lando had thought the ship light on crew, so they'd need every man they had to sail the ship.

"Maybe we should try it," the English voice suggested.

He couldn't be sure, but it sounded like the other man gave the Englishman a soft punch, probably on the man's shoulder.

"Ow. I wasn't going to do it. It was just a joke."

The voices grew louder and the light brighter as they approached Sebastian and Stella's cells. Something clanged along the bars as if to wake them up.

"Breakfast is here," said the Frenchman. "You're lucky we have time to feed you, especially with a warm meal. There'll be a lot to do now that we've set sail. Not sure your next meal will be as timely. And if we hit a storm, you'll be lucky to get water and a few bits of bread."

A scraping sound and the rattle of a cell door opening. Then it was repeated.

"This could be our only chance to play with our prisoners." The Englishman sounded even closer, and Beckworth assumed he was giving Stella the once over. "You wave that middle finger at me again, and I'll show you what a few minutes with me would be like."

Beckworth cringed and was relieved when Stella didn't mouth off. Sebastian would remain silent until directly asked a question, and even then, the man's answer would be obtuse. It had driven the duke mad, or madder than he already was.

"Leave her alone. The captain and his guest won't take kindly to any of your nonsense."

"They wouldn't know." But there was no conviction behind the Englishman's words.

"If you didn't always leave a mark, I'd turn my back, but I'm not willing to take a whipping for your pleasures."

Beckworth released a relieved sigh. He didn't know how anyone could miss these blokes, but there would be a search if he beat them and tossed the bodies overboard. Though the captain might think they simply got drunk and fell overboard themselves. For now, he'd be grateful that it seemed the worst was over.

The extra light began to fade, and the Frenchman mumbled something as they appeared to be leaving. The door slammed shut a few seconds later.

Sounds of spoons scraping bowls and the clank of mugs told him they were both eating. He waited another five minutes, making sure the men weren't coming back before crawling out from behind the crates. He drew the blanket around his shoulders, collected the hardtack, and joined Stella and Sebastian, though his eyes stayed on the door.

"I saved you some." Stella held out her bowl of porridge, but he shook his head and lifted the bread and cheese.

She wrinkled her nose. "Here we are, basically on the run, or at least it feels like it, and we're barely eating again."

"I wish I could make you coffee."

"Did you bring some?"

"A pot and some beans."

"She keeps asking our captors, but they only laugh." Sebastian sounded wounded on her behalf. "She says she's getting a headache again."

Beckworth nodded. "I thought so."

Stella scowled. "How would you know?"

"Because I've spent time traveling with you, and your emotions are on edge."

She didn't respond, but finished her porridge, either because she understood the importance of keeping her energy up or out of spite. He'd give it a fifty-fifty go on either option. He grinned.

"I also have an extra blanket if someone needs it. I doubt either of those dolts would notice."

"Sebastian could use it. He won't take his robe back."

When he returned with the blanket, he found Stella and Sebastian sitting at the corners of their cells waiting for him. He pushed the blanket through the bars, and Sebastian took it without hesitation.

He wasn't sure the best way to approach Sebastian with his question, but he needed to confirm what Maire had told him. "Do you know the name Belato?" Sebastian confirmed he'd hit his mark when the monk sat back, his eyes large as saucers.

"How do you know that name?" His voice was nothing more than a whisper as he tugged the blanket tighter around him.

"After AJ and Finn found me, and we were on our way back to the monastery, men followed us. Let's just say that one of them gave us a name—Belato. Once we arrived at the monastery and discovered you were taken, Maire remembered you mentioned a young monk by that name."

"Yes, he was my protégé, someone I thought I could trust. But his family gained power during the Terror, and he shared his knowledge of the stones with his brothers. He's the one who started all of this. Or perhaps it was me."

Sebastian lowered his head until Stella tapped on the bars. Her expression was fierce, like a momma bird protecting her own. "Positive thoughts, right? You said that."

He smiled. "You remind me of Maire."

She blushed. "Now, I know you're lying." But she seemed pleased by the sentiment.

He turned to Beckworth. "How is Maire?"

"As touchy as always."

"You two can reminisce when I need you to keep my mind off the rocking ship. Right now, I want to know what we're going to do when we arrive in England." Stella fiddled with the edges of the robe. "How do you plan on getting us off the ship?"

---

Stella stared at Beckworth as he nibbled on hardtack. He'd refused their offer of food, saying they got little enough but agreed to share a bit of their water. It was the second day crossing the Channel, and while the ship seemed to toss more than the first time they'd crossed, Beckworth assured her the weather was fair.

That knowledge didn't bode well if they ran into a storm. It meant her experience from the last storm would be worse if the crew couldn't seem to handle smooth waters. The thought alone made her stomach rebel. She choked down another spoon of cold porridge that had been upgraded with one of the herbs Beckworth had given her.

He conversed easily with Sebastian, and she admired his growing beard. It needed a trim, but his roughened look seemed in keeping with his current assignment as a thorn in his enemy's plans. She was still trying to figure him out—his moods, his humor that matched hers, and his eccentricities. He had a few, like his passion for fashion and well-tended gardens, but she suspected there were more layers. She picked up the bag of herbs and tucked it away. The gift of them had almost made her tear up, but it had been the two sheets of paper he'd handed her after rummaging through his saddlebag that first morning that came close to breaking her. Good grief. There was little privacy to hide emotions and too much time on her hands. She glanced at the single swan she'd made, or more correctly, made and remade several times over, but the paper was stiff enough to maintain the shape.

She swallowed a bit of water to force the breakfast sludge down, then tapped her spoon on the bowl which made both men turn toward her. "We're what? About a day away from England?" When Beckworth gave a non-committal shrug, she almost rolled her eyes but decided against it. "You said you needed some time to put a plan together. Are you any closer to telling us what it is?"

"I'm still working through the finer details." His expression was stoic, but amusement danced in his gaze.

"You think this is funny?" She tried to run her fingers through her hair but found more tangles than she thought possible. That must be what he was inwardly grinning at.

"You know as much as the rest of us. We talked through

options yesterday and nothing has changed since then. We still have the singular problem. How do we get off the boat without anyone seeing us? I have no idea if we'll land during the day or at night. We'll need a plan for both, unless your guards give us a hint."

"You would have a better chance of leaving without me." Sebastian set down his empty bowl and pulled the blanket tighter. His gossamer hair looked as bad as Stella's felt.

"No."

"Not happening."

Beckworth got his response out faster with Stella's echoing the sentiment.

"Maire would have my hide if we left you behind." She couldn't imagine facing Maire and giving her the news. It would be better to have Beckworth tell her if the situation got that bad. Maire already had a hate-love relationship with him.

"You need speed of action that I can't give you," he insisted.

Beckworth shook his head and wiped the crumbs of bread away. "Stealth is all we need. And perhaps some type of diversion. It's not just the men on the ship, but anyone that might be waiting for us on the dock. Can you swim?"

Sebastian nodded. "Not well, but I can make it a short distance."

Stella didn't like the direction this was taking. And when Beckworth stared at her with those cornflower-blue eyes, she couldn't look away. "I'm not good in the water."

"Of course not. I've already added it to the list."

She rolled her eyes. His list, which he'd begun shortly after their escape from Gemini, identified all her phobias—horses, tight places, ships, heights. And now water, though she thought that should be lumped in with ships.

"Let me continue to think through possibilities. I'd like to take a stroll around the deck tonight, well after most are asleep."

He swept the crumbs into the empty cell behind him, then scooted closer to Sebastian. "I don't know why they didn't try to trade for the Heart Stone. It would be difficult to take the monastery with Jamie's men guarding it. But it seems they're after something in England that's just as important if they're willing to leave the torc and other stones behind. Or is it possible they already have one or the other?"

Sebastian pulled his legs in until he sat in a lotus position. His face was peaceful, and though she'd only known him a couple of days, she thought he might be reticent to answer, not only because it might be bad news, but that he felt guilty.

"I'm afraid I allowed my naiveté to once again betray us." He shook his head and sipped from his cup. "I separated the stones, torc, and druid's book and hid them in the tunnels. There were two monks who were aware that I was hiding valuables in case the monastery was searched again. I had to keep records so they could be unearthed once peace returned to France. I'm old and not sure how long I have."

"You have plenty of time left," Stella insisted.

He smiled and didn't argue. "One of the monks that was aware of the stones had been bribed to steal them. He'd been at the monastery through the times of the duke and his son. Perhaps he simply tired of the solitary life of a monk and chose a different path. Either way, I received a note that he was remorseful and wanted to return the stones but was fearful of returning to the monastery. I rode to meet him at the smuggler's cave. It was a trap, of course, and so reminiscent of my experience with Belato, but it had never occurred to me that he could be responsible for this.

"As far as I know, the torc and grimoire are still in place. I left a journal for Maire in our secret hiding place that I'm sure she would find, though I didn't tell her outright where the pieces were hidden, just that they were safe." He gave them a quirky smile. "Though with enough time, she might find the hidden message within the text that gives her clues to the items' whereabouts."

"She found the journal." Stella gave them a condensed version of their vacation in France to visit the monastery. She mentioned his workroom behind the timeless statue of the soldier, and Maire's discovery of the first journal which ultimately led them to the second journal hidden in the smuggler's meeting room.

"Maire was studying the journal from the smuggler's room when I left to search for you." Beckworth had moved from a sitting position to lie on his side, elbow bent as he carved lines into the wood planking with a knife. His hair seemed longer in just the few days since she'd seen him, and several locks fell over an eye.

Sebastian nodded. "So perhaps all is not as hopeless as I feared. They don't have all the smaller stones. You have one, as does Ethan. And as far as I know, no one has gathered the other three chronicles, but I have to assume they know of their locations, or believe they do if they're taking us to England. Does Maire have the fourth?"

Beckworth nodded. "Do they know of the other Heart Stone?"

Sebastian had no answer for that, though their consensus was that no one was aware of the second Heart Stone except those closest to AJ and Finn.

Stella laid back and stared at the rough boards of the ceiling. "Maybe they're going to try to retrieve as many parts of the book as they can get before heading back to the monastery. They have us, they'll have most of *The Book of Stones*, and arrive with a lot more in their arsenal."

"All right," Beckworth sat up and put his knife away. "Besides the one in Bréval, you say the other two chronicles are in

England. When we escape, our focus should be on collecting them. That will be Finn's primary goal."

"And then we can meet up with them?" Stella brightened at the thought. All this time in the past, and she'd yet to catch up with her friends—her family.

"If luck is on our side, then yes."

She smiled then scolded herself. Somewhere deep down in her gut, she was convinced that she'd just jinxed their plans.

---

Beckworth slipped behind a short row of barrels and waited for the boot steps to recede. That would be the third crew member up at this early hour of morning. Based on his short patrol the first evening on board, there should be five men roaming the decks, all strolling at random. It made sense, though he wondered if they'd planned it that way, something Dugan would have done, or were just lazy in running their patrols.

The crew didn't appear green, but it was obvious they hadn't worked together before. The ship seemed to struggle with the winds, something that never occurred on the *Daphne Marie*. And that thought was the first spark of inspiration.

He was midship, returning from surveying the aft deck and all points between, when something set that spark to flame. An idea had formed on his way toward the back of the ship, and it crystallized as he scurried from his hiding spot back to the door that led to the forward cargo hold.

He crept through the darkness to the hold. He'd walked the path enough times now to have it memorized. Once inside the room, he found Stella and Sebastian huddled in the corner at the front of the cells, waiting for him.

"Well?" Stella, forever the impatient one. He couldn't help

but grin. Her hair hadn't improved since he'd found her again, but she was still lovely as ever. And the more he stared at her, the more impatient she became.

He sat crossed-legged in front of them.

"Why are you smiling like that?" She squinted and gave him a look he'd seen too often. The one that said she suspected he was hiding something from her.

"I think I found our diversion."

# 12

The day had stretched until everyone's nerves were on edge. Beckworth had been surprised when Sebastian had snapped at them, confirming his suspicions. The Channel crossing, long days in the hold, and the stress of reaching port was taking its toll. It started at breakfast.

When the two guards came with breakfast and to clean out the buckets, they grumbled that the captain decided to wait until midnight to dock, worried about Royal Navy vessels leaving the area. Beckworth couldn't have been more pleased by the news, as he preferred the cover of darkness to slip by their captors and those waiting on the dock.

But his satisfaction with the delay only irritated his compatriots. So, for a good portion of the day, he crawled into his cubbyhole behind the crates and got as much sleep as he could. It would be a long night and most of the following day before he would be able to rest again, assuming they got away.

What he hadn't shared with Stella and Sebastian was his alternate plan if the first one went awry. They wouldn't like it, and if he had to use it, Stella might reconsider her trust in him, but of the three of them, he was the most expendable to Gemini, assuming that was who they were meeting up with. It would probably be the same if it was just Belato. Beckworth was the only one who could mount a more substantial rescue. It made sense if anyone were to escape, it would have to be him. The other two couldn't know his plans for where he'd go to find those resources.

If the captors didn't see him escape, there wouldn't be any questioning. But if he was seen—he closed his eyes, refusing to dwell on the possibility. If it appeared they weren't going to make a clean getaway, he'd have no choice but to abandon them. It was the best possible option. They still needed Stella and Sebastian; they didn't need him. And he would be their only hope. It was a mantra he repeated to himself as he dozed off and on throughout the day.

When the guards left the dinner meal, they appeared to be as prickly as Stella and Sebastian.

"Don't worry," the Frenchman said. "From what I hear, Gemini is right upset with you. I wouldn't want to be in your shoes. You might want to consider finding a protector. Someone who can shield you from her wrath."

Stella laughed at him. He couldn't see her from his hiding spot, but he imagined her with hands on hips, the rat's nest of hair a halo of auburn, her fear tucked behind her bravado. "Gemini would chew you up and spit you out."

The Frenchman yelled several choice expletives Sebastian probably hadn't heard before and stomped out with the Englishman. The slamming of the door convinced him they wouldn't be back anytime soon, and he squirmed his way out of his hole, dragging the saddlebag with him. He'd sensed a change in the ship's movements over the last couple of hours, confirming they were heaving-to in order to maintain their position.

"Let's go over the plan one more time," he said as he dropped next to them and spoiled himself with the last of the food he'd bought at Guerin's Inn. "Our first ride will be a straight shot to Salisbury. We'll stay on the main road for as long as possible then cut to smaller roads for the rest of the journey. I'd like to make it to our destination in two days, but depending on how many are chasing us, we might have to be more creative."

"And what is that final destination again?" Stella asked as she finished her stew and nibbled on the bread.

Beckworth smiled but said nothing.

"I'm sure there's a reason he's not sharing details. If any of us get caught, we'll be encouraged to share what we know." Sebastian had only eaten a portion of his stew and had pushed it back through the bars, holding onto the hard cheese and bread.

"You might as well eat what you can, Sebastian." He returned the saddlebag to its hiding spot. "Try to get an hour of sleep. I should be back by then."

"Be careful. Everyone will be up." Stella's concern was evident in her sharp green gaze.

"Not everyone. Most will be in their hammocks until it's time to dock. The deck should be clear enough to finish our diversion and grab a few other essentials." He didn't wait for second-guessing as he inched open the door, confirmed no one was in the corridor, and slipped out. Lamps had been lit on the top deck, which surprised him. He would have assumed the captain would want to run dark, but perhaps there were other reasons than the Royal Navy for the delay in docking. There were more crew about than he'd planned for, but they looked tired or perhaps bored with the waiting.

He put the finishing touches on their distraction, keeping to the spots of darkness that dotted his path from bow to aft. On his way back, he picked up rope, two belaying pins that weren't being used, and some old rags, which weren't required for his plan, but could come in handy with what he expected might occur just before they reached the dock.

The dock was close. Lights from the multitude of pubs and inns reflected off the water. He estimated thirty minutes to reach a berth once the captain turned the ship. They were too far away for him to determine if anyone waited for them. There was a Royal Navy vessel still moored, so the number of men with horses waiting on the docks would be monitored. He didn't understand why Gemini felt safe using Southampton rather than one of the smaller ports. Maybe she paid off the harbormaster. Either way, this worked to their advantage. It was a busy port, and there would be other distractions he could create on their way out of town if they made it off the ship.

When he arrived back at the hold, he paused at the partially opened door. He'd closed it on his way out. His assumption had been correct and hoped he wasn't too late. He slipped inside, quietly setting down the rope and rags. He gripped both belaying pins as he took in the scene. Both men were facing Stella, who had stepped back, her feet planted wide, prepared for battle if they opened her cell.

"Come here, little bird." The Frenchman fumbled with the keys. "This won't take long. The ship will be turning to port soon. It will take another thirty minutes before they'll want you topside."

"Plenty of time for both of us," said the Englishman, who shifted from foot to foot, anxious to get inside the cell.

Stella noticed him enter the hold, and as he expected, she did what she did best.

"Better men than you have tried. If Gemini's men were here, they'd tell you how I bested my guard who had the same lascivious thoughts."

"What?" The Frenchman stopped and stared at her.

"I think it means wicked," the other man said.

"I know what it means."

"Just open the door. What can one woman do without a weapon?"

"I can do plenty." She showed off a few martial arts moves that impressed Beckworth. Had she told him she could do that? He must have shrugged it off at the time if she did, but when the two men stopped again to stare at her, he made his move.

He used the belaying pins like bats, swinging with his right and hitting the big Englishman on the side of his head. He dropped with a short grunt. Without hesitating, he twisted and brought up his left arm, repeating the same movement. He missed the Frenchman's head but caught his jaw. The sound of cracked bone was enough for Beckworth to drop the pins and confirm both men were unconscious. He dragged them to the back of the hold, gagged them with the rags, then tied their wrists and ankles. As an added precaution, he tied the ropes to an iron ring in the floor used to tie down cargo. They wouldn't be able to roll their way to the door.

The ship had begun its turn to port before he was finished. He grabbed his saddlebag and the keys to the cells, but Stella had already opened hers and was working on Sebastian's door. He walked into her cell and retrieved her raincoat that she'd tossed on the pallet, probably in preparation to fight off their caretakers.

"What if they send more men down?" Stella took the raincoat and shrugged it on, then gave Sebastian his robe in exchange for the blanket. She wrapped it over her head and tied the ends around her waist.

"It's doubtful. They'll assume those two bumbling idiots have everything in hand. They'll need everyone else working the rigging. Can you lift the saddlebag?"

She rolled her eyes and lifted it one-handed.

"Just make sure you keep it with you at all times."

"I know." Her tone was snappish, and she bounced on her toes.

Sebastian laid a hand on her shoulder. "Easy, child. The moments of waiting can test the best of us. The fates are with us tonight."

"Is that just a guess, or did the man upstairs send confirmation?"

Sebastian chuckled. "The lord protects innocents and children."

"I thought it was fools and children," Beckworth quipped.

"I think either applies here." Stella grinned. The banter seemed to settle her.

When Beckworth sensed the shift in the ship, he laid a hand on both their shoulders. "This is it. Stick with the plan no matter what you see or hear. Don't wait for final docking. Jump as soon as the ship is close enough to the dock. Try not to jump in the water, but if you have to, do it." They both nodded. "All right, let's go."

Before he could take a step, Stella wrapped her arms around him. "I know you have another plan. If it looks like everything is going to hell, and you have a way out, take it. We'll be okay."

He leaned back. "You knew I had an alternate plan?"

"You have to ask?"

He grinned. "I suppose not. We'll find you if it comes to that."

"I have no doubt." Then she kissed him. Not on the cheek but a quick, hot one on his lips that seemed to take them both by surprise.

She pushed away, a light blush staining her cheeks, grabbed Sebastian's hand and then the saddlebag. "See you on the other side." And then they were gone.

He stared after her and touched his lips. They still tingled from the heat of her kiss. Other parts tingled as well, and it took a moment to organize his thoughts. He blinked a few times then gave the hold a final scan, noticing something on the floor of Stella's cell. He went back to investigate, hoping it wasn't important since they'd shut and locked the cell doors.

It was a paper swan. He laughed out loud. It probably fell out of her raincoat when he picked it up. It was close enough he could probably retrieve it with one of the belaying pins, but something told him to leave it. It was a sign Stella had been there.

He doused the lamp, using every tactic at his disposal to slow down their pursuers. It wouldn't take them long to relight the lamp, but every minute might count.

Then he crept out, heading for the aft. Let's see how well his carefully planned diversion worked.

## 13
---

Stella held onto Sebastian's hand and the saddlebag as she led them down the dark corridor toward the cannons. All she could think about was the kiss and how stupid she was. It had surprised Beckworth as much as her, though for just an instant, she'd felt his response. She shook her head. *Now was not the time. Now was not the time.* And she kept the mantra going until the monk pulled her to a stop.

"Let me carry the saddlebag."

"It's too heavy."

"Nonsense and don't argue. We'll move faster."

"You weren't so bossy before."

"We must follow Beckworth's plan to the letter, and we can't afford to lose time."

"Yeah, yeah." She passed the saddlebag to him. It did make their travel through the ship faster, and she tightened her grip on his hand. The corridors were dark. If they got separated, and he turned the wrong way, they might lose their freedom before they ever get started.

When they reached the cannons, a light glowed from the far side of the room.

"Hurry up, will you." The voice sounded like a young boy. "How long does it take to check the inventory? It's not like we used anything after we left Saint-Malo."

"This is the last barrel." The scrape of wood on wood made her think the second boy was opening it. "Yep, half-full, just like before."

Stella grinned. Minus a few handfuls. She bounced on her feet, waiting for the light to go out. The two youngsters probably couldn't see them coming in from the other side of the room, but any sound would bring them over.

"Let's go. Captain will need us when we berth."

The light faded as the boys wandered off. The minute it was dark, she took the time to ensure the floor was clear of debris as she stepped gingerly to the gunport. She prayed this was the right side of the ship, and when she peered out the opening, a grateful sigh escaped. The dock was there, though it looked farther down than she remembered.

"This is the spot," she whispered. "It looks like we have the pier to ourselves." She stepped on tiptoes and hung part way out of the opening to assess their surroundings. "I can see the pubs and inns. They look busy, and there are dozens of ships out there." She felt around the floor near the cannon, picking up a rope she'd tripped over her last time out the gunport. It was already tied to something because the end wouldn't give. She followed it to find it tied to the base of the cannon.

"It's a farther jump than the pier in Saint-Malo. I'm going to run the rope out for you to use. Once you're down, I'll pull up the rope then toss the saddlebag down. Then I'll jump."

"You'll injure yourself."

"I'll be all right. We can't leave the rope dangling out the side."

She peeked out the gunport, and not seeing anyone, slowly

released the rope. "There are a couple of crates off to the left. Hide there until I come for you."

He moved to the opening and glanced down. Without another word, he shimmied through the hole and grabbed the rope.

She stuck her head out to watch him and the surrounding area. He fell halfway down but managed to land on his feet. He waved a hand as he waited for the saddlebag. She dropped it, then cringed as she waited for the sound of it hitting. Sebastian had removed his robe and laid it on the wood planking which partially covered the soft thud as it hit the dock. She had to remind herself that the old man had been hiding objects, sneaking around the monastery, and smuggling for years. He knew all the tricks.

She quickly pulled the rope back up, then crawled out the gunport. Sebastian, his robe, and the saddlebag were gone. After one last scan down the dock, she jumped.

It was farther than she'd estimated, and she hit hard, rolling to her side and grabbing her leg. Damn it. Tears welled up, and she shut her eyes against the intense pain. Then she remembered where she was and quickly glanced around. She heard the men on the ship shouting orders and the sound of their boots on the deck as they ran from one spot to another, doing whatever sailors did when arriving at port. They would be too busy to be watching the dock, but a few men were gathering farther up the pier.

She stood, scared to put weight on her left foot, more because of what it meant if she'd injured it past the point of walking than the pain itself. But when she leaned on it, it seemed all right. It was sore and a bit weak, but she managed to hobble over to the crates. She dropped to her backside, letting out a long grunt.

"A change of plan?" Sebastian asked.

"I landed wrong. I just need a minute to work it out."

"There are more men coming. Perhaps we should wait for Beckworth's diversion, then get lost in the confusion."

She stood, tested the strength of her ankle, then walked back and forth a couple of feet. "I think I'll be all right, but that sounds like an excellent idea."

They didn't have to wait long when an explosion rocked the dock and firelight lit the sky. Nothing happened for the first few seconds, and then, like someone had released the bulls, men scurried everywhere. Some ran toward town while others raced toward the ship with buckets of water. Sailors from nearby ships woke, and soon it was impossible to know who was from which ship.

Sebastian pulled the robe around the saddlebag and over his head, while Stella repositioned the blanket draped over her head. She nodded to Sebastian. He slipped from behind the crates and followed two men carrying buckets with her trailing close behind.

Her heart pounded so loudly, she couldn't hear the men yelling anymore. She wanted to urge Sebastian along, but he kept a steady pace, neither fast nor slow. Men pushed them, trying to get them out of their way. All she could think about, besides watching for anyone she recognized, like Gemini or Big and Tall, who everyone else called Gaines, was Beckworth. Had he gotten off the ship without anyone recognizing him? He'd been right about the chaos. With the number of men racing about, they weren't only sailors from other ships. They must have been men from the pubs because the stench of ale and stale whiskey oozing from them made her eyes water as they passed.

She'd have to stop questioning Beckworth's plans. He couldn't have found a better diversion. Everyone was concerned about the fire spreading to other ships and the docks. It was a zoo.

Once they reached the end of the pier, Sebastian made a left. He did as Beckworth advised and kept them within the shadows of the other ships and away from the lights of the inns and pubs. When they reached the last ship, Sebastian let Stella lead. Her crazy memory, which allowed her to remember almost everything she heard, kept her on a narrow path. They zigzagged their way through the city, always steering left, sometimes skipping a street or two. After ten minutes, she worried she'd missed a step and stopped.

"Is something wrong?" Sebastian was breathing hard but still able to match her pace.

"I don't know if I missed a turn or I'm just starting to panic. It seems like we've walked farther than we should have."

"No. Keep going. It won't be much farther."

"I keep forgetting you've lived in tunnels for a long time."

"It's more that I've spent most of my last decade hiding and smuggling. It's fear that makes you question. Take a minute to breathe, then your confidence will return."

She did as instructed, and though it helped, she was still unsure about the last two turns. The streets quieted the farther they moved away from the docks, though they weren't completely empty. The best news was the blaring absence of men racing through the town on horseback, scouring the streets for them. But that wouldn't last long once someone discovered them gone.

After a quick mental review of Beckworth's complicated directions, she confirmed she hadn't made any wrong turns and took Sebastian's word that her anxiety was making her doubt herself. When she turned the next corner and saw the church with the large white cross on its front door, she blew out a ragged sigh. She was breathing as hard as Sebastian.

They scurried across the street just seconds before two men on horseback raced by, heading out of town.

She led Sebastian to a group of bushes. "Okay, in you go."

Sebastian looked at the bushes then back to her. "I don't understand."

"We're going to hide in the bushes. If someone comes looking, they'll check the church, but they won't look in the bushes." When he appeared skeptical, she added, "I do this all the time."

He smiled as he shook his head and handed Stella the saddlebag before working his way into the middle of the bush. She pushed the saddlebag after him, then climbed over the branches before dropping down to sit next to him, pulling the branches over them and fussing with them until they seemed adequately covered.

"Now we wait."

If Stella had worked up a panic over taking a wrong turn or two, it didn't compare to the debilitating anxiety that gripped her waiting for Beckworth. She'd been in this position before, but there were so many men on the ship and two different groups of mercenaries tracking them. How long before they discovered there had been a third person in the hold with them?

The minutes ticked by, and though the air was chilled, sweat dampened her skin, and she grew unbearably hot. When fifteen minutes dragged to thirty, the dull ache in her ankle was overshadowed by a need to strip off the blanket and her raincoat, anything to cool down.

"Did Maire ever tell you about the time Reginald had taken over the monastery, and Captain Murphy launched an attack?"

His question surprised her. This wasn't the best time for chit-chat. "She told me some."

"She had been assigned my protector during the siege. She insisted over and over that we should hide in the tunnels, but I refused to leave my office by the kitchen. We were clearly in plain sight if anyone had bothered to look." He chuckled. "Now that child was not built for patience."

Stella had to laugh. It was true.

"But I can be a stubborn old man, and she had no choice but to wait with me. Dugan found us, and she defended us. Nicked him in the arm with one of her musket balls. The doorframe had to be replaced."

He wiped his eyes and shook his head. "She is a true and loyal friend, and fortunately excellent with firearms."

She chuckled and shook her own head at the realization that she shared something in common with Maire—no patience and firearms. That was definitely an explosive combination.

He continued the story about the two hidden archers and their assistance with Maire in single-handedly stopping the bloodshed within the inner courtyard. She'd heard the story from Finn, rather than Maire, who was uncomfortable talking about her best qualities, or apparently her role in their battles. But there was no question that the little nuances Sebastian added made his retelling by far the best.

After he finished, she mulled over his tale. "If there's a message about patience hidden in there somewhere, I'm not seeing it."

"Oh, the story has nothing to do with patience. It was to help your anxiety. I sense it creeping back."

She snorted, appreciating his attempt to calm her, then shared a story of how she, AJ, and Maire had sneaked through the iron door to find the journal he'd left for Maire. He laughed at their antics but admonished her for keeping Finn and Ethan in the dark, which she agreed hadn't been their wisest decision.

Several minutes later, the steady clop of hooves and a cart approached. This would be the first cart to go by. Other than the two men racing by on horseback, there'd only been a drunk and a single rider since they'd crawled into the bush.

She tensed when the cart slowed in front of the church. Then it inched farther, close to the bushes. Another minute ticked by.

"Stella. Are you there?"

Beckworth.

She sighed with more relief than she'd expected and stuck her head out. "Over here." She heard his chuckle and swore. Sometimes he was such an asshole, but she was smiling when she thought it.

"Hurry. They'll be checking the cells by now."

Stella got out, dragging the saddlebag with her, followed by Sebastian. "What's with the cart? I thought you were getting horses." It wasn't that she minded, it was just unexpected.

"Last minute change of plans. Let's just say an opportunity presented itself, but the cart won't be missed for long." Beckworth jumped down and moved to the back. He swept aside a piece of canvas that covered a couple of barrels and crates. "There should be enough room for you to crawl between them. With the tarp, you should be protected from the wind and some of the chill."

"What took so long? Did they see you?" Stella danced from foot to foot, now that he was here, she was in a hurry to get going.

He helped Sebastian up first, and the monk took the saddlebag and moved toward the back.

"It went better than expected. The explosion was larger than I planned, and I worried the fire would spread too quickly. But there were more than enough men to assist, though I don't know how much damage the ship took."

"Do we care?"

He shrugged. "It depends on whether they planned on using it to get to the chronicles."

She nodded. That made sense. She grabbed the edge of the

cart, but before she had a chance to climb up, Beckworth lifted her by the waist and set her inside.

She scrambled to gain her balance. "I could have done it."

"I didn't miss your limp on the way over. This seemed easier." He was close. Close enough to see the concern in his eyes. Then the sheet of canvas was dropped over her, and he laughed at her curse.

Once he climbed onto the bench, he leaned over and picked up an edge of canvas. "Since we have a cart for now, I plan on heading straight for Salisbury. Once we get out of town, our speed will pick up. We'll run as long as the horses can, so hold tight. The crates and barrels are well tied."

Two hours later, Beckworth stopped by a creek to cool and water the horses. Dawn was still a few hours away and they hadn't seen another traveler. They had passed through a handful of small towns, but the villagers were asleep. Even the inns were dark. Once the horses were rested, they took off, though Beckworth kept them at a slower pace for several miles before he picked up speed again.

They continued on after daybreak, stopping for short breaks, and finally at an inn to gather food. And to Stella's delight—coffee. Somewhere past Salisbury, Beckworth turned them onto a different road. With the sun warming the canvas, it became too hot. Sebastian pushed it far enough away for them to sit up and watch the landscape as they breathed fresh air.

A few hours later, they stopped in a glade several hundred feet from the road. Beckworth ate then fell into a deep sleep. He'd given Stella his handgun, and she took her role as protector seriously, recalling Sebastian's story of Maire.

After a two-hour break, they were back on the road, and she fell into the same time warp as her days riding horseback with Beckworth. She shared stories of what the future was like, and Sebastian listened intently, stopping her often to ask questions.

They spent the night in another glade after eating a warm meal with coffee for her and ale for the men.

Beckworth seemed pleased that no one followed them, but at the same time, she noted the occasional lines that formed between his brows when he didn't think anyone watched him. She understood. What was Gemini up to? She wouldn't have let them go so easily. Had she finally misjudged the situation? Did she know it was Beckworth who'd screwed up her plans again? If she found out, she wouldn't forget it.

It was in the middle of the second day when the cart came to a stop, jarring Stella awake. She had new bruises she hadn't expected from laying in a cart, and each time she crawled back on, she wished she had her own horse. Beckworth had procured more blankets to soften the bed, but it hadn't been nearly enough.

"Stay covered," Beckworth said before he walked away.

Then a woman's voice. "Beckworth, where the bloody hell have you been? Everyone's sick with worry."

His chuckle was warm, and something tightened in her chest. Was this another one of his boardinghouses, or someone closer to him? He still hadn't told them where they were going, even though no one appeared to be searching for them. Then she heard running feet. Were they hugging?

"You worry too much, but it's good to be home, Eleanor."

120

# 14

Maire stood at the railing and studied the ships at the Southampton docks. She wouldn't know what to look for, only understanding bits and pieces of Lando's description of the ship Sebastian, Stella, and Beckworth were on. He hadn't been able to get close enough to the aft of the ship to determine its name, and it was too far away with not enough light by the time it turned to head for open waters.

The Channel crossing had seemed longer than she remembered, though Jamie said they had the wind with them. It was her worry for Sebastian that troubled her. She shared the same concern for Stella, but if Beckworth was with them, they would be as safe as they could be. But Sebastian wasn't young, and with the strenuous conditions of captivity, and the possibility of running for their lives, the strain might be more than he was able to bear.

Strong hands rubbed her arms, and she leaned against Ethan's hard chest—solid and comforting. His warm breath tickled her ear as he tried to bring her comfort. "They'll be alright. Fitz will check the docks for the ship. Jamie won't want to stay long, but there's only one Royal Navy ship anchored on the far side of the pier, so we'll have an hour or two."

"Then what?"

"We'll sail to Poole where the *Daphne* will be safer and decide our next steps."

"Wasting more time." She tapped her foot, antsy and knowing there wasn't a thing she could do about it. Her Irish temper would get her in trouble. She felt it rising with no way to stop it.

He kissed her temple, and his arms wrapped around her waist. Her heart rate settled to a steady rhythm as she turned into him. She might not be able to control her emotions at the best of times, but she could always depend on Ethan to do it for her. She gazed up and never questioned the adoration she saw in his eyes.

He loved her, and had told her so many times. Yet, up to now, he'd made no further commitment. She had to admit the last couple of years had been emotionally turbulent. For six months, she'd been a prisoner held in a cold, dark cell. Before that, she'd been a permanent guest of Beckworth's while Finn and Ethan were time-jumping. Ethan worried about her state of mind. Sometimes, she questioned it herself.

She wasn't the type to dwell on the past. Her focus pinned squarely on the here and now. What she knew without a doubt, was that someone would always come for her. Ethan would come for her. Now, being on the other side again, where she was part of the team doing the searching as they had for Finn when he'd been living his own nightmare in a cold cell, she understood that these friends—her family—would never give up. And knowing that, gave her all the comfort she required.

She pulled Ethan down for a long, slow kiss and reveled for just a moment the strength of his arms as they tightened around her.

"We'll find him." Ethan's words were firm, not doubting them for a minute.

She turned back to the docks and the people hustling from one place to another. The enormity of their task attempted to sneak past her barriers, but she pushed it away. They both turned when bootsteps approached.

Jamie leaned against the rigging. His hair was rumpled as if he'd been running his hands through it for hours, and dark circles had formed under his youthful eyes. She grabbed his hand, giving it a strong squeeze. "Thank you for getting us here so fast. It appears you could use a good rest."

"Aye, that I could, but I'd prefer to wait until we leave Southampton. I'll let Fitz steer us to Poole."

"You think the ship has already left." Ethan jumped right to the crux of what they were all thinking.

Jamie answered Ethan's question, but his eyes were on Maire. "I think it's most likely they dropped off their passengers or collected additional ones before moving the ship to another port. Either way, Fitz and his men will ferret it out." His expression became stern, responding to her change in posture as she straightened and pulled away from Ethan. "Now, don't worry, lass. I trust Fitz won't return until he's turned over every rock to learn what's happened."

"Collecting passengers. You think they picked up Gemini?" Ethan had given her a chance to distance herself, but he kept a hand on her waist. That simple touch kept her grounded.

She hadn't considered they might board more passengers rather than drop off their hostages. "If they did pick up Gemini and her men, where would they have gone?" She didn't expect an answer, and a bit of the comfort she'd felt moments ago began to slip away.

---

Ethan woke when the *Daphne* rubbed against the dock. They must have made it to Poole, but he hadn't heard the typical shouts of the men making port. He glanced down at the woman in his arms with her blonde hair spread around them like a flaxen veil. She didn't stir as he rose. It was the first decent sleep either of them had since learning of Sebastian's disappearance.

It wasn't that she wasn't concerned for the others, but she had a special relationship with the old monk that transcended mere friendship. And that Irish blood of hers wouldn't let her rest from her worry and guilt. She had nothing to feel guilty for, yet he knew she suffered it just the same. The fact they'd both slept through the docking confirmed their need to restore their energy—both physical and mental.

He slipped out of bed, dressed quietly, and left their cabin in search of Jamie. The ship had remained in Southampton for five hours. The plan had been for two, but one of the sailors had returned to report that Fitz had picked up a trail he considered worth the risk of staying. Since the Royal Navy vessel was in preparations for sail, and the British Patrols were busy with repairs and refilling their stores, Jamie had nodded then disappeared into his cabin.

When he entered the galley, he was surprised to find Fitz eating breakfast. "I thought you'd be asleep after being up all day and night." Ethan poured coffee from the pot that had been left on the table.

"Jamie got some rest when he heard I'd be a bit longer. Then I relieved him when I returned, still too jumpy to sleep. We changed shifts once we were well on our way to Poole. I just woke up myself." He shoveled eggs in as fast as he could, followed by a thick slab of bacon and four slices of freshly baked bread.

"How long have we been in port?"

He shrugged. "Three or four hours. Jamie should be up again soon. Once our fair Maire rises, we can go over what I discovered, which should stir everyone's imagination."

Ethan wasn't sure whether that was good or bad, and Fitz's grin didn't supply the answer. The rowdy sailor was always up for a good fight, which wasn't always in the team's best interest.

"Someone should wake Jamie now."

Ethan had to smile at Maire's command as she stormed into the galley, her fists planted squarely on her hips, her eyes a blaze of Irish-green impatience.

"Why didn't someone wake us when you returned to the ship?" She dropped into a chair, grabbing a slice of bread and a piece of bacon while Ethan poured her a cup of coffee.

"Because some of us require sleep on occasion." Jamie strode in, looking mostly rested, though another few hours of sleep wouldn't hurt. "And with the news Fitz brought us, we'll need our minds as fresh as possible."

Ethan didn't like the sound of where this might lead, yet neither of the men appeared concerned. In fact, if he had to guess, they appeared to find the news more interesting than worrisome. The ship's cook brought over fresh-cooked eggs and more bacon.

Maire ate with a gusto that matched Fitz's. She glanced at him sheepishly when she finally pushed the empty plate away. He shook his head and smiled, passing her another slice of bacon which she took without question. He wasn't sure if she was being amiable because of her good night's rest, or whether she was saving her energy for a possible upcoming battle of wills. He decided to wait it out.

Once the dishes were removed, except for a bowl of oranges, a plate of sweet rolls, and a fresh pot of coffee, Jamie placed a map on the table.

"Fitz, why don't you begin with what you discovered?"

Fitz stuffed a sweet roll in his mouth then pushed up his sleeves and chased everything down with a long gulp of coffee. "This lot is almost as tricky as Beckworth. It was lucky that Lando gave us a decent description of the ship, which made it easier to track down. She berthed about five hours before us. Based on her size and approximate number of crew, it tells me they might be decent sailors but not enough of them to handle a ship of her size, which might explain why she hadn't made port sooner, considering her head start."

He leaned back, and with a sigh, the rest of them did as well. Fitz enjoyed telling stories and nothing would make him tell it faster than he wanted. Not even Maire's evil stare, which Ethan thought was rich, considering her own propensity for sharing at her own pace.

"They'd barely made port when there was trouble." Fitz grinned. "It took me and my men some time to put the bits together as to what happened. We were fortunate to find two ships still loading cargo that had been there when the *Phoenix* arrived shortly after midnight and everything went to hell.

"The ship's crew were still furling sails and mooring her when an explosion came from the aft deck. You know what happens when there's a fire on a ship. Men from other ships and the pubs were racing back and forth with water to prevent the flames from spreading. Once they had the fire under control, which took some time, there was another flurry of activity. Horses were brought, and men took off. The one thing everyone we spoke with could agree on—they were searching for someone."

Maire sat up and grabbed his arm. Ethan understood. An unforeseen catastrophe happened the minute they docked, and the easiest explanation was Beckworth's presence on the ship. He assumed that meant Beckworth made the trip without getting caught, though it might be wishful thinking, nor did it guarantee all three had made it off the ship.

"From there the story changes depending on who one spoke with, so I'll tell you what we believe to be closest to the truth." Fitz finished another sweet roll, and when Maire rolled her eyes, he winked at her. "Before I tell you about the passengers on the ship, you need to know that Gemini was in town when the ship arrived. Her and Gaines plus twenty of her men had been in port for a couple of weeks. They probably arrived right after the failed meeting with Finn in Basingstoke. Our best guess is that she never had a ship, or if she did, never had any intention of traveling to France. It seems they were waiting for the *Phoenix*."

"She'd been waiting for Belato all this time." Ethan rubbed his jaw. "If so, how would Belato know to kidnap Stella? We assumed he had Sebastian, but the monk wouldn't have known we'd traveled back."

"Best guess is that Gemini and Belato were using messengers to keep communications open." Jamie tossed an orange back and forth as he stared at the map of England. "She'd probably already sent a message before Stella and Beckworth ever boarded a ship."

"How would they know to look for them in Saint-Malo?" Maire asked.

Jamie shrugged. "I would have put men in several ports along the coast to watch the ships that came from England. They would know they'd make port close to the monastery."

Silence fell as they considered the amount of effort Gemini and Belato had put into developing their plans.

"So, we now believe Gemini and Belato have joined forces." Fitz leaned back and rubbed his stomach, that for all he ate, seemed to stay trim. "We don't know how many men Belato had on the ship. Those that left the ship during their short stay were mostly tight-lipped, and only had an ale or two before heading back."

"Then how could you determine anything about the passengers?" Maire asked.

Fitz scowled at her. "You need to let me tell the tale in me own way, lass. And if you were bothering to listen rather than waiting for a spot to jump in, you would have heard me say the men were mostly tight-lipped, with an emphasis on mostly."

Maire sat back, her cheeks a pleasant shade of pink, though she kept her chin raised. She crossed her arms across her chest, waiting for him to continue.

He nodded their truce, and his demeanor once again became the jaunty sailor. "We found a couple of men who'd been left behind when the *Phoenix* set sail. They were well into their cups, each sniping at the other, and apparently for good reason. It took a bit, but free whiskey tends to get tongues wagging."

"Were they left behind by accident?" Ethan asked.

Fitz grinned. "I don't think so, and their misfortune worked to our benefit. Once we got them going, they couldn't stop talking about the prisoners in the forward hold." Fitz leaned in as if he'd left the juicy pieces for last and didn't want the entire galley to hear, though it was only the four of them around the table. "They only spoke about two prisoners. Somehow, Beckworth did a good job of staying hidden. And while they had something to share regarding both prisoners, they couldn't stop talking about AJ." He winked at Maire. "Now we know that to be your friend, Stella. Seems she has a bit of a tart tongue on her. To hear the men complain, she's a red-headed witch. I have to say, I can't wait to meet her."

Jamie grinned and kicked Fitz's chair. "Just your type, but something tells me you're not her only admirer."

Ethan squinted at Jamie, curious what he meant by the statement. "Go on. What happened next?"

Fitz gripped his mug of cooling coffee. "When they entered the hold to retrieve the notorious AJ Murphy and the old monk, a man knocked them out with belaying pins." He paused when Maire released an audible sigh. "Yes, lass, it appears our Sebastian is well and in good hands. Anyway, they woke tied up. The prisoners and the man were gone. After a severe tongue lashing by the captain, he kicked them off the ship.

"Now, the question was, where did our prisoners go? Since they came to port in the middle of the night, and with only a quarter moon, it would be fairly dark except for the light of the fire. Our friends were already at the bow, so it wouldn't have been too difficult to get off the ship through the chaos, which was most likely a diversion created by Beckworth.

"After speaking with the crew from the other two ships, the innkeepers, the nearest mercantile, and the stables, it seems the lad at the stables was the only one with something of interest to share. A stranger had given him money for two horses, and when the lad had them saddled and brought around, the man was gone, as was a cart the boy had hitched horses to just prior to the stranger's arrival. He assumed someone from the fire had come for it. It was another half hour before someone came for the cart, and the lad realized the stranger had taken it."

"Why the cart?" Jamie appeared perplexed.

Maire grinned. "Stella doesn't know how to ride a horse."

"Beckworth probably took advantage of the situation." Ethan considered what he would have done. "It's slower and more difficult to hide, but easier for Stella and Sebastian considering the distance they'd be traveling. So, do we believe they got away in the cart?"

"Maybe. Probably." Jamie poured a cup of coffee and sat back. He needed a full day in bed, but that was likely not going to happen. Ethan knew what that was like. Too tired to sleep. The mission itself pushing each of them forward. Jamie gave him a sly smile. "I think it's safe to say they found transportation out of town, most likely in that cart. It's equally likely Beckworth stole horses from some other place. Either way, they're long gone."

"The only question is how many men Gemini sent after them."

"If this was a week ago, I'd say she'd send her entire crew. But now, it's guesswork with no clear direction on her motives. She either has no plan and is simply taking advantage where she can, or she's got something much larger at play that I can't even begin to guess at." Jamie tapped the map. "And that's our next question. Where did Beckworth go? He stayed ahead of Gemini before, and there's no reason to think he can't do it again, assuming Gemini did in fact send men after them."

Maire leaned in to review the map. "They could head for Waverly or London. Beckworth would assume Hensley took Mary to catch the last half of the season. Or maybe he went to one of his friends, either Eleanor or Bart."

"Or they could be going to retrieve one of the chronicles as we originally thought." Jamie wasn't surprised when all eyes fell on him. "His first inclination would be to get Sebastian some-place safe."

"Then my money is on Waverly or Eleanor's." Ethan nodded, seeing everything through Beckworth's eyes. He'd been looking for a haven to hide and rest before moving on. No more inns or boardinghouses. If it were him, he'd go to friends. Someone he could truly trust. "Lando said Beckworth stopped for supplies before moving on to Saint-Malo. He'd want enough to get them a safe distance without slowing down. That would have given them a good lead."

"It will be Eleanor's," Maire said with conviction that no one appeared to question. "Gemini wouldn't know about her, and it's close enough to Waverly it wouldn't be difficult to sneak in."

"Do we still assume he'll continue on to Hensley in London, and then onward to Ipswich?" Fitz asked.

"We have no choice." Maire's tone was stern but confident. Something he hadn't seen in her since Sebastian had been taken. "We made plans with Finn, and we need to keep to it."

"Then it's settled." Jamie stood and rolled up the map. "We'll set sail in two hours and put in at Newport. It will give you a more direct path to Hereford, and you'll have less time in the saddle. Once you're on your way, the *Daphne* will head for London. We'll take on some cargo in case we run afoul of the British Patrols."

"Let's hope the chronicle is still within our grasp." Maire gripped Ethan's wrist.

It gave him a jolt. Her hand was cold as ice.

## 15

The first three days on the road to Bréval blended into each other. If Finn had told AJ that she would spend most of her time in 1805 on horseback, she might have stayed at Hensley's while waiting for the team to rescue Stella. Those were her current thoughts as Finn pried her off the horse.

They'd ridden hard, resting the horses frequently, and spent their evenings sleeping on the ground a quarter mile off the road. If Finn ever suggested camping once they got home, she'd stake him with one of her arrows. Her grumpiness abated when she noticed they were in a small hamlet and Finn was leading her toward an inn. The aromas assailed her before she took a step inside, and her bone-weary body turned toward the fire, dropping onto a bench at an open table.

Finn mumbled something in her ear and wandered off. She kept her head down while she quickly scanned the room, as they did each time they entered a town or building. It was smoke-filled and dark, lit mostly by the firelight. There was only a small handful of people—three men standing near the bar, another two on the far side who looked like farmers, and a man and woman with a young boy, maybe five or six, who focused on his food. Their clothes looked old but clean, and they were probably travelers, too.

Not a soldier to be seen, and she breathed a sigh. For most of the trip, the soldiers had been scarce, one or two traveling without any concern for others on the road. But Lando, who sometimes rode ahead and sometimes trailed behind, had noted a troop of twenty heading their way on the second day. They were able to divert to a narrow deer trail that ran alongside the main road, the early leaves of spring offering some protection from prying eyes.

Though they stopped when they could for warm food, this was the first time in the past twelve hours they'd had a decent rest. AJ jumped when a woman dropped three mugs of ale on the table and a plate of roasted pork, boiled parsnips, and a thick slice of bread.

"I've got two more plates coming, dear." She was a stout woman with large, rough hands and frizzy brown hair falling out of a bun, who spoke English, her French accent warm and pleasant. "I have a girl prepping a bath for you like your man asked. Should be ready by the time you finish eating."

She glanced up when she heard the word bath. "Bless you."

The woman laid a hand on hers. "These are tough times for all. We ask no questions here."

She watched the woman head back to the kitchen, and though she should wait until Finn and Lando returned, she was starving. A third forkful of roasted pork was on its way to her mouth when the door opened. It remained frozen in place as her gaze shot to the door, only finishing its path when Finn and Lando entered the room. They both nodded to the innkeeper as they strode toward her. Their server trailed behind them with two more platters of food.

"I'm glad you started without us. I asked for a bath to be

prepared." Finn kissed the top of her head since she didn't slow her eating when they sat.

"I don't think I've ever seen the lass eat so fast." Lando ate a mouthful of parsnips before washing it down with ale.

"I thought I'd never get off that horse," AJ mumbled around a bite of bread.

"And you deserve a bath and a night in a bed." Finn ate the slowest of them all, his gaze constantly roaming.

"We're staying the night?" AJ could have kissed them both. Would have done more than that with Finn if her bones weren't so tired. The thought of walking upstairs was daunting.

"One night, and we'll be on our way early." Finn finished his ale and called for another round. "The next few days will be more challenging as we draw closer to Paris."

And he wasn't wrong. She started day four feeling refreshed after a long soak in a bath until it turned so cold that Finn forced her out before her teeth chattered. His warm body kept her snuggled close to him all night. After a couple cups of coffee and a hot breakfast, they returned to their fast-paced journey.

They had to turn off the main road several times before midday to avoid French troops. Finn decided to follow small roads that ran parallel to the main road. It made for safer travel with fewer disruptions, but their pace had slowed, especially when they were forced to deer trails.

At least twice, Lando discovered large troop movements that pushed them deeper into the trees, sometimes stopping to hide until the soldiers moved past. One such group had gotten close enough she thought Finn would have them flee, but Lando kept the horses quiet with grain, and soon the soldiers moved on.

By the time they reached Bréval, AJ had forgotten all about their one night's reprieve at an inn that felt like weeks rather than three days ago. She and Finn waited near a crossroads, hidden in the trees, while Lando traveled on to scout the town.

They were far enough away for Finn to build a small fire and set coffee brewing. They munched on leftovers they'd procured from an inn the day before. After they finished eating, Finn pulled her close.

"I'm proud of you, you know." Finn's kiss was warm and enticing.

"I'm not sure why. I feel like I've been grumbling the entire trip." She ran a hand down his arm, moving closer until they were lying side by side. The spring sun was bright but not warm enough to dispel the chill. The fire and Finn's warmth were enough to make up the difference.

"We've barely noticed your mumbling, though it might explain why Lando's been riding by himself so often."

She heard the humor in his voice. "I knew the ride would be difficult, but it's not quite what the brochure suggested."

"I thought you enjoyed surprise vacations."

She snorted. "I think it might be best if I plan the next one."

He kissed her temple. "That's a deal."

Her head snapped around when a twig snapped.

Finn followed her gaze. "It's nothing to worry about."

"What's taking Lando so long?"

"Best guess, he's traveling to a nearby town if Bréval doesn't appear safe enough."

"Won't that make surveillance more difficult?"

"Aye, but we'll make it work."

Another snap of a twig had Finn grabbing his sword and jumping up. AJ pushed into a squat, pulling out her dagger. She relaxed when Lando appeared through the trees with his horse trailing behind him.

"It's safe," he grumbled and dropped near the fire. She poured him a cup of coffee. "Thank you, lass. There was a group of eight soldiers in town, but they left as soon as they ate."

"Did you check a nearby town?" Finn asked.

He shook his head. "From what the clerk at the mercantile said, the town is normally quiet, and most soldiers tend to pass by. But they've seen more troops in the last couple of weeks." He bit into a slice of cold beef and a chunk of cheese, and they waited until Lando swallowed it down. "You're not going to like what he else he told me."

"Then it's best to just spit it out," Finn growled, though Lando didn't take offense. He got that way when he knew bad news was coming.

"The countess died six months ago." Lando waited for the weight of that to settle. "And the count has been bedridden since the first of the year. They're surprised he survived the winter."

"Damn it." AJ couldn't believe their luck. For every positive step forward, it seemed they took three back.

"What's the state of security?" Finn asked, apparently undaunted.

"That's where it gets interesting. The count's oldest son moved in a month ago, but the rest of his family only arrived two days ago. I wasn't able to get the whole story, but it seems the two households—the one being moved out and the one moving in—aren't seeing eye to eye."

"Which might give us an opening in the chaos."

"Maybe."

"It's our best option at this point. I doubt the count is seeing guests."

"Do you think the son is aware of the chronicle?" AJ stuffed items into their saddlebags.

"Hard to say." Finn's forehead scrunched in thought. "If there's animosity between the households, this might not be a friendly transition of the manor and title. We need to be closer to monitor the situation. Is the town safe enough to stay in?"

Lando shrugged. "As safe as any other. There are two inns,

and for some reason, one appears to be more popular, though I'm not sure why. They both appear decent enough."

"Let's see if there are rooms at the busiest one." Finn doused the fire and covered it with dirt and leaves.

"Wouldn't the other be the safest?" AJ asked.

"Possibly, but soldiers are more likely to stay at the less popular one to avoid crowds. It will be easier to hide within the crowd if we pay good coin for the rooms."

They waited until mid-afternoon before riding into town. AJ remained near the back door of the inn with Lando and the horses while Finn arranged for two rooms—one for him and AJ and one for Lando, who would play the role of bodyguard.

After a quick meal, the three trudged upstairs to their rooms, weary travelers needing rest before continuing their journey.

In the morning, they split up to run surveillance. They would spend the day gathering information, then meet back for an early evening meal to review what each had discovered. The plan was to infiltrate the manor the following day. Someone had to get to the count. They had to know if the chronicle was still within reach.

# 16

Eleanor. Beckworth's friend. The one he'd gone to the first night they'd escaped from Gemini. Stella would finally see why he'd thought of her in their time of need. Her brain must have short-circuited. Why should she care what their relationship was? He'd said she was a good friend, nothing more.

The next realization had her moving the canvas aside so she could see what was happening. If this woman was a friend, why did they have to stay covered? He couldn't have expected them to stay undercover for their entire stop. She had to see who this woman was. Sebastian tried to pull her back down, but she patted his hand.

"Don't worry. I'll be nice."

She caught the moment Beckworth stepped up to the porch. Eleanor was somewhere in her fifties. Her hair was pulled back, and when the light caught it, there were strands of gray mixed in with her honey-colored hair. Although on the thin side, she appeared strong and healthy. Without Eleanor saying another word, she liked her. She couldn't say why, but there was an independent fire in her. It was in Eleanor's bearing, and Stella felt an instant kinship with her.

Beckworth grabbed Eleanor, and it looked like he might swing her around. But Eleanor beat on his arms, and when he released her from his hug, she slapped his arm.

"The last we heard from you was a note Barrington received from Southampton. On the run, as usual. When will this end?"

She glanced at the cart, and her gaze caught Stella's.

Stella waved along with one of her best smiles.

"For heaven's sake, that's no way to treat guests." She hurried over as Stella pushed the canvas away and helped Sebastian to his feet.

Beckworth jogged to keep up with her. "We're still on the run, just in a different direction. I don't want to put you at risk, and I wasn't sure if Waverly was under scrutiny."

"It is. A small group of men. Watchdogs, I suppose. Barrington says they're only watching the main road, so I use the trail through the woods that runs to the back of the manor. Everything is in order; it's more of a bother to know they're out there."

"And no one has been by here?" When she shook her head, he asked again. "You're positive."

"Yes. Yes. What are they going to do to an old lady? Now let's get out of the weather and into the house. I have a nice fire going. By the looks of everyone, you could use a bath, some food, and a good night's sleep."

Stella became speechless at the promise of such luxury. Her stomach growled in anticipation of something warm to eat. She could sleep for days if they only had that much time.

An hour later, after a soak in a hip bath, she wore a clean dress, and though it was tight across the chest, it was modest enough. She left the guest room, acutely aware this was the first domestic setting she'd been in since arriving in this time period. A lock of hair fell across her eyes, and she pushed it back. It was still damp, but at least it was under control. She was almost human again.

Beckworth was at the table, a mug in front of him that she guessed to be ale. He was speaking with Eleanor, something about fencing and gates. He'd bathed as well. His hair was washed and pulled back in a queue, and he wore a shirt that was rolled up to his elbows and open at the neck.

He'd never looked so appetizing. *Good grief, Stella.* That wasn't the right word. Or maybe it was. She couldn't seem to take her eyes off him. Before she could stop it, an image flashed of him dressed in those turquoise breeches and jacket with matching paisley waistcoat they'd laughed about on the ship to France.

He stopped talking when he caught sight of her. The warmth of a blush rose up her neck and burnt her cheeks under his slow perusal, which was followed by a tender smile. Light danced in his eyes along with something else. Something more dangerous, and her heart beat faster.

"Well, I thought there was a woman underneath all that dirt." Eleanor broke the spell, and when Stella turned her gaze to the woman, she noted the twitch of her lips. She evidently didn't miss whatever that moment was between them.

"I feel more human anyway. I can't thank you enough for taking the time to put a bath together. I feel like I've finally rinsed off two weeks' worth of filth." Instead of sitting at the table, she leaned against the kitchen counter, needing to keep some distance between her and Beckworth until she got used to seeing him in this new setting. He hadn't shaved his whiskers, and it gave him a roguish look that was best if she ignored it. This would be a great time for one of his witty words of sarcasm. Anything that didn't make the room seem so small.

"You should have seen what Beckworth looked like the time Captain Murphy was captured by that horrible Dugan. Three months without a shave and rarely a bath. Claimed it was the best way to hide in plain sight." She filled a coffee pot with water, then crushed the beans before slipping them in.

Stella glanced at Beckworth, who was watching Eleanor, and then his gaze turned back to her. He'd noticed Eleanor smash the beans, just as Stella had suggested when she'd been trying to make the perfect pot. She returned his smile. He lifted a second coffee pot, and she purred with delight.

All else was forgotten as she stormed the table. He was already pouring.

Eleanor chortled. "He said you had a penchant for coffee. More than AJ, so I thought it best to get another pot brewing. He also mentioned you'd eaten more stew and porridge than a person should. I'm warming up leftover lamb roast with potatoes and carrots and just put the rolls in to bake."

"It smells great. Is there something I can help with?" The coffee was the perfect temperature, and she slurped it down like water after a long trek across the desert. She refilled her cup before meeting Eleanor at the counter, where she was putting something together that looked like meat pies.

"You don't need to fuss." Eleanor folded the dough over the meat filling and pinched the ends. "You should rest up. I haven't had guests in weeks, so I'm happy to just have someone to talk to other than myself."

"You wouldn't have to eat alone all the time if you'd move to Waverly, just until this issue with the stones is over." Beckworth leaned back and draped an arm over the chair next to him.

Stella paused with the cup halfway to her mouth. "Where's Sebastian?"

"Fast asleep on Eleanor's bed. After cleaning up, he wanted to help with the food preparation, but Eleanor made him take a short rest. I checked on him a bit ago, and he's sleeping like a babe. I'll wake him when it's time to eat."

"Oh, good. Maire will kill me if anything happens to him. She must be freaking out." Eleanor gave her an odd look, and she grimaced. "Sorry. I meant she must be very worried."

Beckworth chuckled. "I'd say Maire was a bit of both when I left the monastery to search for you. But Lando should have put everyone's mind at ease."

Stella needed to sit down. Right now. The cup clattered when she dropped it on the counter before racing to the sofa. She sat and bent over, her head lowered to her knees.

Beckworth was there in a flash, his hand rubbing her back. "What is it? Are you sick?"

She rocked back and forth as the enormity of the last few days washed over her. What the hell had she done, acting like some comic book hero? She could have been killed or worse on that ship. Her guards might have been bumbling fools, but the person in charge wouldn't have been.

A few minutes later, a mug was stuck under her nose.

"Drink this. All of it. No questions." Eleanor pushed the mug into her hands.

The first whiff was enough to tell her it was whiskey, and she drained it without question. Her eyes watered, and her throat burned like it was on fire.

"I've had smoother," she managed to croak out.

The mug was whisked out of her hands and then pressed back into them seconds later.

"This one is for sipping. When you're done with that, you can have your coffee." Eleanor returned to the kitchen.

Through all of it, Beckworth continued to stroke her back like she was a spooked alley cat.

He stopped when she sat back, but when she glanced at him, his brows were still furrowed, and he wasn't grinning anymore.

"I'm okay. When you mentioned Lando, I remembered the ship and what an idiot I'd been, acting like Wonder Woman."

She sipped the whiskey and shuddered as the liquid went down. It wasn't going to sit well on an empty stomach, but it warmed her and settled her nerves.

"I don't know much about trauma. Only things I've witnessed along the way." He leaned back, and she did the same, turning to face him. "I'll admit, when you showed up on the dock, I saw something in your eyes that might have made some people question your behavior." He gave her a grim smile when her eyes widened. "Or it could have been someone angry enough to want retribution. It wasn't until I saw Sebastian that I understood you weren't mad. That the shock of your arrival in this time period and the continual hardships hadn't gotten the better of you. You'd been adapting well until we arrived in France, but when it was apparent you were acting in Sebastian's best interest, using your skills to determine the best course of action, it was obvious how strong you were. To not leave Sebastian and face your kidnappers—that requires a great deal of courage. And your reaction now reflects the aftereffects of such daring."

She considered his words, not really believing the courageous part. She'd simply been on autopilot, refusing to give up. Maybe it was the same thing, but she was no expert. "I think it was more that I was so pumped with adrenaline, I didn't know any better." She took a longer sip of whiskey, and when the burn ended, she gave him a weak smile. "If you want to call it courage, I won't argue. And I suppose the delayed response has something to do with being here, someplace safe. But how safe are we? If Gemini's men are at Waverly, would they know about this place? About Eleanor?" She glanced to the kitchen, but if Eleanor was listening, it was difficult to tell with her setting the table.

"And that's what I'll find out when I go to Waverly. Now, let's eat so I can get there and back before dark."

When he stood, she rose with him but grabbed his arm. "Promise me you'll come back."

He and Eleanor had stopped her panic attack before it got away from her, but she was still shaky. She straightened her shoulders and mustered enough energy to slide on her best face, but he must have seen something she couldn't hide because he pulled her close.

"I won't let you down."

# 17

Beckworth stared at Waverly Manor from behind the gardens. Winter cleanup had begun, and the gardener was finishing his day of clearing away the beds on the far west side. A delivery cart was being unloaded near the kitchen, most likely bringing the week's hard staples.

He watched for another twenty minutes before pushing his hat down and, keeping close to the trees, made his approach to the solarium doors, which were kept unlocked throughout the day. Barrington would keep to daily habits, ensuring everything appeared normal. He didn't see anyone else, but he wouldn't be surprised if there was a patrol monitoring the perimeter on an irregular schedule.

Before he could step from behind the tree and run the fifty yards to the manor, two men turned the corner of the building. They stopped and scanned the landscaped garden and beyond while Beckworth held his breath. They were his men, but he wanted to get inside without them seeing him in case someone stealthier than he was out there.

After a moment, one took off to the trees on the opposite side of his position, while the other headed toward him before disappearing through the kitchen door. He waited for the one in the trees to move out of sight. The man might find his horse, but at most, he'd take it to the stables.

While he gave the man time to move on, his thoughts drifted to Stella. Her anxiety episode had unnerved him. Though, to be honest, he'd expected it days ago while they were still running from Gemini. There hadn't been a moment since her first kidnapping that she'd been in a safe environment. For some reason, being at Eleanor's had been her first moment of feeling secure. After the episode, she helped Eleanor in the kitchen as if the moment had never occurred, and keeping busy continued to calm her. By the time Sebastian woke for their meal, she seemed back to her old self, or at least the woman he'd come to know prior to their trip across the Channel to France.

She appeared cheery before he rode off, but he sensed her trepidation when he spurred the horse and disappeared down the road. Eleanor would see to her safety. Feeling secure in that knowledge, he snapped his attention back to the business at hand.

He gave the area one last scan, hunched his shoulders, and made a direct line for the solarium. The doors were open as expected, and when he slid inside, he glanced back through the windows to make sure no one had seen him.

He took three steps before he froze.

"Did you really think you could sneak in here without anyone noticing?"

He released a long, exasperated sigh and turned toward the far corner where Barrington stood.

He ignored him and continued on through the manor. Barrington's soft footsteps followed a few paces behind. "I'm not sure if I should be upset that my skills aren't what they used to be or pleased to discover that security is better than I anticipated."

"Would it make you feel better if I said the latter?"

"I'm not sure."

When he reached the study, he went straight for the whiskey, pouring two glasses while Barrington shut the door and strode to the hearth, where he jostled the dying embers before placing a log on the flames.

"Just the one will do. I won't be staying long." Beckworth dropped into one of the chairs and stared at the fire. It was good to be home.

Barrington sat in the chair across from him and took the proffered glass.

"So, what gave me away?"

"Hawthorne saw you on his perimeter check. If it makes you feel any better, he said he was lucky to have caught your movements. They expected you to circle around and come in from the west."

Beckworth chuckled. "Enough. But thank you for the attempt to keep my pride intact."

They drank for a moment before Barrington broke the silence. "Do you still have Miss Moore's friend with you?"

"Mrs. Murphy, you mean?"

"Ah, yes, I do forget myself."

"Stella is with Eleanor, along with Sebastian."

Barrington blinked. "The monk?"

"The one and only." He explained everything from the moment he traveled to meet Gemini's contact in London to discovering she'd captured the wrong person from the future. Barrington responded with questions and snorts as he completed the story of their daring escape from Belato's ship once they returned to England, finishing with his concern that no one came after them.

"Tell me about the men watching the manor." Beckworth refilled their glasses before placing his boots on a footstool.

"Four men living in the woods near the baronet's estate. They watch the road, usually two at a time, rotating their watch. I send staff to the inn and marketplace on a regular basis to monitor them. They rented a room about a week ago, so it seems they might be out there for a while. Hawthorne and his team have been able to monitor their movements and their usual locations. They keep to themselves, but it's difficult to determine if they don't care if they're seen or they're simply sloppy in their surveillance. The first few days, they tried to get closer, but the guards out front have kept them away."

"No other visitors?"

"A few messengers. Mostly from friends seeking you out. Dame Ellingsworth asked to be advised as soon as you returned. She's still in London, and when she heard Hensley and Mary arrived, decided to stay. I imagine she's heard through them that something is afoot."

"And we know little else. If someone did follow us from Southampton, I'm not sure how we could have lost them with the wagon."

"They must have other plans. So far, Gemini's movements haven't been what anyone would expect."

"Making her one of the most dangerous enemies regarding the stones."

"A sign of desperation?"

"Maybe. Or a more clever madness than the duke ever showed. And now, with this Belato chap, who might be the one pulling the strings, the game has become murkier."

"Your plans now?"

"I need messengers sent, more supplies, and then we head for London."

After Beckworth left for Waverly, Stella helped Eleanor clean up and prepare food for their travel to London. Once the bread was sitting in pans to rise and the pork set to roast, she drained another pot of coffee with Sebastian and Eleanor's help. Then Eleanor shooed her from the house, and she grabbed a blanket from a chair on her way to the porch. She'd been told it was the second week of March, but winter was still holding on with gray skies, and a light mist hung in the air.

Eleanor had cleared a spot on her desk for Sebastian where he'd perched with paper, quill, and ink. Whenever the bird chatter ceased, she could hear him scratching away through the slit of an open window. She thought she might write a letter or two, but once she started, she'd end up with a novel. And never handling a quill before, she'd probably also be ink-stained from head to foot.

Instead, Eleanor had given her a couple pieces of paper to make her swans. She had folded the third one and placed it on the chair arm when Eleanor appeared. She thought she might have brought more coffee and was surprised to see her holding a handgun and a rifle.

"Beckworth said you were a decent shot with a pistol."

"A decent shot." She glanced up to the porch overhang and mulled over the comment. There were several ways Beckworth could have worded it. Maybe it was Eleanor's interpretation. And maybe she was being oversensitive to anything Beckworth said. "Yeah, I'm a decent shot. At least with a handgun." She studied the rifle.

"You haven't shot a rifle?"

"Not a flintlock."

"Well, now's a good time while we're waiting." She handed Stella the rifle, stuck the handgun into a pocket of her skirt, and waved for Stella to follow her.

They strolled across a small pasture and into the trees. Dusk was still a couple of hours away, but with the dense trees, the shadows were heavy as Eleanor wove them down a deer trail that eventually opened to a small clearing. There was a shed, a creek, and a small corral with worn fencing that appeared viable enough to hold a horse or cow, though it was empty now. The place appeared abandoned.

"Is this still your property?" Stella asked when Eleanor stopped by a makeshift table and two crates turned on their side.

"No. We left that about a hundred yards back. This is the hunting cabin for old Mr. Littleton, who owns the land just south of me. He rarely comes out this way but twice, maybe three times a year, when his son visits. Since it's closer to me than to his farmhouse, he's given me permission to use it as long as I don't hunt." She smiled. "He likes my rosemary bread and currant preserves."

Stella chuckled. "It seems a fair trade, but why would you need this? You don't keep much livestock other than a cow and a horse. Although I think I saw a few chickens."

"I don't use the cabin, but I like to practice my shooting out here." She set the handgun on the table along with a bag of powder, some shot, and a belt of cartridges.

"Does Beckworth supply your weapons?"

"He likes to know his friends are safe and have the means to protect themselves. They were originally meant for wild animals, but this business with the stones and the toll from the war makes them more necessary."

"Wouldn't it be easier living in town?"

"Maybe, but after living in London for so long, I enjoy the solitude. I get to town when I want to, and I visit with a few women at Waverly. I also have a fair number of visitors throughout the year. It's enough."

Stella watched the woman load the handgun using the gunpowder with precision.

"Now load the rifle. The principle is the same, but you have to use a bit more force to get the ball all the way to the end. Tamp it down good."

Stella fumbled with stabilizing the rifle as she loaded the muzzle.

"Here, let me show you a trick with that."

A couple of minutes later, Eleanor pointed to a tree. "Aim for one of the branches. It doesn't matter which one."

Stella took her time, getting comfortable with the feel of the extra weight. It had been a while since she'd used a rifle but she made an effort to practice with a bolt-action and a lever-action when she visited the gun range. The first shot went wide, and for the next hour, they kept at it until she could load and fire with ease.

"Beckworth said you were good with weapons."

Stella shrugged. "Even where I come from, it's good to know how to use one, though I hope to never have to."

"And now that you're here?"

"It's a different time. One has to adapt."

Eleanor pulled out a flask, took a drink, and passed it to Stella.

She took a tentative sip of smooth whiskey, half expecting it to be moonshine. "How long have you known Beckworth?"

"He hasn't told you the story?"

She gazed off into the trees. "Only that you knew each other in London."

Eleanor chuckled as she tied the bag of gunpowder. "He was a knock-kneed street hustler who came around for Mrs. Brubaker's meat pies. I was working at a whorehouse at the time. Not on my back, but as a seamstress. When he didn't have the money, he scrounged for food, and even at his young age, he charmed me with his silver tongue." She picked at the weeds around the crate, clearing out the ones aged from winter. "When I left the whorehouse for a job with the theater, he tracked me down. Didn't ask for a thing. He'd graduated from a natty boy—that's a pickpocket—to a higher position in the gangs. Said he wanted to make sure where I was so he could check in and make sure I had everything I needed. I was doing well enough, but once a month, like clockwork, I'd find an envelope stuffed under my door with a couple of coins and a short note."

"He was paying you back."

"He never forgets his friends."

Stella returned to scanning the trees, letting the words sink in. Was that why he'd put himself in danger to come back for her? For some misguided idea that he owed her a debt, or maybe one he owed AJ? The thought that it was nothing more than saving the mission made her gut twist. She'd been such a fool— holding his hand on the ship to France, and then she'd kissed him in the cargo hold before he left to set the diversion for their escape. How stupid she'd been. She turned her head so Eleanor wouldn't see her blush.

"How did you get involved with the stones?"

She almost sighed with relief at the change in topic, and she turned back to Eleanor. "One of those in the wrong place at the wrong time scenarios. The kidnappers mistook me for AJ."

When Eleanor waited patiently for her to continue, Stella decided how much of the story to share. To this point, she'd only shared bits and pieces of it—the first part with Beckworth, then a bit more with Sebastian. This was the first time she'd had female companionship, and feeling comfortable with Eleanor, she blurted it all out.

"AJ and Finn were traveling, and I was watching their house. I had stopped by on my daily check when I ran into an intruder who was looking for one of the stones. They mistook me for AJ.

When I couldn't give them the stone, they kidnapped me in hopes of exchanging me for it."

She shared her story from the minute she landed in England to when Beckworth dropped them on her doorstep.

Eleanor never asked a question, letting her talk it out, though she did snort at the parts about the boardinghouses. At times, it seemed it was someone else's story rather than her own. And by the end, she understood the debt she owed Beckworth. Something she'd never be able to repay, except to step up and stop playing the victim. When all her false bravado had caught up with her in Eleanor's cabin, with the enormity of what she'd done and all the things that could have gone wrong, she'd never considered the danger to Sebastian and Beckworth.

"He holds his heart close," Eleanor offered, "but there isn't anything he wouldn't do for a friend. He may, at times, take the easy approach, the direct approach, or the one that might be a little less ethical, but his heart is always in the right place."

"Was he like that when he worked for the duke?"

Eleanor's smile disappeared. "Those were difficult days for him. Men and their fathers. He did everything he could to find some kindness from the man, some small grain of recognition as his son. If Finn hadn't put the man down, I would have eventually found a way to poison his meal."

"I'm not sorry for not meeting him."

"Unfortunately, there are more like him. You don't have to look far these days. Beckworth did what he could to protect the staff and his friends. I can't hide the fact that he went to a dark place, but he's getting better each time I see him. He wants to be respectable. Sometimes he just goes astray."

Eleanor stood and pocketed the handgun. "He'll return soon with more weapons and supplies. Until then, the horses need food and water."

She led Stella back to the house. Instead of going inside, Stella offered the rifle to Eleanor, but she shook her head.

"Keep it until you leave. Beckworth didn't think you were followed, but you never know. It's best if you keep it close."

She nodded and took the cartridge belt Eleanor handed her. Then she turned for the barn. "I'll feed the horses." She couldn't believe the words came out of her mouth, but something told her they hadn't seen the last of Gemini. It was best if she got acquainted with the new horses.

———

The sun had set some time ago, and Stella, feeling like a fifth wheel while Eleanor and Beckworth packed supplies, had grabbed a thick wrap and searched for peace on the porch chair. In her mind, spring was the most fickle of seasons, where every day was a surprise. She hadn't realized how much she depended on weather forecasts. Beckworth could predict the weather by watching the sky. It was a lost art for city dwellers like herself, and she found it odd for someone to stare up at a cloudless day and tell her there'd be rain the next day.

The door creaked open, and she didn't have to look up to know it was Beckworth. He sat in the chair next to her, and from her peripheral vision, could tell he was gazing out to the yard and beyond.

She felt awkward sitting next to him. After their quick reunion on the docks in Saint-Malo, she'd done the most irresponsible of things by basically throwing herself at him, with Lando, who she hadn't even met yet, standing there watching. She'd been holding it together after being snatched from the boardinghouse, especially after discovering Sebastian was in the cell next to hers. But that wasn't enough to feel safe. That only occurred when she'd caught sight of Beckworth on the dock.

Why the hell had she kissed him? It would have been respectable to kiss him on the cheek. They were in France, after all. But on the lips? At least it had been quick. Except, for a split second, she was positive he'd responded in kind, but it must have been her imagination.

Ugh.

Something had changed between them, and it disappointed her. The worst was that she didn't know how to return to the easy companionship they'd shared.

"Eleanor said you fed and watered the horses."

She'd been so wrapped up with her thoughts, his words startled her. "It was a simple enough task. She's done so much to make me feel welcome, it was the least I could do."

Quiet returned, and while they'd ridden for miles in easy silence when on the run, this reticence was all wrong. "How's Sebastian?"

"A day of rest has helped. After another night of peaceful sleep, I expect he'll be more active tomorrow."

When the minutes ticked by without another word from him, she wanted to find a two-by-four and beat him over the head with it. It made her crazy enough to simply ask, "Why do things seem so difficult between us? I don't know. It just seems... we'd grown more comfortable with each other. I was gone for two days, but that was three days ago. Now, there's a distance that feels odd."

He continued to stare at the trees. "We're not alone anymore. We have others to care for."

"Ah. Well, we wouldn't want people to think we liked each other."

When he shifted in his seat but didn't respond, another thought came to her.

"I get it. It was one of those rescue situations where emotions are high. It creates a false sense of intimacy. But you're right. It's better this way." Was that all it had been? Maybe so. She stood and tightened the wrap around her even though she felt over-heated. "It's been a long day, and a soft pallet awaits."

"You didn't have to give up the guest room."

"I wasn't going to make Sebastian sleep on the floor. He's been through enough." She hadn't meant to snap, but he was pushing all the wrong buttons.

He glanced up. His gaze held a surprising warmth. "I wouldn't have expected anything less from you. You're a good woman, Stella." Then he returned his focus to the distant darkness.

She reconsidered his earlier words. He hadn't been faulting her. He'd simply stated a fact—a compliment—and she'd jumped to a different conclusion. Good grief. It hadn't occurred to her that she was the one making more of a situation than it was. Her own misguided thoughts were what had come between them.

"Good night, Beckworth."

She added a log to the fire and wrapped herself in the blankets Eleanor had left for her. Beckworth came in twenty minutes later, probably waiting for her to fall asleep. He dropped onto his pad of blankets on the other side of the hearth. She listened to the slow rhythm of his breaths long after he'd fallen asleep. For the first time since being abducted from Baywood, tears slid down her cheeks until fatigue consumed her.

## 18

Ethan sucked in a deep breath, his chest filling with pride and a longing for home as he gazed at the estate below. Brun Manor had belonged in Lord Brun's family for generations. Soon, it would pass to a nephew the earl barely knew.

Each time he returned, he believed it to be his last. This wasn't his home anymore. He knew that. Yet, it was as if he were looking at his childhood home, and in many ways, it was. Though he wasn't born here and was no blood relation to the earl, he still looked upon the man as a father. Lord Brun was all he'd known.

When they'd arrived a few weeks ago, and he'd seen how time had ravaged the earl, his heart had broken. What would they find when they entered the gates this day?

He felt a hand on his arm and glanced at Maire. Tears shone in her eyes, and while she'd only lived here for a few short months, she'd snared the earl's heart as surely as he'd captured hers.

"He'll be there. And he'll be happy to see you."

He squeezed her hand, and there was a surprising lightness

to his tone. "I think he might be happier to see you. As will all in the manor."

Her smile was angelic, but there was steel in her response. "I'll be just as happy to see them as well, but don't underestimate what you mean to the earl."

Before he could respond, Fitz rode up to his other side. "If anyone's following us, they're miles behind. Either they know where we're headed and are in no hurry, knowing they'd be greatly outnumbered by Lord Brun's men, or there's no one out there at all."

"And if you had to guess?" Ethan asked.

Fitz rubbed the whiskers that had grown since leaving the *Daphne* two days ago. "I don't think there's anyone out there. If I were them, I'd focus on grabbing the chronicle, assuming they know who has them. Maybe they're all in London waiting for us."

"Why London?" Maire asked.

He shrugged. "They didn't come after us at the monastery. It would have been difficult to overtake us there, and they knew it. Without Sebastian, we don't know where the torc or the druid's book are hidden. They weren't worried because they had Sebastian. Time was on their side. Now, they don't have AJ or your friend posing as AJ, and they don't have Sebastian. We're scattered to the wind."

"And your point?"

"They were watching Hensley. Probably Waverly as well. They might have men watching Brun, though I doubt it. He's too far away up here, other than being conveniently located near a chronicle."

"You think they'll go after Hensley." Ethan hadn't thought of that, and he should have. But there was nothing they could do from this side of the country. "Jamie is on his way. Maybe sailing right into a trap."

"You can bet your last crown that Jamie will be thinking the same thing. He might get lucky and run into Beckworth. Either way, he knows several of Beckworth's friends if he needs more men."

"I have no doubt Finn would have considered it." Maire's horse sidestepped, eager to be moving. "All we can do is focus on the task we've been assigned. Keep your eyes open, gentlemen." And with that, she let her horse go, and it raced down the slope leaving Ethan and Fitz to catch her.

When Maire reached the open gate, she slowed as two men rose to greet her. Her horse pranced in place as she tried to hold in the reins.

"Good day, Filmore. It's good to see you again. May we pass? We have business with the earl."

The older guard had greeted them the first night they came through the fog in search of Stella. "Lady Murphy. You never have to ask, and I see Master Hughes has brought a guest. Go, go. Lord Brun will be happy to see you."

She didn't hesitate as she gave the horse its head, leaving Ethan and Fitz behind to speak with the guards.

Ethan shook his head. She was in a hurry because she thought the earl might have news, but he didn't see how a messenger could have arrived before them. Though he wasn't sure where a message might come from. Would Sebastian have thought to post one? Beckworth could have assisted with that. He glanced down at the two guards.

"Filmore and Stewart. Good to see you again. Has there been any trouble? Anyone watching the estate?" Ethan settled his horse so it barely twitched.

The guards glanced at each other. "About a fortnight ago, not long after you left for Bristol, four men were seen passing by on the road to Worcester. We only saw two at a time, but they were together. Randall found them at the pubs in Hereford and followed them to the inn they were staying at. They were there for three or four days and haven't been seen since. Might be nothing."

Ethan nodded. "This is Fitz. He's the first mate on the *Daphne Marie*. Don't be surprised if you find him wandering."

"Very good, sir. And welcome home."

Ethan shook the men's hands and then turned the horse toward the manor. Maire was probably already pouring tea for the earl. While he'd grown tired the closer to the estate they rode, Maire became more animated. His fear was that she'd lose hope if there wasn't some word, even if it was irrational to think they'd hear from anyone until they made London.

Thomas waited at the front steps as they approached. His smile was grim, which meant he'd probably seen Maire and her excitement. He'd come to know her well during the time they'd lived at the manor. He was sure to have guessed her motivation, but his concerned expression was either due to the earl's health or the fact he had no news to share. Either way, Ethan was soon to find out.

"I couldn't stop her. And it only took minutes before the entire manor heard you were back. He's barking orders and demanding to see you and Maire." Thomas led them up the steps.

"Where are they?" Ethan asked.

"In the solarium. The lord rarely leaves it these days. Lydia insists the sun is all he needs, though we rarely see it. But he has perked up the closer we get to spring."

Their boots pounded down the hall. Ethan nodded with a smile at the servants who came out to greet him, then snickered when a couple of the young maids turned their focus on Fitz, who followed behind.

He heard Maire's laughter before he entered the solarium. She was sitting at a table near the hearth, listening raptly to whatever tale the earl was weaving. He almost laughed out loud when he noted Maire was indeed pouring his tea.

When Brun noticed their entry, he stopped mid-story and used both hands to push himself to a standing position.

"Ethan, my boy." His pace seemed slower than just a few weeks ago, but Ethan admitted he might be looking for more than what was there. While his body might have slowed, his eyes were clear, his cheeks full of color, and he was returning Ethan's serious perusal.

Ethan took several long strides to meet Brun, who pulled him in for a tight hug. Then he gave Fitz a quick introduction.

"Who would have thought the fates would have brought Ethan back so soon?" Thomas went to a side table and opened a decanter of what was most likely good scotch whiskey. He poured four glasses and then looked to Maire.

"I'm fine with the tea, though I might beg a glass of wine later." Maire sipped her drink, but her gaze turned to a letter that sat near the earl's teacup. Perhaps he had received some news after all.

Thomas handed out the glasses while Ethan assisted Brun back to his seat.

"Maire gave me a quick overview of your journey, but I'll expect details at dinner." Brun slid his teacup aside and downed a third of his scotch. "Until then, tell me what you're doing back this way, then I'll tell you what news I have."

"I believe you were aware that Sebastian had broken up *The Book of Stones* into four sections, one of which is still at the monastery." When he nodded, Ethan continued. "We believe one of the chronicles is outside Worcester, if Sebastian's journal is correct."

Brun nodded. "Yes, it should be in Bransford."

"You know where it is?" Maire sat up and grabbed the glass from Ethan, drinking a long swallow and grimacing at the burn.

"Why, yes. It should be with Father Dolcet. He became a dear friend of Sebastian's when he lived in France. I believe he spent a short period at the monastery. He's been in Bransford for almost eight years now."

"You never said anything." Ethan stared at the earl, never suspecting him of holding something so important a secret.

"The subject never came up. All the focus to date has been on the stones, and since Sebastian hadn't mentioned to you where he sent the chronicles, it seemed wisest to keep it to myself."

"It seems the game has gotten more serious." Maire fished in her pocket and retrieved a journal where she kept all her notes. "When we arrived at the monastery, we discovered Sebastian had been kidnapped." She dabbed at her eyes, then took a deep breath when the earl reached across the table to lay a hand on her arm.

"We tracked our missing friend Stella, who Gemini still believes to be AJ." Ethan took up the tale for Maire. "At some point, Beckworth became involved and rescued Stella. The two were on the run and were on their way to the monastery. But shortly after arriving in Saint-Malo, Stella was kidnapped again, leaving Beckworth injured or left for dead. We're not sure if they cared which."

"Gemini got to France first?" Brun asked.

Ethan rubbed his head. So much had happened in the two weeks since they'd been at Hereford. "No. As far as we know, she's still in England. There was another man, someone named Belato, who took Sebastian."

Brun gazed out the windows where the sun was peeking through the clouds. "I've heard that name before." He sipped his whiskey and draped a blanket that laid on the arm of the chair over his legs. "That was the monk who worked with Sebastian." When Ethan nodded, the earl continued. "That was what started all of this. Sebastian wrote to me of the raid at the monastery and the betrayal by his intern. I think we both thought we'd heard the last of the Belato brothers by the end of the Terror."

Ethan shouldn't have been surprised the earl was aware of this. "We learned that Gemini was searching for Maire. If they kidnapped Sebastian, there's only one reason they needed either of them."

"For their ability to translate *The Book of Stones*." Brun nodded and reached for the letter, though all he did was hold it in his lap.

"Which leads us to believe Gemini wants to put the book back together," Fitz added as he finished off his whiskey.

Brun studied Fitz. "You sailed on the *Daphne Marie* when Finn Murphy captained her."

"Aye, my Lord. He was a fine captain and trained both me and Jamie, the new captain."

"And what other skills do you possess?"

Fitz seemed surprised by the question, and he rubbed his chin as he considered his answer. "Besides being able to perform any job needed on a ship, I'm excellent with the broadsword or in a brawl. Most of the time, I'm sent in to gather information because I usually go unnoticed."

"Except for balls and parties, from what I've heard." Ethan had a chuckle at the first mate's expense, then refilled his glass as a way of an apology.

"I'm fine as a coach driver but probably couldn't pass for a footman," Fitz agreed and clinked Ethan's glass with his own before downing half of it.

"Excellent." Brun looked around the room before spotting Thomas in the corner. "Thomas, there you are. Come over here where I can see you." He tapped the letter on the edge of the table, and Maire's head bobbed with each whack. "This message was delivered this morning. The rider traveled so quickly, he had to exchange horses several times."

Everyone sat straighter on hearing the news.

The earl smiled at Maire. "Rest your fears for Sebastian. This letter comes from Waverly."

She fell back against the chair, her shoulders relaxing as a soft smile appeared. "Thank the gods. Is that where he's at?"

"No. He's with Beckworth and your friend Stella. You understand the message doesn't provide much detail. They are with a friend and will be heading east to visit another. I don't know who the friend is, but I believe the reference east would be London."

"To Hensley, who should be in London for another month or two." Ethan finished his whiskey and tapped the empty glass against the arm of the chair. "Where would they be if they were near Waverly?"

"Eleanor," Maire replied. She had guessed Beckworth might have gone there after rescuing Sebastian and Stella from Belato's ship. She flipped through her journal. "No one knows about her relationship with Beckworth, and it's not far from Waverly if you don't take the roads."

"The letter also mentioned a cousin up the coast," Brun added. "He was undecided whether it was worth the travel since they'd only be able to visit for a day or two."

"So they're going for the chronicle in Ipswich." Ethan smiled. That also held with the team's previous discussions.

"I hope they leave Sebastian with Hensley." Maire touched Ethan's arm, and he placed his hand over hers in understanding. Sebastian was alive but still in danger.

"There is one piece of bad news." The earl waited until all eyes were on him again. "They haven't been able to confirm it, but it's best to assume Gemini is aware of the general location of the three chronicles. It's unknown whether she knows the specific person who has it."

Fitz grumbled something about the blasted stones, and Thomas growled in agreement.

"That could explain why men had been seen in Hereford." Ethan considered other reasons but couldn't come up with any. "If they were planning on stealing the chronicle, they would have done it already."

"Or maybe they're scouting the area, waiting for us." Fitz set his empty glass on the table, and Ethan guessed he was becoming restless with the need to investigate Bransford.

"We need to assume they haven't found the chronicle, but that is something Fitz can determine." Brun kept his gaze on Maire. "Once we know the town is secure, it will be best for Maire to visit Father Dolcet as a friend of Sebastian."

"And if he still has the chronicle, the danger will be after we take the book." Fitz scratched his stomach. "It will be a long ride to London."

And no one had anything positive to say after that.

## 19

Finn watched the door of the tavern. He'd expected Lando thirty minutes ago, and that itch he got just before something went wrong crawled between his shoulder blades. They'd agreed on waiting an hour before they went in search of each other, so he grasped his mug of wine and picked at a notch in the table.

His task had been the easiest. Determine the exact day the new count officially moved into the manor. The old count wouldn't be leaving. He was to be moved to a smaller room until his death, which was expected at any time. If they weren't able to get into the manor before then, their task would be doubly hard.

Their timing appeared to be working in their favor, but if they couldn't determine the location of the chronicle, it might be lost forever or fall into the wrong hands, like Belato or Gemini. He considered if that would be such a bad thing. Not that it would be easy to steal it back.

This was their best opportunity, and they would have to make it work. It wasn't the first time he and Lando had sneaked into places with a well-crafted story and an ability to adapt to situations. But he worried about AJ. She could improvise as well as him, but the language barrier would be a problem. She'd picked up some French during their vacation to the monastery, but not enough. She wouldn't understand what was being asked of her to be able to attempt a yes or no answer.

The agreed-upon hour was almost up when Lando, out of breath and sweat beading on his forehead, pulled up a chair next to him. He'd been expecting him to come through the front door and almost spilled his wine when he jumped.

"Where the hell have you been?" Finn whispered loud enough to be heard over the rowdy voices.

Lando raised an arm to call the server. "I had enough information to get us close, but before I left, another man joined us."

A finely rounded woman with dark hair piled on top of her head dropped two mugs of wine and gave them a saucy wink. "I assumed you'd want another. No one likes to drink alone."

"Aye, lass, you have the right of it."

"Or maybe I just like the sound of an Irishman." She gave him another wink and added an extra sway to her walk.

Lando smirked. "We're not supposed to stand out."

"I think we're safe from a fetching waitress." Finn's lopsided return grin was brief. "So, who was this second man?"

"A disgruntled butler."

"Aye, that was worth the time. I thought the old count's valet was a lucky find. I never thought we'd get close to the butler."

"I would usually agree, but there's great hostility between the two households. The count's daughter-in-law is a greedy one and created a rift between father and son many years ago. She's quite determined to join the court in hopes of gaining a grander title for her husband."

"In the court of Napoleon, she could also find her way to one of the royal cells."

"I'd rather face pirates on the high seas than a court of lords and ladies."

Finn grimaced at the weak wine, then leaned over his mug. "So, what did the good butler have to say?"

Lando set his elbows on the table as he scanned the room. Four men sat at the table next to them, but they were focused on their food and whatever tale someone was sharing as hearty laughs continued in between bites of mutton and bread. "The household goods will be transferred in two days. The old staff plans a bit of mischief. There should be enough chaos to make our task easier."

Finn nodded. "What about the location of our target?"

"As expected, that information was a bit trickier. The butler mentioned three hidden places the younger count knows nothing about. They've devised a plan to steal the money and gems while the staff creates diversions. They'll meet the following day to split their loot, but he didn't divulge the meeting place."

"People are hungry. If it wasn't for the war, I doubt they'd take the risk. But that doesn't tell us where the chronicle might be."

"No. Not in itself." He smiled as he swigged the wine. "But he mentioned two hiding places he wasn't bothering with. The first was where the deeds and land records were kept, along with some coin. The second location wouldn't be worth the effort because it only contains a single book written in an unknown language."

"Tell me you have some inkling where that second hiding place might be."

Lando grinned. "He might have made a slip or two."

A J tugged at the bodice of the plain brown servant's dress that was too short in the skirt and sleeves and thanked the stars she didn't have large breasts, or the dress would never have fit. She leaned against the manor's wall, a few yards from the kitchen door.

The manor was a flurry of activity, with deliveries and wagons of furniture blocking the side entrance. Finn and Lando had been hauling furniture for the last hour, but so far, they hadn't given her any signal. So, she continued to loiter behind some evergreens, wrapping her shawl tighter.

The only reason she wasn't already inside was her inability to speak French. If someone stopped to give her an order, the response might require more than a nod of compliance. Still, if she stayed out here much longer, her muscles would be too stiff to walk, let alone scurry around the manor as if she knew her way around.

The chaos was more than they could have hoped for. More time was spent moving the same few items in and out with two housekeepers providing different directions. No one appeared to think the activity was suspicious, but that might not last long.

To distract herself, she picked an early blossom and held it to her nose, swaying from side to side as if caught up in the scent and the sun that refused to provide any warmth.

When Finn emerged from the manor, carrying a long side table with Lando, she sashayed over to him. With a wink to Lando and one of the other footmen, she pulled him away. The footman gave her a charming smile as if she might find him more appealing.

She shrugged and shook her head as she pulled Finn to her spot against the wall.

Finn fell into her ruse with more intent than she'd planned, pushing her back to the wall with a demanding kiss. "If you plan on seducing me, lass, you'd better be prepared for a lusty response."

She let him nibble her neck. "What's taking so long?"

"The new count is in the study, going through the land deeds, but I think the noise is starting to get to him. His butler suggested he take a ride to review the property while the furniture is arranged."

"When will I have a clear path to the second floor?"

He tickled the hollow spot at the base of her neck, and she grabbed his shoulders while trying to stop him from moving his leg between hers. "It shouldn't be too much longer. You remember the directions to the servant stairs?"

"The hallway between the library and study. The door to the stairs is at the end of the hall. The count's suites are directly to the left, the countess's on the right."

"You've got this. We just need to make sure the count and countess are completely occupied. It will be easier once the count leaves."

"If I stay out here much longer, I'll be too frozen to move. I need to go in now."

Finn gave her a long, deep kiss, and the chill that evaded her muscles slowly dissipated. "How's that?"

She smiled. "It helped, but I haven't changed my mind."

Finn scowled. "I thought this would be easier without Maire here to goad you."

She tugged on his ear. "You should have known better." She straightened her dress and pulled on her bodice before rearranging the wrap around her shoulders. With a pat to his backside, she strolled away, a smile on her face, the blossom tucked in her bodice. When the footman glanced her way, she gave him another saucy wink, which made him smile before Lando punched him in the shoulder to pay attention to the dresser they'd be moving next.

She kept the same pace and hoped she wasn't making a mistake, but she'd rather find places to hide inside the manor. If anyone paid notice to her, they would just think she was a member of the new household or vice versa. When she approached the side door, she kept her eyes downcast and mumbled to herself. It was a trick Stella sometimes used when salespeople hovered. Many people were uncomfortable around people who talked to themselves, thinking them a bit odd. She bet it would seem even stranger in this time period. She'd learned a handful of words in French, and she strung them together in a phrase she was sure made absolutely no sense. Whenever someone came along that might talk to her, she repeated the words in a sing-song voice and held back a grin when the person rushed past.

The hall from the side entrance connected to the hall from the foyer, and she made a right toward the library, which was busier than she'd expected. She glanced around, searching for inspiration that would make her seem she'd been given a task when her gaze stopped at the hearth and its robust fire. A large stack of firewood had been placed next to it, more than she'd seen at other manors. The staff wouldn't want to bother hauling in wood during the day's turmoil.

Everyone seemed occupied, but before making a move, she realized her wrap was now a problem. She tied it around her waist as if she'd just come from outside, then rove through the room, moving books from one pile to another to appear busy. When she reached the hearth, she glanced around, decided there was no time like the present, and picked up several pieces of wood.

She moved with confidence, remembering the words Finn and Maire had drilled into her head on previous missions. Look like you belong, and most won't question it. She walked straight out a side door and turned right, slowing long enough to peek into the study as she passed.

The count was still there, but he was putting on his jacket as his butler continued to chatter in his ear. She increased her pace, glancing behind her until she slammed into the house-keeper. The woman stood with hands on hips, and she guessed it was the new housekeeper. Without thinking, she began singing her repetitive phrase. The woman looked at her as if she'd gone mad, which was the point. She said something that AJ would never be able to decipher, so she nodded and continued her chant.

The housekeeper attempted her request two more times, but AJ stuck with her lyrical response until the woman threw up her hands and stormed off. Seconds later, another maid rushed by with a bundle of used sheets, nodding briefly before passing by. She blew out a breath and almost ran to the door, yanking it open to dash inside. At the top of the stairs, she paused and leaned against the wall. Little beads of sweat had popped out on her forehead, but there wasn't anything she could do about it with the small stack of wood in her arms. It had been all she could do to open doors, which she did again as she stepped out to the second-floor hall. With no one in sight, she raced the last few steps to the master suite, where the door was already open. Once inside, she kicked the door closed behind her.

She dumped the wood next to the hearth, then noting the room appeared ready for the new count, took the time to stack the wood on top of the existing pile. It was best nothing looked out of place, and after giving the room a quick scan, rushed toward the dressing room. This was the wrong time to second-guess the outgoing butler, but she hoped the old count wasn't as paranoid as Beckworth with all his secret hiding spots.

At the door of the dressing room, she peered in and studied the three walls. The hidden cubbyhole was said to be along the middle of the wall, the third shelf on the right. Rather than take a chance missing it and having to backtrack, she began feeling along the back of the third shelf from the doorway.

The secret was to push on an upper corner, but again, she took the less risky approach and pushed along the top and bottom the entire distance..She moved clothes and boxes as she worked her way down, losing track of how far she'd gone as she moved deeper into the room, which got darker the farther she went. Her fingers brushed against something metal, and when she tried to move it, she discovered it was a heavy metal box with a lock.

She considered going around it, but she should be well past the middle of the wall, and what better place to put a secret door. Since she couldn't lift it, she managed to push it farther down the shelf. Once it was out of the way, as she suspected, part of the wall softened under her touch.

Bingo, as Maire liked to say.

She pressed the upper spot again, felt a slim edge, and pried the door open. Before she could pull out a candle, voices filled the outer room.

"Let's do this with all haste. The horses are already saddled."

"Yes, sir."

AJ cursed under her breath. The count. Of all the luck.

# 20

AJ released another curse. Proper noble etiquette would be just as rigid in France as in England. Of course, the count would require a change of clothes. She closed the hidden door and spun around. There was no time to move the metal box without making noise. In a rush and not knowing any other solution, she split two piles of clothes, making a third to cover the empty spot. With any luck, the valet would be in too much of a hurry to notice the change.

Where to hide? She scurried to the back of the dressing room, dropped into the corner behind a greatcoat and pulled the garment around her, rolling herself into a ball.

Why did people hide stuff in the house? Why not in the stables or under the porch? She'd rather dig through piles of manure than deal with household nobles, who could have her hauled off to jail.

Footsteps approached, then stopped.

"Gray or tan, sir?"

AJ blinked, just now realizing what she hadn't when the count first entered. His valet sounded Irish, and they spoke in

English—not French. That seemed odd. She hadn't heard a single word of English in the manor until now.

"The tan." A ruffle of clothing. "No. The gray. As the new lord of the manor, it's important to impart the correct image. Gray reflects a more business nature between lord and tenant. Let's save the tan for when I ride out as one of the men, stopping to ask questions about their family and harvest as if I'm one of them."

She rolled her eyes. The man sounded like he was running for Congress, or maybe seeking a position in Napoleon's court. Had he always been that way, or had his wife molded him into the man he'd become? She could understand why father and son might be estranged.

A lamp was lit, and she checked the floor to see if any of her dress was showing. The man came close. Those beads of sweat returned, along with her imagination, positive he was searching the clothes she'd moved.

She held her breath.

"What's taking so long?" Thank heavens the count was as impatient as her.

"Sorry, sir, I just found them." His voice began to fade as he moved to the outer chamber. "I'm afraid many of your things are still packed."

After five minutes, the bedroom door opened. "Make sure I have something laid out for the afternoon. I should only be a couple of hours, then I'd like to spend some time in the library before dressing for dinner. The housekeeper assures me the house will be settled by then."

"Of course, sir."

"Have you seen the countess?"

A silent pause. "I think she was in the dining room with the housekeeper, sir."

"Ah. Very good. Well, finish up and take care of this morning's attire."

The place quieted again, but she waited. Soft sounds filtered in, and she assumed his girl Friday was still around. The lamp faded, then the door closed.

Her signal to get the hell out of there. She replaced the clothes as she'd found them and opened the hidden door. If the chronicle wasn't in there, they were sunk. She lit the candle and peered inside. A tin the size of a cigar box was the first thing she could make out. It had a small latch with a lock. Her stomach dropped, then she released a hysterical giggle. The box was too small to hold the chronicle. Then she noticed what it sat on— something covered with oilcloth.

She stuck the candle in melted wax drippings, waited a few seconds for it to harden, then pulled out the tin box. This was it. She blew out a nervous breath and stood on tiptoes to grip the wrapped item. Her heart swelled, not wanting to get overly optimistic, but she knew the feel of a book.

She placed it on the shelf, pulled away the oilcloth, and almost wept when she stared down at the cover that Sebastian must have made. When she opened the book, she held back the giggles that returned at the worst possible time. The first page said it all—Sebastian's recognizable script and the foreign Celtic words she'd seen many times.

After returning the tin box, she closed the secret door and shoved the metal box back in place. She reached into the extra pocket she'd sewn into her servant's dress and pulled out a burlap bag. The book, still wrapped in oilcloth, was stuffed into the bag, and she pulled the strap over her head. She blew out the candle then dripped the last of the melted wax on the metal box. It was still warm when she scraped it off and stuffed it in her pocket along with the candle before running for the bedroom door and leaning against it.

Voices floated from down the hall. She cracked open the door and, not seeing anyone to her right, peered to her left. Three housemaids and the new housekeeper were moving room by room. A maid and the housekeeper disappeared into a room four doors down, but the other two remained in the hall.

She closed the door and spun around, wiping her brow. *Don't panic.* She ran to the windows that opened to a small balcony. With a last look at the bedroom door, she stepped out, relieved to be looking at the back of the house with a view of the gardens. Not nearly as nice as Beckworth's, and the thought made her smile. It was a shame Stella wouldn't have a chance to see his spring gardens.

A drop from a two-story balcony wasn't a bright move, especially when the landing would be on stone. She leaned over to see if a climb was feasible. Chances were slim the housekeeper would inspect an outdoor patio, but after listening to the new count, he'd expect it to be as spotless. Besides, who knew how long the inspections would take? If the count returned and she was still in the house, Finn would freak out.

No one was in the garden. The only thing she'd have to worry about would be the windows on the first floor. She closed her eyes and pictured Finn's rough sketch of the house. If she was in the far-left corner of the manor, the room below the count's suite was the recital room, which was next to the solarium. When the door to the room opened, she snapped into full escape mode.

She climbed over the railing and found sufficient footholds on the openwork of a cornice to hang like Spider-Woman. The next foothold would be a longer reach, and she was determining the best approach when someone opened the balcony doors.

The woman prattled something, and AJ could only pick out a few words. The footsteps receded but stopped too soon.

AJ clung to the wall, her fingers digging into the plaster. Her right foot slipped off its edge, and she shifted her weight to her left leg. Her muscles twitched from the strain, forcing her to grit her teeth. A drop from this height wouldn't kill her if she focused on her landing, but she could still break an ankle.

A long thirty seconds passed until the doors closed, and she stretched her right leg as far as she could until it scraped against an edge. She leaned into her right leg, found a decent handhold, and shook her left leg to release the building cramp.

She braced herself and jumped the rest of the way, landing on both feet with little sound other than the soft thud of the burlap bag slapping against her back. Crouched and leaning on a knee, she glanced around to find herself still alone. The drapes were closed in the recital room. Her luck was still with her.

The solarium windows weren't as dangerous since no one would have witnessed her drop from the upper floor. A quick glance through the windows revealed a room filled with excess furniture and no people.

She rounded the building and passed by the door to the kitchen. Her nerves were fried, but at the same time, she wanted to burst out laughing from the exhilaration of what she'd accomplished. She tamped down her premature celebration when she spotted two well-dressed men speaking with Finn. She strolled by them, her shoulders a bit rounded, and attempted to make eye contact with him.

He spotted her and gave a slight nod as he continued his conversation. She didn't see Lando but suspected he was nearby. She continued walking straight down the path that led to town. She picked up her pace once she was out of sight of the manor, then, after a quarter mile, turned onto an old game trail, only spotting it by the small piece of fabric tied to the limb of a tree.

Several hundred yards in, Lando waited by three horses.

She pulled the burlap bag over her head and pulled out the

chronicle. "I think this is it." She sat on a log. "Who were those men Finn was talking to?"

"I don't know. I was heading back to the cart we'd been unloading when the men walked up to him. He shook me off, so I took the long route back. Did he appear in trouble?"

"They were in deep conversation, but he nodded for me to stick with the plan."

"Let's see what you have, and if Finn isn't back in five minutes, I'll go find him."

She quickly unwrapped the chronicle, and Lando looked over her shoulder as she opened the cover and slowly turned the pages. It was clear from the first page that this was the real deal, though she couldn't read it any better in the light of day. But everything down to the paper and ink appeared similar to *The Book of Stones.*

Lando nodded. "You did good."

Branches rustled as Finn raced into the clearing. "I think they bought my story for now, but if they check further, they might come looking. Did that grin on your sweet face mean we have what we came for."

"Oh, it did indeed." She wrapped their prize, then stuffed it back in the bag and over her head to rest gently on her back.

"Who were the men?" Lando asked.

"The old count's estate manager and assistant. He didn't recognize us and asked if I was with the new count. I told him the butler had recruited a couple of us from the village, that I was in town visiting a cousin but needed the work. They questioned me rather thoroughly, concerned about thieves."

The three had mounted their horses, and when Finn finished his tale, Lando laughed out loud. "Well, they wouldn't be wrong."

## 21

Beckworth woke early and glanced over his shoulder at the sleeping Stella. He'd spent a good portion of the night considering her words, not surprised she felt his distance. He was more shocked that she'd mentioned it, but what did he expect? She'd never been a quiet one. Everything had appeared normal while they'd been on the ship, but Sebastian had been a buffer, and they'd both been worried for his safety. Then the focus shifted to their escape plans. There had been little time to think of much else.

He rose, rolled up his bedding, then crept out the door to wash in the basin outside. The scent of coffee and fresh-baked bread greeted him by the time he'd fed the horses and chopped firewood.

Before he reached the door, Sebastian stepped outside. "I thought you might need some assistance." He backed up to let Beckworth enter. "It seems I'm too late. I haven't been the most helpful, and when Eleanor was kind enough to supply me with quill and paper, I had to jot down our travels before I forgot everything."

Beckworth had to smile. After seeing the number of journals

the monk kept in his workroom, it wasn't surprising to see him hunched over a table all day. "It was a good time to rest while I gathered supplies and information from Waverly. Today, we help Eleanor." He stacked the logs by the hearth and sucked in the added scent of sausage.

"Are we in danger?" Sebastian sat at the table and wrapped his hands around a mug of coffee.

"Always. But not imminently. Barrington has a team of men keeping an eye on four of Gemini's men who are watching the manor, but I don't think they saw me."

"So, we're safe for a while."

"Yes, but I can't say for how long."

"Well, you're welcome to stay as long as you need." Eleanor came through the door, carrying a pail of milk. "But I understand your concern. I haven't seen any strangers, but you can never be too careful."

Stella followed behind with a basket of eggs. She gave him a tentative smile. "It was strange waking up to find the coffee already made."

He nodded. "I think the pallet was the best sleep I've had in a while."

She opened her mouth, then closed it, probably rethinking some clever response, and gave him a weak smile instead. After setting the basket on the counter, she assisted with breakfast, effectively shutting down further conversation.

If they'd been alone, he'd find the courage to explain his distance, his reticence, and his guilt. It wasn't easy to share his weaknesses with others, and for some reason, it was more difficult with Stella. He fetched the coffee pot from the fire and refilled cups before leaving it on the table. When Stella finished preparing the next pot, he placed it on the hook and pushed it into the fire.

The flames caught him in a spell. Memories of Stella sitting at a fire, obsessing over the beans in her quest for the perfect pot of coffee. It was hard to believe he missed those times. The clatter of plates being set on the table shattered the images. He shook himself and returned to the table to sit with Sebastian, who was back to writing.

He tapped the corner of the journal while Sebastian refreshed the ink. "Are you recording current events or summarizing our chances of collecting all the chronicles?"

"I'm recording my journey since I was abducted. I've already left a message for Maire on where to find the chronicles. If she was reviewing my last journal as you stated, then she'll discover the names. That's all that's necessary."

"How were you abducted in the first place? Brother Leclair said you received a message and rode out on your own."

He shrugged, and his lips twitched. "I didn't want to bother anyone. The message said there was trouble at the smuggler's cave. It was signed by a trusted merchant who helps with distribution. They used the man's name to lure me out."

"Where did they abduct you?"

"Just shy of the turn-off to the cave."

Beckworth pictured the route and nodded. "There's a small outcrop of rocks near there. It would make a good hiding spot."

Sebastian closed the inkpot and set the quill in a slim wooden box. "That is correct. There were three of them, and it seemed useless to resist."

Beckworth glanced toward the kitchen. Stella had tilted her head toward them while Eleanor continued her banter. He had no doubt the woman could listen to both conversations without a hitch. "You did the right thing. I believe they kidnapped you because they couldn't find Maire. And while they seem to have their own scribe, I'm not convinced they're very good with Celtic, or perhaps it's the encryption that's giving them trouble. Either way, they need you or Maire."

"Nothing about it made sense until you mentioned Belato. I thought all the brothers had died during the Terror."

"It's impossible to predict when our past might reach out for us. Once we have all the chronicles, we'll need to reconsider the best course of action on how to preserve them."

Eleanor placed a platter of sausages on the table. "No carts before the horses, gentlemen. You stay focused on the task at hand, one chronicle at a time." She picked up Sebastian's journal and the wooden box and placed them on a table near the sofa before pulling a skillet from the hearth.

Stella placed roasted parsnips, fresh bread, and butter on the table, then refilled mugs before sitting across from Beckworth. "So, what's the plan? Are we going to London?"

He couldn't help but notice the excitement dancing in her eyes. "Have you ever been?"

She shook her head. "The trip to the monastery was the first time I'd been out of the country. AJ told me her observations, and I want to see if I agree."

"We'll stop long enough to meet with Hensley and see if he has men to spare for our continuation onto Ipswich." Beckworth pointed his fork at Sebastian. "Who is this person with the chronicle?"

"He's an ironmaster. A very devout man."

"You sent a chronicle to someone with no security to protect it?" Beckworth asked.

Sebastian's gaze twinkled. "He's worked on many structures in and around Ipswich as well as those farther north and some in London. Who's to say where he might have hidden the chronicle?"

Stella snorted. "He buried the chronicle inside his stonework? I hope this guy is still alive, or it'll be like searching for Jimmy Hoffa."

They all stared at her, and she laughed. "Okay, not the right audience to get the reference. Jimmy was a union boss, a leader for organizing workers, and one day he disappeared, never to be heard from again. No one ever found his body. Some say he was buried in a cement foundation."

Beckworth nodded. "It's an excellent hiding spot, but she's right. Is this man still alive?"

Sebastian shrugged. "We haven't communicated other than to know he received the chronicle. He provided a few clues that will help us if he's no longer in this world, but I doubt they'll be meaningful until we arrive. I believe the chronicle will be close."

Beckworth glanced at Stella. Her eyes still glimmered with enthusiasm, holding him in a trance that took a moment to shake off. "This would be grand fun if it was a simple treasure hunt, but we have very dangerous people searching for the same prize who have all but disappeared. They're watching us, and I can't help but think they're waiting for us to gather the pieces."

"What other choice do you have?" Eleanor asked as she nibbled on a sausage and a slice of bread. "You can't leave them where they are. If you ask those who have the chronicles to send them someplace, like to Hensley, they could easily be taken during transport if this Gemini has men in the shadows. Nor can you leave them."

"Do we know how Gemini or Belato discovered where the chronicles are? Maybe they're just following us around, hoping we'll gather them all." Stella's intelligence and the way her mind worked never ceased to amaze him. It was one of her most interesting qualities.

Sebastian sat back, his shoulders drooping. "I don't know how Belato would know the locations, but I have my suspicions. It's possible he took advantage of a young monk with talk of all the artifacts and secrets the monastery holds. Perhaps the monk needed money for his family, or perhaps he was coerced in a different manner. But I believe Belato had a spy in the monastery at the time the chronicles were sent away. Someone who could have overheard or easily discovered where messengers had been sent."

The discussion was making Beckworth's head hurt. "We can speculate all we want. Maybe they know the names of those that hold them or simply which town they were sent to. But the chronicles alone won't give them everything they need, like the Heart Stone. I don't know how they came up with the improved incantation. If they have their own scribe, they're not of much worth if they also need Maire or Sebastian. Belato has been pulling strings since the beginning. Since his previous attempts failed, he's stirred the hornet's nest, and they have us scurrying to bring all the pieces together."

"And what can we do about that?" Stella asked.

"I'm afraid we might have already walked into their trap. Knowing it's a trap gives us some advantages, but we need to know what our other team members are doing, and for that, we'll need Hensley. Let's determine our route to London. We'll need a secondary location to stay until I can scout Hensley's manor."

Once they settled on the next stage, Eleanor stood and collected plates. Stella picked up the rest of the dishes and pushed Eleanor out of the kitchen. "Didn't you say you had a fence that needed repairing to keep the cow from straying?"

Sebastian stood. "I might not be as agile as I once was, but I know a thing or two about fences. And I could use some time outside."

"You'll be getting plenty of that on the road to London, old man, but let's see what we can do to ease some of Eleanor's burdens." He slunk an arm around Sebastian's thin shoulders, the monk's eyes glittering with pleasure to be included in the work.

Beckworth found Sebastian's ideas for fixing the fences

somewhat ingenious, and once done with the repairs, they moved on to fix other items while Eleanor washed clothes.

Stella called everyone in for a quick lunch accompanied by ale. They discussed the making of cider, and Stella updated Sebastian on what the monastery was like in her era.

Beckworth spent most of the time watching her, but the simple truth was that he couldn't take his eyes off her. Eleanor's work dresses couldn't hide her beauty. She'd chosen to wear her hair up in some concoction Eleanor created since her hair wasn't long enough for most modern styles. And even with Eleanor's handiwork, several strands of hair refused to be tamed. Whenever Stella waved her hands at critical parts of her story, she managed to push back the errant strands.

At some point, he removed himself from the conversation to stoke the fire in the hearth. While they continued to chatter behind him, he became lost once again to the flames. This time, he considered security measures for when they left in the morning. He'd discussed several ideas with Barrington, and he'd go back to Waverly before dinner to advise of his decision. A messenger would need to leave tonight to inform Hensley they were on their way. In the morning, Barrington would send a team to keep Gemini's men busy while they made their dash toward London. A simple security precaution in case he'd been spotted at Waverly.

When he became aware of the silence, except for the clatter of plates, he turned around to see that only Stella remained in the house.

"Where did Eleanor and Sebastian go?"

Stella washed a plate but didn't look up. "They went for a walk."

When he stood and started for the door, she must have read his thoughts because she continued, "Don't worry. They're both armed. She said something about collecting honey, and you'd know what that means."

He did. There was an old elm tree at the corner of Eleanor's property. An active bee colony had taken up residence a couple of years ago, and she insisted the bees didn't mind sharing since they were using her tree.

"It will be good to have some fresh honey for the bread." He didn't have any reason to stay in the house. The wagon required a few minor fixes before morning, but all he could do was stare at the loose tendrils she kept pushing back.

He fished in his pocket for the small paper-wrapped object he'd been carrying with him since before Saint-Malo. His heart pounded with an increasing staccato, and he sucked in a deep breath, letting it out slowly, borrowing the count-to-ten method AJ deployed in times of stress. Then he chastised himself. It was a trinket. That was all. And before he made more of it than it was, he cleared his throat. "I saw this in a shop when I was buying supplies."

She finished storing a cook pot before glancing his way, then her eyes lit on what he held. "I didn't think you were going into Corsham."

"This was in France before I found you. I bought the supplies, assuming we'd be on the run once we arrived in England." He held out the small package, waiting patiently for her to realize she'd need to take it from him if she wanted to see what was inside.

Her grasp was tentative, but once she was holding it, she turned it over and over, searching for the opening. She was careful once she began to unwrap it. When the hairpin was revealed, she didn't move.

She appeared to be blinking a lot, but he couldn't be sure with those blasted strands hiding his view. She didn't wipe at her eyes, but she gingerly touched the pin.

"It's beautiful."

He barely heard the words, and that foolish feeling came over him again. "They only had a handful to choose from. This one seemed to suit you best." God's blood. He was selling it like it was nothing more than a new broom. But that was exactly what he wanted it to sound like. His focus had to remain on the mission.

"Well, I don't know what the other ones looked like, but this one seems perfect." She finger-combed her loose strands and captured them with the pin. She turned around so her back faced him, the hairpin in view.

It was perfect, just as he'd imagined.

"What do you think?"

He stared. Whatever words he'd prepared had slipped away. When several seconds went by, she tapped her foot. It was a new affectation she'd adopted while in her cell in the cargo hold. Whenever she was impatient, her foot started up.

"It will do." The words sounded stiff, and he was being an idiot. But he was honest-to-god flustered. He nodded once, then scampered from the room.

The more he kept her at arm's length, the harder it became. He'd noticed their loss of intimacy before she'd mentioned it, and he'd cursed Sebastian half a dozen times for being with them, as if there were another option. It was better this way. She would be going home soon. It wouldn't surprise him if Finn sent her back while he and AJ stayed to finish this nonsense with Gemini and Belato.

He ignored the pressure in his chest and blamed it on indigestion from the morning's sausage. When he stopped his race from the house, he found himself in the barn. He grabbed a mallet and stomped outside. A few minutes with the wagon seemed the best place to start, and for the next twenty minutes, the only sound in the clearing was the mallet pounding the wheel.

## 22

Stella stared after Beckworth as he all but ran from the room. She moved to the window and removed the hairpin, tilting her hand to let the light move across its surface. It was a beautiful piece. She'd never mentioned needing one, though without her gel and mousse, her hair was a creature of its own making. That he'd thought of it on his own made her heart thump faster.

Everything had changed in such a short time. She hadn't been wrong when she'd blamed the emotions from the rescue for creating a false intimacy. But if that were true, why were they stronger now than before? They should have faded. He was her guide and bodyguard, nothing more. Her focus should be on finding AJ and Finn, not taking off in search of pieces from an ancient book. She didn't know what to think anymore and decided to ignore the topic for now.

She found a mug and poured wine from a clay jar. They had a long trip to London and then on to Ipswich for a chronicle, assuming AJ and Finn hadn't beaten them there. She missed AJ, who would give her a good shake if she knew how often Stella watched Beckworth's backside each time he walked away. Or the way she gazed in fascination at the different emotions that crossed his face when he and Eleanor reminisced over their days in London.

She finished the wine, rinsed out the mug, then searched for the broom. By the time Eleanor and Sebastian returned, she'd drunk two more mugs of wine, rinsing the cup out each time, had swept the floor in every room as well as the porch and stairs, and was currently cutting vegetables.

"We didn't mean to be so long, but the bees were being more difficult than normal." She placed a jar on the counter, and Stella looked inside.

"Honeycomb and all. It's been ages since I've eaten from the comb." She'd been a kid, and her youngest brother had found the hive. They'd each been stung, but it hadn't mattered. She squelched the memory.

"Beckworth loves honey. He likes it on his bread." Eleanor took a basket from Sebastian. It was filled with items from the garden.

"The brothers keep hives." Sebastian collapsed onto the sofa and wiped his forehead with a kerchief he'd pulled from his robe. "We usually have enough honey to share with those in need. But to see her take it straight from a tree was fascinating to watch."

Eleanor stepped next to Stella and took the knife from her. "It's time for you to rest. You've been busy since you woke up. If you don't want to go for a walk, you can simply sit on the porch and take in the beautiful day. You might be lucky enough to get a rain-free ride to London."

The thought of being on the road with the rain made her shiver, the memory so recent she felt the bone-chilling cold and the clamminess from a soaked dress. Her only need, besides coffee, was the warmth from a fire. It wasn't that she didn't like rain. She'd lived in Oregon for a long time, but she couldn't remember a single moment where she had to be out in it all day with nothing but a battered raincoat.

"Where did you get that?" Eleanor's question made Stella spin around.

"What?"

"The hairpin. I didn't see it earlier."

Her hand whipped up to touch it and felt her cheeks redden. "Beckworth thought it would help with my hair."

Eleanor stared at her, and a knowing smile touched her lips that made Stella fidget. "It's beautiful. I thought perhaps it was an heirloom."

She shrugged and poured a mug of water, stomping over to hand it to Sebastian, who thanked her with a smirk. "It was just a trinket. I think he found in Saint-Malo." When Eleanor hid a smile and picked up a knife to slice carrots, a change in subject was needed, but she couldn't think of one. "I think I'll take that walk."

Before the door closed behind her, she heard Eleanor say, "He was always a thoughtful man around those he cares for."

*What the hell?* Stella raced down the steps and was halfway to the barn before she considered Beckworth was probably in there working on the wagon. She took a right onto what appeared to be a well-used path, and followed it until she was out of sight of the house.

She didn't have to walk far before she found a small creek and stumbled before collapsing on a log. Did Beckworth care for her? More than someone to babysit in his loyalty to AJ? Did she care for him? It explained her sudden awkwardness. She'd never been speechless around a man before. Even those that piqued her interest never left her tongue-tied. Besides, what did it matter to her? She'd soon be back in her own century. Where was AJ when she needed her the most? She'd talk some sense into her.

She leaned against a tree, glanced up at the waning day then closed her eyes. He was just a man like any other, who'd looked out for her and protected her. She was the kid sister he promised to return to AJ, and she was making more of it than it was. That had to be it. Sure, he was hot, and he had a wicked sense of humor that matched her own. They'd worked well together through intense moments. There was bound to be some sense of camaraderie between them.

The day was warmer than yesterday, but she rubbed her arms. She should have grabbed a wrap before stumbling out of the house like some smitten maiden. *Good grief.* A smile finally replaced the frown. Her world had been turned upside down, and now she was learning this new Stella, who'd faced danger and death. Beckworth had taught her everything she needed to adapt and survive, including those damn riding lessons. She snorted at the memory.

The answer was as clear as the creek that murmured a few feet away. Be herself. She'd allowed the trauma of the kidnapping, the cargo hold, and their escape to take over. She thought she'd overcome her anxiety the night before, but maybe she hadn't. The path forward was simple—stop looking through the rearview mirror and keep her eyes on the target. Get the book, find AJ and Finn, take Gemini down, then go home. Anything else that happened along the way, she'd deal with. And Beckworth? Now wasn't the time to question his motives or her own. She couldn't lose the trust they'd built. Not now.

A twig snapped.

Her eyes popped open, and she froze.

It could be a deer or a rabbit. Another snap. Maybe Beckworth came to find her, but he wouldn't sneak up on her. She reached for her pocket, then closed her eyes with a silent curse. She'd been in such a hurry to escape Eleanor's teasing gaze that she'd run out without her pistol.

*Stupid. Stupid. Stupid.*

She wouldn't have to worry about Beckworth after all. She'd most likely be dead in a few minutes.

"I see you there, girl." The voice was low and sounded like someone chewing on rocks. "Come out and tell me your name."

She wasn't exactly hiding. He was either guessing she was out there, or he'd picked up her trail and assumed she was close. She slowly turned her head toward his voice, but couldn't see him. Not yet. But she heard his quiet footsteps and the rustle of grass.

"I only want to talk. You got nothing to fear from me."

He walked past her, his head turning left to right as he searched for where she might have gone. If he turned around, he'd see her; and if she moved an inch, he'd hear her. If he kept walking, following the path until he moved into the trees, she could make a break for the house.

He'd taken two steps in that direction before he turned around. She was nothing more than a statue, which explained why it took a moment before his gaze focused and spotted her.

"There you are."

She didn't like his grin, and she reflexively wrapped her arms around her stomach.

"Come over here so I can get a look at ya." He waved her closer with the pistol in his hand.

He must be nuts if he thought she'd just jump up and run over to him.

"I said come over here."

She stared at him, forcing her breath to slow and remain calm. If this was one of Gemini's men, he wouldn't shoot her. He couldn't take the chance she was AJ. The most she could do was irritate him. But if he thought he was going to drag her away from her friends without a fight, he was in for a surprise. The question was, did he have a buddy out there somewhere or was he alone?

When he took a few steps closer, his pistol still in his hand but no longer pointed at her, she let her arms drop and settle on the log before slowly reaching around for something she could use as a weapon. He watched her hands, and that wouldn't do.

"Who are you, and what are you doing here? This is private property." She didn't quite scream it, but she'd raised her voice loud enough that someone other than another bad guy might hear.

"Old Bob said to stay close to the manor, but I saw a man sneaking around. It got me thinking."

She snorted. "Your first time?"

He stared at her, clearly puzzled. "What?"

"You said it got you thinking, and I was wondering if that was your first time."

His grin faded as his eyes squinted to slits. "They said you had a mouth on you."

That confirmed her suspicions.

He began waving the pistol again. "I'm not going to ask again. Get over here. You don't want me to have to come get you." He glanced around. "But it's just you and me, so maybe we don't have to do much talking." He took another step forward.

Her hands were behind her now, and she found a piece of wood that might be enough for one good swing. Since he confirmed it was just the two of them, screaming would be her best option. She kept one hand on the piece of wood as she stood, turning her body so he wouldn't see the makeshift club she kept behind her as she straightened.

When he was almost to her, his gun lowered to his side, probably anticipating a good roll in the grass, she took a huge breath. His gaze dropped to her heaving chest. God, she loved predictability. She threw the short branch—not at his head but at his hand.

Her aim was true. The pistol dropped when he shook his hand, and without another thought, she ran. Her cry for Beckworth was loud enough to be heard in London.

She heard the man catching up.

"Stop. I'll shoot. I don't care what Gemini says."

She was fairly certain he was lying, but she glanced around, searching for another path, not seeing an easy way out of this dilemma, when a hand came out of nowhere and snatched her around the waist. She could have collapsed with relief when Beckworth whispered in her ear, "Scream my name one more time. I kind of like the sound of it."

She heard the amusement in his voice and leaned into him, feeling secure in his arms and the fact he had his own pistol.

He released her and shoved her off into the trees.

Everything happened quickly, but she still saw it all before she fell into the bushes. The man had retrained his aim on Beckworth, but Beckworth had already fired.

The man went down, though not before there was a flash from his gun. By then, Stella was stuck in the middle of a bush and fought to extricate herself. She had to see what happened to Beckworth. He couldn't be dead. The man's aim should have been deflected. Still, they hadn't been that far apart.

She cursed, unable to find a strong enough branch to push herself upright. Then she was lifted up and swung around. She stumbled when Beckworth released her, but he grabbed her upper arm to steady her.

She brushed off her dress and the leaves from her hair, breathing a sigh of relief when her fingers caressed the hairpin. After giving him a once-over and not seeing any blood, she turned to the asshole on the ground. She walked over and nudged his shoulder.

"I'm having déjà vu." Stella took the man's pistol and cartridge belt.

"I would agree some things never change." His fingers brushed against her hair, and he produced a leaf. "You do seem to find the shrubbery when sensing danger."

"Funny." It was all she could do to keep a straight face, and wasn't sure it was a complete success. She didn't miss the twitch of his lips. How strange that all it took was killing one of the bad guys for their relationship to fall firmly back in place. Whatever type of relationship it was.

"I didn't have a choice." He stood over the man.

"No. You didn't."

"He would have revealed Eleanor and her home."

"You don't have to explain it. I understand." She stepped next to him and laid a hand on his arm. His muscles felt tight. "And I approve." She didn't know why she said it, but the muscles relaxed, and he released a long breath.

She turned in a circle, scanning the terrain. "What do we do with him?"

"We'll need to hide him for now," Eleanor said matter-of-factly as she strolled by and glanced down at the dead guy. She nodded. "This is one of the men we suspected was working for Gemini. I've seen him in town."

Sebastian said a small prayer as they considered their next steps.

"The food is ready for packaging. There's enough time to get you fed and on your way. You'll want to wait for nightfall." Eleanor found a coin pouch but nothing else in his pockets.

"At least an hour or two after that." Beckworth shook his head when Eleanor offered him the pouch. "I have more than enough to get us to London and beyond if need be. Keep that in case you need to run farther than Waverly."

She stared at him for a while, then stuffed the pouch in her pocket. "Let's get him under those bushes Stella crawled out of. Barrington can send a couple of men over to dig a hole and maybe finish the fencing while they're here."

"I'm sorry for the burden I've placed on you."

She slapped his arm, and Stella's heart warmed at the smile she gave Beckworth. "You didn't start this business with the stones, and we all knew what we were signing up for when we agreed to help. No one expected it to go on this long, but we deal with what life throws in our path."

Sebastian took Eleanor's arm, but before he led her away, he laid a hand on Beckworth's shoulder. "We face an evil enemy. One who would use the power of the stones to change the world's future. It must be stopped. The fact these deaths weigh heavier tells me you're a man on the road to redemption."

Stella turned away from the scene, not sorry that she heard the monk's words, but Beckworth deserved a moment of privacy. She glanced down at the dead man. He'd been of average height, average face, absolutely nothing remarkable. She assumed he either wasn't married or had left a wife long ago if he was working for Gemini. Maybe he sent money home when he had a chance. If there was a wife and children, they'd never see another coin. That saddened her. How many lives were impacted by one fateful decision? But that choice hadn't been theirs; it had been his. And today, he'd chosen wrong.

Beckworth picked the man up by his arms and dragged him toward the bushes.

A flash of something white caught her eye. It came from the man's hat that Eleanor had placed on his chest. She grabbed the hat and turned it over. A piece of paper was tucked inside. It must have been dislodged when the man fell.

"You dropped a swan."

Stella stopped at his words. "What?" She glanced around.

"Oh, I had a couple in my pocket." She began to pick it up when Beckworth stopped her.

He stared at the origami figure and then over at the man before he picked it up. "I've got an idea about that."

She dropped the hat on the man and opened the folded paper. It took a moment as she stared at the tiny handwriting. Then it all came together, and her stomach took a dive. "Beckworth. We've got a problem."

He peered over her shoulder. It was a map with four cities listed. Three of them were the locations of the chronicles. "I guess it answers that question. Gemini knows."

# 23

AJ tugged at her bodice and kept running a hand over the rich fabric of the gown. She glanced at the fine furnishings, feeling awkward and out of place.

Finn stayed her hand. "You'll rub a hole through the dress before we have a chance to speak with the man."

"I wasn't prepared to spend our time in France visiting someone so high up in Napoleon's court."

They'd barely left the count's manor when Finn suggested a stop in Rouen before heading north to find a ship to England. Lavigne, a long-time friend of Hensley's, made them wait a day before he was willing to speak with them. Finn assured her he anticipated the delay. It was critical the meeting appeared to be nothing more than a business transaction. The last time Finn had met with him, he was still captain of the *Daphne*, so he played the same role—a smuggler of fine Irish whiskey. A welcome contraband in any country at war.

This was one time AJ enjoyed playing the quiet wife, and she donned a pleasant smile when an older, stately man, his glasses slipping down his nose, approached them.

Finn stood and held out a hand. "Monsieur Lavigne, it's good of you to meet with me on such short notice. I wasn't expecting to be this far south, but when I knew I'd be passing by your lovely town, I felt remiss in not discussing a new business proposition with you."

"Ah, it's very difficult for the people of France with this war. I normally wouldn't entertain anything at this time, but Monsieur Hensley is a good friend, and I owe him a favor. The least I can do is listen. But no guarantees."

Finn nodded. "Let me introduce my mistress, AJ Moore, from America."

AJ froze, and the blush overtook her before she had a moment to recover.

"Ah, an American. And a rare beauty as well." He winked at Finn. "You never change." He took AJ's hand and kissed it. His eyes danced with merriment as he gazed into hers, forcing a deeper blush.

She was going to kill Finn the first moment she got.

"You still have excellent taste in women. Now come. My study will be more comfortable." Although he'd released her hand, his gaze continued to sweep over her. "Is she aware of your business dealings, or should I have someone show her to the solarium? Perhaps a drawing room?"

"She's trustworthy."

She held back her temper and remembered to play her role, though she was fairly certain Finn was laughing under all that polish and diplomacy.

Once they were safely ensconced in the study, Lavigne led them to a sitting area in front of the hearth. He poured Finn a whiskey without asking, and Finn took it without question. When the man turned to her and offered her wine, she nodded stiffly.

Lavigne chuckled. "Ruffled feathers down, my dear. I meant no offense earlier, but these days, it's difficult to know who in my staff is loyal. I have one or two I can always count on, but these continue to be dangerous times for both our countries." He sat in a chair across from them. "So, tell me, how is Hensley these days? We've kept our communiques brief this last year."

"He's doing well. He's in London currently, finishing out the season."

"I understand you've spent some time at a monastery in Côtes-du-Nord."

"Yes. We just came from there."

"With a stop in Bréval, I believe."

AJ almost choked on her wine, which was the best she'd tasted in this century. She glanced at Finn, using him like a deciphering rod. This man knew more than she'd expected, but Finn's posture remained calm.

He smiled. "You've been following the incidents at the monastery?"

Lavigne shrugged. "It's not an important location, and Napoleon has no interest in the area other than defenses against England. However, it's difficult to ignore tales of two different Englishmen creating grief and bloodshed. Fortunately, the stories of magical riches are seen as nothing more than lore based on rumors of ancient artifacts attracting men as mad as their king."

"Thank heavens for rumors." Finn lifted his glass in a mock toast.

"Agreed." The man settled back and crossed a leg. "So, what brings you to my door?"

"Have you heard the name Belato?"

Lavigne laughed. "How interesting. Another name that is linked to the monastery." He turned his gaze to the dying embers in the hearth. "I should have known we hadn't heard the last of that family."

AJ perked up. After all this time watching Finn and Hensley at work, and she still didn't understand the breadth of their network.

"Were they that well connected?" Finn asked.

"The Belato family had once been a name of recognition and respect in Île-de-France. Their father was a prominent merchant with many connections to the royal court and was quite wealthy. He died—some say killed, though it was never confirmed—several years before the Revolution. From my understanding, he had concerns about his sons' ability to manage the estate, though he'd been training the oldest since birth. But the sons were lazy. Sometimes those born in privilege never grasp the diligence required to maintain a legacy. And so it was with the Belato brothers. Their skill came in gambling and whores. Sorry." He bent a head to AJ.

It took a moment to understand he was apologizing for the impropriety of discussing whores. She ignored Finn's grin and waved for Lavigne to continue.

"There were three brothers. It was the youngest one, the monk, that gave the oldest the idea of the power and riches hidden within the depths of the monastery. At that time, with their father several years dead and none of them having an ounce of brain between them, they'd run through most of their inheritance. Most of the land around the estate had been sold off to pay gambling debts." He shook his head, and a slight smile appeared with a bit of a chuckle. "They had no problems coming up with grand ideas, but none could put a strategy together. The monk was the only one who showed enough gumption to develop a plan."

Lavigne stood and poured more whiskey and refilled AJ's wine. "But Robespierre—" he looked at AJ, "—he was the leader behind the Terror." When she nodded, he continued. "He considered the brothers more like enforcers than advisors. The tales from the monastery were interesting enough, and since the churches were being raided throughout the country, it did no harm to send the brothers north.

"When they came back empty-handed, they lost favor. They still had their roles to play, but they eventually found their fate before the end of the Terror. All except one—the monk."

"Is he still at the estate?" Finn rubbed the arm of the sofa, a sign he was putting events together as he listened.

"No. He was forced to sell it for far less than it was worth due to its poor condition. Although he'd left the brotherhood, he never married. He was the sole provider for his niece and nephew, the only children of the oldest boy. The middle son had a wife, but she died in childbirth along with the babe."

Bells rang in AJ's head. A niece and nephew.

"I suppose it was really just the nephew he raised." Lavigne picked up a marble ball from a side table and took his seat. He rolled the ball around in his hand. "The niece was sent to England when she was young, perhaps nine or ten. This was just prior to the Revolution, when the family money was rapidly depleting. There were rumors they sold her, but who can say? I have no doubt there was some coin exchanged. One can only hope she found a better life."

"What happened to Belato and his nephew?"

"Last I heard, they were renting space above an old distillery in La Bouille, just south of here. If I'd known you were coming, I would have seen to gathering fresh intelligence on the matter."

"Why do you know so much about a monk and his family?" Finn retained his casual posture, leaning back with his whiskey glass settled on the armrest.

Lavigne's eyes sparkled. "I could ask your interest in someone who has fallen so far. But my guess is that his family is once again up to no good. I hadn't thought of the man in years, but his name came up when the Duke of Dunsmore saw his demise. There were rumors he might have had a hand in it. Though I suspect there were others closer to the event."

AJ tensed and glanced around the study rather than meet his curious gaze.

He waved a hand. "I wouldn't worry. Word from the monastery said all was safe, and Napoleon had too many concerns to worry about the loss of an English noble who'd been stripped of all political power and connections."

Finn nodded with his signature grin, and AJ breathed a sigh of relief. The last thing they needed was to be detained in France.

Lavigne leaned over, his expression serious. "I'll speak true. Belato is a stain on Napoleon's new government, but his movements were difficult to track when we had eyes on him. You could stop by La Bouille on your way north, but I doubt you'll find him there. If you have a few days, I can put someone on the streets."

Finn shook his head. "It's not necessary. As you say, with the war, you have other pressing matters. And I don't think he's in France at this time."

Lavigne's brows shot up, and he appeared intrigued. "Really?" He glanced at the ceiling as he rolled the marble ball around. "He's gone to England."

"That's our first thought."

The older man smiled. "Well, no doubt, it won't take him long to run afoul of the law. Perhaps France has seen the last of him."

"Do you know the names of his niece and nephew?"

This required a longer pause before Lavigne answered. "If memory serves, it was Andre and Antoinette."

"Have you heard the name Gemini?"

"Not that I recall. Who is this person?"

"We don't know her real name. She's also been called Lady Penelope Prescott, but we know she borrowed the name from the real Lady Prescott."

"How old is this woman?"

Finn looked at AJ, and she shrugged. She had no idea.

"I don't remember anyone giving a description of her, just that they'd met her and she was a bit forward." Finn had heard about her dalliance with Fitz. "From the way those that have seen her speak, I imagine she's beautiful."

Lavigne leaned back, the marble ball moving faster. "I'll send someone to La Bouille. If I discover anything of import, I'll contact Hensley. If he's still in London, I should be able to get something to him quickly enough. If you discover anything of interest, perhaps Hensley could pass it my way."

Finn stood, and Lavigne led them to the door where the butler waited outside. "You can be assured he'll know how helpful you've been."

The butler saw them out, and Finn said nothing as he helped AJ into a rented carriage. They held hands, each lost in their own thoughts until they reached a livery on the outskirts of town. They walked to the inn down the street where they'd been staying and met up with Lando. After Finn and AJ changed into their traveling clothes, they ordered a meal while bringing Lando up to speed.

"You think it's her. Gemini is Antoinette." AJ gulped her ale and would probably be sorry later because she wasn't going to leave without a second one. "I'm not sure if that's good or bad or what difference it makes."

Finn tore into the bread that came with the lamb and parsnips. "It would tell us we have one foe rather than two, which is a good thing."

"On the other hand..." Lando swallowed a bite and washed it down with ale. "They have more men than we do, and we have no idea what game they're playing. I understand why they have people in England. They still need the chronicles. But they had men in France, and they knew we were at the monastery. They never attempted contact."

Finn shook his head. "I can't see their plan, either. Maybe Hensley can put it together. We have to assume it was Belato and Andre who took Sebastian and Stella."

"No one mentioned Gemini having a French accent. It would make sense if she'd been raised in England." AJ glanced around the room, suddenly and irrationally wondering if Belato had men following them.

"That makes sense," Finn replied. "But Lavigne's information leaves a larger question."

"If Belato is destitute, where is his money coming from?" Lando's question hit the mark.

No one had an answer for that.

"Finish up." Finn pushed his plate away and drained his mug. "I want to make Le Havre by sunrise if possible. That means riding through the night." He squeezed AJ's arm. "Are you okay with that?"

"Oh, yeah, completely looking forward to it. Can't tell you how much fun this has been with all the horseback riding." The two mugs of ale did nothing to lighten her mood, but it was enough to loosen her lips. The thought of hours in the saddle made her consider begging for a wagon, but it would only slow them down.

"I'll make it up to you on the ship to England."

"Let's see if you can buy better accommodations than Beckworth found for Stella."

"I think I have more experience gaining a berth on a ship than Beckworth."

"From your lips to God's ears. Especially if you hope to get lucky in the near future." She walked out the door, grinning at the look on Finn's face and the blush on Lando's cheeks. If it gave him the incentive to procure a warm cabin rather than a tarp and a couple of crates on deck, the comment would be worth every penny.

# 24

Beckworth leaned back in the chair with his boots resting on the porch railing. He'd just ridden back from Waverly while Stella and Eleanor prepared supplies for travel. All he could now was wait.

After they'd returned to the house, with Gemini's man tucked under a bush, the four of them stared at the piece of paper Stella had found. It wasn't a complete surprise that Gemini had discovered the locations of the books, or at least the general vicinity, but it was disappointing and would make their next moves more dangerous.

The map was a rough image of England and northern France. There were four cities marked with an X. Three of the cities, Worcester and Ipswich in England and Bréval in France, weren't a surprise. The fourth marked city was London.

"They have the general locations, but there are no names." Sebastian touched three of the marks but tapped the fourth.

"What does that mean?" Beckworth ran a hand through his hair before tugging his sleeves.

"In my journals, I identified the cities where the chronicles were located, but I never wrote who received them. The only place where I divulged those names was in the journal I left for Maire. That was the only written document of them."

"What if you died before the sections were reclaimed?" Stella asked.

The monk shrugged. "Then they would be lost in time, though it wasn't my intention. I planned on recalling them once it was safe. The entire reason for separating *The Book of Stones* into chronicles was to preserve it in some form rather than have it discovered by the wrong people."

"Why is London marked?" Eleanor asked.

Sebastian scratched his head. "I don't know."

No one could answer the question, so Beckworth had left for Waverly. Now, as he scanned the yard and the landscape beyond for signs of Gemini's men, his gut gnawed at him while he pondered the question of why London had been marked.

Was it possible Gemini uncovered the location of the original Heart Stone? There were only two people who knew where it was located, and he was one of them. Chances were, the mark was nothing more than signifying their final meeting place, the same as their own team had planned. Gemini would have eyes on Hensley, and that made more sense. She'd proven to be a decent strategist. He should have thought to play chess with her to test those skills, but it appeared learning as they went would be the best they would get.

His musings vanished when he heard the sounds of someone approaching. He watched Barrington drive up the overgrown path with two men and waited until they jumped down from the wagon before standing to lead them down the trail where they'd left the dead man. He'd found the man's horse a quarter mile away and retied it near the bush where Eleanor had wrapped a torn piece of rag as if he'd lost his wits and wouldn't be able to find it on his own. They draped the dead man over the saddle, tied him so he wouldn't fall off, then walked the horse back to the wagon.

Beckworth pulled out the origami swan he'd picked up after Stella had dropped it and tucked it in the pocket of the man's shirt. "Make sure it appears the horse is coming from town."

"We'll take care of it." Barrington glanced at him, and his brow rose. "What did you put in his pocket?"

"A test." He took another swan out of his pocket and showed it to his butler. "Stella makes them. It's called origami."

"I'm not sure I understand your point."

He chuckled. "I'm not sure I do, either. If you gave Stella a stack of paper, she'd have dozens of these things spread around the room. She dropped one in the cage inside the cargo hold. Maybe no one will say anything, but maybe someone noticed and brought it to Belato's attention."

"And if Gemini's men discover it..." Barrington didn't finish his statement, just nodded. "It might work. But it will take a few more dead men before they catch on it's the same person killing them. Possibly someone new to the game."

"We're fools if we think there won't be more coming for us. Perhaps a distraction will keep them guessing." He glanced back at Eleanor, who stepped out of the house carrying a burlap bag filled with enough food to feed eight burly men rather than the three of them. "See that you replenish her stores and blankets."

"Of course." When Beckworth continued to watch her, Barrington laid a hand on his friend's shoulder. "We'll watch over her. She'll be safe."

He nodded. "It's best if you leave before us. We'll skirt town from the west, and I'll send word once we arrive in London."

Barrington nodded, then turned an eye to Stella, who approached from the other wagon.

"Were you going to leave without saying goodbye?" She stopped and stared up at him, seemingly not bothered by his grave expression. "That's okay. It takes time for some people to warm up to me." Her gaze was lit with humor. "I'm guessing that's true for you, too."

Beckworth snorted, and Barrington tried to remain indignant but lowered his head to prevent her from seeing his lips twitch.

She stepped back, took Beckworth's arm, and winked at him. "Don't worry. I'll keep him safe."

Beckworth stared down at her, not sure what to make of that promise. When he noticed Barrington give him an appraising look, he was tempted to pull his arm away from her lest his crafty butler read too much into her words. When he felt her firm hold, he changed his mind. He was still figuring her out, and considering the panic attack she'd had the previous evening, it was possible this brave facade was compensating for the map she'd discovered.

Barrington climbed up to the bench and picked up the reins. One of the men jumped up next to him while the other stayed in the back to keep an eye on the horse to make sure the dead man didn't slide off. He gave a short wave as he clucked, and they moved out.

Once they were gone from sight, Stella turned to him. "Will Gemini's men blame the town, maybe take some kind of revenge?"

He shook his head. "They don't have enough men to intimidate the town, and after living with Dugan and his men, they're not easy to scare anymore." He glanced toward the wagon. "Everything packed?"

"Yes. The rain could give us trouble if we can't find shelter."

"We'll stay on the main road as long as we can. It won't be as busy as the one from Southampton to London, but it will get more crowded the closer we get to the city. While I'd prefer to avoid the inns, if the rain becomes a problem, we'll have options."

They reached the wagon, where Sebastian snuggled on a bed of several blankets with a couple more covering him. With the decision to leave after dark under the light of a quarter moon, it was best for Beckworth to drive the wagon with his horse tied to the back. If they ran into trouble, Beckworth knew the less traveled roads wide enough for a wagon.

"This all seems more dangerous with Gemini knowing the locations of the books." Stella, back in pants and shirt, reached into the pocket that held the map she'd found on the dead guy. She'd been touching it off and on, and he didn't think she was aware of doing it. Maybe she was tempted to make a swan out of it.

"Since London is our prearranged meeting place, we'll need to be careful on our arrival. I gave Barrington the new information to send to our friends, although I don't know if they'll receive it."

"Does this change our plans?" While she questioned their intentions to retrieve one of the chronicles, she didn't seem to have any objections. If he had to guess, based on her fingers tapping on the back of the wagon and the way she scanned the yard, she was eager to get moving.

"We can't stay here." Beckworth glanced at Eleanor. It was imperative she stayed safe. He'd ask her to go to Waverly again, just until this was over, but he could tell by the stubborn tilt to her chin she expected him to ask. He wouldn't. She'd go if she felt threatened. It was all he could ask. "It may appear they're not following us, but if one of Gemini's men came here, more may follow. We leave now."

The first hour of travel was quiet as Beckworth circled around Corsham to connect to the main road to London. Stella understood the need for silence until they were clear of Gemini's men, but he seemed to be internalizing something, and as much as she wanted to ask, she focused on watching how he handled the reins.

Once they were well clear of town, she recounted humorous childhood stories of her family's road trips that were meant to keep him engaged while Sebastian slept in the back. Someday, this journey would top them all, and as crazy as it might seem now, it was one she would cherish.

"I have my own, what did you call it? Oh, yes, a road trip story." Beckworth gave her a side glance.

In the moonlight, she barely noticed his grin, putting her on alert that his story might be more of a tall tale.

"I wouldn't think family vacations in a wagon would be common in this time period."

He laughed. "No. It's nothing like what you would expect. But for a young man who grew up with nothing and had nothing tying him down, a spirit for adventure called."

"Now that's something that transcends time. Boys will be boys regardless of the century."

He nudged her shoulder. "Isn't it the same for the women in your century? You had your own journey when you left home and moved west."

"Yes. But this is your story."

"Ah, yes. Well, this was a couple of years after my mother passed. I had worked my way up in the gangs, working with two or three at a time. I had become more of a planner, though I wasn't afraid to jump into a job where needed. After a while, everything seemed too easy, too expected."

"You got bored."

"You do know how to get to the point."

"Sorry, go on."

"I can't wait for you to see the Thames. It will be filled with sailing ships from all over the world. Though not as much as usual with the war, though it will still be busy. The shanty where I grew up was by the river. I spent most of my youth guessing where the ships came and went, but I couldn't leave my mother, then once she was gone, I was too busy building coin.

"However, the more time I spent at the docks, the more an unexplored world called to me. And like every other fool I met, I bartered a few years of my life away for exploits on the high seas. I learned many things during that time, like how to run a ship and how to build alliances. But it wasn't too long before I realized it wasn't the life for me. And it was another four years of hard work and too many pubs to count before my feet landed in London again."

"I had no idea you were a sailor."

"Don't make a big deal of it. I was decent enough with more aspiration of fleecing the crew at a game of dice than working my way up to second mate."

The road split ahead, and he stayed to the left without a second glance. He must have traveled this road dozens if not hundreds of times as the Viscount of Waverly, spending time in London during the season or for various business ventures. He could probably put the horses on cruise control and take a well-deserved nap.

"Did you help on the *Daphne*?"

"Good lord, no. My first trip on her was in chains."

"If I remember, it was well deserved." She rubbed her head though it had been a year in her time since he'd pushed her against the cabinets at the inn while trying to steal the Heart Stone.

He winced when she'd reached for her head and kept his

eyes on the road. "The next time was as a guest, but I spent most of the time nursing Jamie after he suffered a gunshot wound. Besides, I'm better off staying out of the way. My skills at riggings are a bit rusty."

She snorted, then changed the subject now that he seemed in a good mood and appeared exhausted. "You need to teach me how to drive the wagon."

"Well, that only took four hours to ask. I thought you'd wait till morning."

"So, that's a yes?"

"There's no reason not to teach you. It's not the same as riding a horse, and it might come in handy before this is all over."

"Then teach me the basics in the morning before Sebastian takes over. After our rest, you can drive while I watch, but then I get my turn at the reins."

"You never cease to amaze me with your careful planning. You're almost as painstaking as me. We're quite the pair, Ms. Caldway."

His turn of phrase made her pause. They were quite a pair. She'd never met anyone that understood her so well other than AJ. Of course, it would have to be someone from a different time period. She let out a long sigh and leaned her head against his shoulder. "We are a force to reckon with. That's what we are."

She closed her eyes and swayed with the motion of the wagon. Soon his body relaxed as they traveled in silence. This was some road trip.

## 25

When morning dawned, Beckworth continued their trek for another two hours before pulling off a side road that meandered by a creek. Stella made coffee while Sebastian went for a stroll. He took the time to rearrange the blankets in the wagon into two beds.

They ate breakfast under the wide canopy of an oak tree, its leaves mere buds. They spoke of nothing important unless someone considered harvesting honey, a tall tale about a not-so-legendary sea battle, or the best remedy for a hangover as life-changing topics.

Once Sebastian steered them back to the main road, he slept for a couple of hours. Being midday, the road was busy with travelers, and concern for Gemini's men being close faded. But he wasn't willing to risk their safety, so he'd left two loaded muskets resting comfortably near Sebastian's feet and three more laid next to him in the bed of the wagon, primed and ready.

He could have used more sleep, but he woke a bit unsettled. They needed a longer rest in decent beds. For now, he was content watching Stella sleep. He was tempted to brush the strands of auburn from her delicate face. He'd offered several times through the evening to stop and let her climb in back to get rest, but she'd refused.

"I'm not going to let you drive all night long without someone to keep you company. It's too dark out here. We could be ambushed, and you need someone who can shoot. You can't drive the wagon and handle a firearm at the same time. Another reason to teach me how to drive it."

He'd let her talk until she tired herself out, then she would lean against him and close her eyes. The act seemed more intimate than when they'd been on horseback. On the horse, she'd had no choice but to rest against him, but on the wagon bench, it had been a conscious decision. At first, it had surprised him, then he found he enjoyed her company. She'd wake and start a new conversation before she wore herself out, then he'd spend the next thirty minutes guessing what her next topic might be.

Now, looking at her sleeping peacefully as if she didn't have a care in the world, he came to realize she'd touched his heart in a way no other woman had. And it scared him. His gaze landed on the hairpin. He'd been right. It fit her perfectly. His thoughts roamed to an image of her in layers of frilly lingerie from the first boardinghouse in Bournemouth.

He shook himself and sprang up, scanning their location, almost wishing there was something that required his immediate action. There wasn't, but since he couldn't sleep, he might as well keep Sebastian company. He gave one last look at the sleeping princess and climbed onto the bench.

"Good morning." Sebastian was chipper as he handled the reins with a delicate touch.

"Anything suspicious?" He checked the muskets at their feet. Satisfied both were still well-primed, he returned them to their spot.

"A group of six men, but they followed a carriage."

"Probably guards."

"That was what I assumed, or I would have woken you."

He glanced at Sebastian. Eleanor had washed his robe, but he still stood out as a monk to anyone who paid attention. He'd come to the conclusion that if Gemini's men were interested in catching them, they would have by now. It might be a different story once they reached London. If Sebastian refused to wear something less distinguishable, they could at least find a proper hat to hide his balding head.

"Where do you think the others are?" Sebastian never let his eyes stray from the road, which gave Beckworth some idea of how worried he probably was over Maire without actually saying it.

"It's hard to say. They wouldn't leave without knowing all the names of who has the chronicles, and I have no doubt of Maire's ability to decipher your journal. But that's a great deal of land to cover. Murphy wouldn't want to spend weeks tracking them all down."

"You think they'll separate."

"They won't have much choice. You did a good job of spreading them out. Was that done on purpose?"

Sebastian chuckled. "It wouldn't make sense to send them away to have them all in the same general vicinity."

"I didn't realize you knew so many outside of the monastery, let alone in England."

"I joined the brotherhood when I was a young man. My family was poor, but they made ends meet with a farm and a handful of sheep. I stayed with them long after I should have started my own family, but they knew my heart wasn't in it. My mother encouraged me to join the brotherhood. There was a monastery not far from Paris. After a few years, the Prior asked me to be an emissary with other sects. Of course, it never hurt to have friends in the aristocracy who believed in our mission."

"And as an emissary, you traveled to England."

He nodded. "And to Spain." A cart in front of them was loaded down with crates and barrels, and Sebastian clucked the horses to go around. "It was several years before I visited London for the first time. It was during their season, and I was quite intimidated, but the Prior in London was a very political man. I followed him to social events where he introduced me to those he believed would take an interest in France."

Everything was beginning to come full circle. "Is this when you met Hensley and the earl?"

"I met Hensley. Or I should say, he sought me out."

"Interesting."

"He had his toe in almost everything, though that shouldn't surprise you. He was in Parliament at the time."

"I had no idea he was in Parliament. That would explain much."

"Yes. But a faction within Parliament felt he had too many connections with the King's court in addition to a larger network he was building with the aristocrats and merchants. They became suspicious of his motives and pushed him out."

"That must have been hard on him."

"You would think so, but not Hensley. I believe he was building the foundation of his spy network, most likely with support from the Crown."

"I'm only now understanding his worth to England."

"From my understanding, several at Parliament are still at odds with him, but many have seen the importance of his network in the protection of England."

"And why would a man like Hensley, with his secret organization, seek out a monk?"

"Hensley seeks out like-minded sources of information. At the time, I was still living in Paris and, as an emissary, had doors open to me that Hensley would never be able to enter. It was a couple of years later, when I returned to London, that I ran across him again, and he introduced me to the earl. While my friendship with Hensley began as a trusted source for his organization, my friendship with the earl was of a more spiritual nature."

They rode in silence for some time as Beckworth considered the connections and the timing. Stella stirred in the wagon, but when he turned, expecting to see her eyes open, she'd simply turned onto her side, pulling the covers tighter.

Everything the monk shared made sense. He'd been building relationships for years as an emissary for the brotherhood. He understood the monk's reasons for traveling to London, but the chronicles were scattered in a much broader range.

"Why didn't you send chronicles to the earl and Hensley?"

"It would have made sense, and they would have had more security to protect them, but they would also have been obvious choices. I believed the chronicles would be safer in the hands of pious friends whose spiritual beliefs matched my own.

"It wasn't until the duke found a stone and my section of *The Book* that I had to take action. But who would believe such a fantastical tale? When I discovered the duke had sent a stone with the incantation to England..." He glanced at Beckworth, who still remembered the day the letter and stone arrived. The monk patted his knee. "I didn't believe anyone would attempt such a mission, but when the duke held a grand party in celebration of a man disappearing into a strange fog, I had to find a way to save the Heart Stone."

"And because of the earl's spiritual nature, you felt he was the best bet to believe such a tale."

Sebastian nodded. "Who could have guessed what those two events would ignite?"

"Who indeed?"

"Well, that certainly explains everything." Stella's head

popped up, causing both men to jump. Then she punched Beckworth in the arm. "If only the earl and Sebastian knew you'd given the stone to someone who didn't like you, maybe the earl would have told Ethan to seek Finn out for a partnership during their time travel."

He rubbed his arm. She had a decent punch, even without much force behind it. "I thought you were sleeping."

"Dozing. I wasn't quite ready to leave the warmth of the blankets, but I was awake enough to listen. I really needed a recap of events. I don't think AJ knows that much. But more importantly, is it too soon to stop for a break and some coffee?"

Sebastian glanced at her with the same fondness he showed for Maire and AJ. "I prefer tea, but anything to warm my bones would be welcome."

The day was cooler than the day before, and gray clouds covered the sky, but the rain had yet to make an appearance.

"I'll find a spot, and we can have a rest. But we need to finish the day with many more miles before finding an inn for the evening."

"And you'll teach me to drive the wagon?"

He sighed. "Yes, as I promised." He shook his head and smiled when she clapped her hands and began arranging the blankets back in order.

When he leaned over the back of the bench to help her move a small crate, she leaned close and whispered in his ear, "You're a good man, Beckworth. Don't believe anything else."

He turned back to watch the road. His ear tingled with warmth where he could have sworn she kissed the tip, but it was most likely nothing more than the bump of her lips from the swaying of the wagon. Either way, a heat rushed through him he hadn't expected, and he gazed off to his right so Sebastian wouldn't see the grin he couldn't seem to hide.

## 26

Stella steered the wagon to the top of the hill, pulled the team to the side of the road, and stopped. She'd never seen anything like it.

London sprawled before her like some old film reel from the History Channel. Only this was in full color. A smoky brown haze blanketed the city, the remnants of thousands of homes and businesses with wood-burning hearths. Horses, wagons, and carriages dotted the landscape through block after block of houses. Off in the distance, sunshine glinted off short ribbons of water that must be the Thames playing hide-and-seek behind buildings and parks. She might have caught a glimpse of sails, but it was most likely her imagination stimulated by the soft scent of the river that blew through the air, mingling with the more acrid smell of wood stoves, horse manure, and human waste.

The stench would be ten times worse when they entered the city, but it didn't dissuade her excitement. She wasn't close enough to hear the sounds of the city, just the clatter of horses and squeaks from carriages as they passed by. But if she closed her eyes, hooves clacked along a cobblestone street, mingling with the call of hawkers selling their wares and urging shoppers to stop. The scent of lilacs sifted through the flower stands at Whitechapel, where Beckworth found solace as a youngster on these streets.

She opened her eyes, still amazed. London. It was 1805. She could pinch herself, and it still wouldn't seem real.

Sebastian, who perched next to her on the bench, was silent as his head turned back and forth. She wasn't sure if he waited for her to soak it in or if he was caught by the awe-inspiring view. He'd mentioned he'd been to London a handful of times and grew up near Paris, so he was used to large cities, but was it just as amazing each time he saw it?

"Beautiful, isn't she?" Beckworth leaned close from the back of the wagon so she could hear him over a group of passing soldiers.

When she turned to him, his eyes were lit with excitement. Whether it happened each time he returned, or it was simply his eagerness to hear first impressions, she wasn't sure. He laughed when he noticed her reaction.

"I must be grinning ear to ear, and my face feels numb." She touched her cheeks, which were cool from the chilled air. Her fingertips brushed her lips, which confirmed the huge smile. "This was even more than I expected. I'm not sure beautiful is the right word. Maybe awestruck?"

Sebastian leaned over. "It struck me the same way all those years ago. It still gives me chills to see it from this perspective. It looks quite different from a ship on the Thames."

"I hadn't thought of that." She wished she could see it from that vantage point. Maybe not from a ship, but the dock. A nice, solid, not-moving dock. Although, she had to give herself some credit. Two trips across the Channel, and she'd survived. And she'd only gotten truly sick on the first trip over. Though, to be fair, that journey came with a tumultuous ride through a storm. No extra charge, thank you very much.

She was still staring at the scene when the wagon swayed as Sebastian got down, and after helping the monk into the back of the wagon, Beckworth joined her on the bench. It wasn't until he took hold of the reins and tried to pull them from her hands that she jolted into awareness, her grip tightening.

"You can't drive through the city."

"Why not?"

"Because you haven't had enough experience to traverse the traffic and tight streets."

She retained her grip as she stared at the city and remembered a variety of movies set during these times. The streets were narrow, and considering the traffic on the road, the inner city would be chaotic. Then her thoughts turned to Beckworth. If this had been the first few days after their escape, he would have ripped the reins out of her hands. But he hadn't. He held them firmly without tugging, allowing her to work it out on her own, trusting she'd make the smart decision. His faith in her made it difficult to breathe, and she blinked a couple of times. She waited a moment longer before slowly releasing them.

He waited until she dropped her hands before he scooted closer and yelled over his shoulder, "We'll go to a friend I know where no one would think to look for us. I think it best to scout Hensley's house before driving up to it."

"I trust your instincts." Sebastian had settled back against the side of the wagon, his head already turning right then left as if warming up for the sights to come.

Beckworth moved the wagon back onto the road and followed the train of carts and carriages into the city. "You can watch how I navigate through the city, when I slow the horses, and when I start the turns."

She scooted closer until their legs touched. Had he felt the slight tingle? "Can you talk me through the first couple, then I can watch what your hands are doing?"

He gave her a wink. "Of course, luv. And prepare yourself. You'll see the rougher side of the city first, but it won't be for long." And with that, he flicked the reins and moved the wagon faster.

At first, she glimpsed the sights between Beckworth's nudges for her to pay attention to a turn. The houses appeared old and weather-beaten, some barely standing, but they improved as they moved deeper into the city, where they passed business districts and well-tended homes. When he pulled up to a three-story building that looked like a house, he jumped down and tied the horses to a post. She followed him up the stairs with Sebastian in tow.

The door opened before they reached it, and a man rushed out, his head bent low. She stopped and watched the man continue his quick pace until he ducked inside a carriage that took off as soon as the coach door shut behind him.

A woman stuck her head out the door, her gaze pinned on the retreating carriage. Then she turned and set her eyes on Beckworth. Stella bristled at the woman's casual and suggestive perusal of him.

"Well now, darling, if it isn't the man himself. How are you, Beckworth? Libby said you'd gone missing again."

"Now I'm back and in need of a room." He sported one of his amazing smiles, and Stella gave the woman a closer look. With her tiny waist and thick sable hair falling below her shoulders, she appeared young. But on closer inspection, thin wrinkles around her eyes hid beneath well-placed makeup put her a little older than herself.

The woman turned her gaze to Stella. If she noticed Sebastian, who had turned to watch the people on the street, she didn't show it. "How long do you need the room?"

226

"No more than a couple of hours, but I'll pay for the whole night, just in case."

The woman's brow shot up, and Stella snorted.

Beckworth's smile slipped. "Do you have something? Time is of the essence, luv."

"Let me check." She shut the door, and Stella pounced.

"A boardinghouse?" Her whisper could probably be heard the next block over, but she didn't care. "You'll go to hell, you know." She leaned in, aware he could hear her just fine. "We have a monk with us."

"I'm not completely daft. This is a real boardinghouse, and it's close to Hensley's. With any luck, he'll be home and can take us in. Otherwise, I'll contact another house where we can stay."

The door opened before Stella could respond, and the woman waved them in. "Is that your wagon?"

"Yes, but I'll move it once I get my friends settled."

The woman looked beyond Beckworth and frowned at Sebastian, who was smiling at the woman with his stoic expression firmly in place. She glanced at Stella and then at Beckworth. "I'm not even going to ask."

"It's best you don't. This one—" he nodded toward Stella, "—gets mad as a hatter when plans don't go her way." He held out an arm to have her go first, and she strode in, a sudden wave of fatigue hitting her.

When the woman started up the steps with Sebastian following, Stella croaked out, "Coffee?"

The woman glanced over her shoulder. "I'll send up food along with the coffee." She smiled at Sebastian. "Is coffee all right, or would you prefer ale?"

"You wouldn't have any cider, would you?"

The woman chuckled. "Anything you want, my friend. I'll send a pitcher of both."

Stella walked into the corner room where a fire had been lit.

There was a bed that could fit two, a sofa, a table with four chairs, and a plain armoire. She had to admit, this was the best room she'd been in yet. No frilly bedding or lamp, only a flower-print bedcover and two oil lamps.

She dropped onto the sofa in front of the fire and closed her eyes. When she opened them, she found herself laid out with a blanket covering her, still in front of the hearth. She rubbed her eyes and threw off the blanket as she sat up.

Sebastian was bent over the table, the scratch of the quill the only sound except for the occasional crackle from the fire. Plates, mugs, and pitchers were spread around the table. Beckworth was nowhere to be seen.

She rubbed her head and patted down her hair, ensuring the hairpin hadn't fallen out before shuffling to the table. "How long was I out?"

Sebastian continued scribbling until he had to dip the quill into the ink. "Perhaps an hour." He glanced at the fire. "Maybe a bit more."

She peered into the two pitchers—ale and cider. "I missed the coffee."

"Beckworth put the pot by the fire to keep it warm."

Of course, he did. She peeked into the pot, and the scent alone was enough to get her synapses sparking. She took the pot to the table and poured a cup. "Do you want some?"

"No, thank you. The cider is enough."

He continued to write while she scrounged for leftovers, pleased to find the roasted meat still warm and the bread fresh.

"Where's Beckworth?"

"He took the wagon to the livery."

By the time he walked through the door, Stella had three swans sitting near Sebastian's inkpot. He held two wrapped packages tied with twine, but she barely noted them. She wiped her chin in case she'd drooled.

He'd changed clothing.

He wore fresh breeches of a soft dove color with a matching jacket. The waistcoat was a deep purple and royal blue paisley, and the cravat was in the same matching royal blue that brought out the deep hues of his cornflower-blue eyes. His hair was pulled back in a queue, bringing out the fine edges of his face. He grinned at her, and when it seemed she'd lost her ability to speak, his brow lifted.

"Disappointed?"

It took a moment for the question to register, and she smiled, thinking about their talk onboard the ship to France and AJ's comment about the first time she'd met Beckworth. "I was hoping for the peacock."

He gave her a quizzical look and then grinned. "Sorry, luv. They were all out of turquoise."

## 27

Ethan and Thomas played chess in the solarium while keeping an eye on the earl and Maire as they strolled through the garden. A weak afternoon sun was bright enough to bring out the colors of early spring flowers, and Maire laughed at something the earl said when he pointed to one of the beds.

"It's good to see the earl up and about. He has the strength to wander about but never seems to have the desire." Thomas moved a knight and displaced one of Ethan's pawns.

"It seems Maire has given him a purpose." Ethan slid a rook and took one of Thomas's pawns. His mind wasn't on the game, and Thomas gave him a shake of his head as he moved a bishop to take the rook.

"Everything is going as planned. Enjoy the time while we wait for word."

After dinner the previous night, they had drinks and cigars in the library, Maire keeping an eye on them from the corner of the room where she reviewed her notes. Their discussions of what Gemini could be up to changed to stories of their travels. Fitz chimed in with tales from his sailing days that left the earl doubled over in tears of laughter. At one point, he coughed so hard that Maire wanted to take him back to the solarium, but he waved her off, drank a sip of whiskey, then shared some of his own pursuits as a young man in the King's army.

Early that morning, Fitz and two men from Thomas's surveillance team left for Bransford to search for Gemini's men and to confirm Father Dolcet was in town. They would be gone for a couple of days, depending on what they found.

Until then, Ethan would attempt to focus on the earl and enjoy his time home. Thomas was planning a hunt for the next day, assuming the weather held. But for today, it was walks in the garden, games of whist, and rounds of chess. During one particular game of whist where Lydia, Brun's housekeeper who'd become his nurse and confidante, joined them to make the required four players, the earl asked about Ethan and Maire's plans.

"Will you return to the future or settle down in this time?" Lord Brun asked.

Ethan wasn't sure if Maire was waiting for him to speak or if she was at a loss for words as he was. He glanced down at her, and when she met his gaze, some understanding seemed to pass between them.

She stared at her hands, her brows furrowed, and he couldn't begin to guess what she would say. He never spoke of their future, afraid of whether or not her dreams included him, but now he was curious to hear her thoughts.

"This business with the stones doesn't make it easy to plan for a life other than this path we find ourselves on. Until the stones and *The Book of Stones* can be put to rest in a secure place, my freedom and possibly my life will be at risk. I wouldn't know how to make a decision because, for now, there's no choice at all. At least not one where I won't be looking over my shoulder." She took Ethan's hand. "Until then, it's not right to expect more than what I have. And I'm grateful for that."

Ethan was speechless, never realizing her thoughts had been his own, neither willing to put it to words until the crafty earl put them on the spot.

Brun stared at her for a long moment before his steely gaze landed on Ethan. Then a slow smile appeared. "I'm not sure whether to say how happy I am for the two of you, or give Ethan my regrets for the woman he's chosen. What I do know is that whatever the future holds, you'll never be bored."

Maire lifted a brow, but Ethan couldn't stop his grin. Brun had assumed a commitment was in the making when they'd lived with him a year ago. Then Maire had disappeared, kidnapped again because of the stones. Though their commitment was dependent upon things beyond their control, the earl had officially given his blessing—in so many words. The moment gave Ethan tremendous joy, but at the same time, his heart clenched knowing the earl wanted it said before he died.

Thomas stood to break the awkward silence. "I think a bottle of wine to toast to a successful mission is in order." He pulled a cord, and a footman appeared. "We need a bottle from the earl's cellar, and we'll take our afternoon tea in here."

Maire clutched his hand, and he didn't have to ask to know what she was thinking. Neither of them wanted to return to the future, knowing this could be the last time they'd have with the earl. He'd treated Ethan like a son, and it broke his heart he wouldn't be here for him at the end. If they could put the stones to rest once and for all, perhaps the choice would be his. But the last few years had proven that the stones were a curse, threatening to follow them the rest of their days.

The day after the hunt, Thomas returned to his routine, which included running battle drills for whatever part they would play in taking down Gemini and Belato. Ethan joined them for the morning sparring session while Maire coddled the earl, accepting his help as they reviewed her journal and notes, searching for anything she might have missed.

Since the druids wrote in ancient Celtic and added their own brand of encryption, it wasn't odd for her to uncover a clue that forced her to retranslate a word or phrase that changed the entire meaning of a previously understood sentence. Brun, unable to read Celtic but having experience with encryption, reviewed her translated pieces. Ethan had no idea what might come of it, if anything, but to him, it wasn't important. He only cared that two of his most cherished family worked together by a warm fire, always finding time to laugh.

Lunch was served in the main dining room, mostly to keep the earl moving. From the first day of their arrival, Maire had been giving him herbs for his arthritis, herbs for when he didn't feel like eating, and herbs to give him a restful evening sleep so he'd have more energy the following day. Ethan wasn't sure if the earl was aware of it because, as was her way, she went behind his back and spoke directly with Lydia and the cook. Neither had an issue with adding new ingredients to the earl's meals, and the evening herbal sedative carried no taste when mixed with the earl's hot cocoa he enjoyed before bedtime.

Now, three days later, Thomas commented on how well Brun looked. Ethan only smiled and agreed. He'd leave it to Lydia if she wanted to mention anything to Thomas about the new herbs.

After a hearty lunch, he took Maire and the earl for a leisurely ride around the estate. Brun spoke with his renters, who hadn't seen him for months, and with each farm they came to, everyone stopped their chores to speak with him. Maire smiled and laughed as she discussed herbs with the women and seemed more relaxed than she'd been since their arrival in this time period.

When their horses brought them back to the front of the manor, the door opened to reveal Fitz, who stepped out to wait on the landing. From around the corner, Thomas jogged up the steps. A stable boy, who'd been running after him, diverted toward the riders to take their horses. The two men waited patiently for Maire to guide Brun up the stairs with Ethan following. They met around the hearth in the earl's study to warm up from the ride.

Fitz, who'd arrived shortly after the trio had ridden off, had taken the time to clean up, and now leaned back in his chair. Dark circles under his eyes emphasized how tired he was. Thomas had been told the man barely slept while running surveillance. A variety of meat pies, bread, cheese, and sweet rolls had been placed on a side table. Fitz barely registered the food, which reflected how tired he must have been.

Brun sat in his favorite chair with a blanket thrown over his lap. His cheeks were still red from their ride, his vigor as strong as Ethan had ever seen it. "Let's get to it so we can let Fitz get some much-needed rest. Thomas, I understand you've had time to gather everyone's reports."

"Yes, Fitz spent most of his time in town. Henry and Clevon worked the city's perimeter, watching for anyone that might be doing the same thing. Not finding signs of anyone, they traveled to Worcester. After speaking with a couple of inn owners and the mercantile, they discovered two groups of men, six in all, had been wandering in and out of town for weeks. If they branched out to the smaller villages like Bransford, they didn't stay long enough for anyone to give them much notice."

"The first day we arrived, I went into town alone." Fitz scratched his chin and sipped from his glass of whiskey. He wasn't as animated as he usually was, and Ethan had seen it before aboard the *Daphne* after the man had worked three straight shifts. "One man traveling is less suspicious than three. And it gave Henry and Clevon time to check the perimeter and visit an inn on the edge of the village. It didn't take me long to discover Father Dolcet was away, visiting parishioners in the north, but he was due back any day. I took a room at an inn at the center of town, while Henry and Clevon doubled up at the inn they previously investigated. We met twice a day at a pub across the village, though I'm not sure it would have mattered."

Thomas agreed. "There was little activity, with only a handful of strangers passing through. Those that stayed were gone the next day."

Fitz shifted in his chair, clearly needing to find his room before he slept where he sat. "Father Dolcet arrived home around noon of the second day. Several locals visited him that afternoon. If he was concerned about anything, he didn't show it. We waited one more day, but all was quiet. If there's anyone out there, they're a ghost."

"Gemini's men have to be waiting somewhere." Ethan stood to pace. What he needed was another hour on the back of a horse. He wanted to meet these men head-on rather than be chased by invisible phantoms.

"They could be anywhere from here to London," Fitz grumbled and rubbed his eyes.

Fitz would be useless to assist with planning without sleep. While he adjourned to his room, the rest of them ate the food provided while they discussed the earl's morning ride. This would be their last day at the manor. Tomorrow, they'd leave for Bransford.

Hours later, after a pleasant afternoon and evening spent

with the earl, Maire snuggled next to Ethan as he laid in bed and stared at the ceiling.

"What troubles you?" Maire stroked his arm.

With an arm bent over his head, he considered her question. What *didn't* trouble him? Worry over her safety. Where Gemini's men might be hiding. How the other teams were faring. So many things plagued his thoughts, but he settled on one he knew saddened them both. "This will most likely be the last time I'll see the earl."

Her fingers moved to his chest where she ran lazy circles over his skin. "He's been so happy having you home."

"I don't want to leave, but I can't stay. Not with this business with the stones."

"I know. And he knows it, too."

"I still can't believe he knew about the chronicles and never said a word."

"Sebastian, Hensley, and the earl. They hold their secrets tightly, parting with them only when required. In their own way, they're trying to keep us safe. The world safe. It's not an easy road to walk."

"It seems they're trying to hold together a dam that's ready to burst."

She snorted. "That is a likely scenario. *The Book* is the dam, and it's been spread too far for one man to hold it all together. Perhaps Sebastian should have collected the pieces long ago, but how could anyone have guessed where this was leading? Do you think Belato was waiting for the duke to find all the pieces so he could take them? Was he behind all of this from the very beginning?"

"If what Beckworth said about Gemini and Dugan being lovers was true, then I'd say probably so. We'll find out when we catch up to him."

"Do we have to leave right after breakfast? Or can we spend more time with him?"

"It will take several hours to reach Bransford."

"We can send Fitz ahead to procure a room for us. Maybe a stroll through the gardens after breakfast?"

"That's a fair compromise."

The soft circles she'd been creating on his skin were becoming smaller and focused around his nipples. Then her hand strayed farther south, running along the fine hairs that traveled from his bellybutton to his manhood.

"Let me take away your troubles for one evening." She rose and draped herself over him, her breasts brushing across his chest as she kissed his forehead, his cheeks, and then his chin.

Her tongue was gentle but persistent as it trailed the contours of his lips before he returned the kiss with the heat she'd created. He rolled her over, moving between her legs as he caressed a breast and deepened the kiss.

Whatever concerns had filled his mind earlier melted away until his only thoughts were how to make this woman happy. And when she took the lead, murmuring words of endearment, he gave himself to her, as he would until his dying days.

# 28

The ride from Rouen to the coastal town of Le Havre was uneventful, though erring on the safe side, Lando rode either a mile ahead or half a mile behind the entire way. The road to the coast was a popular route from Paris, and while the traffic at night wasn't nearly as busy as the day, it wasn't without travelers and soldiers.

Finn expected to be stopped at some point, but having AJ with them seemed to have made the trio appear less dangerous. More the fools them. Though she'd changed back into her pants and shirt, she'd let her hair flow free. It brushed her shoulders, longer than her normal style, but after their week vacation on the *Daphne II*, then returning to discover Stella gone, she hadn't taken the time to have it cut. It turned out to be a good thing.

They stopped frequently to give the horses a break, but it was mostly for AJ, who needed time to walk around and wake up. Riding through the night could be perilous. Without sights to look at, riding for long hours in the dark became monotonous. Add on the number of miles they'd already ridden over the last week, it was difficult enough for him to stay awake. The last thing they needed was AJ falling from the horse.

She almost melted to the ground when they arrived in Le Havre, and Finn found an inn and a room for the three of them. AJ crawled onto the bed fully dressed and passed out. He left Lando behind to get some sleep while he walked the docks to get a sense of what ships were in port.

After an hour of reviewing the ships and not finding anyone he knew, he returned to the inn with the hope the afternoon might bring more ships. He ordered food and coffee to be brought to the room and after a leisurely breakfast the three of them slept until late afternoon.

"We need to restock our supplies before we leave." AJ rummaged through the duffel bags, half the contents spread across the table.

"Is it necessary?" Finn asked.

"Most of our food supplies are gone, including the coffee, hardtack, and fruit. I know you'll find us the best ship, but I'd rather be prepared and not have to worry when we get to England. We don't know where we'll be dropped off."

"We can do that while checking on the ships." Lando repacked his saddlebag then polished off a mug of ale from the pitcher he'd brought up after their nap.

"It would be faster if I did the shopping while the two of you search for a ship. I'd prefer getting to England as quickly as we can."

"It's too dangerous for you to be wandering around on your own." Finn changed into a clean shirt and tossed her the old one.

She grabbed it in mid-air and rolled it up, stuffing it in what she considered the dirty clothes portion of the bag. Maybe the captain would allow her to wash clothes on the ship. "I'm armed. I'll stick to crowds and wear a hat." She pulled out the one she used on occasion and, after studying its poor condition, punched and pulled it back into shape.

He glanced at Lando, and he shrugged. "If she stays close to the docks, she should find everything she needs and be within reach if there's trouble."

Finn was ready to argue but, noticing the expression on his wife's face, decided it wasn't the time for a battle. "Fine. Get everything done in one hour then back to the room."

The three of them exited the inn together.

When they reached the docks, AJ kissed his cheek. "Don't worry about me. I'll stay on high alert and not get carried away with the shopping." Then she was off, blending in with the sailors, merchants, and customers wandering the busy port.

He glanced at Lando. "I'd prefer a ship heading for London, but we can't be picky. I'd rather be on English soil, one way or another."

"Agreed." Lando slipped into the crowd.

Finn scanned the ships in front of him. A couple from the morning had set sail, and only one new one filled the berth. He wasn't impressed by its condition, but they might have had a rough sail. It would be easy enough to rule out.

He'd taken a few steps when he noticed the tips of two masts steering toward the end of the pier. Something about it caught his eye. He wasn't sure what pulled him, but he changed direction and strode quickly toward the ship. His Irish luck might be with him today.

———

AJ's first stop was the mercantile, where she purchased coffee, a few apples that had seen better days, and dried meat and fish. She also purchased new shirts and pants for all three of them. They'd been on the road a long time, and while their clothes could be washed, the ability to do that onboard ship was slim depending on whether Finn knew the captain. She'd just as soon everyone have a clean set when landing in England. She had no idea of Lando's measurements but anything supersized should fit.

She had checked their first-aid kit before leaving the room. They hadn't required its use, thank heavens, but this was the perfect opportunity to buy fresh herbs, so her second stop was a small apothecary. She'd buy bread and cheese from the inn. They hadn't spent any ammunition, either, but she backtracked to the mercantile and bought more cartridges for the flintlocks. One should never skimp on ammo.

She was still grinning when she stepped out of the mercantile for the second time. Without warning, she dashed to the end of the building, ducked between two groups of sailors, then slipped into an alley where she ducked behind a barrel.

Footsteps followed her trail, and she waited until the man passed by her hiding spot. Once he'd taken several steps beyond her, she jumped up and came up behind him.

"That's a fine way of getting yourself stabbed." She held her dagger at the man's back.

"Point taken." Lando spun around so fast, AJ stepped back, then twisted to her right and shoved the palm of her hand against his left arm before bringing the dagger up to his belly.

She gave him a wide smile. "Nice try."

He chuckled and stepped back. "Perhaps Finn was premature in worrying about you."

"And maybe someone isn't as stealthy as he thinks." She patted his shoulder. "You've been following me since we left the inn."

"You expected it?"

"Of course. I know the two of you well enough to guess what your silent nods mean."

"Then why didn't you say something sooner?"

"I figured it was good practice to follow me around while I

shopped." She slipped her arm around his and guided him back to the street.

"You can be an evil woman, Mrs. Murphy."

"Aye, I've learned from the best." She attempted a poor Irish accent.

They were still laughing when they arrived at the inn to find Finn at a table with a pitcher and three mugs. His lopsided grin didn't change, even when she gave him a perturbed stare after glancing up at Lando.

"I'll not be apologizing for looking after my wife." He poured ale into two cups and refilled his own.

"And I won't waste my time waiting for one." She kissed his cheek, then sat down, dropping her purchases on the floor between them.

"They're bringing us some food. We'll want to make it an early night."

"You found a ship?" Lando asked.

"Aye. And a beauty she is. She'll take us straight up the Thames. We should be in London in two days if the weather holds."

---

AJ stared up at the sails, barely noticing the crow's nest in the bare light of day before taking in the rest of the ship. She was a bit larger than the *Daphne*, and the crew seemed as focused as Jamie's as they scurried around preparing to leave. The sun hadn't risen yet, though there was enough light to notice the gentle sway of the other ships, their decks eerily quiet.

She glanced over to find the ship's captain, who was speaking with Finn and Lando, staring at her. He was older than Finn by at least ten to fifteen years, with a tanned face, a trimmed beard, and warm eyes. The deep lines around his eyes were either from years squinting into the sun or from laughing. Which he immediately did when Lando said something, and she concluded they were laugh lines more than anything else.

She strode over when Finn waved for her.

"This is Captain Lamont." He turned to the captain. "And this is my wife, AJ."

"This is the fair woman who stole my young friend's heart. I didn't think it was possible." When he took her hand and kissed it, she wasn't sure what made her blush more—the warm kiss, the knowing wink he gave her, or hearing Finn introduce her as his wife. That never got old.

"To be honest, I'm not sure who caught who." She couldn't help herself, and she winked back.

The captain laughed then clapped his hands, his eyes darting to his ship, keeping an eye on his men. "As I told Finn, I have one cabin I can offer you. It's small but comfortable."

"It will be fine. I'm just happy to be going back to England."

"We can agree on that." He led them toward the ship. "It's been a long venture through some treacherous seas. The Royal Navy is everywhere down the coast of France. And we'll stick close to French waters until we make our run for London."

"We'll stay out of your way." Finn walked next to the captain as they made their way onboard. "But if you need our help in any way, we're at your disposal."

The cabin fit the captain's description. It held a small table with two chairs, a short bookcase with a handful of books, and a single bed that would barely fit two snuggled together. There was enough floor space for two bed rolls, and the men insisted AJ take the bed.

"It doesn't seem fair, but I won't try arguing with the two of you." She stared them down, her fists planted firmly on her hips. "But if the captain needs your help and either of you come back looking exhausted, you'll use the bed to get a decent sleep. And that is that."

It wasn't long before AJ noted the rocking of the ship that told her they were moving toward open waters. With the living arrangements sorted, Lando left the room to check in with the first mate, whom he'd known for some time. Twenty minutes later, Finn jumped up from the bed where the two had been snuggling.

"Something's wrong." He opened the door and peered down the short hall.

"How do you know?" But the minute the words were out of her mouth, she heard the shouts, followed by gunfire.

Finn opened one of their duffels and pulled out a pistol. "Stay here."

He had a foot out the door before he backed up and shut it. He grabbed a duffel and moved it toward the back of the cabin. "Move the other duffel and saddlebag where they can't be easily seen."

She didn't hesitate. "What's wrong?"

"We've been boarded."

# 29

Stella stared at the wrapped bundle tied with twine that Beckworth had given her. He'd left shortly after dropping it off, taking Sebastian and the second package with him, telling her someone would be up to assist her. Whatever that meant.

The knock came ten minutes later from a petite woman carrying towels followed by two lads carrying a hip bath. They returned soon after with buckets of hot water, a coffee service, and sweet breads. Stella poured coffee and watched the woman prepare the bath with drops of oil. The scent of lavender filled the room, and she sucked in the aroma as visions of her tub back home brought a touch of nostalgia.

The woman stepped away from the tub and gave Stella a look that seemed to suggest she was considering how to beckon a frightened deer forward. "My name is Louise, and I'm here to assist with your bath and clothes.

Stella's wide eyes weren't from fear but pleasure. A second bath in almost the same number of days—she'd died and gone to heaven. Louise continued to stare, and she nodded in return, letting the maid know she'd heard her.

Louise found the wrapped package and untied it. When the

outer packaging fell away, Stella let out a gasp when she saw the scrumptious blue material appear. Louise held up a dress that made her mouth water. From what she'd seen on the streets during their drive through London, this was a typical day dress for someone of wealth. It was a cobalt blue similar to the blue in Beckworth's cravat. There were undergarments and stockings. The shoes appeared dainty compared to the boots she'd been wearing. When Louise held up the dove-colored cape, tears blurred her eyes, but it was the smaller package hidden within the coat that made her speechless. Nested within a pair of satin gloves was an opal necklace, the stone cut in the shape of a teardrop.

Louise gave her a bright smile, but when Stella couldn't take her eyes off the necklace, the woman took a step closer. "The viscount said you weren't used to being cared for like a lady, but he said coffee typically soothed you."

It took a moment for the words to sink in, and when they did, she burst out laughing. "Oh, honey. Truer words have never been spoken." She set down her cup and started stripping. There was no way in hell she was going to let a hot bath go to waste. "And you can call me Stella."

Louise grinned and raced over to help with the simple brown dress Eleanor had given her. Then she paused and pointed to Stella's hair. "Can I take the hairpin? I don't want to harm it while washing your hair."

Stella nodded and sucked in a breath when her toes hit the hot water.

"I'll take these down and have them cleaned." Louise picked up the soiled clothes and bedraggled raincoat. "I'll be back soon."

When she was gone, Stella cupped her hands, pouring the scented water over her shoulders and breasts. A hand towel and piece of soap sat on the footstool next to her cup of coffee, which she sipped before going to work with the soap. She didn't speak a word when Louise washed her hair, but she might have moaned with pleasure.

After drying off, Louise walked her through each step as she was powdered, dressed, and her hair pinned up with the leaf hairpin placed in a prominent spot. She felt like Eliza Doolittle with Beckworth playing the role of a younger Professor Higgins. When everything was complete, Louise showed her to a mirror in the corner. Stella was stunned into silence, barely recognizing the woman staring back at her.

She picked up the opal that laid above the dress's modest décolletage. The stone was warm rather than cool against her skin.

The hip bath was removed and the table cleared except for a pitcher of ale, mugs, and a flock of swans that continued to grow after she'd given several to Louise.

"Make sure you come up and collect the rest of the swans once we leave. I'm sure the staff has children that would enjoy them."

Once she was alone, she added three more swans to the flock and was working with her last piece of paper when a knock at the door made her heart leap to her throat and goosebumps erupt over her arms. She grinned as she pulled on the gloves, remembering Beckworth's propensity for tugging at his sleeves.

When the door opened, she backed up to let Sebastian enter. His wispy hair and robes had been washed, and road dust no longer covered his newly shaved face.

Beckworth followed him in, glancing up and down the hall before he closed the door and turned to the room. Her eyes locked with his for a moment before his heated gaze took a long slow perusal down her body all the way to the shoes, then back up, lingering either at her breasts or the opal, she wasn't sure which, before passing by her face to her hair.

When he finally met her eyes, his smile confirmed she'd be more than presentable to his friends. But it was the heat in his eyes that filled her with emotions she wasn't sure how to dissect. She'd seen that look in men's eyes before, but she wasn't prepared for her body's response. She glanced at Sebastian, which was as good as dumping cold water over her.

The monk hadn't seemed to notice her change in appearance and was already opening his journal and inkpot.

"I knew that shade of blue was the right color." Beckworth strode in and handed her a linen card. "Hensley is sending a carriage, and it should be here soon."

She read the card with its fancy lettering, which confirmed his words. He avoided glancing at her while he picked up their odds and ends, packing them in the saddlebags. He'd brought back another larger package she hadn't noticed.

"This has our other clothes, freshly cleaned, though we'll want to air them out when we get to Hensley's. I'm not sure they're completely dry."

He continued to babble about trivial things, something she'd never seen him do. Sebastian fighting over his robe being taken, a silly spat between two women in front of an apothecary, and stopping to buy more paper for her swans and a fresh inkpot for Sebastian. He finally stopped and stared at her.

It was an awkward moment, made doubly so with the scratching from Sebastian's quill, reminding them they weren't alone. If they had been, would they have needed to call Louise back to redress her? The thought brought a tightness between her legs that snaked up her belly and eventually made its way to her lungs, threatening to suffocate her.

She jammed her fists on her hips and narrowed her eyes. "What you're telling me—" She was surprised her tongue worked and there was enough air in her lungs to make sound, "—is that you had a full morning while waiting for me to get ready." When he continued to stare, she continued. "I'll have you know that if we were in Baywood, it would take me exactly thirty-two minutes to get ready, including a shower. And if it had been a bath rather than a shower, then you wouldn't have had to return at all. Those, my dear Beckworth, are meant for full-on girl days."

He grinned as a chuckle burst out of him. "Well, there she is. For a moment, I thought all that extra polish had taken the spark out of you."

She laughed in return before pouring a cup of coffee to steady her nerves. At least the sexual tension had dissipated, though when he stepped close to pour a mug of ale, his masculine scent triggered a tingle that spread over her.

"Do you think Gemini's men are watching Hensley?" She sat down, getting a feel for the layers of fabric that encased her body.

"Absolutely." He poured a second mug and set it in front of Sebastian, who didn't seem to notice. "I hope Hensley's had time to figure out what she's up to."

"They'll recognize us, won't they?"

He shrugged. "They might have men watching who'd seen us at Gemini's camp. I'll be recognizable for sure. But you?" He gave her another quick glance, and his lips twitched. "I don't think anyone would recognize you without that bird's nest of hair."

She touched a tendril and laughed. "I barely recognized myself. I don't know how Louise did it, but I feel like one wrong move and it will all pop out in dozens of knots."

He was still chuckling when a knock broke the moment. One of the boys who'd brought the water buckets told them a carriage waited downstairs. He gave the boy a coin and let him take the saddlebags.

The carriage looked grand as she surveyed the rest of the

street. When she reached the door where a man held it open, she considered the small step.

"Remember to lift your skirts or you'll enter face-first." Beckworth's warm breath tickled her ear.

Without responding, she lifted her skirt with one hand while grabbing the door with the other. Beckworth placed a hand under her elbow to assist.

Once inside, she dropped to the bench, surprised there wasn't more padding. Sebastian followed her in and sat across from her. His smile was warm, and his eyes sparkled with excitement. She smiled back at him until Beckworth popped his head in.

"I'll ride alongside."

She glanced out the window and watched him mount, curious why he chose to ride rather than tie the horse to the carriage. Then she noted the narrow streets and two-story buildings. Men were looking for them and might have already found them. Beckworth needed the ability to react, and he couldn't do that from inside the carriage.

After fifteen minutes on busy streets, the carriage pulled up to a three-story manor that met all her expectations. She waited for someone to open the door while she surveyed the neighborhood. It was obviously an expensive area, and she was curious where Gemini's men could be hiding without being obvious.

When the door opened and Beckworth greeted her, she sighed with relief. He held out a hand, and she took it, remembering to lift her skirts as her grip tightened on his. The exit went better than her entry, and if she did nothing else right the rest of the day, she had this one small victory to hold onto.

Sebastian had barely left the carriage when the door to the manor opened and a plump woman hurried down the steps, two young girls racing to keep up with her.

"Teddy!" The woman had Beckworth in a bear hug before

Stella could blink. And he surprised her when he didn't pull away.

"It's good to see you, Mary, but it hasn't been that long since you've seen me."

She pulled back and slapped his arm. "That was long before you got into all this trouble, and we hadn't heard anything except for quick snippets in a letter."

Before he could apologize, Mary left him and rushed to Stella, grabbing both her hands as she took a step back. The woman was a small tornado of energy.

"You must be Stella. I hope you don't mind the informality. We all started that way, and I don't see a reason to change. You're all our family."

Her cheeks warmed, and her eyes filled with moisture. Family. The woman just met her, and she was already considered one of them.

"Now, Mary, we haven't been properly introduced." A large, robust man, who stood a foot taller than the petite woman, shook Beckworth's hand. "Good to see you made it. You gave everyone quite a scare." He moved past Beckworth to Sebastian. "Brother Sebastian. It's been too long. Mary and I are honored to have you in our home."

Beckworth went over formal introductions before Hensley led Sebastian up the steps. He turned and held out an elbow to each woman. Mary immediately took the right and Stella took his left. Halfway up the steps, he faltered for an instant when Mary patted his arm and gave him a wry smile. "We weren't sure when you would arrive, and I'd already invited dear Dame Elizabeth for the weekend. She should be here in a couple of hours. However, I'm afraid I wasn't clear in my invitation. I believe she's bringing Lady Agatha with her."

The names rang alarm bells for Stella, then her knees almost buckled when she reached the top step and remembered where she'd heard the names. These were the two women who'd terrorized AJ on their first meeting. Well, as they say, forewarned is forearmed.

---

Beckworth watched Mary lead Stella away, chattering about plans for the weekend while Hensley walked Sebastian in a different direction toward his study.

He'd stopped listening to most of the conversation after hearing Elizabeth was on her way. He'd wondered how Stella and her would get along, but Lady Agatha added an awkward twist to the weekend. Elizabeth could hold her tongue about Beckworth and Stella being in town, but Agatha was impossible to control. Tongues would be wagging by midday tomorrow.

Maybe there was a way to use that to their advantage. He mulled over the possibilities, but the scent of lavender Stella left behind was distracting. In more ways than one. He couldn't believe his luck when the dressmaker had a gown in cobalt blue he thought would fit Stella's curves. It hadn't been difficult to imagine her in it, but the image didn't do the real woman justice. She was radiant, and the opal was the perfect touch.

If Sebastian hadn't been in the room, he wasn't sure what would have happened. It was likely Hensley's coachman would have had to send another missive reminding them he was still waiting outside. He shook off his overactive imagination, noticing he was the only one still standing in the foyer.

He found the men in the study where Sebastian was seated in Hensley's usual chair and a footman was pouring tea. Hensley had pulled another chair over, and the two were already in deep conversation. After two minutes of listening to their banter, he felt like a third wheel. He stepped next to the footman and opened a decanter of whiskey. The footman picked up a sliver of ice, but he shook his head and poured half a glass. Something told him he'd need the extra fortitude for the conversation to come.

He leaned back on the sofa and listened to the two men catch up. They were in the middle of reminiscing about Sebastian's days in London when the door opened and Stella strode in, quickly scanning the room before taking a seat next to Beckworth.

"I don't know whether to apologize for being late or interrupting your man time." The footman stepped next to her, and after reviewing what the men were drinking, she asked for a red wine. "I have thirty minutes before I'm needed for a fitting. Apparently, Mary keeps a handful of dresses around in case AJ or Maire show up, although I don't think they were expecting to cover a more shapely figure."

He and Sebastian hid a smile while Hensley stared at her. It was one of the few times he'd seen the man speechless.

"Beckworth should have warned you about Mary." Hensley's gaze warmed, and he sat straighter, brushing away non-existent lint. "She can be an exacting woman."

"Then we have something in common." She sipped her wine, nodded with approval, then studied the men. "Have you been planning or talking about the old days?"

Hensley grinned. "We thought it best to wait for you. I'm also somewhat meticulous and want to hear your story from the moment you met your kidnapper in your own time. Don't leave anything out. I can better assess our enemy when I understand their moves."

She responded with a sly smile. "You must be an excellent chess player."

His smile matched hers and would tell Stella all she needed to know. They were interrupted by a footman carrying in a tray of refreshments that he laid on the short table between them. In between nibbles of cheese and sips of wine, Stella began her story with a day that was already going wrong with spilled coffee, her stop at the inn, some nonsense about a seagull, then finding Gaines in the kitchen.

For the next hour, Stella continued the tale, stopping for a refill of wine while Hensley shooed away the lady's maid who'd been tasked to retrieve her. Beckworth stopped her when she got to their escape from the farmhouse so he could add the events that led up to his arrival, then only added to her story if she left out something important Hensley needed to hear.

Hensley listened intently, only breaking in to ask for clarification when needed. Stella and Beckworth's stories required separate tellings after the second abduction until they were joined together on Belato's ship with Sebastian. The story ended with the killing of Gemini's man who snooped too close to Eleanor's home.

Hensley wiped his brow once Stella sat back as if he'd experienced it all himself. Sebastian had fallen asleep sometime after the lady's maid interruption, but appeared to have an inner clock that woke him once their story was completed.

"Have you received any messages from Ethan or Finn?" Beckworth had hoped some word would have reached Hensley.

"No. I sent a message to the earl and expect an answer any day, but nothing yet. And nothing from France."

Muffled voices floated in from the hall. One particularly loud voice could be heard above the others—Elizabeth.

Hensley glanced at the door, hearing them as well. "We know the men watching the manor and can have them picked up at any time, but Gemini would simply replace them. Then we'd waste time identifying the new men. It's best to leave them in place for now. I wouldn't worry about them; we keep eyes on them. I'll send men to Ipswich and see what they can discover."

"I'd like to send two of my own with them." Beckworth

trusted Hensley's men, but his crew viewed things from a different perspective and could go places Hensley's men couldn't. When Hensley nodded in agreement, Beckworth asked, "Until then?"

His question wasn't necessary. He knew what the answer would be, but Sebastian and Stella needed to hear it.

"Mary has planned an entire weekend of events. I've asked her to put our guests in the west wing with us, leaving the three of you with private rooms at the opposite end of the house. You can use the back stairs if needed. It will give you extra freedom to come and go without too many questions."

"And what will we say about Stella?"

Stella answered the question. "I'm a friend of AJ, who just arrived from America, hoping to catch up with her in London."

Beckworth wasn't sure it was wise to bring up AJ, considering her difficulties with Agatha. But when he glanced at Stella her chin was held high, and she had what she called her game face on. Agatha would be surprised to meet AJ now, who was no longer the timid time traveler, but Stella would be an entirely different situation. They were in for a whirlwind weekend.

# 30

Finn kept his eye on the cabin door as he stuffed his pistol inside the duffel then threw a blanket over it. He scanned the room. AJ had tossed the bed covers and let some of them fall over the duffels. She rubbed her pants pocket like she always did before a perceived attack, assuring herself her dagger was close.

He shook his head. This wasn't the time to show force. He turned to stand in front of her when the door burst open. Two men barged in, and suddenly the room was much smaller than it had been.

One man, with beady eyes and a belly that showed how he spent most of his free time, stood behind a taller man. His unkempt beard hung halfway down his stained shirt.

The tall man was the more dangerous of the two. He was lean and most likely quick on his feet. His dark blond hair was tied back in a leather thong, and he sported a goatee. There might be muscle hidden beneath his shirt, but nothing Finn couldn't handle. The one thing that screamed danger was the crazed look in his brown-eyed gaze.

The burly man bounced on his toes as he leered at AJ. Finn

held his ground, and though he didn't ignore the man, his focus remained on the taller one.

"Is it Captain Murphy? Could we be so lucky?" The tall man spoke with a French accent. He wasn't old enough to be Belato, the ex-monk. Finn estimated him to be a few years younger than himself, and could be Andre, the nephew.

Finn didn't respond.

The man took a step closer and peered around him to give AJ a full perusal. "I understood your wife to be a redhead." He chuckled as he took in the messy bed covers. "I understand." He winked. "A man of your virility can't go long without female companionship. Who could blame you, being departed from your wife for so long? How long has it been? A month?" He let his gaze linger on AJ for a moment longer.

All Finn could do was watch and wait. Looking wouldn't get them dead. Touching? That was an entirely different matter.

"Don't worry. We don't have time to play. Not until we have the ship under control. For now, you will stay locked in here. Then we'll take what we came for." He gave AJ a wicked grin. "And perhaps have some fun."

"Who are you?" Finn wanted information. He also wanted to test them.

The man considered the question then shrugged. "I understand you took a trip to Rouen after Bréval. I don't know who you met or why, but I hear you're a resourceful man, so I would be naive to think you haven't heard the name Belato."

Finn glanced at the ceiling as if he needed a moment to place the name. "Isn't he the only surviving brother of three who squandered their family's inheritance through incompetence? And now he's gone mad with plans for some misguided revenge."

AJ sucked in a breath and stepped closer to him.

He knew this was a dangerous tactic, but he was tired of the game. He wanted to know his enemy and stop running from shadows. And he got what he wanted.

The man's composure cracked. "Belato is a great house that was cheated out of its wealth."

"If you say so."

The punch came fast, but Finn was ready for it. The first one split his lip, the second took the air from his lungs. AJ caught him when he stumbled back, and the bulky man grabbed the tall one.

"The ship, master." The heavy-set man had an English accent. That was interesting.

The tall man struggled out of the other man's grip then pushed him toward the door before turning on Finn. "I am Andre Belato. No one tarnishes my family's name. Certainly not some Irish peasant. I'll enjoy our talks. I have no doubt they might become a bit physical." Then he winked at AJ. "I'll be sure to find some time with you as well, my sweet."

"Put two guards at this door." He pushed past his lackey, who slammed the door shut, leaving them alone.

AJ pushed him onto the bed and held his face with both hands. Her thumb was gentle as it brushed over his lip. "What were you thinking getting him aggravated?"

"I wanted to know who he was, and I didn't think he'd give it up without an incentive."

"You could have tried harder."

He laughed but grimaced. The punch to his gut had a lot of anger behind it. "He's touchy. Part of it's his age. He's young and doesn't know how to hide his emotions."

"And what does that tell us."

"It's all a guess, but their plan is taking longer than antici-pated. They might be having a difficult time keeping up when we do something unexpected."

"Well, they still think Stella is me." AJ ruffled through a bag and brought out the first-aid kit.

He smiled then touched his lip. It wasn't as bad as he thought, though it would sting for a while. "Their other problem is keeping in touch with Gemini in England. It takes too long to get messages back and forth. We know they want the ship. They're probably moving everyone to England."

"How did they take over the ship? With the number of men they need, it would be difficult to hide onboard."

"Not difficult. Impossible." He relaxed under her gentle ministrations as she dabbed the blood away then followed it with one of Maire's herbal salves. "There must be a second ship. The bay has a narrow opening, and if I wanted to board a ship, I might have a couple small ships sail in with boarding crews while the second larger ship blocks the exit."

"Where do you think Lando is?"

"If he wasn't shot during the initial skirmish, I imagine he's plotting with the crew."

"Do you think the captain's dead?"

"This is a crew who's been together for a long time. Whether Belato knows it or not, shooting the captain will most likely make the crew more difficult to manage. They might have thrown some of the crew overboard. It's difficult to know."

"What are we going to do?"

He grabbed her around the waist and pulled her close, giving her a gentle kiss. He laughed when she made a face at the mint-scented ointment on his lips. He held her tight, more terrified for her than for him. He'd die before letting anyone touch her, and they'd brought an arsenal with them. But there wasn't much they could do from a locked room. "We're going to do the most difficult thing there is. Wait and see if Lando can rescue us."

A J sat next to Finn on the bed, his arm around her as they waited. Andre Belato had stormed out of their room two hours ago. Finn had listened by the door after he left, and while he couldn't make out the words, men had been stationed outside their door.

Finn pulled the bookcase in front of the door. It wouldn't keep them out, but it would slow them down, giving them time to react. They loaded and primed two pistols and a musket. Extra cartridges were kept within easy reach in the duffels and in Finn's pockets. AJ might not like the pistols, but she knew how to load and fire one. The room would make for close-contact shooting, and it would be difficult to miss. While she wasn't comfortable shooting a man, she wasn't feeling charitable considering Andre's veiled threat of rape. If it came down to her or them, it wasn't much of a decision.

Her dagger was in her pocket, and her bow and quiver laid on the floor in the corner covered by a blanket that appeared to have been tossed haphazardly. Her skin prickled with nerves, and when her stomach growled, Finn forced her to eat hardtack. What she needed was coffee. What she wanted to do was open the door and beat the guards senseless with a baseball bat. She didn't have a bat, but the musket would work fine.

"The waiting is killing me." She burrowed closer to Finn.

"You've been held prisoner before."

"When I had a concussion, and all I cared about was sleeping and making the headache go away." Finn shivered next to her. He never liked to talk about the ordeal she'd gone through when she fell off the horse and was grabbed by Reginald's men. He'd thought he was going to lose her, and she was surprised he'd mentioned it. But she had her own demons whenever she remembered the time when their roles had been reversed, and he'd been the one lost and close to death. "At least I have you with me. If I only knew Lando was all right."

"I'd be more worried about him doing something foolish if we were on the *Daphne*. He's most likely keeping his head down, waiting for word from either the first or second mate, assuming either is still alive."

"Why didn't they search for the Heart Stone and chronicle?"

"They either have their hands full gaining control of the ship or they're waiting for someone else."

"From the second ship?"

"Aye. If there is one."

They fell silent, holding hands, both seeming satisfied to listen to the other's soft breathing and thumping hearts. She had no doubt he was more worried for her than himself, just as she was feeling protective of him. When another half hour passed by, she rolled close to him.

"Tell me a story."

He chuckled. "It's too early for bedtime."

She poked him in the stomach. "I mean something from your past. Maybe a story about you and Lando, or Jamie. There must be dozens about Fitz."

He kissed the top of her head. "Those might be too racy for you."

She leaned back and stared at him. "My best friend is Stella. What could possibly be too racy for me?"

His brows wiggled. "You'd be surprised at some of Fitz's antics."

She giggled. "I doubt it." She slid down and ran a hand over his stomach. "But it might turn my mind toward something naughty that we can't do with men outside our door."

"Now who's being racy."

They both laughed but slid apart to put an inch or two between them.

When she leaned over and rested her head against his shoulder, she couldn't get thoughts of the other teams out of her head. Two hours locked in a room, and she was already going bonkers. "How about a sailing story or some mission that didn't go quite as planned."

"You mean something other than one of ours."

She snorted and sat up straighter, leaving the comfort of his warm body and protective arms. "We'll have plenty of stories for our children."

"Once they have children of their own."

She laughed, but it was cut short by harsh words yelled from the other side of the door.

"Let me see what you have there." The gruff voice sounded like the burly man they'd seen earlier.

"It's nothing, sir. Just a meal for the captives."

"A warm meal? Who said they could have a warm meal?"

"I was just told to bring it down."

"He must have meant for us, not the prisoners." There was a bit of a scuffle. "That will teach you to argue with me. Here."

Finn had jumped from the bed at the first spoken words. AJ followed suit, crawling across the bed to stand next to him. They stood ready. Neither pulled a weapon, but they were close at hand.

Nothing happened, and seconds ticked by. How could Finn keep so perfectly still? She fidgeted, her weight shifting from one foot to the other, restraining herself from springing to the door and beating on it until someone opened it. Anything to know what the hell was happening.

*Thud.*

They glanced at each other, and Finn shrugged before turning his attention back to the door.

A second thud and the sound of cloth sliding against something.

Finn pulled out his pistol, and she reached into her pocket, keeping her hand on the dagger.

Another minute went by before the door slowly opened, and a head appeared.

"Captain Murphy?" The voice was English.

Finn cocked his head to the side, then said, "Johanson?"

The man threw the door wide and stepped over a body. "Sorry it took so long. We needed time to put a plan together and wanted to get farther away from shore."

AJ followed Finn's gaze over the man's shoulder. Two bodies were slumped on the floor.

"How long will they be out?"

Johanson glanced back. "Permanently."

"Who has control of the ship?"

"They do, but not for long."

"AJ, this is the second mate, Johanson."

The second mate nodded at her. "The captain and first mate are locked in one of the cargo holds with three men standing guard. Belato took the captain's cabin, and three guards are posted at his door. With the two down here, that hasn't left many to control the entire ship. The second ship was gaining on us until we caught the wind and they're now quite a bit behind us."

"We caught the wind, but the other ship didn't?" Finn sounded skeptical as he considered the second mate's story.

Johanson grinned. "It appears we have a new crewman on board who has a unique way of trimming the sails. Some of the men thought it sounded better to make our change of fortune seem more like fate."

Finn nodded, and AJ's concern over Lando vanished.

Johanson glanced at AJ. "He's come up with a plan that we have some misgivings about. Since you have more experience with the man, we wanted your thoughts."

AJ crouched behind a barrel and stared up at the crow's nest that didn't look any higher up than the one on the *Daphne*. She'd be able to climb the ratlines all the way.

Finn hated the idea and refused on general principle. "I'm not going to have my wife become a prime target while I sit around and wait for the captain's call to bear arms."

"So, you'd rather jeopardize this ship because you don't want me taking a risk, even though you know I'm the best person for the job."

She smiled when she recalled Johanson's eyes growing round as cannonballs as the two squabbled. The man was almost out the door with Finn's first swift no, until her stern voice made them both freeze. It seemed her tone that sounded eerily similar to that of an irritated mother made men instinctively come to attention well into their adulthood.

Now, Finn was hidden under a tarp on the aft deck, stewing and most likely planning revenge while he waited for the signal.

No one was in the crow's nest. The clanging of a bell sounded the alarm, followed by the yell of, "Ship starboard!"

At the same time, Johanson nudged her. "Now."

She barely scanned the deck as she pushed her quiver of arrows behind her, her bow already strung around her neck, and ran for the rigging, jumping on the first ratline, her fingers gripping tight to the shroud. Her focus remained on her hands, feet, and each step in front of her. She ignored the men below, her muscles tense as she waited for a musket ball to slam into her. She'd been up and down the mast of the *Daphne* enough times that she could do this with her eyes closed.

She climbed into the nest from the starboard side and, once inside, stayed low as she removed her quiver and bow from around her neck. She pulled out six arrows and leaned three on one side of the nest and three on the other side. There would be several targets on the ship, and she needed the arrows within easy reach each time she loosed one.

Finn had given her the choice of hitting each target in a place of her choosing. She understood what that meant and would make her decision when the time came—which was now. She counted to ten, picked up an arrow and nocked it. Ever so slowly, she rose until she could make out the men being pushed back to their stations by the enemy force. The second ship had proved to be a false alarm, just as they'd planned.

She picked her first target. Since it would be impossible for her to know which sailors were part of the crew and which ones were the pirates, each man who was near a target had wrapped a scrap of fabric around their left upper arm. She didn't want to kill anyone, but the first couple of shots had to hit the target, and aiming for legs or arms was a risk from this distance.

The dilemma surfaced each time she was put in this position as it had earlier in the cabin with the possibility of someone coming for her. She closed her eyes and focused on why they were here at this time and this place. It had been weeks since she'd seen Stella, who'd been kidnapped. These were bad men with a lust for power and greed, who would kill anyone in their way. It had to end. She couldn't control everyone, but she could stop those in her path.

She sucked in a deep breath and released it slowly. Then she trained her arrow on the man standing next to two sailors. He appeared to be yelling at them based on the way his arms were waving about. The two sailors had lowered their heads to the deck. Both wore the handmade armbands.

She blew out another breath, then loosed the arrow. It hit the man in the upper left shoulder, and he dropped. The two sailors immediately dragged the man toward the railing, tucking him next to spare canvas.

Not waiting to see more, she turned to her next target, who was on the port side, staring out to sea. His legs were braced wide, hands on hips as if he were the captain. A sailor washed the deck near the man's feet, and he glanced up at the nest. A red bandanna was tied around his arm. The next arrow hit the target square in the back, and he'd barely dropped to the deck before the sailor pulled him to the side and tossed a few bundles of rope over him. It wasn't the best cover, but they only needed to keep the downed men unseen for the first ten minutes.

She turned to the other side of the nest, surveying the foredeck as she nocked an arrow. That's when she caught sight of Lando. He worked the rigging, staring up at the sails. His eyes locked with hers for an instant before moving on. There was only one man next to him, his stare focused on Lando's hands at the ropes. Probably making sure he wasn't doing anything more than trimming the sails.

Her shot should have hit his shoulder, but he turned at the last minute and the arrow flew wide, sailing over the rail. She nocked the next arrow within a heartbeat as the man turned to see what had flown by. This time the arrow hit him in the lower back, and she flinched. That one would hurt. Lando caught the man, and in a blink of an eye, tossed him over the railing.

That was unexpected. But the man would have yelled out as soon as his body acknowledged the injury and flagged his pain receptors. Lando made the only call he could.

When she bent to grab another arrow, she heard the shot, and the yard arm above her splintered. There were more shots and men yelling. Soon, in addition to the gunfire, the sound of steel meeting steel could be heard above the wind. The yelling soon became screaming.

Staying low, she surveyed the situation, scanning the area

where Finn had been hiding. She might have seen a flash of his hair, but there were too many men. She watched the fighting, the scent of gunpowder reaching her nose and making her sneeze. That was when she spotted the man climbing toward her. He glanced up, and when he saw her, his smile made her stomach sink.

He was moving fast, and she wouldn't have time to nock an arrow. She pulled out her dagger, and the minute a hand grabbed the edge of the crow's nest, she stabbed it. The man howled and the hand disappeared. It reappeared a foot away, and she stabbed it again, then waited.

She pictured the underside of the nest, and she walked the circumference, expecting him to come up from a different spot. The pain in his hand had to be excruciating. It was likely she'd hit a nerve or two, and if so, chances were slim he'd have the strength or the functionality for it to be of any use.

She took the risk and peered over the side. The man was working his way back down, blood dripping from his left hand, which he held near his chest as he fumbled his way down with one good arm.

Not wanting to deal with anyone else making an attempt for the nest, she kept an arrow nocked and her focus on the base of the mast while keeping an eye on the skirmish. After what seemed like forever, and was probably fifteen minutes at the most, the ship was back in the hands of the crew. Captain Lamont pushed his way through the men, who cheered and patted him on the back. Several crew members had lined up the boarding party, and after checking each face, she cursed the fact Andre Belato wasn't among them.

For the first time, she turned to scan the water and saw what she assumed was the other ship trailing in the distance. Her best guess was that Belato had left the ship while they were still making their way out of the bay, feeling satisfied his men had control. It was nice to know their enemy wasn't infallible. The question was whether they could learn from their mistakes. She hoped not.

She slung the quiver and bow over her head and made her way down to the deck. Finn plucked her from the shroud before her feet touched down, and he hugged her fiercely. Then he kissed her so passionately, she heard a few catcalls.

When she leaned back to stare into his emerald eyes, she gave him a wink. "I don't know about you, but I'm starving."

## 31

It was early afternoon before eight of Brun's men followed Ethan and Maire out the gates of the manor toward Bransford. After a leisurely breakfast and a long walk around the gardens, Maire and Ethan said a tearful goodbye to the earl. They rode in silence, and Maire kept an eye on Ethan, who stayed aware of his surroundings but had mentally turned inward. Though their focus was now on Bransford and what awaited them there, she couldn't help but notice the sorrow in his eyes. They had left the earl in good health, but Ethan seemed to be burying this part of his life. And though her own heart was breaking, they had a mission to complete, and the earl would expect nothing less than their devotion to that cause.

Fitz had eagerly agreed to ride ahead and procure rooms at three different inns. It was easy to see he battled his own concerns for Jamie and the crew of the *Daphne*. Jamie's sole mission was to get the crew to London, which seemed an easy task if there wasn't a war. Even staying close to the coast, the Channel could be problematic with British Patrols.

They arrived close to midnight, the party breaking into

groups, each heading to one of the inns Fitz had identified before he'd left the earl's estate.

Maire followed Ethan into the inn, more than ready for bed. Two men drank by the hearth where low flames kept the room warm enough. The men appeared to be well into their cups and were most likely locals. When they reached their room, Fitz materialized out of the darkness, making her jump.

She scowled at him. "Why didn't you wait downstairs? You gave me a start."

His grin made her relax. "Sorry. I don't want anyone to know we're together. The innkeeper knows, but let's keep it like that. I'm probably over cautious, but it seems too quiet."

"It's been a long ride; we just want to get some sleep." Ethan opened the door to the room, and Fitz followed them in.

"The other two groups have settled in. Thomas will meet you downstairs for breakfast while his men scout the area. He'll know where I am and how to find me if I'm not in my room, which happens to be across from yours." He tipped his head to Maire and left.

Once gone, Maire's dress slipped to the ground, and she stepped over it to crawl into bed. She laid her head on Ethan's chest and didn't stir until he slid out of bed the following morning.

She threw the covers over her head and tried to go back to sleep, but all she could think about was their next step. This priest knew Sebastian, had worked beside him, and had been entrusted with a valuable artifact. They couldn't just walk up to the door and demand the chronicle. She had no letter from Sebastian giving the man permission to hand over something so valuable. It would require finesse. Perhaps sharing part of Sebastian's journal would be helpful.

With a huff, she crawled out of bed, grateful Ethan had

stoked the fire before leaving. She dressed quickly, and stopped short when she reached the top of the stairs. The room was full of men, but it didn't take long to spot Ethan, Thomas, and one of his men in a far corner.

She pulled her wrap close, not because she was cold, but to avoid any straying hands among the twenty men, who were clearly from the King's army. Many of them watched as she pushed her way through to Ethan. When the soldiers noticed the three men at the table rise at her approach, their gazes dropped but not before a few glanced at their friends with a remorseful shrug. She couldn't help but smile.

"A grin will only encourage them." Ethan put an arm out to the open bench next to him.

"Where those boys are going, a little encouragement is the least one can provide." Thomas took a long drink from his mug.

"True enough." Henry, who'd remained in town with his partner Clevon while Fitz returned to update the earl, devoured his breakfast of eggs and sausage.

"It appears you're outnumbered." Maire gave Ethan a pat on his arm. "They seem harmless enough, but being a soldier doesn't mean they're honorable. I feel safe enough with the three of you at my side."

They discussed the other two teams while they ate, estimating where they might be on their missions and whether they were successful at finding the other chronicles. Once their plates were taken away and more coffee and ale were poured, the men rested their arms on the table, gathering close so they wouldn't be overheard.

Thomas pulled out a sheet of paper. "Fitz and I made a map while at the earl's." It was detailed, and she had no doubt Fitz had drawn it. She'd seen his work before. He was an excellent sketch artist. "I have an archer on the top of these two buildings.

There's another in a tree behind the church." He tapped at each location as he mentioned them. "The other four will remain a block away and patrol the perimeter at varying intervals, keeping an eye on who comes and goes." Thomas pointed to a third building. "I'll watch from the livery across the street. It has a decent view of the front and east side of the church."

"I'll go in with Maire, offering her and the priest protection if needed." Ethan looked at Henry. "What will you and Clevon be doing?"

"We'll be spending time at the inns and pubs with Fitz. We have a fair handle on who's local so we can keep an eye on any new arrivals."

The three men nodded in agreement, and Thomas was folding the map when Maire shook her head.

"No."

Thomas and Henry glanced at Ethan, who turned his head toward her. She knew what was coming next. He'd have his armor in place, ready to fight for his position. It was something he'd feel strongly about, so she braced for the inevitable and turned to face him.

"What do you mean, no?" His gaze didn't hold its usual warmth. In fact, his silver-gray eyes were the reflection of a stormy sea.

"Everything Thomas has laid out for his men are fine. Unless Gemini has sent her own army of men, we have more than enough to carry out this mission. But there's no need to enter the church's courtyard." She looked each man in the eyes. "There will be no bloodshed on church property. There's been enough of that at the monastery."

This next part would be the hardest. "And you, my love, must stay outside as well." Her smile was soft and endearing. She played a rotten hand by calling him her love rather than using his name, which put him in an awkward position with Thomas and Henry listening. But deep down, she'd come to the conclusion this would be their best play with the priest.

His brows grew together, but the storm in his gaze receded to the gentle Irish sea they always reminded her of. "Explain."

Got him. It really was becoming too easy, but she was only getting away with it because the risk of danger had been greatly reduced with the number of men they'd brought with them.

"I'm meeting with a priest, who was given a sacred duty by someone he's known for many years. Someone who shares Sebastian's beliefs and values. If you were him, holding onto a sacred artifact, would you be willing to discuss it with a woman arriving with an armed escort? Perhaps he would consider the men as the security they are, or he might believe he's being cowed into handing over the chronicle. Having even one of you beside me could be enough to scare him. I have enough of a burden to get him to believe me."

"You expect to just walk into the church alone while I sit here and drink, hoping for everyone's safe return?" Ethan puffed his chest a bit.

She grinned. "No. That wouldn't be wise, either. It would be best if we had a coach, but a wagon would do. I thought Fitz could act as the coachman, and you can wait inside as my doting and overprotective husband. That will keep you and Fitz close enough to run in if there's trouble."

The three men glanced at each other, performing their silent ritual of coming to an agreement.

"I'll find a conveyance," Henry offered. "I'll need a few hours."

"That will give me enough time to send a message to the priest asking for a meeting. I'll let him know I traveled from Brun Manor to discuss a mutual friend in France. If he's been gone for a few days, he might not have an opening this afternoon. We might have to wait a day or two for an appointment. Either way, he might have some idea what the meeting is about and will have time to prepare."

Ethan put a hand over hers. "Then let's find some paper and quill."

# 32

Stella turned her head this way and that as she studied her hair. Sarah, the lady's maid Mary had assigned her, was a sweet young girl with magic hands. Not only did she tame Stella's hair into a glossy updo, curling the tendrils around her face, but had also applied a rosy powder to her cheeks that brought out the varying hues of green in her eyes, making them look larger.

It wasn't, however, her rosy cheeks that made her blush to her auburn roots. When Sarah led her to the standing mirror in the corner, Stella was once again amazed at her transformation. She thought her appearance in the cobalt-blue dress was the best she could hope for without the aid of a blow-dryer and expensive makeup.

She'd either been wrong or was staring through a window at a woman in the next room. Her evening gown was a deep periwinkle, and when she'd first seen it lying on the bed, she'd snickered. AJ had said periwinkle was the color Beckworth had been wearing at their first meeting. Onboard the ship to France, he'd insisted it was turquoise. It seemed odd that Mary would have this color of dress laying around and assumed Beckworth had a hand in it. Regardless, the deep periwinkle complimented her hair, and the low neckline emphasized her other attributes.

Sarah handed her long gloves in the same shade as the dress. Once she'd pulled them on, she ran a hand over her neckline, then smiled when the opal necklace was fastened around her neck. She glanced around the room she'd been assigned. It had a woman's touch, as the rest of the house did, but the decor wasn't overly feminine or masculine. Though it didn't have the modern amenities she'd grown accustomed to in her timeline, it wasn't a bad way to live—as long as you had money.

Nothing different about that in her time period, other than the poor suffered more in this one. That had been easy enough to see on her coach ride through London. Now, she understood Beckworth's determination to rise above the station he'd been born. A position that usually required a birthright or a good marriage. The fact he'd risen on the coattails of the duke didn't bother her. How else was someone in this era supposed to make something of themselves? And he was a duke's son, bastard or otherwise. She touched the hairpin, and her nerves settled.

"Lady Stella? There's one more item before you go downstairs."

She'd fussed with the woman all through her long soak in the bath for the maid to use her first name, at least while it was just the two of them. Sarah had refused, and it was obvious she was uncomfortable, so they settled on Lady Stella.

She ran a hand over the silk fabric of the gown, unable to feel the softness under the glove. If she only had a phone so she could take a picture. When Sarah approached with a long, slim box, her brows furrowed as she stroked the opal around her neck. She liked the opal and didn't want anything different.

The woman opened the box, making sure it was faced toward Stella so she'd see it first.

"Oh, my god." Stella reached in and pulled out a bracelet

made of small opals. Each stone was in its own silver setting, and there were a dozen stones. She counted each one of them.

"It matches your necklace." Sarah held out her hand to take the bracelet. "Let me put it on for you." She clasped the bracelet over Stella's gloved wrist. "The color of the gloves brings out the different shades of the opal."

"It does."

"You're ready now." Sarah scurried about cleaning up the mess the two of them had made in getting her ready. "I'll be back this evening to help you with the dress."

Stella faced the door but couldn't seem to take a step forward until Sarah nudged her.

"If the women are snappish, remember, it's only because all the men will have their eyes on you this evening."

Stella snorted. "That's something I can handle."

Sarah grinned as Stella sashayed out the door.

Once she was out in the hall, her jittery nerves returned. She wasn't worried about holding her own against other women, no matter how ill-tempered, jealous, or snarky they might be. Beckworth hadn't advised her about proper mannerisms, word choices, or how to deal with aristocrats. She hadn't had any problems with Mary or Hensley, but they both knew what century she came from.

No one else did.

Now she understood AJ's dilemma when meeting others. Well, she'd figured out long ago that it paid to listen before opening one's mouth. The difficulty would be to remember that before something unfortunate was said. And she found it odd that she wasn't worried what the guests might think of her. Instead, she didn't want to embarrass Beckworth.

The hall and stairs were empty, as was the foyer. She peered to the left, then had taken a step to the right when a footman appeared and confirmed she was headed in the right direction.

Another footman stood in front of a door halfway down the hall, and voices filtered out as she approached. She stopped when she heard boots behind her.

She shouldn't have been stunned when Beckworth strode toward her. He fussed with his cuffs, and when he lifted his head, he stopped midstride. His heated gaze devoured her, and her skin grew hot and tingly as she drank him in.

*My god, he's beautiful.*

His jacket and breeches were a dark gray, almost charcoal. His waistcoat was striped with two shades of periwinkle and his cravat was the deeper, bolder tone of the same color.

She smiled. "How did you find so much periwinkle in such a short amount of time?"

He moved toward her like a panther stalking its prey, and a chill ran up her spine. The good kind of chill.

"I have my ways. And if I share my secrets, I won't seem as mysterious." He stopped just short of her and reached for her hand. When she complied, he ran a hand over the opal bracelet. "I knew this would be perfect on you."

His gaze never strayed from hers, and she ran a hand over his jacket, tugging at the edge where it opened at the top of the waistcoat. "We're starting to look like twins."

He leaned in, his thumb tracing a circle over her glove just above the bracelet. "I don't want any of the men here tonight to have any illusions about who you belong to."

The sentence hung for several seconds before he added, "For appearance's sake, of course."

But the look in his eyes told her his last statement was the real fabrication, and this time the chill was one of excitement. Suddenly, she was looking forward to whatever was in store for the evening.

"You have that look in your eyes, Lady Caldwell."

She batted her eyes. "What look might that be?"

"The one that tells me rumors will be all over London tomorrow about the viscount's new lady."

She frowned. "That makes it sound like there's a new one at each of these events."

He lifted her chin, forcing eye contact again. "There's never a lady at these events."

"Oh," was all she could say as he pulled her arm through his and led her down the hall.

His warm breath whispered in her ear, creating goosebumps along her bared skin. "Let's give them something to wag their tongues over."

She straightened her shoulders and heaved a large breath, pleased when Beckworth gave a quick glance at her neckline, then marched into the sitting room with him at her side.

For a moment, all eyes turned toward them. At least a dozen people milled about the room, and she swallowed. Hard. And suddenly, facing this many of Gemini's men didn't seem as daunting. Beckworth squeezed her hand, and she immediately fell into realtor mode. She was Stella Caldwell—the best broker in Baywood, dammit, the entire county. And she was no wallflower.

"Could you get me a glass of wine?" she asked as she smiled at the people, who seemed to have taken a large, synchronized sigh before returning to their conversations. The guests returned her smile when they glanced at her, and she held back a chuckle when a couple of the women's shark-like intensity changed to curiosity.

When Beckworth handed her the glass, she almost purred. "Let's start the introductions."

They worked their way around the room, and she filed away names using her standard cataloguing system that matched some tidbit about the person with their name. It didn't always work, especially if too much time had passed since meeting them, but it had over a seventy-five percent success factor if it was within a year. With each introduction, they stayed for a few minutes while the men prattled on about current events and the women asked about her travels as they eyed her bracelet. The entire time, she gave side glances to two women who watched her from across the room. One of the women looked to be in her sixties or a well-aging seventy-something. The other woman was probably in her forties if she had to guess.

Each time she seemed to get closer to them, the farther they moved away until she realized Beckworth was steering her away from them. He was apparently saving them for last.

She almost clucked her tongue when it came to her. They must be Dame Elizabeth Ellingsworth and Lady Agatha something or other. She never caught the woman's last name. She'd spotted Sebastian, still in his robes, playing chess with Lord Osborne. The older gentleman had been so focused on the game, he barely glanced up, and when he did, he gave her a warm smile before abruptly returning to the board.

Beckworth scowled, and she patted his arm, chuckling at his misplaced chivalry.

"You can't blame someone for having his mind elsewhere when we interrupted his game."

"He should expect nothing less when playing games at a social gathering." His chin rose, and she stifled a laugh.

This must be the viscount AJ had first met. If she considered the guests she'd met and the two barracudas, as AJ called them, she was yet to meet, it was easy to see how AJ would have been off her game. Beckworth could be intimidating for someone who lacked confidence. Not a normal behavior for AJ, but she'd been out of her element in a hostile environment and had been at odds with Finn at the time.

Stella wouldn't have been cowed by him if she'd first met him at one of these affairs. There was no question she'd have spent a moment admiring his looks. But as beautiful as he might be, if he'd been this pretentious man rather than the captivating one she knew, she would have ignored him.

Well, she'd had enough of the proper Beckworth. It was time to add tinder to the embers.

She finished her second glass of wine then made a show of fussing with his cravat while running a hand down his arm. Several eyes took note as she anticipated, and she finished it off by going on tiptoes to whisper in his ear, "Take me to AJ's barracudas." She pinched his chin and grabbed another glass of wine from a passing footman.

She caught the fire in his gaze as she took a sip, and she hoped the glare she gave him was enough of a challenge.

It was. He tugged her from one couple to another. The more she laughed with the other guests, the more stilted he became. The question was why. When she set down her third empty glass, Beckworth took her elbow and spun her around, coming face-to-face with Dame Ellingsworth and Lady Agatha.

The older woman had a pleasant enough smile, and Stella didn't miss the humor in her bright, intelligent eyes. Lady Agatha, however breathtaking she was, appeared to have eaten something sour as she ran an unimpressed glance over her. She stopped long enough to appreciate the opal necklace, and her gaze kept shifting to the matching bracelet.

"Teddy, I thought you'd forgotten all about us, but I can see why it took an extended time introducing your lovely companion." Dame Ellingsworth reached out a hand, which Stella reflexively took. The woman's grip was strong but only gave hers a slight squeeze.

"May I introduce Lady Stella Caldway from America?" His words seemed stiff, and Stella didn't miss the amused glance the older woman gave him. "This is Dame Elizabeth Ellingsworth and Lady Agatha Osborne."

Stella let the Osborne name roll around her head as she waited for Agatha to give her a quick nod before sticking her pert nose back in the air. Now she had it. The old man playing chess with Sebastian must be her husband, though he looked old enough to be her father.

"I can see why Teddy's been keeping you close all evening. A couple of the single men have an eye on you." Dame Ellingsworth covered her mouth with a fan and leaned over. "And I imagine of few of the married ones as well."

Stella laughed. "To be honest, I hadn't noticed. There are so many names to remember."

She felt Beckworth's gaze on her but refused to look at him. He would be trying to figure out what she was up to and was probably terrified she'd make a scene in Hensley's home.

"I imagine, coming from America, you're not used to such fine affairs." Lady Agatha barely glanced at her when she said it, but when she turned her catlike eyes on Stella, she gave her a wicked smile. "Although I've heard Boston has enough English aristocracy to make the town livable."

"I wouldn't know how many stayed after the war; I grew up farther west." Her expression was sweet as maple sugar, and she hid a grin when her mention of England losing the war scored a hit. Lady Agatha's face pruned up again, and Ellingsworth hid a smile behind her fan.

This time she gave Beckworth a side glance and found his expression interesting. She'd expected him to be mad at her, and his lips twisted in a way that suggested a forthcoming lecture, but his eyes told a different story. She relaxed at what she assumed to be pride in his star pupil.

She was surprised when his arm snaked around her middle. "Much like my friend AJ Moore, who's also from America if you remember—" his steady gaze fixed on Lady Agatha, "—the women from America tend to be made of sturdy stuff."

"I do find much of the working class to have that attitude for some reason."

"In America, we call it work ethics and pride in a day's accomplishments, but then, I'm just an estate agent."

Lady Agatha looked aghast. "You work?"

"After my parents and both my brothers were killed in a horrible mill accident, it was either make money selling rich people homes or end up on my back."

This time Ellingsworth couldn't hold back a snort of laughter, and when she noted the steam coming from Lady Agatha's ears, placed a hand on the woman's arm. "Well, Agatha, I think you've met your match. I think she'd fit right in at our garden parties."

Beckworth attempted to steer her away when the butler announced dinner. His expression said he wanted to swat her backside, but then it changed to dismay as Ellingsworth took her arm and guided her toward the dining room. "Teddy, you don't mind if I take this lovely woman from you? You've monopolized her long enough. Please escort Agatha, if you don't mind."

That was the last she saw of him for the rest of the evening, except from across a long dining room table. As she expected, after dinner the men adjourned to another room for cigars. Sebastian made his apologies and left the group, no doubt to write in his journal before calling it a night.

Before he left the room, Beckworth's heated gaze landed on her, and she smiled as he tugged his sleeves before following Hensley out the door.

She stayed with the women for an hour, surprised she found most of the conversation stimulating, and a few of them made her blush. Lady Agatha kept her distance, which was fine by her. There would be no changing the woman's low opinion of her now that she'd confirmed Stella's low station in life. When the discussion turned to spring garden parties and the ending of the season, Stella made her apologies, claiming fatigue from her arrival earlier in the day.

The room would be buzzing about her once she was out of earshot. No bother. Mary seemed happy with her, and Dame Ellingsworth appeared to have accepted her. For Beckworth's sake, that was all she cared about.

She'd hoped to see him before the evening was over, wanting to know his opinion of how the evening went. Had he been upset with her assertive nature? It didn't bother him when they'd been on the run, but now she was among his friends, and she worried she'd taken it too far.

When she reached her room, she'd expected Sarah to be waiting for her. She desperately needed out of her dress. The fire was ablaze in the hearth and provided the only light in the room. The maid couldn't be far. Maybe she hadn't expected Stella until the dinner party started winding down.

She was halfway across the room when she stopped, sensing someone else.

He stepped out of the shadows, and she sucked in a breath.

Beckworth was still in his evening attire, though his cravat hung around his neck like a scarf. And damn if that didn't make her heart go pitter-patter.

"I was expecting Sarah." The words came out like she had a mouthful of molasses.

"I gave her the night off."

# 33

---

Beckworth stared at the woman before him. After hours in a wagon, two major dress changes, and a few hours mingling with high society, Stella looked as fresh as a ripe garden strawberry. One he wanted to taste and devour. Even with the bright flames from the hearth, part of her face remained shadowed, and he couldn't read her expression.

This might be the worst mistake of his life. There had been something between them from that first day in the rundown cabin, and as they learned more about each other, they'd developed a friendship. At first, the intimate contact during their long hours in the saddle hadn't bothered him, but as the hours and days grew, there were moments he couldn't help but notice the woman pressed against him.

When she reached for his hand on the ship to France, he'd been speechless. It wasn't that it didn't please him, but he wasn't sure what to make of it. Had it been the comforting hand of a friend or something more? Neither of them were blushing virgins. She hadn't spoken of other men in her life, but things were different in her time period. He doubted she would shy away from intimacy, assuming she was of like mind.

He wasn't sure why, but their few days' separation in France had changed something between them. Had it been the kiss? He'd assumed she was pleased to see him when they'd found each other. Had she felt the spark? Then they were trapped on the ship, and she'd become subdued around him, and they'd lost their easy banter. After they escaped from the ship, the tension between them grew. It wasn't hate that created the rift. If she was mad at him or no longer trusted him, she wouldn't have been shy about letting him know. All that put aside, there could only be one thing that created the strain between them.

That was the thread he held onto when, after seeing the playful heat in her gaze earlier in the evening, he decided this would be the night. If it was ever going to happen, it had to be before they left for Ipswich and whatever waited for them. And right now, this night, there wasn't any possibility of him leaving this room until morning.

When he looked past the way she filled out the dress, the opal that nestled between her breasts, and the hairpin she always wore, there was a woman who'd given her full trust to him. She'd saved his life as surely as he'd saved hers. And if he had any doubt whether she wanted the same thing, he would walk out the door—no harm. But there was no question about her intentions as she strolled toward him, a seductress that captured him under her spell.

He couldn't help but smile.

"Are you sure it was a good idea to let Sarah have the night off?" She plucked at her gown like a woman wanting to shed a second skin.

"I can assure you, I know how to undress a lady."

He caught her involuntary shiver, but her slow and determined steps never faltered. She stopped mere inches from him, her head tilted up. He was tempted to kiss her, but something told him to wait.

There was a hint of a smile as she turned around. "Let's confirm your skill at getting this blasted thing off me." The words were all Stella, but the tone was the seductress.

His fingers almost shook as he untied the drawstring at her waist and then took his time to unloosen it, inch by inch up her back until he felt her squirm with impatience. His knuckles scraped along her shoulder and down her back as he peeled the dress from her to let it fall to her feet. He took the gloved hand she held out to steady her as she stepped over the discarded cloth.

She kept her back to him and stepped by the fire. "Perhaps you can see better over here."

He grinned. She was in a playful mood. When he placed his hands at her waist he felt her twitch. He leaned down to place the lightest of kisses on the side of her neck, and he let out a low growl when she arched her back.

That was all it took to lose himself as he pressed soft kisses across her shoulders, along the base of her neck that made her giggle, and then down her back as he stripped the layers away.

She turned, and he couldn't take his eyes off her. All he saw was Stella. A goddess in the firelight. She smiled and pulled the cravat from around his neck. Her movements were excruciatingly slow as she unbuttoned the waistcoat. When her fingers worked at the buttons on his pants, his breath caught.

---

Once Stella started down this path, she had no plans on stopping. In fact, the moment Beckworth made his presence known in her room, she knew where this evening would end. His heated stares throughout the evening, gazes that stripped the dress off her—didn't he know he was so easy to read?

KIM ALLRED

When she replayed the night's events, she couldn't remember anyone giving them strange stares, except for Lady Agatha, but she was probably like that all the time. Maybe she'd imagined his responses. But she didn't mistake what she saw when she entered her room.

Now that she was here, her hand on his pants, his arousal obvious, this was the worst of times for her brain to reengage. She couldn't remember ever getting this far with a man and feeling fear. Not fear of the man, but outright terror at how this could change her life. But how could it? Once they had the chronicle and they met up with the others, she would be on her way back to Baywood. This wouldn't be her first fling. So what was the problem?

Before she could analyze it further, Beckworth nuzzled her neck and goosebumps erupted. Her fingers returned to their task. When the last button was undone, one arm snaked around his shoulders while she held her hand over his erection. Their kiss was deep, intimate, and heated her blood.

Then she was in his arms, and after three quick strides, he tossed her on the bed. She laughed as she fought her way through the pile of blankets. By the time she oriented herself, Beckworth had gotten his pants off.

Her breath caught. For a man of leisure, he didn't have a drop of fat on him. What did he do to keep those toned muscles?

When he moved over her, driving her into the depths of the bedding, her brain short-circuited, leaving only her base senses to come to life. And she drank them in—drank him in—accepting the pleasure and the intimacy. She'd worry about everything else later.

Stella opened an eye and assessed where she was and why she couldn't seem to move anything. She was laying on a hard lump, but she was warm and so satisfied. Then the lump moved, his scent washing over her, and she smiled. She remembered now.

When she was younger, her situation would have created a blush to her toes, but not anymore. She was comfortable with who she was and with her body, so her desire to stretch like a well-fed cat was only hampered by the lack of response from her muscles.

Somehow, knowing she required assistance, strong hands ran over her back before moving under her arms and dragging her off him as he slid her to his side. Then he threw a leg and arm over her as he turned into her, bringing the bed cover with him until they were cocooned.

His warm breath brushed a lock of hair, tickling her ear. "Morning."

She glanced at the fire, the embers nothing but a glow. The heavy drapes over the windows told her nothing. There wasn't a hint of daylight bleeding past the edges.

"Is it? For all you know, it's the middle of the afternoon and tongues are wagging all over the manor."

"Would it bother you if that were true?" His arm moved farther south, hugging her to him.

"Not at the moment. But I reserve to change my mind once I'm dressed and have to face everyone."

"I wasn't sure how the evening would go, so I told Sarah you were recovering from long days of travel and would require a long sleep-in. She's not to disturb you before nine. And if my internal clock is working, there should be a knock soon, which means a tray will be waiting outside your door."

"That tray wouldn't be delivering coffee by any chance."

"If we're lucky, a few bites of breakfast as well. Mary is quite informal when she has a houseful of guests. Everyone comes and goes at different times. It would be different if we were at their estate in Bristol, but in the middle of the London season the days are filled with teas, lunches, and shopping trips."

The idea of coffee gave her a bit of energy. "Are you sure they haven't already knocked?"

He chuckled, and it was a deep, rumbling sound that woke other appetites. "I promise I would have heard it even if you worked me into unconsciousness."

She smiled but added a pout when she replied, "I don't remember any complaints."

His hand slid from her hip to her breast. "Perhaps we should find something to do while we wait for the coffee." He kissed her breast then her shoulder before moving past her neck to nibble on her ear. He rolled on top of her and drew her into a slow, languid kiss. All thoughts of coffee disappeared into a haze of reawakened passion.

After thirty minutes or so—she wasn't positive because she'd lost all sense of time—she lay spent, unsure how she'd found the energy for another round of lovemaking. She grinned. She'd be lucky to get out of bed before noon.

Beckworth moved the arm she'd laid across his chest and gathered a blanket that had fallen off the bed. She watched in delight as he tucked it around his waist, and with the edges trailing behind him, strode to the hearth where he stirred the embers before dropping two logs on top of them. Then he moved to the door and peeked down the hall in both directions before picking up a tray, closing the door with his bare foot. After reengaging the lock, he placed the tray on a dresser, looked under the silver domed lids, then poured two cups of coffee.

He waited until she managed to sit up, fluffing pillows for both of them to lean against, then handed her a cup. She ran it under her nose, letting the aroma give a swift kick to her synapses before taking a sip. She purred and snuggled next to him once he'd climbed back in, throwing the covers over both of them. Leaning against the headboard, they watched the flames catch and build as it consumed the logs.

"I could get used to this." The words slipped out without thinking. They shouldn't mean anything more than a wishful observation, but this moment in time wasn't anything either of them would ever get used to—at least not with each other. She thought he tensed, but it was probably her own realization that as much as she enjoyed the evening, and as happy she would be with more like them, there was no future for them. It hadn't bothered her last night, but she'd be a fool to say it didn't bother her now.

If he sensed her sudden discomfort, he didn't show it. "Have you given any consideration to what you'd like to do while in London?"

The change of topic relaxed her, and she snuggled down and sipped her coffee. "My only thoughts were arriving safely. How long will we be here?"

"A couple of days, possibly more, depending on what Hensley's men discover in Ipswich. I'll need to meet with him in an hour, and then each morning to discuss any messages he's received and consider our options. With any luck, some of the other teams will arrive."

"AJ and Finn?"

He nodded. "And Maire and Ethan."

"As much as it would be nice to just sit around and do nothing, I'll be bored before lunch."

"The women will expect your occasional attendance at their activities, but I think there will be more than enough time to show you around London."

"Really? You wouldn't mind? Because I want to see all of it, and not just the places the rich people go. I mean, I'd love to see Westminster Abbey and Hyde Park. I'd say Tower of London, which is nothing more than a tourist attraction in my time period, but I have a feeling it might still be in use in this one."

"I agree we should forgo a trip to the Tower."

"I want to see your London. Where you grew up and all the places you spent your youth."

When he just smiled, she amended with, "But no more boardinghouses."

He laughed. "I can promise you that. But it will be safer if we attend the more appropriate places a proper lady would go."

She cradled the cup in her lap and turned to give him an earnest look. "Sarah can find a day dress where I won't look like an aristocrat. You can take me to all the ritzy places tomorrow. It won't mean the same if I don't see your London. I want to meet your friends, and not just the ones that fit in at dinner parties and balls."

He took her empty cup and rose from the bed, placing them on the table with a clatter. "I grew up in dangerous places that haven't gotten any safer."

She snorted. "And they're probably just as unsafe in my time. AJ said you had friends and crews you still worked with all over the city."

He opened the silver domes and began moving eggs and sausage to two plates. "I do."

"And would they be a danger to me?"

"Never." The sharp gaze he gave her softened. "Sorry."

She threw the bed covers off, unconcerned about her nudity, and taking some satisfaction in the immediate change of mood coming off the surly Beckworth. Something raised his hackles with her request, and she had to understand why it bothered him.

She changed her approach, knowing full well she would be

using her state of undress to cool his stubbornness. She sensed his gaze on her when she sauntered to the tall dresser where Sarah had stored most of her clothing, including several items that magically showed up since her arrival. She flipped through her wardrobe before finding the moss-colored silk robe. It fell to her ankles, and she tied it loosely around her waist. Now that he'd seen all of her, revealing bits and pieces of naked skin should keep him off-balanced for the rest of the conversation.

She picked up a sausage and nibbled the end. It took all of her strength not to glance down his body when his expression turned sultry. She took another bite before putting it down, noticing he'd already refilled her cup. After a sip of coffee, she gave him a thoughtful look. "Does where you grew up embarrass you? Because I never got that feeling when you spoke of it before."

"Of course not. I have nothing to be ashamed about. My mother did the best she could." He glanced at her robe, the part above the belt, then cleared his throat. "I know what you're about with this request, but there's no reason to see those neighborhoods. It's not the man I am anymore."

She stepped close enough to run her hand over his arm, but rather than reach out, she waited until he met her gaze. It was a struggle to keep her hands off him, to comfort him. "But that's not true."

Before she could explain what she meant, his immediate response was a look of shock and dismay. She grabbed both his arms, ready to shake him until she noticed her touch alone had calmed him.

"Let me finish. No one is just one thing. You look at me and see a successful businesswoman. And I am. But I didn't get there without earning a few scars in the process. I've told you about my early days, though I admit, not in great detail. But it's not like I wouldn't have told you someday—if things were different." She sucked in a breath, not wanting to think of the short time they would have together. "I wouldn't be who I am without that background. And the same goes for you."

She took his wrists and led him to the sofa, sitting close beside him. "You're a man who walks in two worlds. One as the viscount, a title and standing you worked hard to achieve. I know the story. You had to do some unsavory things working for the duke. Your father. Some might consider them irredeemable, but that only applies to people who have no desire to change, to make amends. That isn't you."

There was doubt in his eyes. She'd never seen that before. It twisted something in her. She ran circles over his hands with her thumbs. "You fit the viscount role well, but I think your need for the title is more about security rather than power or greed. You enjoy the time you spend with your crews, even now. Taking a job with Hensley was a way to continue living in both worlds without having to explain it or hide it. The reason I want to visit those places is because the bad part of town and the good part of town are who you are today. What makes you the kindhearted, loyal man you've become."

She released his hands and sat back. There wasn't anything more she could say. It was his turn to either confide in her or turn her away.

Several minutes passed while his expression went through several changes. Some she recognized—fear, acceptance, amusement, and satisfaction. Others she couldn't read at all, though the last one looked like regret. Then his cocky grin returned.

"All right. It's a date. I need to finish up breakfast and meet with Hensley first. Ask Sarah for a dress similar to what she might wear to church. I'll make apologies to Mary that we'll be out for the day. It will be a smaller group for dinner, and Elizabeth will want to spend time with you."

"Excellent." When she stood, he pulled her close and buried his head in the gap of her robe, his kisses heating the sensitive skin of her breast.

"But breakfast will have to wait a few more minutes." He tugged her back down and worked the robe off her inch by inch.

When he left thirty minutes later, still cramming eggs and sausage in his mouth while grabbing a chunk of bread, Stella fell back into bed and hugged a pillow. She wouldn't take back a single moment with him, but something grew inside her that filled her with longing and despair. It took every ounce of strength to push it down, relieved when Sarah knocked and came in, immediately picking her evening gown off the floor.

She jumped out of bed a new woman. Today it was all about Beckworth, and she refused to ruin it with thoughts of an untenable future.

## 34

Ethan and Maire ate lunch in their room, going over their afternoon plans while Thomas checked on his men. Their duffels were packed and would be transferred to whatever conveyance Henry was able to find. Once they had the chronicle, there was no reason to stay.

Maire's appointment with the priest had been confirmed for two o'clock. They would be getting a late start for London, but Thomas and Fitz agreed that putting miles between them and Bransford through the cover of darkness would be a good thing.

At ten minutes to two, Ethan and Maire left their room, duffels in hand, and found Fitz waiting for them on the bench of a carriage. It wasn't the best carriage, only one step above Bart's old carriage they'd used for previous missions. As far as Maire was concerned, it fit her expectations perfectly—not too rich and not too poor.

She gave Fitz a pleased smile, and he gave her a wink as he jumped down to store their duffels.

"Where in all the heavens did Henry get a carriage?" Ethan walked around the coach, checking its wheels. "And I see our horses are now harnessed."

"They did fine." Fitz opened the boot and stuffed the duffels next to his saddlebag. "They were a bit disagreeable when we backed them in, but a bucket of grain seems to have soothed them."

"And where's your horse?" Maire asked. "Or are we taking this all the way to London?"

"Thomas is holding onto mine. It wouldn't be wise to take the carriage. It might give us cover, but if we get in a scrape, it will be a hindrance. Henry rented it for the afternoon and gave the stable master extra coin to pick it up at an inn on the outskirts of Worcester."

"He agreed to that?" Ethan's brow rose.

Fitz nodded with a grin. "He has a couple stable boys who get restless. It will be good for them to pick it up from the other livery."

Maire waited by the door for Ethan to open it, then climbed in, checking her pocket for her pistol. She preferred rifles or muskets, but a pistol was her only option for a face-to-face meeting, though no one expected Gemini's man to be inside the church. She grinned as she looked out the window at the people wandering by. What would they say if she marched into the church with a rifle in one hand?

The coach swayed as Ethan climbed in and sat across from her. "I'd ask if you were ready but, based on the glimmer in your beautiful summer eyes, I'd say this is something you've been waiting some time for."

"Having another part of *The Book* in my hands, a piece I've never read before..." She clenched her hands together and glanced out the window before looking back at him. "It will be a difficult ride to London without having time to read it. Couldn't we get another carriage?"

She didn't expect anything less when he shared a tolerant smile. Regardless of what mysteries might be answered in the

KIM ALLRED

chronicle, they had to wait for the safety of Hensley's manor, and London was days away.

He pried her hands apart and rubbed them, keeping his gaze locked with hers, even as the coach began to roll. "I know how much you want to read it, but our first concern is ensuring its safety. Once you retrieve it, the road to London will be the most dangerous of our travels, even with the earl's men with us."

She nodded. "Aye. I know. Just having it near will be good enough."

He clucked his tongue. "Let's not start the journey with lies."

She laughed and squeezed his hands. "You know me too well."

The carriage stopped several minutes later, the village not being that large. Before Maire got out, she glanced at him. "Are you going to be all right waiting here?"

"And now you know the most difficult part for me."

She snorted. "You were never good about sitting still. I promise to be as quick as I can without being rude."

Fitz opened the carriage door, playing the bored coachman, but as she stepped down, he whispered, "Keep to a nice gentle stroll in and back out. You'll be all right."

Maire approached the church and its well-tended courtyard as a woman stepped out of the front door. The woman nodded but barely glanced at her as she passed by. When Maire reached the door, she took a deep breath, opened it, and stepped inside.

The interior was cool with the soft scent of sandalwood incense. It was a simple church with a handful of statues and plaques. Candles burned at a small altar to her right, and large stained-glass windows reflected myriad colors over the dark, age-stained pews and stone floor.

She walked up the main aisle, her boots leaving the echo of soft taps in her wake. At the front altar, she crossed herself but didn't genuflect. She was more a spiritual woman than a religious one. The priest in the Irish parish where she grew up was always cross with her even though she'd attended mass most Sundays. But she dabbled with old Celtic texts and met with the Tinkers whenever they passed through town, learning her herbs. Not something a proper Irish lass should be doing, but considering her childhood, or the loss of it when her parents died, Finn let her do almost anything she wanted—within reason.

She was staring at a painting of the Crucifixion when she heard footsteps behind her.

"Are you Miss Murphy?"

She turned to find a man of average height and build holding a leather-covered bible, which she assumed from the cross imprinted on the cover. He didn't wear the typical cassock of a priest but robes similar to Sebastian's. His chubby face gave a welcoming presence, and his eyes sparkled with intelligence, and if she had to guess, a bit of curiosity.

"You can call me Maire." She reached out a hand, and he took it in both of his. Then she noticed his gaze shine with unshed tears.

He wiped them away with the cuff of his robe. "I must apologize. I never thought this day would come." His voice was a rich timber that must give his parishioners a great deal of comfort. He stood straighter and cleared his throat. "I'm Father Dolcet, a very dear friend of Brother Sebastian."

She smiled, and her own eyes misted over. "I can't tell you what it means that you know him well. It's been some time since I've seen him."

"Come. Let's go to my office. I have a fire warming a pot of tea."

"I have to admit, I was a bit concerned whether you'd understand my message."

"Not many speak the older Celtic languages. My Breton is a

bit rusty. I'm more familiar with the Cornish language, but I was able to decipher enough of it."

He led her through the nave to a side door, then down a short hallway to a simple room lined with bookcases. There were two chairs next to a plain wood desk where a tea service had been set with fresh cups and a plate of biscuits. She kept an eye on his movements as he made the tea. She had no reason to suspect him of anything, but Ethan had instilled caution in her, and it had served her well.

They made small talk about the village and the last time he'd been in France as they nibbled the biscuits and drank a pot of tea, each sharing short stories of their time with Sebastian. And it wasn't lost on her, nor on him, that they were testing each other for their sincerity.

When she'd had more than enough tea, she pulled an envelope from her pocket. "We've been dancing around each other, but I want you to be assured the chronicle will be in good hands." She handed him the envelope, then sat back and waited.

Inside was an aged piece of paper she'd pulled from Sebastian's journal. He should recognize the handwriting, but she made sure the page she brought identified the four locations of the chronicles.

The priest sat back and rubbed his eyes. Without a word, he opened the bible he'd been carrying and removed a folded piece of parchment with a broken wax seal. He handed it to her.

It was a short message written in Breton Celtic. Its English translation read:

*Dear Father Dolcet,*

*The time is near at hand when I might call upon you to return the package I entrusted with you many years ago. I will send a special envoy from the monastery. Her name is Maire Murphy, and she is quite knowledgeable of the teachings of* The Book of Stones. *Please*

*know that she has my full confidence in protecting what you have so
carefully cared for.*

*Your humble friend,*

*Brother Sebastian*

"When did you receive this?" Maire's chest tightened with
the knowledge of how much Sebastian trusted her.

"It's been about nine months now. I was beginning to think
something dreadful had happened."

She wiped her eyes and smiled at him, holding back the
hysterical giggle trying to bubble out. "It has been a difficult
journey." Inside, all she could do was shout over and over again
—*how had Sebastian known she would return to fulfill his missive?*

He rose and took the letter back from her. "If you follow me."

She trailed behind him as he scurried back down the hall,
turning right instead of returning to the nave. He opened the
second door to the left and led her into a room that hadn't seen
use for a long time if the layers of dust were any indication. On
the far wall was a half-filled, equally dusty bookcase. Without
disturbing the dust, he pressed a stone on the floor bordering
the wall. The bookcase scraped along the stone floor, revealing
an opening large enough for a person to enter. It brought back
memories of the bookcase in the monastery where she and AJ
had first met Sebastian.

Nerves trickled up, along with a threatening giggle, which
she hoped wouldn't turn into hiccups. She wished AJ could be
here for this. And, for a fleeting moment, wondered what AJ's
endeavor with the other chronicle entailed.

The priest lit an oil lamp and led her down rough and
chipped stone steps.

"Watch your footing. I've considered fixing the stairs but
decided to leave them as they are. Should someone accidentally
open the door, they might question the wisdom of going any
farther."

She didn't want to suggest if someone found the door, it was most likely for a reason. But it was possible a maid or child might step on the stone accidentally from either cleaning or playing.

The steps ended at one end of a long hallway. They passed several doors made of oak with locks that appeared to have been made a hundred years ago.

He seemed to have heard her thoughts. "The church was built in 1658. The previous priest showed me this just before he died. This tunnel runs from the church to an old cabin about a hundred yards in the woods beyond the courtyard. It was used to hide and relocate known Catholics during the Protestant persecution shortly after the church was built. A few rooms, similar to those at the monastery, were used to shelter families until it was safe for them to leave through the cabin. Those were dark days indeed."

At the third door, he used a key to unlock it. The room was overfilled with items made of various precious metals or stone. Dozens of books were stacked on tables or filled the bookcases. There didn't seem to be any organization to the place, as if people placed things in any open spot depending on their mood. It could take days to find anything, assuming one knew the object was in there.

"It would be best if you stayed here while I retrieved it. Besides the maze, there are a few traps that, while they won't kill, can be rather unpleasant."

He disappeared behind several stacks of crates, books, and a large statue of a winged angel, perhaps Michael. She heard another scraping of stone and assumed another secret room. Unable to stop herself, she used a fingertip to turn a book around, discovering a French journal from about the time the church had been built. She was reading the first page when the priest returned with something wrapped in cloth and tied with twine.

He smiled when he noticed the open journal. "I've been known to spend long days with a single oil lamp going through everything. It might not look to have any organization to it, but I've cataloged a quarter of it and purposely left it in organized disarray."

"You've done a good job of it."

She followed him back the way they came, but instead of going back to the nave, he led her to a different door.

"I'm afraid I have another appointment, and they're probably waiting in the vestibule. It would be best if you left through the courtyard. There's a small path that will take you around to the front of the building. Many people come to the garden for self-reflection, so it won't be odd if you left that way."

He handed her the cloth-wrapped package, and when she placed a hand over it, he laid a hand on hers. "It's been an honor to meet Sebastian's good friend. Please give him my regards and tell him it's a blessing to be considered a trusted resource. We must continue to protect this world from those that would diminish its light."

When he released her hand, she tugged on his robe and pulled him closer. "You are an honorable and holy man." She kissed his cheek and smiled at his blush. "I have no doubt Sebastian will be forever grateful for the care you've given the chronicle."

Without another word, she turned and walked out into the gray day, feeling a sense of accomplishment and, simultaneously, the heavy weight of a new responsibility. She would do whatever was necessary to get the chronicle safely to London.

# 35

Stella might have regretted her words to Beckworth that she'd be bored staying at the manor all day. She hadn't expected her time in London would be the whirlwind it became.

True to his word, he took her to the East End. He skirted the area, keeping her away from the worst of the poor, sick, and struggling people. He used the trip to check in with his crews, introducing her as a close friend to AJ and Finn Murphy, and though most had never met either of them, they'd heard of their exploits with Beckworth's half-brother, Reginald.

It hadn't taken her long to see how welcome he was with the locals. And by extension, though cautious, they had given her the same courtesy. If they were concerned about her social status being hidden beneath the common day dress, they became perplexed then seemed to accept her more when she pitched in to help one of the women with hanging her clothes to dry. The woman had one kid on her hip, one crawling around on the muddy ground, most likely eating some of it, while two young boys raced circles around them. Stella never made a scene, she simply struck up a conversation and began picking clothes out of a basket as they spoke.

Beckworth never said a word, but his small grins and quick glances told her everything she needed to know about her attempts to fit in. They visited half a dozen people on their carefully guarded walk around town and shared an afternoon meal with one couple and their two teenaged boys.

Chester was the leader of one of the larger crews, and although he was roughly ten years Beckworth's senior, they'd known each other since they were both street rats. Katherine, his wife, worked as a seamstress at one of the new factories, but only two days a week. Whether it was because that was all the hours she could get, or they used it as a cover, she wasn't sure. They lived in a modest house and rented two of their rooms to two older gentlemen who were part of the gang, their specialty surveillance.

"We heard you went missing. Some said you went to France again." Chester lit a pipe, and the sweet scent in addition to the cooking stew was an aromatic balm from the smells of the city.

"Good to know you're receiving decent information." Beckworth took a sip from his mug and grimaced, then smiled after the burn settled. "Also good to know your moonshine is just as ghastly." He grinned again, this time taking a larger swallow.

Chester caught Beckworth up on local news while Stella rolled up her sleeves to help Katherine with the meal. Their sons raced in without warning and ate so swiftly, Stella was certain they were practicing for a speed-eating contest.

While she helped with the clean-up, Katherine shared a story of her early days as a pickpocket in the West End until she met Chester, and she moved up the chain until she handled disbursement of their ill-gotten goods. Once she was pregnant with their first son, she used her seamstress skills to create costumes for the crew. Stella wondered if she'd ever met Eleanor, who, according to AJ and Maire, had mad sewing skills.

"I hear you've been running from someone named Gemini."

Chester had lit his pipe again and leaned back in an old stuffed chair.

"Any word on whether she's in town?" Beckworth asked.

Chester's eyes widened. "A woman. We heard it was a man."

Beckworth shrugged. "She works with a man named Gaines, who sometimes acts on her behalf using the same name. It's been a good deception until recently."

"I haven't heard anything, but unless they're up to something or she has a sizable crew of her own, it's hard to keep track."

"We know she has a couple men watching Hensley, but we think she's currently in Ipswich."

"Unless they're meeting up with smugglers, not much reason to be up that way."

"They're working with another group that sailed in from France. It wouldn't be surprising if they brought contraband with them."

"Or maybe picking some up," Stella said. They all nodded, and she returned to drying the dishes, a grin on her face, feeling like one of them. It was also interesting that Beckworth wasn't sharing anything about the chronicles. She doubted it had to do with trust and more keeping the crews out of their mess.

The four of them sat and listened to Chester and Beckworth share stories. Based on Katherine's shaking head, many of the tales were most likely exaggerated. When they said their good-byes, Katherine gave her a hug, and Chester nodded with a smile. "Good to meet a friend of Beckworth's. You're always welcome at our door."

The following day, Mary insisted that Stella spend the day with the women. She wasn't sure what to expect with Mary, Elizabeth, and Agatha, but she had a surprisingly good time as they went from one social gathering to another. Agatha was civil most of the day, and Stella chalked the day up to another success.

Beckworth refused to take pity on her sore feet and spirited her away on the third day to walk through Westminster Abbey. They returned for lunch with Sebastian, Mary, and Hensley. Since Elizabeth and the Osbornes had left after breakfast, Beckworth talked Hensley into taking everyone for a ride through Hyde Park. Mary sat between Sebastian and Stella, leaning over to point out a particular person or some statue.

Dinner was a quiet affair, but Mary kept them to social protocols of cigars for men and the drawing room for the women. Late on the evening of the third day, Hensley's men returned.

After breakfast, Hensley called Sebastian and Stella to join Beckworth and the other two men to share the news from Ipswich. Hensley's men couldn't confirm one way or another if Gemini's crew were there. Being a port town, the docks were busy with privateers, smugglers, British Patrol, and one Royal Navy vessel. They did, however, find a ship that matched the description Beckworth had given them, right down to the name —the *Phoenix*.

That meant Belato was in town. The consensus was that Gemini and Gaines, or Big and Tall as she called him, were most likely there as well. Not sure what else to do, they made plans, one after another, as each was discussed then discarded as too dangerous or too risky.

When they adjourned, Stella retreated to the small outside garden. She'd been out there a couple of times, but never when the sun was shining as it was that day. The roses were in full bloom along with the wisteria. It was too early for the lilacs. Beckworth had taken her to the flower hawkers at Whitechapel when they'd been in the East End. They'd stood in the middle of the sellers and closed their eyes like five-year-olds. The scents were similar to Mary's garden, except for the single vendor who had fresh bouquets of daphne.

The simple recollection of the flower and its name made her

think of the ship, which led her to worry over why AJ and Maire weren't in London yet. She found a bench in a far corner of the yard, lifted her face to the sun, and closed her eyes. She had a bad feeling about Ipswich. Maybe they should leave the chronicle there and be satisfied with the others, assuming those missions were successful. She'd suggested it, and Hensley had considered it, and the others felt it was worth considering, but what they meant was that it would be their last resort.

"We're leaving Sebastian with Hensley." Beckworth sat next to her, his leg rubbing hers. "He doesn't add anything to the mission other than being a liability. He's safer here and, if Gemini or Belato had hoped to recapture him, we can keep him out of the game and mess with part of their plan."

"A plan we're only guessing at. Maybe it's best to just wait for the others. We'd have a larger group."

"Which would be more of a disadvantage in this situation."

"Why?" She knew he'd want to go. He was willing to take the risk. When they'd been on the run, she was fine with taking chances. But taking on a mission and knowingly walking into danger sounded foolhardy. Yet, AJ and Finn had done it time and time again. Now, she remembered why she'd never been interested in time travel. Each time she watched the fog take AJ, she'd feared she'd never see her friend again. Then it hit her. This wasn't about her, or the stones, or the chronicles—not really. This was about AJ and Finn never having to worry about the past. This was about Maire being able to make a decision of whether to stay in this time or come back with them. This was about having a choice without worry of being kidnapped again or someone showing up in Baywood and hurting their family. And seeing it from that perspective, there really wasn't a choice about retrieving the chronicle.

"We have a situation where we know where our target is," Beckworth said in answer to her question. "With a letter from

Sebastian, it shouldn't be difficult to convince the blacksmith to hand over our prize. We don't believe Gemini or Belato know who Sebastian sent the chronicles to, just their general location. It's easier for a few to slip in without being seen. A larger group creates more potential for discovery. Hensley hasn't been able to determine their numbers. Right now, we know nothing, other than they're in town and will be watching."

She leaned her head against his shoulder. "I don't want to end up in Gemini's hands again."

"Maybe you should stay here. I can go with one of Hensley's men. It would be easier that way. Less risk."

"I don't like that, either. Maybe we could have the blacksmith come to us. Not all the way to London, but some spot along the way." He leaned back and stared at her until it made her fidget. She pushed a loose strand of hair back. "What?"

"That's an excellent thought. If we assume Gemini and Belato truly have no idea who has the chronicle, that could work."

"I still think having more of our team with us could work. We could create a distraction like you did on the ship. Then send one or two in to grab the book while everyone is distracted elsewhere."

"That's what makes this so difficult. Hensley's men weren't able to find Gemini or her men. We don't know their numbers or where they're hiding. Without that knowledge, a distraction might not be enough to pull them all away from our target." He squeezed her hand. "Hensley wants time to consider options and he'll tell us in the morning what his decision is. Maybe the others will arrive by then. If you insist on going, you'll want to have your traveling clothes ready, which means back to your pants and shirt."

"Why is Hensley making the decision?"

Her question seemed to stump him. Then he shrugged as he

picked a leaf from a nearby bush, folding it in half, then half again before letting it spring back to its natural form. "He doesn't have the final say, but he's a master strategist, and it would be foolish not to give his suggestions a solid considera- tion. With these types of missions, we go in knowing we might have to reassess once we get there. It's always best to have options ready."

Stella rubbed her hands along her dress. It was dove gray and one of her favorites. It wasn't the flamboyant colors she preferred, but the empire-style dress made her feel more like a princess than any of the evening gowns. Maybe that was because of the way Beckworth looked at her in it. Like he was doing now.

She'd made a decision after their first night together, then had pushed it away, preferring to enjoy every second of being with him, both in and out of bed. The last few days had been like a dream, and now that they were leaving, she had to stay focused. Once the chronicle was retrieved, it was just a matter of waiting for AJ and Finn, then they would go home. And though it was against everything she wanted, she had to put Beckworth at a distance.

She grasped his hand. "I've made my own decision."

He didn't pull away, but she felt a change in mood through their physical connection. "What is that?" He sounded like he was expecting unpleasant news, and she supposed it was.

She tapped her foot, not sure how to say it. And like a bull in a china shop, she barreled through it. "I don't think we should sleep together again after we leave London."

He didn't say anything, but he might have clasped her hand a bit tighter. "I see."

"I've given it some thought. Everything that's happened between us here, meeting your friends, seeing where you grew up, the dinner parties, and the amazing evenings..." She shook her head. "This has been a fairy tale where the monsters aren't allowed. But I have to face some startling facts. This next journey is going to be dangerous. We're actually walking into what's probably a huge trap. And once we have the chronicle and AJ and Finn show up..." The breath rushed out while she tried to suck some in and almost choked.

"Then you'll go home," Beckworth finished for her.

"And then I'll go home." She had to say it out loud. Her chest ached as if someone were standing on it, suffocating her.

She grasped his arm and leaned into him, and he wrapped an arm around her. They stayed like that for a long time, not speaking, just holding each other.

Then they rose. She wasn't sure which of them stood first. He placed her arm through his as he walked her into the manor and up to her room.

"Tonight?" he asked.

She placed a hand on his cheek. "Our last night." Then she closed the door and without waiting for Sarah—and sorry to mess up the dress—she crawled onto the bed, pulled the covers over her, and wept.

## 36

Beckworth leaned back in the chair and stared at the ceiling of Hensley's office. He twirled his glass of scotch and purposely didn't think of Stella. She'd been right. Once they left for Ipswich, the game would be dangerous indeed. Their only focus set squarely on retrieving the chronicle and racing back to London.

They would need a small, tight unit. Get in and get out.

Hensley continued to read his messages that had arrived earlier in the day, occasionally making notes. It didn't matter. None of the messages would help the decision before them. After another five minutes, Hensley laid down his quill, took his glasses off, and leaned back, locking his fingers together over his stomach as he joined Beckworth in staring at the ceiling.

The man had aged in the last couple of days. They'd both expected some word from one of the other teams by now, but there was nothing but silence.

"How long do we wait?" Beckworth finally asked the question he knew Hensley was mulling over. "Gemini tends to get impatient once she's put a plan in motion. Who knows what she's been up to or whether she's anywhere near Ipswich. And we know nothing of this Belato. Sebastian's knowledge of the man isn't reliable after all this time. It's impossible to know how the Terror and the loss of his brothers and family's wealth might have shaped him. All we know for sure is that he's been playing a long game of revenge. No doubt he's as mad as the duke was."

Hensley turned his gaze to the messages he'd piled in a stack. "Even if Finn or Ethan had sent word, I fear Gemini has been building a small army as she waits to play her hand. A small strike force is still the best answer, but if they have any idea the blacksmith is our target, you'll be walking into her hands."

"How critical is it to get the third chronicle?"

"From what Sebastian says, he believes all four chronicles are required to decipher how the torc works. However, if someone has three of them, it's possible, with enough time and trial, the correct incantation could be pieced together."

"And we don't know if the other teams were successful in retrieving the other chronicles."

"At this stage of the game, I believe you should go. Tomorrow if possible. See if the blacksmith is being watched. Find your best path in and out, execute, and return. Nothing you don't already know."

Beckworth nodded, although if he had his choice, they'd leave the third chronicle where it was. But Gemini had three of the five small stones, and someone had knowledge of the incantations. They had no choice but to go after the chronicle. "How long will you stay in London?"

"For another few weeks unless something calls us home. I'd prefer to be here until all the teams return or send us word. Sebastian will remain in our care. I only trust Jamie to get him home safely."

Two hours later, Beckworth was late to dinner, arriving to a strained atmosphere. After Elizabeth and Agatha's departure, it left the household quiet as the tension of the pending mission and missing team members plagued the manor. Fortunately, for his sake, Mary's mood improved instantly when they were called to dinner.

Stella wasn't her normal vivacious self, though it hardly mattered. Hensley and Mary could keep a conversation flowing all by themselves. To emphasize that fact, Mary shared stories of previous dinner mishaps that got several chuckles from Stella. Then Sebastian shared humorous tales about the monks' first attempts at making cider.

Everyone knew the stakes. Beckworth and Stella would be departing early the next morning, so there were no cigars in the study or small talk in the drawing room. Mary made some excuse about preparing the house in anticipation of the rest of the team, though even that seemed to increase the dour moods.

Beckworth caught up with Stella as she mounted the stairs and forced her to take his arm. This was their last night in London, and he intended to do whatever it took to make her forget about tomorrow.

When he opened her bedroom door, he stood aside and waited for her to enter. She took a few steps before stopping. The fire had been stoked and dozens of lit candles adorned dressers and tables, leaving the room in a golden hue.

She spun in a slow circle, taking it all in. "What's all this?"

He strode to a side table near the hearth where a tray had been set with an opened bottle of wine and two crystal goblets. He poured the wine, feeling her steady gaze on him. "This is your most perfect romantic evening. The only item I wasn't able to obtain was the music." He handed her one of the goblets. "I'd hoped we could make our own."

Her expression almost crumbled, but she gulped the wine and managed a smile. It wasn't her usual bold one. This one was tender, the one she shared after they made love.

"Come sit by the fire." He picked up his glass and sat in the middle of the sofa, pulling her down next to him. She leaned into him as they watched the flames.

"Something feels different about this mission." She picked at the edge of his sleeve, then ran a thumb over it before repeating the action. He took her hand, interlacing his fingers with hers.

"That's because this is your first one. Until now, you've been running, hiding, and surviving. This time you're walking into a situation you don't have to. Other people's lives will be on the line. Not that they weren't before, but it's different than when you're running for your life."

She took time to consider his response, then slowly nodded. "And this is what you do for a living."

He shrugged. "I don't have to work for Hensley, but being a man of leisure isn't as fulfilling as I thought it would be."

She turned so she could face him, and the smile he'd come to know was back. The one that told him she had an entirely different explanation, and the most he could hope for was that she wouldn't have a list.

"First, I'm not sure how you could ever think you could be a man of leisure." When his brows rose, she patted his thigh, which made his cock twitch. When her smile turned coy, he knew he'd given her the response she was looking for. It was all he could do not to shift in his seat. "Don't take it personally. You've spent your whole life running cons, working for food and rent. After all those years, I don't know why you'd think you could just sit in your manor and watch other people do all the work. I'm sure there are plenty of tasks for a viscount to do, but this leads to my second point."

He smiled. She did have a list.

"You're a man of action. You might not be one who creates the intrigue, but you like to puzzle them out, find ways to make people share their secrets, and you're willing to take the hard road. I understand how working for Hensley completes your need for something more exciting than a manor in the middle of nowhere."

"I love my manor in the middle of nowhere, and I don't get nearly enough time there."

She finished her glass of wine, took his empty glass, and set them down before taking both his hands in hers. "I love my home and my garden, and I barely get the time to enjoy it. Yet, it's rare for me to take time off, and I can't remember the last vacation I took. I savor every moment I have at home, but if I'm there too long, I get itchy."

"Itchy?"

She nodded, gathering steam. "That feeling that gets under your skin that won't let you settle down. You start walking around the house with no real destination. You just feel the need to move. You probably go riding or hunting, but even those activities aren't as fulfilling as they were days or weeks earlier. I imagine most lords of the manor find that a perfectly pleasant life. But you weren't born to it. You had to fight tooth and nail to get where you are, but that fire inside you didn't go away like you thought it would. You need to get out and do something meaningful, and Hensley's network of spies is right up your alley."

He gripped her hands, his head buzzing with churning emotions. She'd figured him out in such a short period of time. Part of it was how they'd met and the forced intimacy of being on the run. Even knowing his jaded past and his continued dalliance with the crews, she accepted him for who he was. Why did it have to be someone from a different time to truly understand him?

"Is there a point to your list? Or is there more?"

She laughed, but then her face grew solemn. "You take risks. I suppose you're like Finn in that way. And Ethan. That's why, despite what you might think, you all get along well." She pinched his chin. "Don't say it. I know you don't want to be compared to Finn or Ethan, but that's only because deep down, you don't think you're as good as them." She stabbed a finger in his chest. "You don't believe you're a good man. You think your heart's been tainted, but it hasn't." She pulled up her skirts and knelt on the sofa. "All I have to do is see you with your friends, with Mary, and the staff here. You have a gentle heart. You have more love in there, but you're scared to let it out because you've kept it guarded for so long. But it leaks out to everyone who means something to you. Even to those where you see goodness. And that makes you just as good as Finn and Ethan."

She undid his cravat and slowly pulled it from his neck, running it through her fingers before dropping it to the floor.

"And this is why I work for Hensley?" He could barely breathe. She'd seen through his mask—and shattered it. She'd heard the tales from AJ, had seen firsthand when he was in Baywood what kind of man he'd become working for the duke, trying to please his father. God, he'd actually hurt her when he'd slammed her into a cabinet, though it had been an accident, not what he'd meant. He'd been so crazed at the time. Yet, she saw past all of it.

She nodded as she undid the ties on his shirt. "If it wasn't Hensley, you'd probably arrange some partnership with Jamie. You, my dear viscount, are a man of action not of leisure. Give it another twenty years, and I might change my mind." There was a slight shake in her hands. She would have no idea what he would be doing twenty years from now. By the time she made it home, he'd be long dead.

She pulled up his shirt, and he raised his arms as she tugged it off. Her gaze locked with his, her hand running over his bare chest. "You found a fur rug."

He nodded, unable to say anything over the gigantic lump in his throat. She was so beautiful in the firelight, and he removed the leaf hairpin, scattering the rest of the pins so her hair hung loose.

Then she was on him.

He laughed as she pulled him to the floor then reached for the buttons on his breeches. She was laughing too when he pushed her hands away and flipped her around so he could work at the ties of her dress. He tickled her in between her squirming as he stripped her bare before rising to remove his pants. When he stared down at her, she'd rolled over, her arms raised above her head, tangled in her hair that caught the fire-light, giving her dark auburn tresses golden highlights.

She was a sight, and as she laid there, he saw more than hunger in her eyes. He saw the love neither of them would speak of, but it was there just the same. When he finally dropped to his knees, he ran his hands up her legs, over her hips, slowing to caress her breasts before lying next to her as they kissed. It was a deep kiss, filled with longing, desire, and a thrill of excitement laced with fear of what tomorrow would bring. But soon, the only thing that remained was the desire, and the flames burned to embers before the two of them fell into a deeply contented sleep.

---

Sarah nudged Stella. "Wake up, my lady." The maid's footsteps receded to the other side of the room.

Stella was still on the fur rug, a blanket thrown over her. She didn't have to open her eyes to know Beckworth was gone. It was better that way. Their last night of intimacy, and damn if he didn't provide.

"There's fresh coffee, and breakfast is ready in the dining room. You need to eat before your travel."

Sarah was right. It would be a long ride to Ipswich, and she didn't want to face it on an empty stomach. She pushed the memories from the previous night aside and stretched like a well-pampered pet. Her memories from these nights with Beckworth would have to last her a lifetime. She couldn't afford to think about the future and what it would be like without him.

"Ugh." Where was AJ when she needed her? She tossed the blanket aside and dragged her naked body up.

"I have a warm basin waiting for you. Why don't you wash up while I prepare your traveling clothes?"

"I'll need my pants, shirt, and boots." Stella drew a warm rag from the basin that had been scented with lavender and began washing her body.

"Should I pack the other items?" Sarah folded the blanket she'd picked up from the floor. Then she collected the candles, placing them together on a dresser.

Stella considered the pending operation. Her pants should be enough, but best to be prepared for anything. "Pack my second pair of pants and shirt and also a day dress. Nothing too fancy. Ooh, and a brush. And my stationary." Beckworth had bought her a stack of writing paper. No quill and inkpot, just the paper. No one else understood the present, but she did. They were for her swans.

Once dressed in her pants and shirt, she hurried to the dining room. Everyone was already eating, and Hensley smiled at her when he took note of her outfit. "Ah, Stella." He set down his fork and wiped his mouth. "Get yourself a plate from the sideboard. We have a fresh pot of coffee right here next to me."

She smiled, happy to sit by Hensley. He always had the interesting stories. She glanced around for Beckworth but didn't see him. Ignoring her disappointment, she scooped eggs onto her plate, and added a large piece of bacon and a roll. This was more than she should eat before a long day of travel, but the amount of coffee she was going to drink this morning would require frequent stops until lunch. If her stomach got upset, there would be time to walk it off.

Sebastian sat across from her, and his eyes twinkled. "Are you ready for your journey?"

She grinned at him. "It better be worth the ride."

"Oh, I have no doubt." His tone grew serious. "But don't underestimate Belato. He wasn't the quickest of my interns, but he was always determined. I never considered him a great strategist. He was horrible at chess. He might have been seeking the stones and book for years, but I believe his niece and nephew to be the planners."

"I haven't met Belato or his nephew, unless he was one of the few men I saw onboard his ship. If that's the case, then neither are very bright. They bumbled our escape, after all. I do, unfortunately, know Gemini, and I have no doubt she's excellent at planning. We'll be on our guard."

They ate breakfast, and the light conversation eventually turned to the topic of the blacksmith. Stella hadn't been privy to the discussion of why a blacksmith would have the chronicle, but she'd learned quickly that Sebastian had his own way of looking at things. They were discussing the best way to approach the blacksmith when two men entered the dining room.

"Good timing." Hensley pointed toward his two guests. "This is Sebastian, a Brotherhood monk from France, and this lovely woman is Stella Caldway from America. She's a good friend of AJ and Finn Murphy, and Beckworth has been assigned her bodyguard until Gemini is stopped."

He waved toward the two men. "This is Morton and Lewelyn. They're two of my best guards and scouts. They'll accompany you to Ipswich."

"The horses are ready. We just need your dispatches." Morton poured a cup of coffee and chewed on a piece of bacon and a roll unlike Lewelyn, who sat with his hands in his lap, a bored expression on his face.

They were husky men, at least six feet tall, and reminded her of Lando. Morton was blond with hardened features and stunning baby-blue eyes. Lewelyn was dark-haired with broody brows that reflected his expression and probably his entire personality. But his dark eyes missed nothing, and she was a bit surprised by the twitch of his lips when he caught her perusal.

"Give us another thirty minutes." Hensley cut into a sausage. "Beckworth should be back by then."

"Where did he go?" Stella was grateful for the opportunity to ask without seeming nosy.

"To dispatch some letters and retrieve your transportation. He'll be back soon." He finished the sausage and soaked up the yolk of his egg with a piece of roll. He kept his eye on the door, and now that she knew where Beckworth had gone, she assumed his watchful eye was hopes of a last-minute message from Finn or Ethan, or even better, the teams themselves.

She drained the last cup of decent coffee she'd see for a while and excused herself for final preparations. After a slow walk around her bedroom, keeping her gaze averted from the bed, she stopped to say goodbye to Mary. When she returned downstairs, Hensley waited for her.

"It's time. The horses are out front." He held out an arm then led her through the foyer and out the door to where they stopped at the top of the steps.

She frowned at what waited for her. Morton and Lewelyn were already mounted. Next to them, Beckworth stood in front of two horses. Her saddlebag was on the back of one the ugliest horses she'd ever laid eyes on. It wasn't so much its features as it was the dull mottled color. It wasn't a flattering look. Then her frown deepened when, even from this distance, the horse appeared to be assessing her and determined she was the one coming up short.

They couldn't possibly think she could ride solo all the way to Ipswich. Her backside hurt just thinking about the ride back.

She glanced at Beckworth and noted the twitch of his lips. He found this amusing. Her fear of being in control of the horse, or more accurately the lack of it, pushed the anxiety of the entire mission to overload, landing her squarely in the box of pissed off. She was overcompensating. She knew it and didn't care.

With a flip of her hair, which was now left to fall its full length to her shoulders, she stomped down the steps and stared up at him.

"I thought there would be a carriage or wagon." She didn't bother to mention riding with him. Even she was aware of how foolish that would look. Then she considered the intimate contact of riding a long distance together and gave the horse a side glance.

Beckworth held her gaze with an expression that was impossible to read, but his tone was somewhat formal. "A carriage is too obvious and would be problematic if we have to run. A wagon poses the same issue. You've been on a horse by yourself enough times to be able to handle the ride."

She narrowed her eyes. He was once again playing the role of viscount, and she didn't like it. Maybe it was because of all the eyes on them. It might be a reflection of her attitude that he wasn't going to entertain in mixed company. She couldn't blame him.

"I see. And what if we run into trouble on the way?" Or the horse got tired of her and ran off in the hopes of tossing her into a ditch.

"Then I'll swoop you off your horse, and Morton will have to take him. But let's do our best."

She could have smacked him, especially when she noticed

his blank expression turned to amusement. He was baiting her. Well, she learned long ago, you never play your enemy's game, you make them play yours. Not that he was the enemy, but at this moment, the idiom still fit.

After a long look in the horse's eyes, and a stern discussion with it of who was in charge, she mounted without difficulty and ignored the men watching her, who all seemed amused.

She nodded to Hensley and Sebastian before managing to turn the horse in the general direction of Beckworth. The horse seemed to understand the rules and followed without much effort on her part. The horses clopped down the road in a leisurely manner. Beckworth would wait until they were clear of London before picking up the pace, which gave her time to get comfortable with her mount.

The sun was out, and the air was brisk. Her gaze narrowed like a laser beam on the center of Beckworth's back. If she focused her annoyance directly on him, maybe it would diminish the spidey-sense that screamed this trip was all a horrible mistake.

# 37

Ethan glanced behind him. Something was wrong, he just couldn't put a name to it. They'd left Bransford straight from the church. Fitz drove the coach while he'd been inside with Maire. Thomas and the men followed until they stopped at a livery in a small hamlet where they dropped off the coach, transferred the duffels to the horses, then took off again.

The ride to London would take two days and a bit more, assuming they kept a decent pace and didn't run into trouble. After their days at the manor and a night in Bransford, the team was well-rested. Thomas spread his team out, two riding a half-mile in front, and two just as far behind them. They'd ridden through the darkness on a decent road.

The first night, they slept a few hours in the woods, feeling safe enough to build a fire and keep a rotating group of lookouts.

Maire constantly worried about the chronicle. She'd buried it under clothes and weapons in one of the duffels, but if they were overtaken, it wouldn't long for someone to find it.

There was no way around it. The journey to London was when they were at their most vulnerable.

When they came to Oxford, it was late afternoon. Thomas

wanted to rest the men before their final run to London, which would be a long day, but the closer to London they got the less chance of trouble as the number of travelers increased. They continued southeast out of Oxford and found a quiet inn. After a quick meal, they found rooms and slept until a couple of hours before dawn when they were back on the road.

Now they drove the horses as quickly and safely as possible through a wooded pass. Instead of keeping men far ahead and behind, Thomas brought them all in so they were eleven strong.

Dawn had broken a couple of hours earlier as the rain started. They were a few miles out of Stokenchurch, and Ethan looked over his shoulder again. They hadn't ridden a half mile when they came across a large group on the road. Two carriages and three wagons were lined up with a number of horses tied to the conveyances or nearby trees.

Ethan glanced at Thomas. "Something's up."

Fitz rode up next to them. "Hold my horse, and I'll go see." He dismounted and strolled through a crowd of men who were conversing between the wagons and carriages. He stopped for a few minutes, talked to a couple of them, then continued on.

While they waited, Thomas's men surrounded Maire and Ethan, keeping them partially hidden from view by those watching from the roadblock.

Fitz returned twenty minutes later, and by his expression, he didn't have good news to share. "Someone chopped down a couple of trees, which are blocking the road. They're waiting for men with axes. It will take them a while."

"We could help them if we had the tools." Thomas didn't look pleased. "But with the rain, this could take longer than I feel comfortable standing still."

"I agree." Fitz took his horse back from Thomas and waved toward the group of travelers. "These people aren't fighting men.

If Gemini's men are out there, and they're the ones that felled the trees, these people won't provide any help."

"Most likely, there will be casualties among them from being in the way." Maire glanced around while struggling with her horse that refused to stand still. It stomped from one foot to another, most likely feeling Maire's tension through the reins.

"From what one of the men said, a few riders took off through the woods to catch a small road to High Wycombe."

"Is there no way around the tree?" Ethan asked. He didn't like this at all.

Fitz shook his head. "The land is steep on both sides for a fair distance. If we want to go around, we'll have to cut over to another road or trail."

"How many men could Gemini have compared to what we have?" Maire asked.

"Hensley's never been able to determine an exact number, but if this Belato brought more men with him, it could be more than we care to deal with." Ethan considered their options. "We could go back to Stokenchurch and wait, but they might have planned for that. Did anyone say how long they think it would take to clear the road?"

Fitz scratched his scruffy chin. "They figured several hours by the time they get the men here and cut through the trees. Whoever did this spent most of the night taking them down. They're decent sized."

After gathering opinions from Thomas's men and further discussions, they were of like mind to push forward and take the road to High Wycombe. No one was comfortable with the decision, but second-guessing the enemy was never a good strategy.

They followed a deer trail in search of the secondary road. Thomas kept the group tight, with Maire and Ethan in the middle. Thomas led, and Fitz rode behind, pushing them forward. The rain didn't let up, and with the dense canopy, the trail was dark. They kept an even pace, slower than Ethan preferred, but the road was dangerous with the low branches and rocky terrain.

They found the road, which wasn't much wider than the deer trail they were on, but it was wide enough for a wagon to pass as long as the cargo didn't stick out past the sides. At least they didn't have to worry about low branches, and they picked up their pace.

They'd ridden a couple miles when the first shot rang out. They pulled the horses together and moved into the trees. Thomas, who'd been in the lead, was fine, but the shot had taken out a branch near his head.

After a minute, a deep voice called out, his accent giving him away as a Londoner. "We know you have something Gemini has been seeking, and we know you have the scribe with you."

Maire reached for Ethan, her hand squeezing his tightly, before sitting back and pulling her pistol from a pocket. No one spoke, waiting to see what Gemini's man would do. There had to be more of them out there.

"I know what you're thinking. You should have stayed on the main road. How many men are with me? Maybe you should have returned to Stokenchurch. And they're all excellent questions. So let me explain the situation to you. All we want is the scribe and the package she carries."

"Have they been following us the whole time?" Maire whispered.

Ethan shook his head. "No. If they knew the locations, they're betting on us retrieving the chronicles. It only makes sense we'd head for London. From what Beckworth said, Gemini had guessed his move before he had. Her men were on the main roads leading to Southampton. She'd scattered them to pick up a trail. If it worked before, she probably assumed it would work again."

"With the dense trees, it's impossible to see how many are out there," Fitz said.

"We need them to show themselves." Thomas glanced around. "They'll have to get close to flush us out, but I agree with Fitz. With how close the trees are, they could sneak up and pick us off without leaving a target to shoot at." He nodded to one of his men, who nodded at the others, and they tied their horses to branches before disappearing into the trees.

"How far will they go?" Ethan asked.

"A hundred yards. They'll want to keep tight so no one sneaks between them."

The voice yelled out again. "If you're worried you made a mistake leaving the road, you should know there's a group waiting on the other side. You were never going to make it to London. And if you're thinking of heading back, you're already surrounded."

"We need to confirm that." Fitz looped his reins over a bush and pulled out his broadsword. "I'll be ten minutes, fifteen at most."

Ethan wanted to say no, that it was too dangerous, that they could wait for dark, which was a couple hours away. But they didn't have nearly enough time. Fifteen minutes was probably too long. He nodded. "Be careful."

Fitz was gone in an instant, disappearing into the foliage in two strides.

Several minutes ticked by, and with each second, Maire paled in the dimming light and became still as stone. She didn't see a way out of this. Ethan didn't, either, but he'd made her a promise that no one would kidnap her again. He would do whatever it took to ensure that didn't happen.

"I've been a reasonable man." The man's tone was even, not a trace of impatience. The sign of a dangerous man who had the upper hand. "I've given you time to consider your lack of options. You don't want to take a chance of the lady being injured—or worse."

He'd barely finished his statement when Fitz burst out of the trees, his sword bloody.

"They're coming."

The flash of flintlocks sparked, and the sound of steel on steel rang through the trees. Ethan held up his sword, keeping Maire behind him as he turned, waiting for someone to come at them, knowing it could be from anywhere.

Maire wasn't cowed. If he had to guess, she was raging mad. She tended to get quiet at those moments. Fortunately, it didn't happen often, which was why he hadn't considered it when he'd noticed how quiet she'd become. But seeing her now, pistol primed and aimed toward the dark trees, her eyes a stormy green, she was channeling her rage.

"I took out two when they began to move in. I checked all but west of here. There were five men just outside our perimeter at three different points. I'd bet a week's worth of Mrs. Brubaker's pies they have the same number on the west side." Fitz wiped his blade clean with debris from the forest floor.

"That's too many." Thomas whistled, bringing his men in, if they could hear over the noise. When the first two arrived, one was half-carrying the other, who had blood dripping down his arm.

A man screamed, then Thomas's men appeared, all of them with blood staining their shirts. Whether it was their blood or others it didn't matter. They were all standing. No one followed them, but they were missing one.

"They'll pick us off until only Maire is left," Fitz said, no emotion in his voice.

A single shot rang out, and it grew quiet.

"This is your last chance. We gave you the opportunity to leave us the lady and her possession, but you refused the hospitality of my offer. Now I give you one last chance to slip away into the darkness. But the lady remains where she stands."

"Chances are they have a weakness on their west side." Fitz stared into the darkening forest. "At least that's what I would do. They know we're not going back. It's better to strengthen the other teams. If we had some type of distraction, we could get through that line and swing around from the north."

"And what kind of distraction did you have in mind?" Thomas asked.

"I can't think of one at the moment," Fitz replied sheepishly.

Ethan closed his eyes. He didn't want to suggest it. It seemed a coward's way out, but it had worked once before at Waverly. With the tight quarters they were in, it was sure to work again. It was one thing to hear about the power of the stones, assuming these men were aware of the stories. Either way, seeing it in action was something quite different.

"No." Maire's gaze locked with his. "It's impossible."

"We don't know that. We've never tried it with a smaller stone."

"Exactly. We have no know idea what could happen."

"We'd either end up at Parliament or wherever AJ is."

"You're talking about using the stone?" Thomas asked.

"Aye." Fitz's spirit improved. "It worked at Waverly. Reginald's men scattered when the fog came."

"Yes, that's right." Thomas nodded. "It's the perfect distraction. The fog will also deafen the sounds of hooves."

"You won't be able to hear them, either," Maire snapped.

Ethan hadn't expected her to be happy about his suggestion. She hadn't been happy the first time. He took out his stone. They needed a decision now before the men moved in.

"Please, Maire. I know how you feel, but this is the best way to save everyone, or give them a fighting chance. Just like before."

Fitz dropped their duffels next to them. When she glanced around and saw all the men ready to mount, she slowly nodded. "All right."

She removed the powder from the pistol and slowly released the cock before shoving it in her duffel, which she then swung over her shoulder. She held out her hand. "Give me the stone."

Ethan took his duffel and handed her the stone. "This is the right thing."

Tears ran down her face, but she held her head high and her shoulders rigid. "Get on your horses and start riding as soon as I start speaking the incantation. Don't hesitate, and don't look back. Godspeed, gentlemen."

Thomas touched her shoulder, and Fitz shook Ethan's hand before giving a quick glance to Maire. Then they mounted their horses.

Ethan stepped next to Thomas, who leaned down from his mount. "Take care of the earl."

Thomas took his hand. "Of course."

"All right, gentlemen. You've made this most difficult." This time, the voice held an edge.

They'd run out of time.

Maire took Ethan's hand and closed her eyes. She spoke the words that would take them to the Heart Stone.

This would be a different jump then the ones he'd taken before. Both Heart Stones were in this time period. Something Maire was keenly aware of, so when the fog came, and he met her eyes, he understood this was most likely a huge mistake. There was nothing he could do other than hold her hand tight as the fog descended and sucked them away. But before the terrible twisting ache in his stomach came, he felt a burning pain slam into him. His last thought was of Maire and what she would do when she found him on the other side—shot and bleeding out.

# 38

AJ leaned against Finn as they watched the ship makes its way up the Thames, the sun just breaking over the horizon. After the captain had regained control of the ship, he'd ordered the crew to dump the pirates overboard. It was up to the ship behind them to save their men or let them perish as they kept up their chase.

The other ship had stopped to pick up their men, confirming his assumption that the captain was aware he'd never catch the faster ship. With one of the Belatos onboard, they would probably head for London. If they'd been in contact with Gemini, they probably knew about Hensley.

At this point, Gemini and Belato had to be getting desperate. They'd lost their hostages, and while they were aware of their stop in Bréval, they hadn't been there, and didn't have the chronicle. Most likely, they didn't have any of the others.

Once the river led them to London's inner city, she bounced on her toes, anxious to dock.

Finn kissed the top of her head. "It won't be long, lass."

"They have to be here. Right?" It had been several weeks since she'd last seen Stella in Baywood. She'd only heard from others that her friend was safe, in good spirits, and still with Beckworth, who was also protecting Sebastian. She grinned. He would have his hands full. She trusted him to keep them safe, but it wasn't the same as being with Stella. No one would care about Stella as much as she did—not when it counted.

"They should be here, but it's possible they moved on to Ipswich. We'll know soon enough, and there's nothing you can do to make the ship go faster."

Lando took that moment to step next to her. "Don't worry, little one." He pointed to the left. "We're heading to that second berth up there. You'll be on land and hopping into a wagon soon enough."

Finn squeezed her arm each time she fidgeted. She watched the men at the rigging and was in painstaking agony while the ship moored and critical cargo was unloaded.

Finn and Lando stayed on either side of her as they slid between two groups of men hauling crates down the plank. Then she tapped her foot the entire time she waited with Finn for Lando to return with a wagon.

She calmed when she exited the coach and stared up at Hensley's manor. Then she almost cried with relief when Mary ran down the stairs and enclosed her in a warm embrace.

"It's so good to see you, my dear." She held AJ at arm's length as she was wont to do and gave her a perusal. "A little on the skinny side, but that always happens when you've been racing all over the country." She tugged AJ behind her, leading the three of them up the stairs as footmen dealt with the duffel and saddlebags. "It's a shame you just missed your friend and Beckworth."

Finn grabbed AJ's elbow when her knees buckled, and while the squeeze of his fingers told her he'd heard her soft swear, Mary seemed unaware.

Hensley waited at the door as he ushered them in, then gave

the street a long stare before the door shut behind him. "I gather from the look on your faces, Mary told you Stella and Beckworth left this morning. Come to the study. Mary, please have baths drawn for them and a meal prepared. I have a feeling our friends will be leaving us after they clean up, eat, and get a short nap."

He shook his head at AJ as Mary scampered away, already calling for her lady's maids. "You'll do all three of those things because you'll need your wits about you. Now come, I have at least one thing to put you at ease."

They followed on Hensley's heels, and when she entered the study, breathing deeply of the cigar scent that made it feel like home, she squealed.

"Sebastian!" She raced to the monk, who stood in front of the hearth. Careful not to barrel into him, she gave him a solid hug, grateful to feel the strength of his arms around her. "It's so good to know you're all right."

Finn and Lando both shook the monk's hand as Hensley begged everyone to sit.

"I'm sorry I wasn't able to meet you at the monastery." Sebastian sat and moved his robes around, pulling a journal out of a pocket. "Beckworth told me Maire discovered the proper locations of the chronicles."

Finn nodded. "We assumed since Belato's ship sailed from Saint-Malo with rumors of heading to Southampton that Beckworth would try for Ipswich."

"Why did you assume that?" Hensley asked.

Finn shrugged. "He wouldn't be able to get the one in France, and his first instinct would be to go to Waverly before seeking you out. You're typically in London this time of year, so Ipswich made sense."

Hensley nodded. "And since Maire and Ethan aren't with you, I assume they headed north to Worcester?"

"That was the plan. You haven't heard from Ethan?"

Hensley shook his head. "You're the only word we've received."

"Not even Jamie?"

"No. Which is why Beckworth and Stella decided to move for Ipswich. We had no idea when you would return. We have confirmed the ship that carried our friends from France is now in Ipswich. It makes sense that Gemini is most likely there as well, though my men weren't able to confirm that. I fear it will be a difficult task to retrieve the chronicle. Using a small strike force seemed the best option. They travel with Morton and Lewelyn."

"I know them." Lando, who stood next to the door, moved toward the group. "I've worked with them before, they're excellent."

"But greatly outnumbered." Hensley took a glass of whiskey from Finn.

"Of course, we'll go," Finn said. "Who is this person with the chronicle?"

"Martin Smith, who follows his heritage's profession as a blacksmith."

"A blacksmith?" AJ had a hard time picturing how Sebastian came to know an English blacksmith. "That's different."

"He takes his faith very seriously. But I don't know how well he'd do under pressure." Sebastian mopped his forehead.

He couldn't say the word torture, even if that was what he was thinking. And Beckworth took Stella into that? What was he thinking? They all sat there like it was just another mission with the stones. Missions that always went wrong. Everyone acted like Stella did this type of thing for a living. Her temper rose quickly.

"Why did you let Stella go to Ipswich?" AJ's tone was as controlled as she could manage, considering the circumstances.

"It wasn't my decision." Hensley gave AJ a stern look, not willing to bow to her emotions.

Her irritation grew with her inability to cow him. "Then whose was it?"

He gave her one of those smiles that said she wasn't going to like the answer, and she closed her eyes when he said, "Stella's."

She drank the two fingers of whiskey Finn gave her then asked for a refill. The second one did the trick, and she relaxed, though her anxiety would return after food and a nap. But it would be enough to get her through the meeting before she could hold Finn and not let go.

Hensley gave them the plan he and Beckworth had developed. He didn't have to tell them the dozen different things that could go wrong.

Before they finished discussing when they would depart, shouts came from somewhere near the foyer. Boots raced down the hall. Finn and Lando stood, both reaching for their knives. Their pistols and swords had been stored in the duffels.

The door flew open as Fitz and Thomas stormed in, looking like they'd been riding non-stop for weeks. They looked exhausted and were breathing hard.

"An ambush. Maire and Ethan. No choice." Fitz huffed out the words. He was bent over, hands on knees, and she wondered if he'd run on foot part of the way.

"What happened?" Finn barked.

"There were too many." Fitz seemed to have gained some oxygen. "Gemini's men had us surrounded and weren't going to let us go. They wanted the chronicle and Maire."

"What happened? Get on with it." Finn's impatience flared, and AJ gripped his arm.

Fitz straightened, his breathing under control, and gave Finn an apologetic stare. "They jumped."

# 39

Beckworth sighed with relief when they came to the village two miles from Ipswich. All he wanted was to stable the horses, get a meal and a pint, and sleep until morning. It was too late to do anything else. To be honest, he had to get away from Stella.

The first two hours had been a litany of swearing and complaining, either at the horse or whoever seemed to crowd her space. By lunch, she was petting the horse, and he'd noticed the braided mane when he fed the gelding oats. The next two hours she spoke only to the horse. He couldn't understand half of it, but the parts he did hear made him smile.

He knew he'd acted like an ass that morning, and this was her payback. Morton and Lewelyn had dropped farther back, completely perplexed by what was clearly an issue between the two of them. And for all her stubbornness, she appealed to him even more. He understood her reason for stepping back, but he couldn't look at her that morning without remembering their evening. And at times, their situation frustrated him past reasoning.

Once the rooms were procured, the four found a corner in the inn's common room and ordered hot meals with mugs of cider and ale. Stella's mood had mellowed, probably from sheer exhaustion, but she had enough sass left to engage Morton and Lewelyn, who smiled for the first time since Beckworth had known him.

After dinner and a final review of their plans, everyone went to their rooms. He stared at the fire, tired but unable to sleep. After an hour, he dragged himself to bed and stared at the ceiling. Thirty minutes later, a soft tap woke him from a light doze. Before he could get up to investigate, his door opened then closed quietly.

He saw her form against the backdrop of the firelight, but it was her scent that hit him first. She must have brought the lavender soaps with her from London.

"Are you asleep?" Her whisper was barely loud enough for him to hear, though he was fully awake.

"No."

He waited to see what she wanted, forcing down his instant physical response to her. She hesitated, and he assumed she was building up her courage to ask whatever it was she wanted.

"I'm so exhausted, but every time I close my eyes, I'm waiting for someone to barge in the room and grab me."

Beckworth could have slapped himself. What had he been thinking? Of course, she'd be nervous. This was the first inn she'd slept in since her kidnapping from the boardinghouse in France.

"Come here." He patted the bed. "I'm clothed, and we'll sleep like we used to."

If he thought she was going to mull it over or state her list of requirements, he was wrong. It took her two steps to launch herself into bed, then she rolled over to watch the fire. He got up, added another log, then made her move over.

"I wanted to watch the fire."

"I know, luv, but that also puts you closer to the door."

"Of course. I guess I am tired." She scooted over to let him in.

"If it helps, I won't look at the fire, either." He turned toward her and didn't take offense when she rolled over to give him her back. He nestled as close as was proper for the two of them and shut his eyes. Sleep was quickly overtaking him, and he didn't miss the fact the reason for his restlessness was her being across the hall and not directly under his protection.

He vaguely heard her small voice before sleep fully took him.

"Thank you."

---

The next morning, Stella woke and stretched, then remembering where she was sprung up, rubbing her eyes. A new log in the hearth was fully engulfed, making the room almost too warm. Beckworth was nowhere to be seen, but her saddlebag had been moved to his room.

She'd barely finished washing her face when there was a knock.

"Are you up?" Beckworth's voice floated through the closed door.

Surprised he waited on the other side, she opened it and discovered why. He was burdened down by a heavy tray with a complete breakfast service. He dropped it on the table and the plates clattered together. She took a step forward in case she had to save the coffee.

"I thought you could use your sleep while Morton and Lewelyn went to find the blacksmith."

It didn't take them long to fall into the pattern they'd developed while on the run. He filled coffee cups while she moved extra eggs onto his plate and slid the cheese to hers.

"How long ago did they leave?"

"It's been almost two hours."

She frowned. "That seems too long."

"We'll give them another hour before we go looking."

"Both of us?" The original plan was for Stella to remain at the inn if Beckworth had to leave for any reason.

"After last night, it occurred to me it would be better if we stuck together."

"Thank you for that. Last night, I mean. I didn't think it would bother me, and it was foolish, but I don't think I would have slept at all."

He squeezed her hand. "There's nothing to apologize for. I should have thought of it myself, but so much has happened since that night in Saint-Malo."

She didn't think he referred to their nights together, though it was part of it. It had been a tumultuous journey since Saint-Malo, and they'd grown complacent during their stay at Hensley's.

They were fifteen minutes from leaving the inn for Ipswich when Hensley's men returned. They came directly to Beckworth's room when they didn't find them downstairs.

"From what the business owners on both sides of the blacksmith says, he's been gone for two days without a word." Morton delivered the unwelcome news as he picked at the leftovers. "It wasn't unusual for him to leave if he'd been called to a farm, but he would typically let them know if he was going to be gone for longer than a day in case any of his customers stopped in."

Afraid Morton might start licking the plates, Stella left them to get more food, coffee, and ale. When she returned with a young lad carrying a tray, she was pleased to find they had waited for her before completing their report.

Once the men were eating, Morton finished the bad news. "They were more concerned by the fact he left his forge burning. We checked the docks. The *Phoenix* is still in port, and we discovered a heavily guarded warehouse about three blocks from the ship.

Lewelyn, who didn't talk much, grunted. "They're sloppy. They don't rotate their guards properly, leaving gaps of five minutes at entry points, one of which is access to the roof."

"It might have been done on purpose," Beckworth suggested.

Both men nodded, but Morton responded. "Agreed, but we thought it was worth the risk, considering we didn't know what happened to the blacksmith."

"Or we didn't before going up to the roof." Lewelyn stuffed another roll in his mouth, his left leg bouncing as he played with one of Stella's swans, attempting to see how it was made.

She took the swan from him, slowly unfolded it until the paper laid flat, then refolded it with the same methodical pace so he could see each fold. His eyes lit up when she handed the swan back to him. "For good luck."

He grinned and stuffed the figure in his pocket.

"I take it they have the blacksmith?" Beckworth asked. He'd pushed his chair away from the table to face the door. Maybe someone had spotted Morton and Lewelyn and followed them back, or maybe he was as antsy as Stella was.

Morton nodded. "And it appears they've worked him over pretty well."

"So much for all that planning. What's the new one?" Stella, who nursed her coffee, folded another bird. Her leg bounced to match Lewelyn's increasing one.

"There's too many men for an extraction." Morton scratched his head. "We could bring in more men, but we'd need at least a dozen well-trained ones. We can send a message to Hensley and continue surveillance."

"How long will that take?" Stella dropped a half-folded swan. "Two to three days before we can get to him."

"I understand your concern. I have it as well, but this is most likely a trap." Beckworth ran his hands through his hair, a new behavior he'd started during their stay at Eleanor's. She knew she was partly to blame for it.

She nodded. "But what will more men do other than create a gun battle on the docks at Ipswich? Aren't there Royal Navy ships in port, or one of those British patrols?"

"The Royal Navy left earlier this morning. There's one British patrol, but it's on the other side of the docks, and they're mostly sailors, not mercenaries." Morton stood and walked to the small window in the corner that had a view of the street. "We might be able to create some type of distraction near their ship. That might pull enough men away for us to get in."

"We did something like that in Southampton." Beckworth turned his gaze on her. "Gemini will see it for what it is. Though if the ship is in danger, she wouldn't have a choice but to split her force, or she might have enough men at the ship to deal with the threat."

"Would they be that diligent at midnight?" Stella asked.

The three men stared at her. She shrugged. "I don't know how long they've been here, but it's been at least a week. Can she keep the men away from the pubs?"

"Somewhere around one or two would be better," Lewelyn said.

"And what about the chronicle? Do you think he gave it up?" Stella wanted to save the blacksmith. He was an innocent in all of this, but they couldn't take their eyes from the prize.

"Considering the condition he appears to be in, I wouldn't blame him for giving them the book." Morton gave Stella an apologetic glance. "Sorry, but they weren't playing games."

"They might have beaten it out of him, or maybe he said the wrong thing to the wrong person after too many ales," Beckworth said.

Morton scratched his chin. "There was a table with several

stacks of books. It's possible Gemini had the blacksmith's home and shop ransacked for any book the men could find."

"Which sounds like a trap to me." Stella had to admit Beckworth was right. "I would have expected the blacksmith to have hidden the chronicle. They might have taken all his books and when they didn't find the chronicle, they tortured him. If they did get the location from him, I doubt she'd leave it with the rest of the books."

Beckworth tapped his chin. "Or she left it with the rest of the books and is keeping it well guarded. She knows it will take more than a tortured blacksmith to lure us out."

"If she has the chronicle, it's either in the warehouse or on the ship." Lewelyn bit into an apple and wiped the juice from his chin.

"There's only one way to find out." Beckworth refilled the men's mugs with ale.

The three men glanced at each other, and she didn't like what passed between them. And once they laid out their idea, she hated it even more.

———

**B**eckworth stared at the warehouse from the roof of the building across the street. He and Stella had crept to the top two hours before dawn. The building was the same height as the warehouse, and he used a spyglass to search for men on the other roof. He didn't see anyone. They could be asleep. He'd be foolish to think Gemini wouldn't post someone on the roof, but there hadn't been anyone on this one.

Stella walked the perimeter before focusing on the north side that faced the warehouse and the south side that faced the docks. She held a rifle, and every few steps, she lifted it and tested her aim. Or perhaps she was checking to see if she had enough light to spot anyone.

They had the light of the quarter moon, which was good and bad. It was bright enough to see Gemini's men, but in turn, they could be spotted as well. There were plenty of shadows to hide in, which still favored both sides.

When Stella returned to where he stood, he reviewed the plan. "From what Morton said, they use this main door, which makes sense since it's the most direct route to the docks, but there's a door on the other side as well. That's the one I'll go through."

She nodded.

"If anyone comes in or out of the door, leave them be. Only shoot after Morton creates the distraction, then pick off whoever you can. Don't shoot more than once from any one spot or they'll be able to pinpoint your location."

She nodded again.

"Once I have the blacksmith, and with any luck the chronicle, I'll drop him off at the church the next block over, then meet you at the livery. You have exactly fifteen minutes after the distraction begins. No more than that. Even with you moving around, it won't take them long to figure out where the shots are coming from."

When she nodded the third time, he turned her to him. "Are you listening to me?"

She stared up at him with squinted eyes. She was annoyed. At least she wasn't ignoring him.

"I heard you fine. As usual, this is the fourth time you've reviewed the plan in the last hour." She shrugged off the hand he placed on her shoulder. "I'm not an imbecile."

He snorted. "No. And you know that's not the point. The more you hear the plan, and the more you go over it in your head, the more automatic it will become. You can't waste precious time trying to remember the next step once all hell breaks loose."

She took a deep breath and let it out slowly. "Why do you have to go in alone? Wouldn't it be better with two?"

He smiled and pulled her to him, forcing her to look up. He held her gaze and ran his knuckles over her cheek before fingering a lock of her hair. "We've been over this. If you had any skill with a dagger or sword, I'd take you with. But your special talent with a rifle puts you on this roof. It's as simple as that."

Her eyes shined in the moonlight. "So you'd take AJ in if she were here?"

He laughed. "If I didn't need her skill with the bow, then yes. She's deadly with a dagger."

Her head tilted to one side, and she gave him a long look. "That makes sense." She placed a hand on his cheek. "Don't get killed."

"Don't shoot me coming out the warehouse in case I have to come out the front door."

She gave him one of her not-so-innocent smiles. "I thought you said you trusted my talents."

His grin became more of a leer. "I appreciate all your skills."

She blushed, which was what he'd been aiming for.

"Just keep your wits about you. Keep one rifle at each point then just duck and run back and forth."

"I've got it. Now get in place. There's only a few minutes before Lewelyn lights the first torch."

Beckworth stared at her a moment longer then nodded. He was halfway to the ladder on the other side of the building when she grabbed his jacket. Then she was in his arms. Her kiss wasn't sweet. It was demanding and thorough, and he let himself go for just a moment. She felt so right in his arms, but this wasn't the time, and their ending wasn't going to be any different.

They both pulled back reluctantly. Then he turned away,

running for the ladder, knowing they'd lost a minute or two, and he needed to be in place before the chaos erupted.

———

S tella ran to the ladder as soon as Beckworth disappeared over the side. He moved swiftly, jumping the last few feet after he'd searched the darkness. Then he was gone behind a building that would shield him from notice until he reached the entry point into the warehouse.

After doing her own search of the street below, she walked the perimeter of the building, the two rifles laying at her predetermined shooting points. There were only two ways up to the roof. The ladder Beckworth had just used, and the stairs that led to the interior.

They'd used those stairs to get to the roof after Beckworth familiarized her with the building. It was a warehouse similar to the one Gemini was using. At least, that's what Morton said, which was good because it gave Beckworth an idea of what he'd be walking into.

The main floor was mostly open space, currently half-filled with cargo. From what Beckworth told her, the warehouses were mostly holding facilities for shipments going out or coming in. This one had a workshop for repairs. There was also a string of rooms that ran along one side.

The second floor didn't cover the entire warehouse. There were offices along one side and a six-foot-wide catwalk that ran the other three sides. Two staircases, one at each end of the building, provided access to the second floor. An additional staircase led to the roof.

Their biggest concern was how many men would be bunking in the second-floor offices, or whether they were all staying on the main floor. Morton wasn't able to determine that, so Beckworth would have to make adjustments as needed. Something Morton and Lewelyn agreed was one of Beckworth's natural talents. She'd seen those talents in action. Let them be enough this time.

Once she'd scanned the perimeter, she double-checked the rifles to ensure they were primed. She looked out over the other buildings to the docks where the tips of masts stood out in the soft moonlight. Her stomach grumbled as a response to her churning emotions. Her nerves were wrecked, fear for Beckworth making her antsy. She walked the roof one more time before grabbing a rifle and positioning herself on the side of the building that faced the main door of the warehouse.

She gripped the rifle tight and waited. It wasn't one of her better talents.

# 40

After dropping from the roof ladder and racing around a building, Beckworth slipped behind a stack of crates and waited. A minute later, two men stumbled by, both of them weaving. Sailors returning to the docks after a long night at a pub. Once they were out of sight, he hurried to the warehouse, stopping to search for guards. Satisfied there weren't any, he crept toward the back door of the warehouse. It appeared closed, but when he stepped up to it, someone had left it open a few inches. Whether it was always open, someone got careless, or it was part of their trap, he couldn't be sure, and he didn't have time to worry over it. He slowly squeezed through without making a sound.

He tiptoed to a spot along the wall and waited for his eyes to adjust to the darkness. Moonlight leaked through the small bank of windows above the second floor, giving off enough ambient light to make his task easier. He listened, but the building was quiet. Morton said the blacksmith would be in the center of the room. His legs and arms had been tied to a chair, and he'd been beaten. There was no telling if the man would be able to walk, or he'd have to carry him. Best to anticipate the worst case.

The plan was to wait for the diversion before moving inside, but he wanted to know where everyone was. He wasn't fond of surprises. He moved swiftly along the wall of rooms. The first couple were empty. The last two had three bedrolls in each, and only one appeared occupied. He backtracked, this time his focus turned to the main floor.

The blacksmith was where Morton said he'd be. His head hung toward his chest. He was either unconscious, asleep, or dead. Two men guarded him. Neither appeared to be awake, but were probably light sleepers.

He crossed the expanse of room, sticking to the shadows, and slowly climbed the stairs. There was no one on the landing. He crept to the first door, which was open, and he peered inside. No guards or bedrolls. He glanced down the walkway, noted the second door was closed, and stepped inside the first room.

Little light filtered through the open door, but it was enough for him to see the array of pillage stacked on the two long tables. He walked the length of each table, spotting swords, daggers, coin purses, a box with jewelry, stacks of books, and other odds and ends. Who were they stealing from, and was this how Gemini financed the men and a ship? Even if they spent an entire month looting, he didn't think it enough to finance a long-term mission.

Once he'd checked both tables, he went back to the stack of books. Nothing. He walked the rest of the room. It was mostly crates with a single desk and chair. Then he discovered a small table tucked between two barrels. There was a second chair, an unlit lamp, a quill and inkpot, and a book.

Heart racing, he stepped closer. It was the right size. The book was open, but the writing was too small to make out details in the available light, though the words didn't appear to be English. He closed the book and reopened to the first page. *The Third Chronicle* was written across the top in Celtic. Sebastian had reviewed the wording with him before he left for Ipswich. A canvas bag lay next to it, and he shoved the book inside, then tucked it under his arm before moving back to the staircase. He was halfway down when the first explosion rocked the night.

---

Finn slowed his horse as Ipswich came into view. After their meeting with Hensley, they'd cleaned up, eaten a hearty meal, and fell into a restless sleep. He'd held AJ, as much for himself as for her. He had a bad feeling—they both did—and it didn't make the miles from London to Ipswich any easier. The closer they got to the city, the weight of oppression bore down on him.

Lando, Fitz, Thomas, along with five of his uninjured men, and two of Hensley's rode with them. Those that survived the ambush hadn't gotten much sleep. But no one complained when they'd mounted fresh horses. With any luck, they'd make Ipswich before first light and wouldn't be too late.

It was an hour before dawn when they reached the inn where Beckworth and Stella were supposed to be staying. Finn apologized to the innkeeper when he woke him, and handed him several coins, only to discover the team had left late the previous evening.

Now, as they approached Ipswich, Finn considered where the group might have gone. There was one place to start, and he led the group toward the blacksmith shop.

Lando walked through the building and stopped at the forge. "The fire has been out a day, maybe two. The ash is still warm."

Fitz came out of a door that led to the living area. "There was a pot in the hearth with stew in it. It's been cold for some time. There's a bookshelf but no books."

"Did he leave on this own?" Thomas asked. He searched the

floor and the worktable. "It's hard to tell if there was a struggle without knowing how clean he kept his workroom."

"Or he got spooked and left. Maybe Beckworth took him someplace safe." AJ paced, her head was down, and she mumbled to herself. She didn't get that way often, but she was absorbing too much information that provided no answers. This was more than her journalist instincts kicking in. It was a pattern she'd developed over the last six months. She was working through various scenarios, determining which made the most sense, barely hearing those around her. He was rubbing off on her, and he wasn't sure it was a good thing.

He stepped into her path and put an arm around her shoulder. "The fire's been cold for a while. Longer than today."

She nodded, but her mind was still at work.

"We need to check the docks." Finn walked AJ back to her horse and motioned for her to mount.

"Let's split up. Four teams." Thomas pointed at the men, dividing them into groups of three. "This is a scout mission only. Stay out of sight. We're looking for Belato's ship or our missing team members."

"Where do we meet up?" Fitz asked.

"There's a church two blocks west of the docks." Finn glanced at the men. "We'll meet behind it. If you discover a situation where you can't get to the church, find a secure spot, and we'll find you."

Once the other teams had ridden off, Finn took AJ's hand. "Listen to me." He squeezed her hand until her head jerked up. Her eyes were red, but they were dry. "You need to be with us. Stella needs you to be with us." She nodded but without much enthusiasm. She was frustrated, angry, and stressed. He wouldn't allow her to shut down.

He kept hold of her hand, and after a few minutes, with Thomas's man waiting patiently, he felt her squeeze back. Her gaze was bright with rage, but it wasn't directed at him. He'd seen it before, but he wasn't able to determine the point when her anger had turned to fury. Instead of worrying about her not paying attention, he'd have to worry she'd do something she'd regret later. At least he was familiar with that emotion.

---

W hen the sound of the explosion and a bright light came from the docks, Beckworth missed the next step but caught himself.

A man stumbled from the ground-floor office. He glanced around and yelled, "What the hell!" Then he raced out the door.

Beckworth ran toward the two men guarding the blacksmith, never slowing as the two men jumped from their chairs. He pulled his dagger, a distinct disadvantage to the men's swords, and took the first one while he still swayed, stabbing him in the neck.

After he pulled the dagger out, and with two quick steps and a twist to his right, he sliced the throat of the second man as he lifted his sword above his head. He ducked as the man's arm came down, and almost toppled when the flat side of the blade hit the edge of his shoulder.

He glanced up in time to see Gemini reaching the bars of the second-floor landing. She stared down at the disarray but hadn't seen him yet. Gaines strode up behind her.

He moved to the blacksmith and cut the ropes at his legs. When his legs fell stiffly to the side, he pushed up the blacksmith's head, but it was already frozen in death. They'd been too late. The man had been killed several hours ago, probably not long after Morton and Lewelyn had been there. He'd been an innocent.

The men guarding him had been a trap all along but had been caught napping.

The stomping of boots on stairs snapped him out of his thoughts. The sound of shots came from the street. Stella performing her part.

He was almost to the back door, the sack still under his arm, when a second explosion, this time in the direction he was running, went off. The charge wasn't supposed to create flying debris, but he stopped long enough to check. The diversion had been perfect—enough to scare and disrupt. The first explosion would be keeping the crew of the *Phoenix* quite busy, as well as the other ships as men were startled from sleep.

He pushed his way out the door, then raced for the livery, keeping an eye behind him to make sure he wasn't followed. When more gunfire erupted, he second-guessed waiting for Stella. His brain said wait, but his gut said go. He followed the path they'd discussed over and over to the church in case she had to hide from Gemini's men. Not spotting her anywhere, he ran for the warehouse and climbed the ladder to the roof, and once on top, discovered he was too late. He ran the perimeter of the building, scanning the streets below as he ran. The rifles were gone.

Maybe she'd taken a different route to avoid Gemini's men. He was turning for the ladder when a commotion caught his eye. Two men were dragging a kicking whirlwind, her hair whipping around as she appeared to be—biting them?

He surveyed the area. Men were everywhere. He'd never get to her without at least Morton or Lewelyn, but they'd be making their way to the second meeting point, and there wasn't time to find them. There was no way in hell they were going to take Stella without him.

He flew down the ladder and raced after the men, keeping to the shadows as best he could. Men coming from the docks were headed for the warehouse. Only a few were headed toward the docks, so he picked an alley between buildings to make up time.

By the time he reached the docks and the *Phoenix*, which was smoking, the flames already extinguished, he was too late again.

Gemini and Gaines waited at the bottom of the gangplank. Two men dragged Stella to face them, then forced her to her knees. Each man leaned a hand on her shoulders to keep her down. She must have spit because Gaines stepped back and wiped his jacket. Gemini stepped up, grabbed her by the hair, and slapped her. It took the struggle out of her, but she held her head high, always defiant.

He was ready to step out, when Gemini lifted her head and scanned the area.

"Teddy!"

The voices of the men grew silent. The only shouts came from the crew as they worked to fix the damage to the ship. Sailors had returned to the other ships, most likely persuaded by Gemini's men.

"You must admit, it's time to allow me to call you that." Gemini squinted as if she might see him, but she glanced in the wrong direction. "You know how much I want to kill this bitch, right?"

A coldness swept over him. The only thing that held him still was the knowledge she'd rather have the chronicle.

She tapped her boot for a minute then huffed. "If you want to save her, come out, and give me the chronicle."

He considered his options. If he said something, her men would be on him. He surveyed his surroundings, identifying the best path to take once he responded. His attention was snagged when he turned back to Gemini. Two men, ducking low, scurried behind a wagon. He'd know the big man anywhere. Lando. That meant AJ and Finn would be close. There were no guarantees they had more of the team with them. It wouldn't matter. They'd still be outnumbered and would suffer fatalities. But there was one way to keep that from happening.

Taking a chance that AJ and Finn were close, he stepped out of the shadows and walked toward Gemini. He held his right arm out to show he didn't have a weapon. The book was still tucked under his arm in plain view. "I think a trade is in order."

"I'm not talking about a trade. Can't you see you have no choice?" Gemini gave him a sterling smile.

"It's a simple trade. The chronicle for the woman before you."

"Come now, Teddy, you're smarter than that."

"First, I don't remember allowing you to call me Teddy. My name is Beckworth. Second..." Good Lord, he was ticking off a list like Stella. "I don't think you counted correctly. When you counted the woman and myself, did you add in the two men on the rooftops? They have rifles aimed at you and Gaines. And lastly, while I'd be fine if they hiccupped and accidentally fired, your death would only rile up these men, which would create fatalities on both sides—should you care."

Gemini couldn't help glancing to the roofs, but there were too many shadows for her to discern the truth. The two men in front of her turned to look, as did Stella. But rather than lift her gaze, she stared straight at him. Her eyes glistened in the moonlight, but he was too far away to see if tears had fallen. Her chin was still upturned.

He was taking a risk with this next step and glanced toward the wagon. This time he saw Lando, who gave him a signal. He sighed with relief. They'd brought more men.

"Here's the thing, luv. I have the advantage because the chronicle is the only thing of value here. Not me, and certainly not that woman. She's not AJ Murphy."

Gemini stared at him, then down at Stella, and burst out

with a hearty laugh. "What game is this? She looks just like the little bird Gaines brought me."

"Oh, she is that same woman." When Gemini appeared confused, his smile broadened. "The problem is, Gaines kidnapped the wrong woman. AJ and Finn were away on a sail. Stella stopped by to water the flowers. That's something they do in the future. She's an innocent. And haven't you killed enough innocents already?"

Gemini shook her head and glared at Gaines, who mumbled something he couldn't hear. Most likely pleading his case. He almost had her, but she needed more.

"Didn't you wonder why the rumors about AJ—her skill with a dagger and bow, her ability to ride a horse, her general ability to fit in—didn't suit with the woman before you?"

Her eyes widened. Now she believed.

"We just want her back." He hoped that hadn't been a step too far.

Gemini's smile returned. "So, you played me from the beginning, or perhaps from the moment you saw my captive." She turned to Gaines. "See why he's so dangerous." She swung back to Beckworth. "I'll trade this woman, who might not be Murphy's woman but is certainly a pain in my backside, for the chronicle and you."

Beckworth stilled. He should have known it would come to this, or maybe he had. If he tried to barter, would Gemini simply kill Stella, then take him and the chronicle anyway? This required a sacrifice.

He glanced at Stella, who was shaking her head no. Now he saw the tears and her fierce determination. Her unspoken words rang in his ears that she'd kick his ass, assuming they'd ever see each other again.

When he glanced at Gemini, he understood she'd caught the exchange with Stella. Her smile turned wicked.

"Come now, Teddy. We'll find someone to keep you warm on these chilly nights. Someone a bit more pliable. Is it a deal?"

It wasn't even worth the question. He'd do anything to keep Stella safe. He stepped forward, keeping his right arm out. When he'd gotten a few feet from them, his arms were grabbed from behind. The bag fell to the ground.

"Be careful, you fool. Bring me that," Gemini snapped.

She pulled out the chronicle, looked inside, then nodded, stuffing it back in the bag. "Let her go."

"Gemini?" Gaines protested.

She turned on him. "All this time, the wrong woman." He stepped back. Gemini snapped at the two men, who still restrained Stella. "I said let her go, or is discipline required?"

They immediately stepped back, and Stella didn't hesitate to rise to her feet. When she tried to go to him, a man blocked her path, shaking his head.

Beckworth had to say something, but Gemini couldn't know how important she was to him. He gave Stella a wink. "Sorry, luv. It was fun while it lasted, but the end was bound to catch up with us sooner or later."

Out of nowhere, Fitz was there, hands raised. He looked at Gemini. "I'm just here for the woman."

Gemini smiled at him. "Fitz. I'm surprised to find you here." She glanced at Beckworth. "Or maybe I'm not." She shooed him away with her hand. "Go. Go. You have a free pass out of town. But don't return."

Gaines whistled and yelled up to the ship. "Tell the captain to prepare sail. We leave now."

Men scurried to the ship, and the last Beckworth saw of Stella was Fitz pulling her away until she disappeared into the sea of men. Her eyes had been filled with regret, irritation, and an emotion he didn't want to name. Not now.

---

This couldn't be happening. Stella struggled against the man holding her. Gemini called him Fitz. If that were true, AJ and Finn must be close. They had time to get to Beckworth.

She was still kicking herself that Gemini's men had caught her. When the first explosion went off, she nicked a man running out of the warehouse, who'd stumbled into a second man. She'd only fired a flintlock rifle a couple of times, and she hadn't had the time to fine-tune her accuracy. When she ran to the other station, she fired at the group coming up from the docks. It stopped them momentarily while she ran back to the other station and reloaded the rifle as she surveyed the street. No one was leaving the warehouse. Instead of waiting for someone, she ran back and carefully chose her target from the men running from the dock. She selected one in the front, and when the shot landed, he stumbled, forcing those behind him to stumble over the falling body. She took two more shots, then picked up the rifles and made for the stairs.

She'd run a block from the warehouse, when a man sprang out from an alley and grabbed her. She hadn't expected anyone to come from this side of town. He must have been at a pub and been in the right place at the wrong time. He was a big man; otherwise, she could have taken him. When the second man showed up, she cursed her lousy luck. If she got out of this, she'd demand a dagger and speed training course on how to use it.

When the second explosion went off, she almost got away, but the big man was too quick. She kicked and bit all the way to the docks. Her only satisfaction was their swearing when she landed a few good blows and tasted blood from one of her bites. She almost cried when they dragged her in front of Gemini and Big and Tall. But she'd be damned if they saw her fear.

The moment Beckworth stepped out of the shadows, she could tell she wouldn't like his plan. She'd never been truly afraid for her life until that moment when she gazed into Gemini's eyes and saw nothing but anger and madness. She had to remind herself that this woman thought she'd killed her lover. That might make anyone a bit mad.

Then he gave up the ruse and admitted she wasn't AJ. She'd expected Gemini to shoot her right then and there. But the crazy woman had lost interest in her. She pinned her focus on her next conquest—Beckworth. Her assurance there would be someone to warm his bed grated on Stella's last nerve. She'd bet her life savings that Gemini was thinking of herself in that scenario. And who's the bitch now?

Fitz hadn't dragged her far by the time most of Gemini's men passed by them on the way to the ship. But Gemini, Gaines, and Beckworth, along with his two guards, hadn't moved.

Beckworth kept his head down. He'd said his goodbyes. And even though his words were meant to sting, she knew they were for Gemini's benefit. He couldn't fool her. It had taken some time, but she could read him now. And when she'd stared into those cornflower-blue eyes, the truth was there for anyone to see, whoever cared to look.

They turned as a group toward the gangplank while Stella plucked at Fitz's grip to no avail. Big and Tall moved slower until he was behind Beckworth. Then Stella saw it—the two-by-four he held in his hands. Within another blink, the two men stepped aside as the makeshift bat was swung full force, hitting Beckworth in the back.

He fell.

She screamed.

The two-by-four was coming down again when Gemini turned and yelled at Big and Tall.

"No. No. No." Stella couldn't stop screaming as the word

repeated over and over. Were they killing him? She'd see them all in hell. Then the two men grasped Beckworth under his arms and lifted him. His head lolled to one side, his beautiful ash-blond hair darkened with blood.

She couldn't stop shrieking and lunging. Then other arms held her.

"Hush, Stella. It will be all right." Finn's voice should have comforted her, but it didn't.

"Stella, honey. We're here. It will be okay. You need to calm down."

AJ. Finally. Where the hell had they been? Why didn't they stop this?

They pulled her back inside a warehouse that fronted the docks. It smelled of old hay and manure, and probably held live-stock until the ships were ready for them. But all she saw was Beckworth falling. That bat would have done a lot of damage. And his head? Suddenly she couldn't see anything through the blur of tears.

"I can't breathe." Her struggles increased.

"Let her go." AJ was at her side when she dropped to the ground.

She sucked in air, and she excepted the burn as oxygen rushed in.

"Step back and give her more room. She's not going anywhere." AJ hadn't moved away, but didn't touch her.

Their words were nothing more than angry buzzing. She watched the ship as it moved away from the dock, then the wind filled the sails, and the ship caught the tide.

When silence descended, Stella glanced up to see Lando had joined the group as well as other men she didn't know.

Finn bent down and touched her elbow. "Let's get you up."

She stood, then AJ's arms were around her. "We'll take you back to Hensley's, then send you home."

Stella pushed away from AJ. She took several more steps until she'd put distance between her and the rest of them, most of them strangers. Her voice held the edge of a royally pissed-off and heartbroken woman. "I'm not going anywhere."

"We can't go with you." AJ didn't seem to understand. "We have to stay to gather the rest of the chronicles, but you need to go home. You've been through enough."

Stella straightened, her shoulders back, her chin raised. "Like I said. I'm not going anywhere." She pointed out to sea. "We're going to find Beckworth and bring him home."

She made the mistake of glancing at Finn, who gave her such a sad smile she almost choked from the raw emotion that stormed through her.

*He is not dead. He is not dead. He is not dead.*

It seemed she had a new mantra. She glared them down, no doubt looking as nutty as Gemini. "I don't care if you help or not. Make your own choice. But I'm getting Beckworth back. Gemini can't hide forever." When everyone just stared at her, she looked at Finn before pinning AJ with her stubbornness. "You know I can't."

AJ appeared confused. "I don't understand."

She gave Finn a quick glance. "I can't leave him without knowing he's safe." And dammit, this wasn't time for tears. She blinked rapidly, but they still fell.

Then AJ's gaze widened. "Oh, Stella." She ran to Stella and hugged her. "I'm so sorry."

Stella turned with AJ to watch the ship move farther away, so close yet it might as well be miles. "I can't leave him. He saved me. I have to save him."

AJ leaned her head against Stella's. "We'll find him, honey. I promise. It's what we do."

Thank You for Reading!

---

The stakes have escalated and no one can stop the one woman who won't let anyone stand in her way to save Beckworth.

**The Book of Stones**
**The Mórdha Stone Chronicles - Book 9**

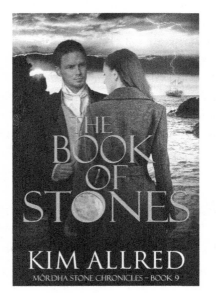

E veryone believes Beckworth, the Viscount of Waverly, to be a man with no regrets because he's hidden the pain of who he'd become when trying to win his father's favor.

Stella Caldway sees the real man behind the mask—a loyal

man who would drop anything to help a friend in need. His only fault lay in seeking acceptance from a man who didn't possess the ability to give it.

When he's taken, Stella is gripped with guilt, and she'll do whatever it takes to find him and bring him home.

But Gemini's game plan takes an unexpected twist. Teams from two different worlds come together to thwart her end game in an attempt to put the secrets of *The Book of Stones* to rest— once and for all.

Buy Now

———

Keep reading for a preview from *The Book of Stones*

———

Enjoy!

# BOOK OF STONES
## CHAPTER ONE

*England - 1805*

The ride from Ipswich to London was painful, numbing, and unforgettable. Stella Caldway, a woman out of time, seemed more isolated than she'd ever been. Her horse followed the one in front of her, keeping pace without having to do much thinking other than not falling off the horse. Not nearly stimulating enough to stop the images from bombarding her—kneeling in front of Gemini, Beckworth giving himself up for her, the two-by-four as it came down on his back, then again on his head, him falling before being dragged off. It was a manic reel that played over and over, her own personal nightmare.

For the first several miles, she followed Morton and Lewelyn, who, from what she'd gathered, had returned to the warehouse and then the docks when she and Beckworth never arrived at the meeting place. They said nothing. What was there to say?

Her gaze kept falling on Beckworth's riderless horse that trailed behind Lewelyn's horse. The sight a constant reminder of her failure. If she'd paid more attention when running for the meeting spot. If she'd been able to get out of the man's grasp before the second one arrived. If. If. If. Unable to stand it anymore, she kicked her horse faster until she rode next to them and asked if they couldn't ride ahead and let Hensley know they were coming.

"Finn already sent Fitz ahead." Then Morton noticed her staring at Beckworth's horse, and she caught Lewelyn's nod. Morton squeezed her hand. "Of course. We'll be waiting for you." And without so much as a nod in Finn's direction, they took off.

If Finn wondered about the exchange, he never said a word. AJ rode alongside her for a while, but Stella couldn't look at her. She finally understood the wordless days AJ had spent on the back deck of the inn, staring out to sea, wondering why Finn hadn't followed them home. Had she spent those days kicking herself for leaving or not doing more?

When the sight of London appeared, the city still several miles away, she didn't see it with the same excitement as that first time on the knoll. Her chest ached, remembering how Beckworth had waited patiently, watching her emotions as she'd taken it all in. He'd wanted to hear her first impressions.

The city didn't look the same. Instead of the bustling metropolis she'd originally seen, now she only saw a monstrosity harboring the poor and sick while the rich went to their parties. It was wrong to be looking at it now without him. She closed her eyes. He couldn't be dead. Gemini had plans for him. If there was only one thing she was grateful for, it was the spiteful woman's personal interest in him. That alone would keep him alive—for now.

When they reached Hensley's manor, Finn helped her off the horse, and AJ wrapped an arm around her as they trudged up the steps. There wasn't a happy greeting with Mary running down the steps, though a couple of footmen arrived to collect bags, and stable boys took the horses.

Mary waited just inside the door and took Stella from AJ, clucking at her friend. "You've had your own harrowing journey. You have to take care of yourself before you can take care of others."

Then Finn pulled AJ away as Mary guided Stella to her room, where Sarah waited with a bath.

"I'll have food brought up. Sarah has strict orders to make sure you eat something. What would Teddy think if you're nothing but a mere shadow of yourself when he returns?"

Though she didn't respond to Mary's words, they nestled in the back of her mind, knowing she was right. But as she'd always told AJ, everyone deserved a pity party, and she sure as hell earned this one. And if it lasted more than a day, they'd have to deal with it.

Sarah was an angel who pampered her to a point. She took Mary's orders quite seriously and sat on the bed as she coaxed Stella to finish the light meal. Fortunately, neither she nor Mary forgot Stella's penchant for coffee. There was always a fresh carafe provided until shortly after lunch, when Sarah replaced it with a bottle of wine. These women were too good to her and more than she deserved.

AJ watched Stella stumble up the stairs. In all the time she'd known her, she was typically upbeat. She had her moods, mostly an overload from her clients, and she'd disappear into her garden. It would be a day, sometimes two, before Stella rejoined the world. But she could count on one hand and, quite frankly, a couple of fingers when Stella had been upset over breaking it off with a man. It was always Stella that walked away—all for solid reasons—but she took each of them to heart.

All the time she'd worried about Beckworth watching out for Stella, she'd never imagined them becoming that close. She tilted her head as Stella disappeared down the second-floor hall. It was obvi

ous she had strong feelings for him. They'd been on the run for a long time which might put them in intimate settings. The question was how long their relationship—or whatever it was— had been going on.

Beckworth would never take advantage of Stella. Not without the knowledge that either she or Finn would kick his ass. But this wasn't the time to ask. Stella had disengaged from the world, and something told her it was going to take more than a day's worth of pity party to come out of this one.

Finn put an arm around her shoulder. "Let's go to the study. Hensley will want to debrief. You know there's nothing you can do for her now."

"I know. It just wasn't the homecoming I was expecting."

He kissed the top of her head. "I know. We'll work it out."

Hensley was already behind his desk while Sebastian sat by the hearth, staring into the fire. Morton and Lewelyn stood against the wall near Lando, and Fitz sat on the floor in a corner. Thomas pulled two chairs over for them.

Hensley wasted no time. "What happened?" He looked at his two men to start the replay. Morton gave a detailed report from when they left London to their role in setting the diversions to give Beckworth time to sneak into the warehouse. After setting their charges, they went to the livery, which was their second meeting point. They were to arrange for a wagon in case the smithy needed to be transported to London for his injuries. Lewelyn had a bad feeling, so they'd run to the church where Stella and Beckworth were to take the smithy if his injuries could be treated locally. When no one was there, they followed the most likely route to the docks in time to see Beckworth fall.

Finn took over and gave their account of going to the blacksmith's shop. The smithy hadn't been there for a couple of days, and they found his body in the warehouse after the *Phoenix* had set sail. "We didn't want to leave him there, so we contacted the local constable."

"We told him we'd been looking at warehouses available to store cargo." Thomas looked exhausted. He'd been racing from one city to another since leaving Bransford and dealt with a harrowing ambush that took one of his men. Two others were in upstairs guest rooms, healing from their injuries. "The constable had been concerned when he heard of the smithy's strange disappearance and was genuinely upset to discover he'd been tortured so close to home."

"He'll never get the answers he wants," Finn said. AJ stroked his arm, remembering her inability to look at the man's body, and knew Finn had found it difficult. They all had. "The man was a loner, and though he'd been a devout man, the constable knows we all have a history. And this time, his past caught up with him."

"He was a good man," Sebastian said from his seat by the fire, never turning away from the flames. "Your story wasn't far from the truth. He had a troubled childhood and ran with the wrong crowd until a few years before I met him in London. He was visiting his mother, who'd been sick and didn't recover. He'd turned to the church for salvation. I never thought he'd give his life for the chronicle."

"I'm not sure it would have mattered if he'd given them the chronicle the minute they stepped into the smithy," Lando said. "They somehow discovered he had the book. Gemini had been in Ipswich a long time, and she had plenty of men to scour the area. She knew we'd be coming for it and used the smithy to lure us in. And it worked."

"The smithy was most likely past saving when we first saw him in the warehouse, but he was heavily guarded." Morton's remorse was plain to see, as was Lewelyn's, but they were most likely blaming themselves for the loss of Beckworth. "Our plan was solid. Only Stella can tell us what happened once the diversion started."

"And I expect that will take some time to get from her." Hensley tapped his desk as he stared down at it.

"Once we made it to the docks, Stella was on her knees in front of Gemini and Gaines." Finn continued with his report. "I can see why men fall for Gemini's guise. She's a beautiful woman but hard as nails from what little I heard. There were too many men for us to do anything, and it was sheer luck we got as close as we did. We were all surprised when Beckworth walked out of the shadows with the chronicle, ready to trade it for Stella."

"Do you think he knew I had a man on the roof?" Thomas asked.

Finn shrugged. "I think he was bluffing, though he'd seen Lando and must have known we had more men. He probably guessed we didn't have as many as we needed to make a difference. Thomas's man had orders to take out either Gemini or Gaines or whoever threatened Stella. But it would have been a bloody scene if fighting had started."

Hensley nodded. "Which is why Beckworth suggested the trade. He must have known Gemini could have easily walked away with both him and Stella."

"He blew her cover." Finn tapped his finger on the armrest, his brows furrowed. "He wanted to remove Gemini's need for her since she would no longer be a valuable trade for the Heart

Stone. But in doing that, Stella became collateral damage. He traded himself for her safety."

AJ had been holding it together up to that point. All the time they'd been chasing Stella and Beckworth, she'd been worried that no one would look out for her when it truly mattered. To put their own life on the line for her. Beckworth was a good friend, a trusted friend. Yet, when he gave himself up for Stella, she'd known then he was a better man than she ever gave him credit. She would never have guessed something deeper might have developed between them.

Was their unique relationship the simple fact of him rescuing her in the first place? Perhaps some reverse form of Stockholm syndrome. She'd have to wait until Stella was in a place to discuss it. One thing was for certain, something serious happened if Stella refused to go home.

AJ vaguely listened to the plan, which was nothing more than sending men to watch the coast to see if they could find the *Phoenix*. All bets were on Southampton or back to France and the monastery.

Until they knew more, her focus would be set squarely on Stella. Then another thought came to mind. Stella and Beckworth had been in London for several days before leaving for Ipswich. If anyone knew what went on in this house, it would be Mary.

# BOOK OF STONES
## CHAPTER TWO

*Baywood, Oregon - current day*

Maire desperately wanted to grab her stomach, but she clutched the chronicle to her chest with one arm and held tightly to Ethan with the other. The duffel over her shoulder weighed heavy and threatened to topple her over.

She kept her eyes shut tight in an attempt to ward off the blinding light and grimaced against her need to vomit. Her last thought before she was pitched aside was whether the books held any advice to make the time jumps smoother.

She hit something so hard her teeth rattled and vaguely remembered the duffel. Ethan let go of her hand, and she immediately clasped her stomach and rolled over, the strap of the duffel slipping off her shoulder. All she did was gag, her stomach still twisted in knots. She hadn't eaten anything since early that morning in Stokenchurch, and it had only been cheese and bread. There wasn't anything left to throw up.

Then she remembered the ambush and their need to jump.

She rested her forehead on the wooden dock, hoping their gamble had been worth it and that Fitz, Thomas, and the men found safety. In a frantic movement, she searched for the chronicle and thanked the heavens when her hand touched it. It took a minute while her eyes adjusted to the natural light of the sun rather than the intense whiteness of the jump.

She reached out for Ethan, who lay on the dock motionless. That wasn't right. She crawled to him. "Ethan? Ethan? What's wrong?"

He was on his side, the duffel still against his back, acting as a prop to keep him upright. She pulled the duffel from him, and he fell onto his back.

That's when she saw the blood.

## THANK YOU FOR READING!

I sincerely hope you enjoyed a glimpse of *The Book of Stones*. Don't miss the exciting conclusion to *The Mórdha Stone Chronicles*.

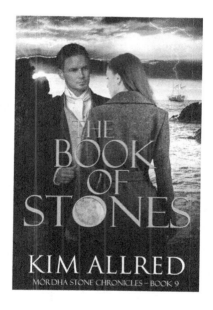

Buy Link

If you're interested in other stories written by me, you might enjoy my new series, *Of Blood & Dreams*, a paranormal romantic suspense series. A touch of mystery...with just a pinch of spice.

*Seduction in Blood*
*Of Blood and Dreams - Book 1*

*A thief. A vamp. A walk on the wild side.*

Cressa Langtry is the best cat burglar on the west coast. But she owes a large debt to the wrong kind of people. Her only way clear is to steal something for the city's notorious and ancient vampire – Devon Trelane.

Devon Trelane can't forgive the one man who cost him a seat on the Council. Luckily, a thief has fallen into his lap. A woman with the skills he requires to take down his greatest enemy.

There's only one hitch—a simple business arrangement becomes complicated when their dreams collide.

**Pick up your copy today - available on Amazon, Kindle Unlimited, print and audio**

**Buy Now**

Want to know when my next book will be available?

Sign up for my newsletter here.

Or follow me at a location of your choice:
Amazon, Goodreads, BookBub, FB Heart-Racing Romance Group, Facebook, or Instagram

# ABOUT THE AUTHOR

**Kim Allred** grew up in Southern California but now enjoys the quiet life in an old timber town in the Pacific Northwest where she raises alpacas, llamas, and an undetermined number of free-range chickens. Just like her characters, Kim loves sharing stories while sipping a glass of wine or slurping a strong cup of brew.

Her spirit of adventure has taken her on many journeys, including a ten-day dogsledding trip in northern Alaska and sleeping under the stars on the savannas of eastern Africa.

Kim is currently creating worlds while shooing cats and dogs away from her lap, and the mighty parrot, Willow, from her keyboard. Willow can peel the keys from the board in fifteen seconds flat.

Kim's current works include her time travel romance series, the *Mórdha Stone Chronicles*, and the urban fantasy romance series, *Of Blood & Dreams*.

To stay in contact with Kim, join her **newsletter** (https://www.kimallred.com/contact/), her **Facebook** group (https://www.facebook.com/groups/588539362866139), or visit her **website** at **www.kimallred.com**.

Made in United States
North Haven, CT
23 July 2023

39426688R00232